THE MAN IN BLACK LOOMED OVER HIM...

SIMON SWUNG WILDLY AND earned a wicked backhand for his trouble.

Then, faster than any big man had a right to, the man's hand shot out again and his fingers wrapped around Simon's throat. Simon tried to throw him off, but the man had fifty pounds on him and arms like iron. Simon's hands gripped the man's wrists trying vainly to pry his hands away.

Simon coughed and gasped as the hands tightened over his throat, slowly squeezing the life out of him. The more he struggled, the weaker he felt. The world outside of his body became muffled as if someone had a laid a thick cloak over everything. All he could see now was the hulking black figure of the man above him.

Simon felt himself start to slip away and clawed for a handhold, but he was fading. "Eliza—" Simon said in a rasping whisper, but the word wouldn't form. Simon closed his eyes and felt the dark begin to take him...

Out Of Time Series: Monique Martin

"Featuring charismatic characters, vividly portrayed time periods, and historically accurate details, Monique Martin's Out Of Time romantic time travel mystery series displays literary acumen, dedication, and sophistication."

From *Toplist:Bestfictionbooks.com*

ALSO BY MONIQUE MARTIN

MONIQUE MARTIN

Sands of Time

Out of Time Series
Book #6

Cover Photo: Karen Wunderman
Cover and Interior Layout and Formatting: TERyvisions

ISBN 10: 098466078X
ISBN 13: 978-0-9846607-8-0

For more information, please contact
writtenbymonique@gmail.com
Or visit: www.moniquemartin.weebly.com

ACKNOWLEDGEMENTS

This book would not have been possible without the help and support of many people: Robin, who helps me in too many ways to count; Dad and Anne; Mom and George; Eddie and Carole; Ian Recchio, for generously sharing his time and snake expertise; Michael; JM; Melissa; Cindy; the Diasporians.

I'd also like to thank the thousands of people who help preserve the past through books, websites, museums and sheer will.

Sands of Time

(Out of Time Book #6)

Monique Martin

CHAPTER ONE

Egyptian Desert, 1920

IT WAS A SCENE straight from one of his nightmares—Elizabeth's hand slipped from Simon's grasp. He called out her name in a panic, but the wind threw it back in his face. He twisted and turned, trying in vain to catch a glimpse of her white dress in the unrelenting fury of the sandstorm. But he saw nothing.

It had come upon them so suddenly they'd barely had time to head for the small outcrop of rocks and ruins they'd passed just a few moments before. A fifty-foot wall of sand and dust and earth overtook them before they could reach the relative safety it could provide. He'd dismounted his camel and raced to Elizabeth's side, barely able see his own hand by the time he reached her. Sand cut into every inch of exposed flesh as they struggled to orient themselves. They had to find shelter. Simon saw the faint outline of something more than desert sand and pulled Elizabeth toward it.

A ferocious gust of wind came. Like a giant hand it had shoved him aside. He struggled to stay upright, and in that instant of struggle, he'd lost her.

And now he couldn't see her at all.

"Elizabeth!"

Raising his forearm to shield his eyes against the sand and dust that ripped into them, he reached his other hand out into the emptiness in a vain attempt to touch what he could not see.

She couldn't be far. He took a stumbling step forward, but didn't dare take another. He could be going in the wrong direction. Another step could be another step away from her. His breath was hot and heavy against the scarf that covered most of his face.

"Elizabeth!"

The wind howled and roared around him. Tiny pieces of sand bit into the palm of his hand like a thousand needles.

"Simon."

He thought it might have been a trick of the wind at first. He turned around and saw nothing but the storm raging around him. Then, he heard it again.

"Simon!"

He took a step toward it and thrust out his hand into the void.

Fingers gripped his and his heart started beating again. He pulled her toward him so fiercely, she lost her feet, but he held her upright.

Holding her close to his chest, he allowed himself just one moment of triumph, of relief, before knowing they had to move again. They didn't dare stay where they were, out in the open. They'd be buried alive.

His arm wrapped tightly around her now. Not bothering to shorten his long strides, he half carried her along with him as he started them up the small hill toward what he hoped was the shelter. A brief break in the wind told him he was right. Barely visible, but there, just twenty feet away, were the remnants of a stone wall. It seemed to take forever to cross the short distance, but finally, he felt the hard stone against his hand. He felt his way around to the leeward side of it. It was scant protection against the storm, but it would have to do.

"Down here!" he yelled over the roaring winds as he pointed toward the ground. Elizabeth nodded quickly and wrapped her *keffiyeh* scarf more tightly around her face. She knelt down and leaned against the stone wall. Simon crouched down behind her, shielding her with his body as best he could. Pulling the edges of his jacket around them both, he bent his head down, held her and waited.

He'd been a fool to agree to this. It had sounded simple enough. Didn't they all in the beginning? But here they were, barely 48 hours into their mission back in time, and they'd already nearly been killed. If the wind didn't stop, there was still a good chance they wouldn't see the dawn.

Simon started to grind his teeth, but felt the omnipresent sand in his mouth. He couldn't even brood properly in this damn place.

It could have been ten minutes or thirty, he couldn't tell, but the wind began to abate and the roar dulled, until finally, it stopped altogether.

Slowly, Simon lifted his head and felt the accumulated sand fall from his shoulders and run down his back.

"Mister Cross!"

It was Hassan's voice, but he ignored him. He had someone more important to tend to. Simon eased back from his position behind Elizabeth and tilted her scarf-covered head up. "Are you all right?"

Elizabeth's blue eyes blinked back at him from the small slit in her scarf wrappings and she nodded. She tugged at one end of the *keffiyeh* and puffed out a relieved breath when her face was finally exposed. "Holy moley."

"Indeed."

Simon stood and held out his hand to help her stand.

"Are you okay?" she asked.

He nodded. His eyes stung from the grit and his body felt bruised and welted, but he knew they were lucky.

"Mister Cross!" Hassan said as he came to their side from his sheltering place.

Hassan, the dragoman they'd hired in Cairo to be their guide and interpreter, was short and round around the middle. Despite that, he moved through sand with surprising ease, his long robes billowing out behind him. His weathered face was relieved and a little amused. His long dark mustache twitched as he fought down a smile.

Not finding anything the least bit amusing in what had just happened, Simon glared at him. Hassan schooled his features and raised his hands in apology, but the broad smile he'd worn when they'd met him at the docks couldn't be contained. Everything is fine, trust in Hassan it said. They could have been on fire and he would have smiled that smile. Everything is fine, trust in Hassan.

"You are both all right?" he asked.

Simon wanted to find fault with him, to blame someone or something for this disaster, but the man had acted quickly and decisively when he saw the storm approach. He could hardly be blamed for the capricious nature of this damnable place.

"We're fine," Simon said tersely as he reflexively reached into his pocket to make sure the watch hadn't been lost in the sands. He felt the familiar outline of his grandfather's pocket watch and sighed in relief. It was safe. As long as it was, they had a way to return to the future.

"That was some storm," Elizabeth said, her Texas accent more pronounced than usual.

Hassan shrugged. "It was fierce, yes, but tiny." He held up two fingers to emphasize his point. "A great *khamaseen* can last for days or even weeks here in the desert."

Elizabeth glanced up at Simon. "Weeks?"

"And swallow an entire town until there is nothing left to see but the shifting sands."

Simon frowned. "Wonderful."

Hassan laughed. "Welcome to Egypt, my friends."

CHAPTER TWO

$\int$ IMON SQUINTED AGAINST THE sun and the sandy grit that filled his
eyes. He reached up to rub them when Hassan grasped his arm.
Hassan shook his head and barked out an order in Arabic to one of
the men of their small company.

"Water," Hassan said, pointing to his eyes.

When the man didn't move quickly Hassan yelled again and
clapped his hands impatiently. It had the desired effect. The other
man hurried as fast as he could through the deep sand to their side.
He held out a large goatskin that served as a canteen.

Hassan snatched it from his hands and sent him off with another
order. The other man nodded his head repeatedly and hurried off to
see to whatever it was Hassan had been on about. All communication
Simon had seen in Egypt so far involved a great deal of hand waving
and pointing and no small amount of yelling.

Hassan turned to Simon and pasted his broad smile back upon
his features. He held out the goatskin and gestured for Simon to use
the water to flush his eyes.

While his eyes were irritated beyond measure, he hated to waste such a precious resource.

Hassan noticed his reluctance and waved a placating hand. "The oasis is not far. Wash your eyes. We will have more water soon."

Simon frowned down at it.

"Trust in—"

"Yes, yes," Simon said as he took the bag. "Trust in Hassan."

Hassan beamed and then bowed. He left Simon and Elizabeth alone as he went to bark more orders at his men.

Simon looked for his mark on the bag. Satisfied it was one they'd treated with iodine, he uncorked the waterskin. Bacterial infection from untreated water was a very real danger here.

Sadly, it was just one of many diseases that threatened the unwary traveler. He and Elizabeth had also gotten a raft of vaccinations and taken several different kinds of medication in preparation for their trip. The rest was, as they say, in the hands of Allah.

"Here," Elizabeth said. "Sit down and I'll do it."

Simon handed her the skin and took a seat on a bit of the ruined wall they'd sheltered behind. The ruins could have been a hundred or a thousand years old. In the desert, it was difficult to tell.

Elizabeth touched his chin. "Tilt your head back."

He did and she flushed his eyes with the refreshingly cool water. When she was finished, he nodded for her to take the first drink.

"Oh, that's heaven," she said after she swallowed and handed the bag back to him.

He drank a little, but not much. Despite Hassan's assurances, Simon was not going to get stuck out here with nothing to drink. He would conserve water until he had a cool pint of whatever passed for beer here firmly in his hands.

Simon re-corked the bag and watched Hassan lord it over his men. One of the camels had apparently wandered off in the storm.

A few of the men were sent to find it while the others made sure the remaining camels and supplies were unharmed.

Elizabeth sat down next to Simon and leaned into his side, resting her head on his shoulder as she stared out at the seemingly boundless expanse of desert before them. "It's beautiful, isn't it?"

In spite of its apparent desire to bury us alive, he thought. In the two days they'd been on caravan following George Mason, the desert had proven every bit as formidable as he'd feared. Stark and endless. Flat and featureless. Rare sandstone formations seemed to rise out of the desert floor only to be cut down and shaped by the whims of the ceaseless winds. It was dusty and hot and cruel.

Simon looked down at Elizabeth. She smiled dreamily at the horror. "Beautiful," he said.

She lifted her eyes to his and then her smile was for him. He leaned down to kiss her—

"Mister Cross!"

Elizabeth giggled.

Simon turned his head. "Yes, Hassan."

Hassan beamed at them as he walked up the small hill. "Good news! We have found the camel."

"That is good news," Simon said as he stood and put out his hand for Elizabeth.

"And your hats!" Hassan said triumphantly as he held out the misshapen masses that used to be their hats.

Elizabeth took hers. "Thank you, Hassan."

He bowed. "We are ready to continue when you are, Mister Cross."

Simon slapped his fedora against his thigh to shake off the dust and sand. Fitting it back on his head, he pulled the brim down, grateful for the shade it provided. He glanced over at Elizabeth who had managed to secure her large brimmed sun hat again.

Simon nodded and they started down the small hill to the camels. "How far to the oasis, Hassan?"

"An hour, perhaps two, no more."

Simon knew that meant three, at the very least. He glanced up at the sun and hoped they'd reach it before dusk.

At the bottom of the hill the men and their camels waited. Simon helped Elizabeth mount hers. Despite the animal kneeling on the ground, the saddle was still a good four feet high. For Elizabeth, at just over 5′ 4″, mounting by herself was a tall order, and hardly the custom for a lady.

The first time she'd tried, one of the men had simply put a hand on her bottom and hoisted her up. After that, Simon had made it clear that he preferred to perform that particular task.

Once she was secure in her saddle, he made his way to his beast. It glared at him with inscrutable eyes and groaned as he neared. Simon climbed onto his saddle and then the men gave the order for the camels to stand. As usual, it took several tries before they moved. It was incredibly awkward at first, but Simon knew what to expect now. He gripped the roped reins and held onto the front pommel as the camel lurched forward slightly and upward onto its knees. Quickly, Simon leaned back in his saddle as the back end rose before the front. He'd learned that lesson the hard way. In another jerky movement, the front legs joined the back and he was fully upright.

The height had been unnerving at first, but it was the swaying walk that had given him the most trouble. Simon was used to the walking gait of a horse—a four-beat gait—where three feet were on the ground at any one time. The camel's two-beat pace meant that both the right front and right rear legs were off the ground at the same time causing the rider to sway from side to side as well as up and down. It had taken nearly an hour for the seasickness to wear off.

Despite the camels being pungent, stubborn and uncomfortable, Elizabeth appeared to be having the time of her life. She'd even gotten so comfortable in the saddle that she could cross her legs in front of her and lean back as though she were kayaking through the desert. Perhaps her ease with it all was because she tended to let things come to her, instead of trying to shape them to her will as he did. Maybe it was her age, but somehow he doubted it. He'd never been as open as she was when he was twenty-five. It was just who she was—open, adventurous, and painfully optimistic. Just a few of the very many reasons he loved her.

While he worried about practical things like water and catching up with Mason in Fayoum, Elizabeth passed the time trying to learn a few words of Arabic from the men, much to their amusement.

"*Gamal,*" she said, pointing at herself and then at the camel. "*Gamyl.*"

The men laughed.

"You have called yourself a camel," Hassan said. "And the camel beautiful."

Her camel bellowed and the men laughed harder.

Elizabeth grinned and joined in. "Well, he *is* handsome."

They rode for another three hours before Simon spied what looked to be an outcropping of date palms. He'd thought it was a trick of light at first. He could imagine how the mind would play games with someone who'd been out in the desert sun too long. But as they neared, he saw it wasn't a mirage, but an actual oasis. A powerful sense of relief flooded through him. While he trusted Hassan, and they weren't hundreds of miles from civilization, the primal fear of not having enough water was surprisingly intense. He breathed a sigh of relief.

Hassan pulled his camel up next to Simon's and smiled broadly. "You see? Trust in Hassan."

The oasis, fed by a natural spring, was meager, but welcome. A few date palms and little trees lined the banks of a very small spring. The camels drank while Simon and Elizabeth found a spot to rest. Simon spread out a blanket and Elizabeth sat down. She took off her hat and unwound her *keffiyeh*, and put them both aside. She unbuttoned the top few buttons of her dress and pulled the fabric away from her throat and chest. Tilting her head back, she let the gentle breeze cool the heated skin.

Simon stretched out next to her, happy to have a chance to work out the kinks from the long ride. He used to ride often as a boy at his estate in England and later during his years at Oxford, but he didn't recall ever feeling this tired. Of course, he reminded himself, that was twenty years ago and he'd been on a civilized animal.

As if it had heard his thoughts, one of the camels bellowed and craned its long neck around to stare at him.

Simon ignored it and turned his attention to something more pleasant. The setting sun cast everything in a golden glow and he pushed himself up onto an elbow to admire his wife. Her white dress was dusty, sweat dripped down her neck into her cleavage and her hair was windswept and in disarray. She had never been more beautiful.

She smiled down at him and then sighed contentedly. She squinted off into the distance. "Do you think Jack's all right?"

Simon took off his hat and fanned his face with it. "I'm sure he's fine. Probably half way to Libya by now, but I'm sure he'll catch on eventually."

Elizabeth frowned, then arched her eyebrows in reluctant resignation. There was nothing they could do about it now.

When they'd started out after Mason, they knew the time might come when his trail would leave them at a crossroads. It had happened barely a day out of Cairo. Two roads diverged from the small village

Mason had stopped in and there was no way to know which route he'd taken. Or, honestly, if he'd taken either of them. He was, however, as far as they could tell, traveling alone and with no extra pack animals. That meant he couldn't stray too far into uncharted land. Besides that, they were fairly certain he was meeting someone and a random spot in the desert was hardly optimal for that.

There were villages and towns both to the west and to the south of his last known stopping place and so they'd split up. Jack had continued on to the west and they'd gone south. About ten hours later, they'd come across a tribe of Bedouins who had crossed paths with Mason. He was headed south which meant they were on his trail and Jack was on a wild goose chase.

Simon tossed his hat down onto the blanket and ran a hand through his hair. "He can take care of himself, Elizabeth," he assured her.

She smiled and nodded again and leaned back against the blanket. "I'm sure he'll have stories to tell."

Simon had little doubt of that. He turned away from her to watch the men hurry about, tending to this and that when he noticed that Hassan was not watching them, but surveying the horizon. Simon excused himself and stood, and walked over to join him.

He stared off into the distance trying to see what Hassan seemed to see. "Everything all right?"

Hassan kept his eyes on the desert to the west where the sun was sinking low in the sky. "We should not tarry here long."

"We're not making camp here?"

"We are too vulnerable here."

Simon didn't understand how they could possibly be more at risk in an oasis than they were out in the harsh desert. However, Hassan didn't take his eyes off the horizon.

"Why would a predator wander the wilderness for prey when he knows it will come to the water," he said. "The prey will come to him."

Simon didn't like the sound of that. Was there some wild beast he'd never heard of out there? Predators? In the short time he'd known Hassan, the man had been painfully jovial. This sudden shift in temperament was discomfiting. "What on earth are you talking about?"

"Bandits," Hassan said softly.

"What?"

"Bandits," Hassan said, this time urgently. He spun around and barked orders. The men froze for a moment, before he bellowed at them again.

Simon looked out onto the horizon, but he couldn't see anything. "What are you talking about? Bandits?"

Hassan hurried to where Elizabeth had been sitting on the blanket. She'd stood and started to walk over to them. Hassan gripped her fiercely by the arm. "You must stay quiet." With that, he practically yanked her to the ground.

"What the hell do you—" Simon said as he ran to stop him.

Hassan pushed Elizabeth down and hurriedly flipped the blanket over on top of her.

Simon grabbed his arm and spun him around. "What in the bloody hell do you think you're doing?"

Simon started to lift the blanket off Elizabeth, when Hassan stopped him. "Please, Mister Cross. Trust in Hassan. It is better they do not find her."

"Who?" Simon demanded.

Hassan didn't need to answer. Simon could hear them now, the approach of a dozen or so riders. They wore black robes and *keffiyehs* covered their faces. Their horses began to rim the small rise that ringed the far edge of the pool.

Hassan took Simon's arm and led him away from the blanket, away from Elizabeth. It was all Simon could do to not look back.

"Do as I say," Hassan whispered. "And we will live."

A large man on an even larger horse rode up into the middle of the line of men. Unlike the others, his face was not covered and he wore a large, wolfish smile.

"Probably," Hassan added.

CHAPTER THREE

THE LARGE MAN IN the center of the line of men, presumably the leader, shifted in his saddle and stared down at them with keen, appraising eyes. He scanned their little company and then said something in Arabic to one of his men.

Simon had a pistol in his saddle bags, for all the good it would do him, even if he could reach it. As the line of men shifted, Simon could see clearly now that they were well-armed. Some carried rifles and most had swords and daggers and looked the sort who wouldn't hesitate to use them.

One of the men moved his horse to his leader's side. The leader spoke to the man, nodding toward Simon and Hassan as he did. The other man nodded and then began to translate.

"Who are you to come to this place?" he said in English with a precise upper class accent. Cambridge, possibly, and young.

"We are—" Simon started, but Hassan gripped his forearm.

"We are but humble travelers, *Effendi*. We meant no—"

The leader raised his hand and Hassan stopped talking and bowed his head in deference.

The leader nodded his head toward Simon and said something to his translator.

There was a momentary delay before the translator relayed the question. "You are English?"

Simon kicked himself for having spoken, but there was nothing to be done for it now. "Yes."

There was little love lost between the Egyptians and the English in 1920. The British occupation had begun to more than chafe and violent protests had erupted just a year earlier.

"You are not welcome here," the man translated for the leader. "You and your kind have trespassed against the great people of Egypt for too long. The day is coming for freedom and today you will play your part in our revolution."

Simon tensed. If history had taught him anything, it was that revolutionaries seldom acted benevolently toward their occupiers, especially when they had such an advantage as twelve against one.

Between the Ottoman Turks, the French and now the British, the Egyptian people had grown tired of overlords. Simon knew a little about the 1919 revolution and the path toward independence from British rule. It had been marked with violence in the beginning, mostly against the Egyptians, however. In the end, the revolution was considered by some to be a textbook case of successful non-violent civil disobedience. He could only hope these men, despite their warlike trappings, were not part of the fringe that seemed to exist in every insurgence.

"I support your cause," Simon said. After the moment it took for the man to translate his response a round of surprised discussion broke out among the men.

The leader silenced his men with a raised hand. He spoke to his translator once more.

"Then you will not mind giving generously to it."

The leader motioned for two men to dismount. They shouldered their rifles and strode toward Simon and Hassan. Simon tensed, but kept still. Their long shadows stretched out in front of them like ominous specters.

One of the men lingered behind the other and scanned their makeshift camp. He unshouldered his rifle and walked to the far side of the camp where he began inspecting their supplies. Hassan's men knelt in the sand, hands clasped before them in supplication and surrender. The man inspecting the camp waved to another man who dismounted and untied the sacks of their provisions and carried them back to his horse.

The man in front of Simon said something in Arabic and lifted his hands and curled his fingers inward in the universal, *give it to me* gesture. Simon barely hesitated. The money he had with him was a fair sum, but thankfully, Simon had had the sense to visit the Bank of Cairo as soon as they'd arrived and deposited most of their money into an account there. He hated to lose what cash he had on hand, but it would be a small price to pay if they could get out of this alive.

Slowly, he reached into his jacket pocket and took out his wallet. He started to open it when the man snatched it from his hand and pulled out a wad of bills. He waved it in the air to show the leader, who was unmoved.

Next to him, the young translator shifted uneasily in his saddle and looked nervously between Simon and the leader.

The man tossed his wallet into the sand and stuffed the cash into a small bag at his waist. He turned back to Simon and gestured again.

"That is all I have," Simon said, as he raised his hands, palms out.

The leader nodded his head once and the man strode forward and patted Simon's jacket. It was only moments before he discovered the watch. Simon could hear Hassan groan and mumble something next to him, but he ignored it. Simon's mouth went dry as the man turned the watch over in his hands. If they lost the watch, they'd be trapped here, back in time, forever.

"It's an heirloom," Simon said as he looked up at the leader. He raised his hand to shield his eyes from the setting sun. "Hardly of any value."

"One does not hide something that is not valuable," the young translator relayed.

The man who had taken their supplies had finished digging through their saddle bags and began circling the camp. He would stop every few steps and poke the bundles of their clothes or blankets with the tip of his bayonet. Simon's jaw worked with the effort it took not to turn and look at the blanket that covered Elizabeth. If they found her, God only knew what they would do and he would be powerless to stop them.

His heartbeat raced as he tried to find some way, any way out of this mess. Swallowing hard and trying to remain calm and focused, Simon watched the man out of the corner of his eye as he moved closer and closer to her hiding place.

The man stopped and stooped down to pick up a gunny sack, but found the contents wanting and tossed it aside before resuming his inspection. Simon felt sweat bead on his forehead. His breath came quicker, harder. Just a few more steps and he would find her hiding place.

"You are nervous."

The words snapped Simon's focus back toward the leader. Simon tried to appear unaffected, but he could feel the sweat running down his temples now, knew the rising and falling of his chest had given away his anxiety.

"Perhaps there is something even more valuable that you are hiding from me?" the translator said in an uneasy voice that did not match the pleasure on the leader's face.

The horse shifted beneath him, as anxious as his master was patient. The leader's eyes studied Simon intently.

The man with the rifle jabbed a saddle bag with the bayonet and then moved to the tree near where Elizabeth was hiding. Simon's heart raced with every step. A cold fist tightened in his stomach as he watched him inch closer and closer until he was standing at the edge of the blanket.

Simon tried to take a step toward her, but he was held back. "Don't," he said. "Wait."

The man raised his gun, ready to stab the blanket. Simon's heart flew into his throat.

"Stop! Please!" Simon strained against the man that held him.

The man with bayonet remained poised, ready to strike.

Simon turned to the leader. "Please, tell him to stop."

The man holding Simon jerked him back and pressed the sharp curved blade against Simon's ribs and grunted in warning.

The leader watched him with a cool expression, eyes narrowed and nodded imperceptibly. The man with the bayonet lowered it, but kept his rifle trained on the spot where Elizabeth was hiding.

"*Alhamdulillah*," Hassan said with a relieved sigh.

Simon swallowed and tried to restart his heart when the leader barked an order and several more men dismounted. One came to hold Simon's other arm and the others hurried toward the blanket.

Simon strained against their grip. "What are you doing?"

They raised their guns and pointed them at the small mound in the middle.

Simon's heart thrummed in his chest again. Dear God, were they going to shoot her? "Please—"

The sound of the metal bolts of the rifles sliding the rounds into place echoed in the quiet oasis. One of the men gripped the edge of the blanket and nodded to his men. Simon couldn't help but surge forward, in a desperate attempt to help her, to stop this madness, but the two men held him back.

"Don't! Don't shoot!" Simon pleaded with them as the man flipped the blanket back. The men leaned forward in anticipation only to find Elizabeth curled into a tiny ball. Slowly, she lifted her head and the men lowered their weapons.

"She...she was resting," Hassan said, trying his best to cover for them. "It was a long—"

"Iskit!" the leader called out and Hassan fell silent again and bowed his head obsequiously.

The leader nodded to his men and two of them grabbed Elizabeth by the arms and roughly tugged her to her feet.

Elizabeth blinked against the sudden bright light, confused and frightened as she saw the men surrounding her with guns. She caught Simon's eye and the fear and confusion in her expression was like a hand squeezing his heart.

"Simon?"

Simon started to move toward her, but the men still had a grip on his arms. "Leave her—"

Hassan stepped toward him and put a hand to his chest and whispered. "Do not make things worse than they already are, Mister Cross."

Simon's chest heaved with the effort to remain where he was as the men dragged Elizabeth forward.

"What's happening?" she asked, trying to take it all in.

"It will be all right," Simon reassured her. He would find a way out of this, he promised her silently. Some way.

The men dragged her to stand in front of the leader who leaned forward in his saddle and smiled. This time he spoke for himself. His accent was thick. "Beautiful woman. Very valuable."

"Please," Elizabeth said. "We're just travelers."

He ignored her and nodded to his men who dragged her toward the horses. Elizabeth squirmed in their grip and called out to Simon, her voice on the edge of panic.

The sound of it cut through him and he struggled in vain against the men that held him. He clenched his jaw and glared up at the leader who finally pulled his attention away from Elizabeth and turned to look at him. He sized Simon up through narrowed eyes and then spoke through his young translator once more.

"Your clothes, your accent, they are from wealth. You could have returned to Cairo and paid dearly for the safe return of your wife."

Could have? Simon's heart and mind raced. He tried to twist out of the grip of the man that held him, heedless of the dagger pressed into his ribs.

The men bound Elizabeth's hands and then hoisted her up onto a horse, shortly followed by a man who sat behind her. Simon could see her searching desperately for any means of escape. His mind raced for something, anything he could do.

"I can see you would be a problem, however, should I take only the girl," the younger man translated.

The leader stared at Simon for a long moment and Simon couldn't help but wonder if it would be his last. He glanced over at Elizabeth. She'd stopped struggling, and now was focused solely on him. The fear in her eyes no longer for herself but for Simon.

Simon could feel the leader's eyes on him, but he would not look away from Elizabeth. If this were to be his last moment, it would be with her.

The leader said something to the translator, who, for the first time, replied back in Arabic. After an eternity, the leader spoke again and after a pause the translator said, "You will come with us as well. Two will fetch twice as much as one."

Elizabeth sagged forward in relief. Simon exhaled. He'd been spared. For now. Simon kept his eyes on Elizabeth as they tied his wrists together. The relief and joy in her expression gave him strength. As long as he was alive, as long as she was alive, there was hope.

The two men holding Simon by the arms started to pull him toward the horses.

"I will spare you, brothers," he added to Hassan and the other men.

Hassan bowed. "You are most gracious, *Effendi*." He avoided meeting Simon's glare.

"You will not speak of this," the translator said to Hassan. "If you want to pass this way ever again and live."

Hassan bowed his head and tilted it toward Simon. His expression was intense, but whether it was regret or shame in his eyes, Simon didn't know.

The men gathered the reins of the camels and lead the animals up toward the horses. Hassan and his men might be spared, but they would be on foot from here on out.

The men jerked Simon forward and hauled him toward another horse. The Arabian pranced anxiously in place as they forced him up into the saddle and a man climbed on behind him. The other men returned to their horses.

Simon's rider turned the horse around so they were facing Elizabeth.

"Do not be foolish," the leader said in his thick accent. The man behind Elizabeth showed the long knife in his hands and pressed it between her breasts. Simon clenched his hands into fists.

Elizabeth swallowed nervously.

"It will be all right," he said with much more conviction than he felt.

The rider behind him spun his mount away as the leader called out a command. As one, the group of men spurred their horses and rode off into the desert. Toward what fate, Simon could only imagine.

CHAPTER FOUR

IT WAS DARK BY the time they arrived at the raider's camp and Elizabeth couldn't see exactly where they'd taken Simon. She'd heard him call out her name once and then nothing more. She had no idea where they'd taken him or what they might be doing to him. All she knew was that he wasn't with her and it made her heart ache in a way she hadn't felt before.

She closed her eyes and pushed away the thoughts of what might be happening. If they'd wanted to hurt him, they'd had ample opportunity. Surely, he was simply being kept in a tent similar to hers, waiting for the ransom demand to be made.

Of course, that was another problem. Not having any relations or anyone at all they could contact other than Jack, who was God only knows where, this little kidnap for ransom plan was going to fall short of the pledge goal.

The initial shock at what happened had started to wear off, but it was still a jumble. Everything had happened so quickly. She'd nearly lost Simon and then he was spared and, the next thing she knew, they were being carried off into the desert. The long ride had given her plenty of time to think, but her mind just raced in circles. She'd only managed to catch a glimpse of Simon a few times. Each time broke her heart and gave her strength in equal measure.

Elizabeth shifted her legs out in front of her. She'd been tied up for several hours now and they were starting to cramp.

Outside, she could hear the men singing. Through the thick fabric of the tent, she could just make out the glow of a large fire and the sounds of men laughing and enjoying their victory.

She and Simon would make for a pretty ransom, or so they thought. While they had brought a fair amount of money with them, it was undoubtedly not the prize these men were hoping for.

Poor Simon. She could still see his expression when she'd emerged from her hiding place—the worry, the love, the strength.

When they'd spared his life and taken him prisoner as well, she'd never been so relieved. The thought of losing him...she refused to let it take root. They might be captives now, but at least they were alive. At least, they could be together, she'd thought. Except, it hadn't quite worked out that way.

She had to find a way out of here before their time ran out. Their captors would cut their throats before they'd cut their losses.

Way to stay positive, Elizabeth, she chided herself. She and Simon had been in worse situations before and gotten out of them. They'd find their way out of this mess, too.

Escaping wouldn't be easy. When they'd brought her to her tent they'd eased her down gently enough onto a large cushion, but then they'd bound her ankles and tied her to a tent post. If she managed to get her tether undone, she could probably untie her feet, but then what?

Her prison walls weren't cinder blocks and iron bars, but they may as well have been. With armed men outside, the canvas walls or walls of some sort of animal skin by the smell of it, would do just as well. Although, she had to admit, as she looked around her quarters, as prisons went, this one wasn't too shabby. It looked like some Bedouin chieftain's private quarters. Posh as far as desert prisons went, she thought, trying not to think about the private quarters part.

The tent was fairly big, maybe fifteen by fifteen. A large hanging lamp at the center pole gave off a glowing yellow light. A small hand mirror hung from a peg and a white pitcher and large bowl sat on the floor at the base of the post.

The room, such as it was, had no furniture, but it did have several large and colorful faded pillows with a worn oriental carpet that served as the floor. Smaller carpets hung on twine strung up along the walls like wall tapestries. What looked like they might be camel or horse saddles, covered by felt blankets, were situated on the far side of the room creating a makeshift seating area. A small leather chest sat between them. She was, she thought with a sinking feeling, undoubtedly in the bedroom section.

Her imagination started to run away with her, but Elizabeth tripped it up before she felt too queasy. There was no reason to jump to the worst conclusions. The not-quite-worst ones were bad enough. She and Simon were prisoners of an armed group of raiders, who were going to seek a ransom that couldn't be paid. That hardly needed the embellishment of imagination.

The flap to the tent flung open, interrupting her train of thought and the large man who'd given the orders earlier strode inside. He was followed by another man, whose face was still hidden behind his *keffiyeh*.

The big man surveyed the area for a brief moment, apparently making sure things were as they should be. Then he strode over to the sitting area and untied a small bag from his belt. He tipped the contents into his hand.

It was Simon's pocket watch. Elizabeth tried not to look as relieved as she felt to see the watch and suddenly found her fingernails, which were filthy, fascinating. Out of the corner of her eye she watched him turning it over in his hand, inspecting it, judging its worth.

His grunt sounded disappointed. If only he knew how valuable the watch really was. He flipped open the lid of the small chest with his toe and tossed the watch carelessly into it. He turned back to her, his eyes narrowed. He closed the lid of the trunk and approached her.

He was tall, at least he looked tall from the ground, and broad shouldered. He looked every inch a general. He was in perhaps his late forties. His face was leathery and dark and the hair of his short beard jet black. The black fabric of his robes was dusty and nondescript, except for the elaborate wide cloth belt he wore. It was some sort of gold brocade and far fancier than any of the other mens', clearly marking him as their superior.

His dark brown eyes were sharp and alert as they ran over her body. There was, much to Elizabeth's relief, nothing salacious in the look. It was matter of fact. An inventory. He was assessing her in the same way he'd assessed the watch and making sure his property and her value hadn't been damaged. Satisfied, he turned to the other man and spoke several sentences in Arabic.

The other man nodded and then, with one last look at Elizabeth, the big man left. The other man watched him go and then slowly approached Elizabeth. She leaned back away from him and he stopped mid-step.

He held up his hands in front of him. "Do not worry," he said in perfect English. "I am not here to hurt you."

He looked quickly toward the tent flap, and then back to her. He closed the distance between them, and knelt in front of her. "I am sorry it came to this."

Elizabeth felt a surge of hope spark inside her. She held out her bound wrists. "Then let us go."

The man nervously glanced back at the doorway. "You will be treated as our guests."

"You tie up all of your guests?"

She could see the regret and even a hint of a chagrined smile in his light brown eyes. "This is not how things were supposed to be."

He sounded genuine, at least, she wanted to believe he was.

Elizabeth sighed and looked down at her hands. It could be worse. Maybe it was for Simon. She looked up at him, pleading. "My husband—"

"He is unharmed." He sighed and seeing her distress reached out to comfort her, but thought better of it. "Please, be patient and in time—"

The tent flap was pulled open and one of the other men stepped inside. He glared suspiciously at the man in front of her who quickly pretended to assess her wrist bindings. The other man stood in the doorway and said something. His tone brusque and impatient.

The young man in front of her narrowed his eyes and barked back at the man in Arabic. The man at the doorway looked nervous for a moment. The young man stood and turned to him and said something in a commanding tone. The other man bobbed his head, looked at Elizabeth in what seemed to be shame, and ducked back out of the tent. Whoever this man was, he might be young, but he had some power here and he was sympathetic. If she could just get him to help them.

Once she was sure the other man was gone, she said, "Please, help us—"

He looked back at her and she could see the conflict and fear in his eyes.

"Please?"

He paused for a moment and then glanced back over his shoulder before leaning in very close. "I will do what I can."

Relief and hope coursed through her veins. "Thank you."

"I can make no promises. But I will try to help you."

With that, he turned and left the tent.

It wasn't much, but it was hope and Elizabeth would take any she could get.

CHAPTER FIVE

ELIZABETH STARTLED AWAKE. In that fuzzy moment before full sense returned, she couldn't remember where she was. A sound outside her tent brought her instantly awake as what little adrenaline she had left shot through her body. She tried to sit up, but could only manage to lift herself up onto one elbow.

She tried to slow her heart and listen. Her eyes slowly adjusted to the darkness, but the night was still again.

Suddenly, the flap to her tent opened and one of her guards stepped inside. The moonlight outside cast his shadow across the carpet for a brief second before the flap fell shut again.

She could barely make out his silhouette as he crossed the short distance between them. He was tall and, even though he wore robes, she could see he was broad-shouldered and muscular. She tensed as he grew closer.

He knelt down in front her and laid down his rifle. Her heart raced and she tried to press herself back against the cushions. She clenched her hands into fists and raised them up in front her. She was just about to hit him with her best double-fist Captain Kirk when she heard the quick grating sound followed by a sharp snap and whoosh of a match being lit. Quickly, the small flame lit the space between. The man looked at her and tugged down the *keffiyeh* that covered his face.

"Hey, kid."

Elizabeth's eyes stung as tears threatened and she let out her breath in a rush. "Jack!" she said too loudly and then added in a whisper. "Am I glad to see you."

He flashed her a smile and then glanced around the tent. "Damn, I thought he might be here, too."

Elizabeth shook her head needlessly. "I don't know where they have Simon."

He nodded and looked at his match already burning down. He scanned the tent quickly and found a candle. It was nearly guttered, but he managed to get it to light. He put it down next to her and reached for her hands.

"Don't worry, we'll find him."

Elizabeth had never lost hope, but hearing from Jack made it solidify into truth. He pulled a knife from his pant's pocket beneath the black robes he wore.

"How did you find us?" Elizabeth whispered.

He made quick work of her bindings and tether. "Later," he said. "Let's find Cross and get out of here. They weren't expecting company, but the guards I knocked out won't stay down forever."

Elizabeth nodded and accepted his hand up. Her legs wobbled unsteady beneath her and Jack put an arm around her waist. His forehead creased with worry.

"Are you hurt?"

Elizabeth shook her head. "Just been trussed up like a Christmas turkey too long."

She shook some life back into her legs and they steadied beneath her.

"All right?" Jack asked as he carefully let go.

She nodded and then turned to him. "Oh, Jack," she said as she pulled him into a quick, tight hug. "Thank you."

"Thank me when we get out of here." Jack blew out the candle and tossed it aside. He picked up his rifle and took hold of her hand, and started toward the tent flap.

"Wait." Elizabeth pulled out of his grasp and rushed over to the small leather chest. She flipped open the lid and felt around inside. It was filled with small trinkets and jewelry.

"What are you doing?" Jack whispered harshly behind her.

"The watch," she said. "It's in here."

After a moment, her fingers landed on the rounded edges of the watch. She snatched it and felt along the outside of the case. Her fingers ran over the familiar etching and she clasped it tightly in her hand. "Got it."

She stood and Jack brushed her arm as he reached out his hand in the darkness. She grabbed it and they hurried to the tent opening. Jack eased it back and peered outside. The moonlight was bright outside. It would help them navigate the camp, but it also made them easier to find.

He let the flap close and lowered his head close to Elizabeth's ear. "There are three smaller tents to the left and one to the right," Jack whispered. "Three men are bivouacked outside by the fire near the single tent, but they're asleep. There are crates and supplies about thirty feet at ten o'clock."

Elizabeth nodded in the dark. "Right."

Not for the first time, Elizabeth was grateful for Jack's military training. The skills he'd acquired as a spy in WWII sure did come in handy.

"When we leave the tent, we're gonna head right for the crates, all right? There's a pretty good view of the rest of the camp from there." Jack squeezed her hand. "Stay close."

He opened the tent flap again and then turned and nodded to her. They dashed out into the night. Elizabeth could see the burning embers of the fire to the right where Jack had said it would be.

She saw the outline of the crates and barrels ahead, and let Jack lead her behind them.

"Watch your step," he said, nodding to the ground.

At her feet was one of the men, tied up and unconscious.

"I'm glad you're on our side," she whispered.

She sensed his smile as they crouched down behind the crates. All of the tents looked alike to her. She had no idea how they were going find Simon.

"What do we do?"

Jack surveyed the camp and then knelt down in the sand. He sighed. "My money's on the single tent by the fire."

"Why?"

"The men out front. It's separate from the others. If I had a prisoner that's where I'd put him."

That made sense. "How did you find me?"

Jack shrugged. "Dumb luck."

Elizabeth had been hoping for more than that. "Well, let's hope it hasn't run out." She looked at the lone tent and the men by the fire. "What do we do? We can't exactly walk in the front way. Not with those men there."

"Sneak around to the back, dig our way under," Jack said.

Elizabeth nodded. "And hope he's alone."

They circled around the long way out of the camp and back into it. She hadn't realized it before, but the camp was at the base of a small rise that turned into a cliff that disappeared into the distance. They skirted the edges of the cliff and made their way silently to the back of the single tent.

Jack held up his hand and crossed his fingers, and then knelt down in the sand. He laid down his weapon and then quietly started digging. It was slow going. For every handful of sand he pulled away another seemed to slide back to fill the hole. Between them, they finally made enough progress to slip under the taut tent canvas.

"Wait here, while—" Jack started to say and then shook his head with a smile. "Ah, forget it. Just stay quiet." He wiggled under and disappeared inside.

Elizabeth glanced around. The night was still. She took a deep breath and then followed him.

The interior of the tent was dark, but some light from the fire outside let them see vague shapes. She could just make out the silhouette of a man sitting near the center post. Her heart raced in anticipation.

"Elizabeth?"

Simon's voice was hoarse and dry. She saw him turn his head and strain to see behind him. She hurried to his side as Jack took up position by the tent flap.

Even in the dark, Elizabeth could see the worry in Simon's eyes. She cupped his cheek and kissed him.

"Are you all right?" he asked.

She nearly laughed. Shouldn't she be the one asking him that? She nodded and kissed him again.

"If you two are finished," Jack said, holding up his knife and flipping it over handle first to Elizabeth.

She took it and set about cutting Simon loose. She cut the ropes that bound his legs and then moved around behind him.

"Jack," Simon said.

Jack spun around and shushed him. He waved for Elizabeth to hide as he slid to the side of the doorway.

Elizabeth ducked behind Simon, who let his head fall forward as if he were asleep. She grabbed her skirts and gathered them up and tried to make herself as skinny and small as possible.

The tent flap opened and a man stepped into the doorway. He held the flap open to let the light from the waning fire illuminate the inside of the tent. Elizabeth stayed crouched down. The moment dragged out into another. She could just see his legs through a gap between Simon's arm and his body.

The man's feet shuffled and then he stepped forward and the tent flap fell closed. Elizabeth swallowed her gasp and held her breath. He leaned down to pick up the cut ends of rope that lay around Simon's ankles. Just as he did, she heard a grunt and then a crack.

At the sounds of the struggle she looked up and saw Jack with his hand over the man's mouth and the other around his neck. They grappled in muffled silence. Elizabeth jumped up and glanced around the room for something, anything to use as a weapon. She grabbed the first thing she found — a metal coffee pot and swung wildly at the man's head. It connected with a crack, but he was only stunned, until Jack spun him around and hit him square on the jaw. The man lost consciousness immediately. Jack grabbed him before he hit the ground with a thud.

He eased the man to the ground and they all froze waiting to hear if the sounds of their scuffle had alerted anyone. All Elizabeth could hear was her heart beating out a drum solo like Animal from the Muppets. She and Simon caught each other's eyes as the silence stretched out, until, finally, Jack moved again and quickly bound and gagged the guard.

Silently, he finished cutting Simon's bonds and they all crawled through the hole near the back of the tent. Once they were outside, Jack picked up his rifle and nodded toward the way they'd come.

Simon gripped Elizabeth's hand and squeezed it. He looked down at her and they both knew the million things they wanted to say would have to wait.

Jack peered around the edge of the tent and started at a run toward the edge of the camp. Elizabeth and Simon followed him.

Jack led them out into the darkness. They ran in the deep sand until Elizabeth thought her legs would catch fire they burned so badly. Jack stopped; he was far ahead by now and waved for them to hurry. He gestured toward a small dune and they scaled it as quickly as they could.

Once they were on the other side, Simon said what Elizabeth had been thinking. "We can't run all night."

"Won't have to," Jack said when they reached the bottom of the other side of the dune. He nodded into the distance and there stood four beautiful horses. Their reins were gathered and held by a short, portly man.

Jack grinned. "Trust in Hassan."

CHAPTER SIX

Wanting to get as much distance between themselves and the bandits' camp as possible, the four of them rode hard for the first half hour. Even then, Elizabeth knew they'd measured their pace for her. She wasn't as strong a rider as the others, but she did her best and held on for dear life. Hassan took the lead, since he was the only one who knew where the heck they were, much less where the heck they were going. Jack brought up the rear, his pilfered rifle and robes discarded now. And Simon, Simon never strayed from her side.

She was grateful to sit down in the saddle when they finally slowed as they neared the first in a series of small towns that would lead them to Fayoum and the train station. Although her joy was short-lived. Riding a horse while wearing a dress and nothing else but short cotton tap pants? Not recommended. Luckily, they rode at a moderate walk through the towns.

The endless desert had faded behind them and was replaced by actual vegetation and makeshift roads. She'd never been so happy to see a scraggily shrub before. More plants meant more water, and more water meant people and civilization. They'd only been out in the desert for three days, but it had felt like a lifetime.

Soon, the towns grew closer together until they merged into the small city of Fayoum. The oasis of the same name was a large man-made creation. A series of canals funneled water from the Nile to create the Venice of Egypt.

The mud houses and thatched roofs could have been from another century. Even another millennium. Heck, they probably were. It was hard for her to wrap her mind around it. Used to life in the United States, she'd been stunned by the breadth of history she could feel and touch when she and Simon had traveled to England. Even more amazing was that centuries there were thousands of years here.

It all would have made her feel very small and insignificant if it weren't for the country itself. There was something about Egypt, something unlike anywhere else she'd been. She didn't feel like a tiny speck on the timeline of history. She felt part of the whole of it. All of history seemed to coexist in this place. It was mysterious and magical, and filled with bandits and sandstorms. And her legs were definitely beginning to chafe, she thought with a frown.

"Here," Simon said, as he brought his horse closer and shed his jacket. He folded it up and held it out to her. "Sit on this. It should help a little."

She shook her head. "It's not that bad."

He arched an eyebrow and then tucked his jacket into the saddle in front of him.

She turned and watched him. His face was dirty and his five o'clock shadow had grown into a ten o'clock. His clothing was dusty and wrinkled. He was exhausted, down to the bone weary, and his thoughts were still only about her comfort. It was humbling.

He must have felt her watching him because he turned and looked at her curiously.

She smiled in reply to his unanswered question. "Just thinking about how much I love you."

A small, startled smile came across his face, but it faded and he grew serious. And then his eyes softened in that way that always melted her heart.

"You confound me," he said with a shake of his head.

She grinned. "Then I must be doing something right."

THEY WERE IN THE heart of Fayoum now. Vegetation and life grew more vibrant with every mile. The arid desert was gone now and a lush sanctuary had taken its place. Flowers blossomed amid the papyrus grass along the shores of small canals. Tall palms and other shade trees lined the roads. Small and large tracts of land were ready to grow a harvest of sugar cane, sweetcorn and Egyptian wheat. And she was ready for a bath. But it would have to wait, they weren't quite finished with this part of their adventure just yet.

While Jack had been busy looking for them in Fayoum, he'd learned that George Mason was in town, but wouldn't be for long. Mason had purchased a train ticket for the morning train to the main line along the Nile. From there he could go just about anywhere. If they didn't catch up with him now, he was lost for good. They had to get on that train.

When they first arrived in Cairo, having jumped back in time, they'd been there for less than four hours when they discovered Mason was on the run. They'd barely had time to make arrangements for their bags to be sent to Shepheard's and rooms to be reserved for whenever they might return. Now, they were in their fourth day of the hunt. She could only hope it was their last.

They arrived at the small train station just in time. The steam engine was building up power and large bursts of steam shot out from the sides of the cars. Black smoke billowed out of the smoke stack on the engine.

They quickly dismounted and dashed for the train. Hassan lingered behind.

"Aren't you coming?" Elizabeth asked, once she realized he wasn't with them.

He held up the reins of the horses. "I will see you when you return to Cairo."

If they returned and, *if* he wasn't caught and punished by the bandits. "Right," she said confidently. "In Cairo."

Simon tugged on her hand. "The train," he said, nodding toward the now moving locomotive. The wheels had already started to spin and grind against the tracks as the heavy train began to slowly pull out of the station.

It seemed like hardly enough to say considering Hassan had risked his life to save theirs, but it was all she had to offer at the moment. "Thank you," Elizabeth called as Simon led her toward the last few cars.

Hassan waved. "Everything is fine. Trust—"

The train whistle drowned out the rest and, with one last look over her shoulder, she ran toward the moving train.

Thankfully, it wasn't going more than a few miles an hour. Jack jumped on easily. He stood on the second step and leaned down, reaching out for Elizabeth. She jogged alongside for a moment. Her skirts weren't heavy, but they were long and she had to pick them up in her right hand. By the time she did, the train was going a little faster. Then faster.

"Elizabeth," Simon said as he ran along next to her. "Now would be a good time."

She glared at Simon. "You try doing this in a dress!"

Simon looked moderately sympathetic, but nodded toward the rapidly approaching end of the platform. "Darling."

She looked at the stairs Jack was standing on. The gap wasn't huge, but it was intimidating and getting more so with every step. He was right though, she had to go. She gripped the handrail and timed her leap onto the steps. She made it with room to spare. Jack grabbed her free hand and pulled her up to the space between the last few cars. The platform was really running out now and the train moving faster. But it was no problem for Simon as he reached out a long arm, grabbed the handrail, and leapt up with one long stride.

They huddled briefly in the small passageway as the train picked up more speed and the platform and Hassan disappeared into the distance behind them. The shimmying of the plates between the two cars grew more precarious and Simon put his arm around Elizabeth's waist and pressed a hand against the car door with the other to brace himself.

"Let's start at the end," he said.

The last car was crowded with people, jammed onto long, thin wooden benches that ran along the sides of the car. Some people held onto handrails that hung down from the ceiling, while others simply squatted on the floor. Despite all of the windows being down, the car was stiflingly hot and stuffy.

The clackity-clack of the wheels against the tracks and rumble of the train were intensely loud. Jack picked his way through the third class passengers, walking all the way to the end. He opened the door there to make sure Mason wasn't standing on the small back platform. He closed the door, shook his head and rejoined them.

Next, they made their way into the second class car. The long thin benches were replaced with two-seaters in rows from back to front. Slowly, they walked up the aisle. Only two men wore western clothing and neither was Mason. When they reached the far end, Simon doubled back to make sure. Mason could have ditched his suit for a galabiya, one of the long outer robes men wore. When he reached the end, Simon turned back and returned to them. "Not here."

They were passing through another second class car, when they came upon the conductor.

"I'm afraid this one is on you," Simon said to Jack as he patted his empty jacket. Puffs of dust came off his chest and he waved them away.

Jack arched an eyebrow, but dug into his pants pocket and paid for their passage. Once their tickets had been punched, the conductor moved out of the way and let them enter the first class car.

It was nearly empty. Only three people sat amongst the half-dozen rows of facing leather banquettes. A couple to the far right sat close together and looked out of the windows, and an unaccompanied man sat in the middle of the car. They couldn't see his face though. His back was to them and he was bent forward, his forehead in his hand as his elbow rested against the table.

Slowly, they walked to the far end of the car. The man stayed hunched over some piece of paper, his fedora pulled down and shielding his face.

Simon motioned for Jack to stay put and he and Elizabeth approached the man's seat.

"Mr. Mason?" Simon said.

The man's head jerked up and he quickly reached into his jacket, but Simon grabbed his wrist.

"Let's not do that," Simon said as he firmly held Mason's arm in place with his right hand. With his left hand, he reached into Mason's pocket and pulled out a small revolver.

"I'll keep this," Simon said quietly, and he slipped the gun into his own pocket.

Elizabeth looked back at Jack, who had taken two steps forward, but stopped when he saw that Simon had it under control. He moved back to his position at the door behind them where he could see Mason clearly.

Elizabeth and Simon slid into the seats opposite Mason as the other young couple, less interested in the scenery now and more interested in getting the heck out of there, grabbed their hats and hurried down the center aisle and into the next car.

Finally, Elizabeth thought, they'd caught up with the elusive Mr. Mason. He looked exactly as he had in the photograph in the dossier Travers had given them. Same pencil thin mustache, and small sharp features. His eyes danced nervously between Elizabeth and Simon.

"This might come as a surprise to you, Mr. Mason," Simon said. "But we're on your side."

Mason smirked, but she could see the uneasiness in his eyes. "Are you?"

"Travers from the Council sent us to help you retrieve the watch," Elizabeth said.

Mason's eyes shifted to hers and narrowed. "That was thoughtful of him."

Simon sighed. "He said to say, 'Over the rolling waters go.'"

Mason's eyes lit up immediately, but he quickly schooled his features. "Come from the rising moon, and blow. Blow him again to me."

"While my little one, while my pretty one, dances."

It was a clever code. A simple verse from a Tennyson poem with a few select words changed.

Mason huffed out a breath as he took off his hat and ran his fingers through his hair. "Thank God. I thought you were one of them."

"Definitely not one of them," Elizabeth assured him. "Wait. One of what?"

"I'm not sure exactly." He smiled weakly. "I was beginning to think everyone here was working for the Shadow Council." He looked even more exhausted than they were. "It plays tricks on you, this country. You search so long and you don't know who to trust. Can't trust anyone really."

"Have you found it? Have you located the watch?" Simon asked.

"I think so," Mason said. "At least I'm close. It's been an odd sort of thing. I should have known, you know? I knew Shelton. I suppose we'll never find out what happened to him, will we?"

"No," Simon agreed. "Probably not. But the watch—"

"Right, the watch."

The door to the far end of the car opened and a man in a dark galabiya and *keffiyeh* scarf covering his face looked around. He stared at Mason for a moment, and then he raised his hand. He had a red and black checkered scarf wrapped around it and Elizabeth wondered if he'd been injured.

And then she saw the flash of the muzzle and the angry sound of a gunshot rang out.

Simon pulled Elizabeth to him and twisted away from the assailant. The gunshot rang in her ears, made all the louder by the small enclosed space of the railcar.

"No!" Jack cried from behind them.

Elizabeth heard the door slam shut and then footsteps. She looked up just as Jack passed her, running toward the doorway. And then Mason, blood dribbling down his chin, eyes frozen in surprise, fell face first into the table.

Elizabeth's breath caught. "Oh my god."

The bullet wound to the back of his head was small, but brutal. Simon slid out of their seat. "Stay here!" he said and rushed to join Jack.

Elizabeth stared in shock at Mason as more blood spread out beneath his head. She shook herself out of it and pushed out a bracing breath as she slipped out of the seat, and ran to the door. She found Simon and Jack standing just inside the next car.

Simon started to say something, but settled for a frustrated sigh.

"Where'd he go?" she asked.

Jack held out the dark robe and red and black *keffiyeh*. The ends were charred from the flash from the gun. The shooter must have shed them immediately in the space between cars and then blended in with the rest of the passengers.

If the passengers had heard anything or seen anything, they gave no sign of it.

Simon grunted in frustration and went back into the first class car. Elizabeth and Jack followed.

To no one's surprise, Mason hadn't moved. The blood pool under his head was already starting to look sticky.

"We need to search him," Simon said.

Jack, used to grim business like this, didn't hesitate. He leaned Mason back in his seat and made quick work of going through his pockets. He found Mason's watch and handed it to Simon. It was identical to the one Simon's grandfather, Sebastian, had given him. Other than his wallet, the only other item he had with him was an envelope. Jack put that into his own pocket and eased Mason back down onto the table.

Elizabeth felt queasy.

"Now what?" Jack asked.

Simon looked at Elizabeth and took hold of her hand. "I don't know," he said, honestly. "I really don't know."

CHAPTER SEVEN

IT WAS EARLY AFTERNOON by the time they arrived in Cairo. They'd successfully managed to mix in with the rest of the train's crowd when Mason's body was discovered. They, like everyone else on the train, had nothing helpful to offer. The couple who'd left the car and everyone else who'd seen them searching for Mason had instantaneous amnesia. For the first time, Elizabeth was happy people's urge not to get involved was stronger than their desire to help. Even the policeman seemed more put-out by the crime than eager to solve it.

The carriage ride from the busy train station to their hotel was a blur. Elizabeth was hungry and tired and had sand in places where sand should never go. She was too tired to take in the city as their carriage paced along. The splendor and insanity of Cairo would have to wait until tomorrow. She needed a sandwich and a bath, preferably at the same time.

Their rooms were large and elegant, and it took all of her strength not to simply plop down on the large brass bed and call it a day.

But she knew she wouldn't feel completely human again until she'd bathed and brushed her teeth.

The bathroom was big and bright. White tiles covered it from floor to ceiling, and a lovely small chaise sat in the corner. She plopped down on it and felt herself melting into the cushion. She took off her shoes and wiggled her toes. Her filthy toes.

That was enough to get her moving again and she walked over to the tub, pleased to see that it came equipped with a shower. It was one of the few in the hotel. Apparently, Americans were keen on them, but Europeans hadn't made the leap yet. Showers were generally reserved for athletic clubs, barracks and other manly places. Women were considered by many to be too delicate to withstand the powerful blast of water.

Elizabeth turned the tap on the overhead shower. Not exactly a fire hose, but water, and running water was all she needed. She shed her clothing and stepped in, pulling the fabric curtain closed to keep the water from splashing all over creation. From the large shower head above her, a cool drizzle of rain fell down onto her. She stood there in an exhausted stupor for a few minutes before summoning her reserves and shampooing and bathing.

She would have been content to stand there for an hour, but Simon was waiting. She toweled off and slipped on her robe.

"It's all yours—" she started to say, as she re-entered the bedroom, but the sight before her brought her up short.

Simon sat in one of the large wing backs in the sitting area, one boot on and one boot off. His head was tilted back against the cushion, his eyes shut and his breathing deep. A lone sock dangled from his fingers. He'd fallen asleep mid-undress.

Elizabeth couldn't help but smile. He was such a giant doodlebug. The poor man probably hadn't slept in days. His hyper-awareness and perpetual DEFCON-3 status had finally caught up with him.

Elizabeth walked quietly over to his chair and gently moved his disheveled hair away from his eyes. She thought about leaving him and letting him sleep there, but chair sleep was no sleep at all.

She caressed his cheek, the stubble rough under her palm.

Slowly, his eyes blinked open and a gentle smile came to his face. He looked down and realized where he was. "I fell asleep," he said needlessly.

Elizabeth nodded. "I think the bed will be better."

Simon nodded and stood, giving an enormous stretch and dropping the sock onto the floor. He frowned as he noticed he still had one boot on.

"Do you want to shower first or just conk out?" Elizabeth asked.

He took in a deep breath and wrinkled his nose. "Unless that's you, I think a shower is in order."

Elizabeth laughed and pointed him toward the bathroom and then turned back to their room as he closed the door behind him.

Feeling strung out, but oddly invigorated now, Elizabeth opened their trunks and aired out their clothes. She found her hairbrush and sat down at the small vanity. She frowned at her reflection. Ugly dark circles hung under her eyes. She looked as tired as she felt. She tossed a silk slip over the mirror so she wouldn't have to look anymore.

It had been a hell of a few days and hardly what she'd expected. They'd been planning on moving down Sebastian's list. Having a list of people, places and times where the forces of darkness threatened made their life simpler, except for the nearly dying every time.

Their most recent trip to Natchez was a case in point. They'd had several close calls and Simon's arm took over three weeks to heal, but all that remained now was a thin red scar. However, the part of the mission that shadowed Elizabeth, shadowed both of them, was Old Nan's prophecy—that their child, their future child, would die. They'd discussed it and then discussed it again, finally deciding that they could not live in fear of what might be and put their worries aside as best they could. Despite that, it was never far away, this fear for a child they did not yet have, lingering just on the edge of thought.

Trying to move on meant a return to normalcy. Of course, normal for them was planning another time traveling adventure. They'd been about to do just that when a different sort of ghost from the past appeared at their door. Peter Travers, a member of the Council for Temporal Studies, arrived and brought with him disturbing news from the Council. Was there any other kind?

The Council had apparently split into two factions, one even less trustworthy than the other. This new Shadow Council, as Travers had called it, the enemy within, was secretly trying to collect all of the time traveling watches. To what end, Travers didn't know, but it surely wasn't anything good.

Of the few loyal members, one had disappeared completely and another, Charles Graham, fearing for his life, had gone on the run. In order to stop whatever nefarious plans the Shadow Council had, Travers and the handful of remaining members he trusted made plans of their own to recover all of the watches. They'd sent George Mason to find one that had been lost in time, its location unknown. But when Mason himself hadn't returned as scheduled, Travers had come to Simon and Elizabeth for help.

While they wouldn't have wept at the demise of the Council, the idea of its corruption was the stuff of nightmares. Each member held a powerful privilege, the ability to travel in time, and if it were turned toward evil....

Elizabeth shivered, shook her head and went back to brushing her still damp hair. She couldn't get caught up in the giant what ifs, she had to concentrate on what she knew. Which, sadly, wasn't very much.

They had no idea what Mason knew about the location of the missing watch or why he'd gone out into the desert in the first place. Or, honestly, what they should do now that he was dead.

Elizabeth sighed and put down the brush just as Simon emerged from the bathroom, a towel around his waist. He scrubbed another towel over his hair and then held onto the ends and put it behind his neck.

"Feel better?" she asked.

He ran a hand through his hair, slicking it back. "Marginally. No food yet?"

On cue, there was a knock at the door.

"Ask and ye shall receive," Elizabeth said with a flourish.

She started to get up to answer it, but Simon waved her off. He ducked into the bathroom and re-emerged belting his robe.

Answering the door, he took the tray of sandwiches and two bottles of Perrier, and set them on the small table in the sitting area.

He patted his robe pockets. "I'm sorry, I don't have anything today. But, tomorrow," he assured the bellboy.

"Wait," Elizabeth said as she dug into her trunk. She pulled out a small clutch purse and pulled out one of the of-the-era pound notes Travers had supplied them with. She hurried to the door and handed it to the man. He blinked at it for a moment and then grinned, bowed and hurried down the corridor.

Simon closed the door. "That was extravagant. Probably fifty times what he's used to receiving."

She shrugged and went straight for the food. "Let him live a little."

She bit into her sandwich and said in between bites, "I don't know what it is, but it's good."

Simon took a sandwich and carried the tray over to their bed.

49

"Oh, breaking Cross House Rule Number Seven," Elizabeth said. "Food shall not be eaten in bed unless: A) The person in bed is ill or B) It's a very, very special occasion."

He swallowed and put the tray down at the foot of the large bed. "This qualifies under the second exception."

Elizabeth arched a questioning brow.

"We're alive."

"Good point," she agreed and stacked the pillows against the headboard before she crawled up onto the high bed.

Simon took the damp towel from around his neck and tossed it into the bathroom before sitting up at the head of the bed with her. Elizabeth slid the tray between them and took another bite of her sandwich as he uncapped one of the green pear-shaped bottles of Perrier and poured each of them a glass.

Elizabeth clinked her glass against Simon's. "To staying that way."

He looked into her eyes and nodded solemnly.

"Do you think Hassan's all right?" she asked. The man had risked his life for them and not knowing his fate had started to eat away at her.

"Yes, I think so. He's rather...resourceful, I'm sure he has things under control." He took a drink and set his glass aside. "However, on that front, I'm not sure we should pursue this."

Elizabeth shifted to the side. "The watch?"

"Yes, all of it." Simon's brow furrowed.

She put her sandwich down. "After all we went through?"

"Precisely *because* of that," Simon said. "We are out of our element here. I understand we have to accept some dangers, but..."

She reached out and laid her hand on his forearm. "We made it through the worst of it."

"We don't know that, Elizabeth," he said with a sigh. "And if this mission is anything like the others, and I have no reason to suspect otherwise, things will only get worse the nearer we get to our goal."

He picked up his drink again. "No, I think perhaps we should leave this for someone else."

Elizabeth frowned. Something wasn't right. Simon was definitely not one to dive into anything headfirst, but he'd come to terms with the dangers inherent in what they did. Or she thought he had.

He looked down into his glass and then finished it and put the empty glass on the end table.

"What's really wrong?" she asked.

He glanced over at her and opened his mouth to speak, but closed it. His eyes danced over her face until he shook his head. "Nothing. I'm just tired, I suppose."

She didn't quite believe that. There was something else going on, but she didn't want to push him. Not yet, anyway.

She was about to change the subject when an enormous yawn overtook her. Maybe it was just fatigue. They'd barely slept or eaten for days and had spent half of the time tied up and the other half running for their lives. It tuckered a person out.

"Finished?" Simon gestured to what was left of the sandwiches she'd wolfed down.

Elizabeth nodded and Simon set the tray aside. He smoothed down the pillows and lay back against them. She followed suit and rolled onto her side.

Simon's head turned toward her and he smiled tiredly and lifted his arm, his silent plea for her to join him. Elizabeth nestled into the crook of his shoulder. He wrapped his arm around her and pulled her more snugly against his side.

Elizabeth ran over the days in her head, but the usually crisp IMAX feature was running slowly and increasingly out of focus, until sleep finally claimed her and the picture stopped altogether.

CHAPTER EIGHT

Jack ran a smoothing hand over his hair and then knocked sharply on the Crosses' door. He waited a minute and when no one came, he knocked again. He checked his wristwatch. Almost eight o'clock. They'd only had four or five hours rest since they'd arrived at the hotel, but it would have to do.

He was about to knock a third time when the door opened and a frazzled Elizabeth greeted him.

"Sorry, we overslept." She turned back into the room and hurried over to her large steamer trunk. "Jack's here!"

She gestured for him to come in. "Simon's shaving."

"You want me to come back?" he asked.

She waved the thought away and pulled open one of the trunk drawers. "He's getting pretty good with the straight-edge, it shouldn't be—"

"Dammit!" came the cry from the bathroom, followed by some low-level grumbling.

Elizabeth stifled a laugh. "Usually. We're both still a little googley-eyed."

Jack nodded. He hadn't gotten much sleep himself the last few days and the few hours shut-eye he'd managed that afternoon were hardly enough.

"Aha!" Elizabeth cried and held up the shoes she'd apparently been searching for.

"Take your time," he said.

Elizabeth smiled her thanks and sat down at the vanity. She slipped on her shoes and then turned to look at her reflection, needlessly touching up her perfect make-up. A small frown tugged at the corners of her mouth and she sighed heavily.

Jack walked up behind her. She looked beautiful, as always, but a little worried, maybe even sad. It was an expression she seldom wore and he didn't like seeing it on her face. "Something wrong?"

She looked at his reflection and tried to brighten, but quickly gave up the pretense. "Simon thinks we should go home."

That wasn't all that surprising. As far as he could tell, Cross felt that way every time they'd traveled anywhere. And, frankly, Jack could hardly blame him. Putting yourself and your wife in mortal danger didn't come easily, shouldn't come easily. Hell, if the roles were reversed, he wasn't sure that he could do it.

Jack squeezed her shoulder encouragingly. "He'll come around."

Cross entered the room, wiping the last bits of shaving cream from his neck with a small towel. "Who'll come around?" he said as he plucked a tiny bit of toilet paper that covered a small shaving nick from his chin.

Elizabeth turned around on her bench. "You."

Cross made a sour face and tossed his towel back into the bathroom. "Let's just say I'm unconvinced this is worth the risk."

He picked up the dress shirt that had been laid out for him. Slipping it on, he worked on the buttons and looked at Elizabeth in a gentle challenge as he waited for her inevitable counter-argument.

Elizabeth raised her hands out in front of her, balancing out the options as she ticked them off. "Maaaybe getting hurt, versus the end of the world as we know it."

Cross opened his mouth to say something, something harsh judging from the set of his eyes, but caught himself with noticeable effort and settled for one of his mildly chiding "Elizabeths."

She might have been a bit dramatic, but from what that weaselly little man Travers had told them, it was a possibility.

"The power of the watches in the wrong hands?" she said. "If there is this Shadow Council like Travers said and they really are secretly trying to gather all of the watches…"

Cross tucked his shirt in. "I'll admit that is troubling, but it doesn't mean we have to be the ones to stop them."

"There aren't exactly a lot of qualified applicants," Elizabeth said.

Cross shouldered his suspenders with a snap. "I'm sure they can find someone." He turned away to search for his jacket and Elizabeth looked pleadingly at Jack.

He was sympathetic to Cross's concerns, but his time in WWII had taught him that hoping the other guy would take care of it rarely worked out.

"I know I don't have as much skin in the game as you do. I'm new to this whole time travel thing," he said. "But I do know that nothing good happens when people who can do something don't."

Cross pushed out a long breath through his nose. Jack could see the tension in his shoulders as he turned back to face them. He glared at Jack, but didn't argue the point.

Elizabeth stood and walked over to her husband. She straightened a twist in his suspenders. "The only thing necessary for evil to triumph is for good men to do nothing."

Jack could see Cross weakening. His eyes softened as he looked down at her.

"If this Travers guy is right," Jack said. "And the bad-guys on the Council have plans for the watches, the good guys better get them first." He peered at himself in the mirror. "Like it or not," he said, straightening his tie, "that's us."

Cross shot him another glare, but Elizabeth patted his chest and the fire in Cross's eyes dimmed. Not for the first time, Jack thought a beautiful and compassionate woman was the best weapon ever invented.

Jack dipped his hand into his jacket pocket and pulled out Mason's watch. "Ya know, now that we have two of these, if you wanted to go, I could stay and see it through."

As expected, Cross's eyes lit up at the possibility while Elizabeth's forehead wrinkled in worry.

"You'd have to teach me how to use it," Jack said, as he put the watch back into his pocket. "But—"

"And you'd have to wait until the next eclipse," Elizabeth said quickly. "And we have no idea when that is."

As exciting as the idea of having his own time travel device was to Jack, having to travel back and forth during an eclipse made things a little dicey. Not knowing when the next one was, made it even more so.

"Or we could give him the key," Cross said, deflating her balloon in one stroke.

There was that, Jack thought. The watchmaker, Teddy Fiske, had made a special watch key for Elizabeth that allowed the bearer to travel without needing an eclipse. Problem was, there was only one key.

She looked at Cross briefly and nodded. "We could."

"But you don't want to," Jack prompted.

"It's not that," she said. "We could give it to you, but then *we'd* have to wait for an eclipse to leave."

Cross grunted, clearly displeased his idea embraced flawed logic. "True."

"Besides," Elizabeth said softly, her eyes lowered briefly before she looked up at Cross. "I want to stay. I know this is dangerous, but three of us have a better chance of success than one of us. No offense," she added.

"None taken," Jack assured her.

"And," she said. "This is who I am."

Cross looked at her. The unease and admiration mixing in his eyes.

"It's who I want to be," she said.

Jack saw Cross's jaw muscle clench and unclench as he fought his instinctive reaction to argue. Cross reached out and caressed her cheek tenderly before remembering Jack was standing there. He dropped his hand and cleared his throat.

"If I do agree to this," Cross said somewhat pompously, clearly more comfortable standing on imperious ground. "Where can we possibly start? Mason didn't reveal what he knew about the missing watch to Travers. It was pure luck Travers discovered Mason had traveled to Egypt at all."

Cross slipped his jacket on and continued, "And need I remind you that our one lead died this morning and any chance of picking up the trail for the missing watch died with him."

"Not necessarily," Jack said as he walked across the room toward them. "We know Mason was here looking for a watch that some other Council member lost or left behind here, right?"

Elizabeth nodded. "Travers said that Mason had somehow traced it here, but he wasn't sure exactly where."

Jack reached into his jacket pocket and pulled out an envelope. "On the train Mason said he was close to finding it."

"Yes," Cross said. "But he died before he could tell us anything more."

"I think he did anyway." Jack took a piece of paper out of the envelope and unfolded it. "He had this on him."

Cross took the paper and he and Elizabeth frowned as they looked at it. "I don't understand," Cross said. "It's just a long series of numbers."

Jack pointed at the top line. "It's a code. I'm not sure what kind yet, but you don't code messages that don't have valuable information in them."

Jack jabbed at the paper. "He knew something. Something he didn't want anyone else to know."

"Except the person he was sending that to." Elizabeth examined the envelope. "Louche, Blomster & Blackwood."

She looked up at him questioningly, but all he could do was shake his head and shrug.

Cross took the envelope from her. "Solicitors. A very old English firm."

"The plot thickens," Jack said.

Elizabeth worried her bottom lip for a moment. "The code, can you break it?"

Jack wasn't sure. He'd had some training in it, but he was far from an expert. "Eventually."

Cross arched an eyebrow. "That's hardly comforting."

"This isn't all we have to go on, ya know," Jack said as he took back the paper and envelope and tucked them into his jacket. "Everyone leaves a trail. And Mason might have been good at what he did, but he left us a trail a mile wide in the desert. Five'll get you ten, we can pick up his trail here in Cairo too."

"He was staying here at this hotel," Cross reasoned. "He must have chosen this particular place for a reason."

"What do you mean?" Elizabeth asked.

"If you want to stay off the radar," Jack said. "You don't fly high."

Elizabeth frowned and looked to her husband for an explanation.

"Shepheard's is the hub of the Cairo social scene," Cross said, warming to the mystery. "If someone didn't want to be seen, this would be the very last place they'd stay. He must have come here because he needed something here."

"Or someone," Elizabeth added.

"Right," Jack said with a grin. He tugged on his shirt cuffs, ignored Cross's obvious hesitancy, and held out his arm for Elizabeth. "I say we go downstairs, have some dinner and make some new friends."

CHAPTER NINE

$\int$ IMON HAD BEEN TOO tired to appreciate the wonderfully grand absurdity of the lobby and entrance hall at Shepheard's before, but now, rested, it stood before him in all of its overwrought glory. He might as well enjoy it while he could. He was still unconvinced staying here was wise. He'd see it through tonight and hope he could talk sense into Elizabeth in the morning.

As they descended the grand staircase into the main hall, they passed two life-size bronze statues of bare-breasted women with ancient Egyptian headdresses, holding up electric lamps. Thick columns topped with lotus flowers led to an enormous octagonal Moorish hall with a sixty foot ceiling. What appeared to be a canopy of glass was the centerpiece of wildly detailed and adorned walls, floors and ceilings. Grand pointed Coptic arches, intricate latticework and mosaics evoked the lavish feeling of the great Cairo of centuries past for the European traveler. Divans, rattan chairs and tables were scattered on and around ubiquitous oriental carpets. Among the potted palms and trays of champagne were princes and marquis, generals and titans of industry. Europe's elite called Shepheard's home. As he understood it, it was more of a social club than a hotel really. A place to see and be seen. Simon could only hope Mason was one of the latter and not just the former.

As they walked through the long hall and toward the front desk, Simon absently tried to place the tune the small orchestra in the loggia played. Anything to take his mind off last night. The memories of those long hours, not knowing, imagining the worst shadowed him still.

Reflexively, he reached out to touch Elizabeth. His hand landed lightly on the small of her back. Just a small reassurance, but one he needed.

Jack had suggested they stop at the front desk and make an inquiry before dinner. Simon let Elizabeth precede him through a knot of British soldiers. The hotel and the rest of Cairo wasn't dominated by their presence the way it surely had been during the war years, but they and their uniforms were still omnipresent.

"Hello," Jack said to the clerk, as he casually leaned against the front desk. He pointed to Simon and Elizabeth. "We're friends of George Mason. He's also staying in the hotel. We tried his room, but there was no answer. Did he change rooms?"

The slender clerk bowed his head slightly and quickly consulted a ledger behind the counter. "Mr. Mason is still in room 226, but I believe he is away at the moment."

Jack turned to Simon. "I told ya." He looked at Elizabeth for confirmation. "Didn't I tell ya? And he knew we were coming."

He sighed and addressed the clerk again. "You don't know when he'll be back, do you?" Jack leaned in conspiratorially and lowered his voice. "We have some business and it's getting a little...urgent, if you know what I mean."

The clerk nodded again and smiled. "I understand, sir. I am afraid I am not privy to Mr. Mason's schedule. But perhaps Professor Whiteside can help you. They spent a great deal of time together."

Jack snapped his fingers. "Whiteside. Right. Mason mentioned him. Is he around?"

Simon was impressed. Wells didn't miss a beat. His lies sounded more natural than his truths. He'd not only managed to find out Mason's room number, but a contact as well.

"I believe the professor and his daughter are in the dining room."

Jack pointed in one direction and the clerk corrected him by pointing in the other.

Jack rapped the counter with his knuckles. "Good man."

He turned to Simon and Elizabeth with a grin. "Shall we?"

The dining room was large, holding at least fifty tables, elegantly set with white linens and silver service. Like the entrance hall, it too had an enormously high ceiling and was decorated in classic Moorish design with embellished columns patterned with green diamonds, an emerald carpet and large gilt mirrors.

A dozen or so waiters in white robes with wide maroon sashes about their waists and matching fezzes, or tarbooshes as they were known locally, lingered around the edges of the room ready to meet a diner's needs. Simon stopped one of them and asked for the professor's table. The man bowed and directed him to a table near the cascading, tiered fountain at the far end of the room.

The table next to Whiteside and his daughter was empty giving them the perfect opportunity to meet them both. Whatever Mason wanted with Whiteside, it had something to do with the missing watch. At least, that was the logical conclusion. It could simply have been part of his cover, but Simon's instincts told him it was something more.

Simon pulled out a chair for Elizabeth, and then he and Jack took their seats. Whiteside was perhaps in his late fifties or early sixties. His hair had gone mostly white and what there was left of it sprouted off his head in unruly short curls. He was slightly disheveled, not from lack of money, but lack of care. His suit was well-made and expensive, but wrinkled in a way university professors' often were. He looked to be the sort who would perpetually have chalk dust on his forearm and neither notice nor care.

"I'm sorry, my dear," he said with a vague hint of a Lincolnshire accent. "I simply must meet Jouvet tomorrow at the museum."

The young woman, presumably his daughter, teetered between childhood and womanhood, probably no more than eighteen. She pushed her glasses back up on her nose and looked at her father with alarm.

"But, papa!" she started in an excited voice, before regaining her composure. "I can go alone. I don't need George to escort me. Really."

"Don't be absurd, dear."

The girl chewed on her lip and tugged nervously on a tendril of blonde hair that had escaped from her bun as she furiously searched for a counter-argument.

Whiteside looked up from the book he was reading and patted her hand. "I'm sure you can amuse yourself here for the day."

The girl continued to fret, but in silence, and Simon took advantage of the opening. "I'm sure Mason will be along before too long," he said, somewhat loudly.

Jack grunted. "It's just like George to do this."

"I'm sure he had a good reason for running off," Elizabeth said, joining their little play. "I hope he's all right."

Whiteside cleared his throat and turned toward them. "I'm terribly sorry to intrude, but did you say something about George Mason?"

Simon shifted in his chair to face him. "Yes, we did. Do you know him?" Simon glanced back to Jack and Elizabeth. "We're a little concerned."

"As am I," Whiteside said with a frown. "Forgive me," he stood and stuck out his hand. "Arthur Whiteside. This is my daughter, Christina."

Simon stood, shook his hand and bowed slightly toward the girl. "Simon Cross. My wife, Elizabeth, and Jack Wells. So, you know George Mason?"

Whiteside's forehead creased in worry. "Yes, we share common interests."

From the short dossier Travers had given them, Simon knew Mason's areas of expertise. While they varied from ancient literature to philosophy, combining his clear love of antiquity with their current location, it was hardly difficult to guess. "Egyptology?" Simon asked.

"Yes," Whiteside said with a broad, dreamy smile as if he were thinking of a lover and not a field of study. He came back to himself and said, "Mason was an avid collector. Very well versed on the subject."

"Cross here is no slouch himself," Jack said winning a quick glare from Simon.

He had studied the subject, of course, both at university and in his own pursuits, but... "Compared to Mason and yourself, Professor, I'm merely an amateur."

Whiteside was pleased at the compliment and his smile broadened. "Won't you join us?" He gestured to their large, empty table. "We have plenty of room, as you can see. The Everetts seem to have disappeared as well."

Christina rolled her eyes and shook her head in obvious exasperation with whomever the Everetts were. "They're probably drunk again."

Whiteside laughed uncomfortably and shot his daughter a surprised and confused look as though he didn't realize she knew what drunk was. He cleared his throat and looked back to Simon who saved him from further embarrassment and steamrolled right over the awkward moment, thanking him profusely for the offer.

"You mentioned that you were worried about George, too," Elizabeth said as she settled into her seat at the new table. "Do you have any idea where he went?"

Whiteside summoned a waiter with a wave of his hand. "Not the foggiest, I'm afraid. Mason's a bit of an odd duck." He laughed and then clapped Simon on the forearm. "But then I don't need to tell you, do I? And not that there's anything wrong with that, of course. I've been called far worse."

The waiter appeared at their table and Whiteside tapped his own Old Fashioned and raised a finger, signaling for another, before casting his glance around the table. "What would you like?"

They placed their orders and the awkward silence that always followed an interruption settled in around them.

"So, Christina," Jack said. "Is this your first time to Egypt?"

"Oh no," she said, with a shake of her head. "Daddy and I come every season. Except for that one year we spent in Singapore. It rained so much nearly all of my books were ruined. But then I suppose that's to be expected in the rain forest, isn't it? But I still miss my copy of Songs of Innocence and Experience. Keats, you know."

The girl seemed to suddenly realize she'd wandered far off topic and blushed prettily. Elizabeth smiled kindly at her.

"Egypt is wonderful," Christina said softly, but there was a twinge of wistful sadness in her voice. "I'd rather be here than London or Paris."

"Well, you're way ahead of me," Elizabeth said. "This is my first time and I want to see everything."

Simon sighed dramatically. "She means that quite literally, you know?"

Whiteside chuckled.

"Mason was supposed to show us around the museum, but..." Simon let his bait dangle in the air.

"Cairo Museum?" Whiteside said. "I have an appointment there tomorrow, but it won't take long." He ignored the look his daughter shot him at that remark and pushed on. "Perhaps, you'd join me? I'd be more than pleased to stand in for Mason, as it were."

"That's very kind of you, Professor Whiteside," Simon said.

"Arthur," Whiteside said. "Any friend of George's and all that."

Simon felt the familiar warmth of Elizabeth's hand as she slipped it into his under the table and gave it a "well done" squeeze.

Jack sighed. "Museums." He held up his hand in apology. "No offense, Professor. I was kind of hoping to see a little of the city. Poke around a little."

"We can meet up later," Simon said and then added with a conspiratorial whisper in Whiteside's direction. "He's not the academic type."

Whiteside smiled in understanding.

"Speaking of, is that Budge?" Simon asked, nodding down at Whiteside's book.

"Yes!" he said, pleased and obviously not realizing Simon could read the author's name at the top of the page. "It's quite good. Really quite good. Have you read his Legends of the Gods?"

"No," Simon said. "I—"

"Fascinating!" Whiteside said as he ran his finger over the text and read with dramatic flair. "The legend of Heru-Behutet begins with Horus holding the hippopotamus-fiend with a chain and spear! Behind him stand—"

"Father," Christina admonished. "Not at dinner. Remember the rules?"

It took Whiteside a moment to stop the freight train of his enthusiasm, but when he finally did, his face filled with chagrin. "You're right, of course, my dear. Forgive me?"

She smiled kindly at him. The shy child was gone, and a lovely, compassionate young woman appeared.

Whiteside put his hand over his daughter's. "Her mother, God rest her soul, made me promise not to bring my work to the table. Said the sand got into everything." He smiled and laughed lightly, but it was clear to everyone that the thought of his late wife still grieved him deeply. Simon did not blame him for that. He cast a quick glance at Elizabeth. He did not blame him at all.

Dinner was surprisingly good. The food wasn't quite up to the level one would find in the finest French restaurants in Europe and New York, but it was still excellent. Both Whiteside and his daughter were pleasant enough company and, as far as Simon could tell, genuine. There was always the risk that anyone they might meet could be an agent of the mysterious Shadow Council Travers had mentioned. However, Simon found that highly unlikely in the Whiteside's case.

They spoke openly and freely of their lives in England where the Professor had retired from teaching and his position as curator for the Ashmolean, a venerable and well-respected museum at Oxford. Representatives from every major museum in the world were in Egypt for the season, all vying for the best artifacts to send back home.

"A nest of vipers," Whiteside called them. "Don't let Winlock's winsome good looks fool you," he added with a nod toward the excavator from New York's Metropolitan Museum, who was anything but handsome. "Beneath that broad smile and broader mustache lies the heart of a brigand. Mata Hari in tweed."

Whiteside's eyes flashed with humor and he couldn't contain his smile.

"Oh, father," Christina chided him gently.

"In all seriousness, it is nasty business—acquisitions. There's a great deal of money at stake."

"And no small measure of pride," Christina added with a sly smile.

His eyes glittered. "It is quite the dangerous game."

"Don't believe everything my father says. He's prone to exaggeration."

He might have been overstating things a bit, Simon admitted, but considering the money involved in antiquities, he might not be far off. Had that been why Mason befriended Whiteside? Was the watch mixed in with other collectables?

"Are you here to acquire for the museum?" Elizabeth asked.

"Oh, I'm retired. Although a little business, a little pleasure."

"And speaking of," Christina said, ignoring her father's glare. "I don't see why I can't go to the Bazaar alone. I've been dozens of times."

"Never alone," he said. "This is a wonderful country," he said and then grew serious. "But you'll be hard pressed to find a man who won't try to cheat you."

"Father!"

Simon wasn't surprised by Whiteside's attitude. His was typical of the British of the day. The occupier always thinks the people he conquers are better off by his occupation than they were before. Of course, the occupation of Egypt had little to do with improving the life of its citizens and far more to do with unfettered access to the lucrative Suez Canal.

Whiteside's expression was unashamed. "Well, it's the truth, my dear. And the gyppos at the Bazaar are the worst of the lot. It's not at all safe for a young lady alone."

Christina sulked, but only for a moment. Her eyes lit up and shifted to Jack. "What if I had an escort?"

Whiteside's eyes narrowed. "Who?"

"Mr. Wells," she said brightly. "He's new to Egypt and wants to see some of the city. The least I can do is to show him around and he can be my protector."

Whiteside frowned. "I'm not certain that's entirely proper, Christina. You understand, of course?" he added to Jack.

But before Jack could say anything, Christina jumped in. "Diana will be back in the morning. What if the three of us go? She can chaperone."

Whiteside considered it.

"I would like to see the Bazaar," Jack said. "And I promise to be a perfect gentleman."

"Yes, of course," Whiteside said quickly, embarrassed to be seen questioning his guest's honor. "Of course. If you can make arrangements with Diana," he said as his daughter beamed in response.

"And we three shall go to the museum," Whiteside continued. He lifted his glass. "Quite the day!"

CHAPTER TEN

"**D**O YOU WANT MY COAT?" Simon offered. The night was cool, but not cold. Elizabeth's green silk halter dress didn't afford much in the way of warmth, but she didn't mind. The air felt good.

She shook her head and leaned into him as they walked. The grounds were lush and large. Paths lit with tiki torches wound their way through the palms and flowers and fountains. Fairy lights lined the edges of the hotel and looked like fireflies winking on and off as they went deeper into the garden.

Simon was quiet as they walked, which wasn't all that unusual. He was comfortable with silence. But Elizabeth could feel the slight tension in his body, in the way he held his shoulders. This wasn't the easy silence of an evening at home reading or sitting by the fire, this silence was hiding something.

"Are you all right?" she asked. She squeezed his arm. "You're all tense."

"Fine," he lied.

She frowned, but didn't press him and leaned back into his side as they walked along a path. "I think things are going pretty well really."

Simon looked down at her about to argue the point, but didn't. "We did make progress," he conceded. "It is a daunting prospect though, isn't it? The watch could be with anyone, anywhere in the city. Assuming it's still even in Cairo."

"True, but Mason went out of his way to befriend Whiteside. He only would have done that if he thought Whiteside could help lead him to the watch." Elizabeth chewed on her lower lip. "Or thought that Whiteside had the watch himself."

Simon nodded. "Possible, but it seems unlikely. Mason didn't seem the sort to play games. Why not simply take the watch and leave town?"

Elizabeth thought about it for a moment. "Well, even if Whiteside doesn't have the watch, I don't think Mason would have gotten close to him if he didn't believe he needed him to get to the watch."

"Mason was quite paranoid on the train," Simon agreed. "And that fellow who lost the watch in the first place, his simply disappearing without a trace does complicate things immeasurably."

Elizabeth tucked a stray curl behind her ear. "I understand why Mason was so cagey with the details of what he found out, the fewer people who know and all that, but it does make our job a lot harder."

Simon ran his hand down her arm. "At least we know he thought it was here. Now."

"Maybe it's in a collection somewhere or mixed up in a museum archive?"

"Possibly," Simon said and then brought them to a halt near a large gnarled sycamore tree. "There's something else that makes our job more difficult. We mustn't write off Mason's paranoia as simply paranoia. If what Travers says about the Shadow Council is true, there may well be other operatives here right now."

"Operatives?" Elizabeth said as she turned and slipped her arms around his waist. "That sounds so...Bondish."

"Elizabeth—"

"I know," she said before he could. "This is serious." She put one hand on his chest. "I'm not taking any of this lightly, Simon. I understand what's at stake."

Simon took hold of her hand and kissed it.

"At least Travers bought us some time. I'd always kind of wondered why the Council didn't come and try to take your watch away," she said.

Whatever his reasons, Elizabeth was grateful for Travers running interference for them. He'd known the details of each of their last adventures, and yet, the Council hadn't come for the watch. For reasons she wasn't quite sure she believed, he'd hidden their presence and destroyed any trace of their involvement as the Shadow Council grew in power.

Whatever mechanism the Council had used to keep tabs on the watches, Travers had destroyed as well. Without it, the watches and their owners were basically wiped off the grid, untraceable. It had been a difficult choice, he'd said. But they had to do everything they could to keep the watches out of the hands of the Shadows, even if in the process it made it nearly impossible for the good guys to find the watches as well. It bought them time, and in their business time was everything.

Simon had been reluctant to believe Travers, but he had protected them. Although, she knew their anonymity would not last forever.

Simon's forehead wrinkled in worry and she knew he was sharing her train of thought.

Elizabeth reached up and cupped his cheek. "We can do this. Together."

Simon covered her hand with his own and closed his eyes. When he opened them again, they were filled with an emotion she couldn't name.

"What is it?"

He let out a deep breath and stepped away from her. "I can't get last night out of my head."

Elizabeth shook her head. "What do you mean? It was scary, but it all worked out."

Simon shook his head. "But what if it hadn't? I spent all night in that tent wondering what was happening, what they were...doing to you, and—"

Elizabeth closed the distance between them. "But nothing happened."

"But it could have, Elizabeth. The not knowing..." Simon said, his voice rough.

Elizabeth's heart dropped. She'd never stopped to consider what it must have been like from his perspective. She felt like such a fool. The men had treated her well, but Simon had no way of knowing that. She'd been so busy trying to save the world, she'd ignored the one part of it that meant the most to her.

"I'm sorry." Elizabeth said as she shook her head and sighed. She took hold of his hand and traced the contours of his palm. "If you want to go home," she said and then looked up into his eyes. "We'll go."

He shook his head and took a firm grasp of her hand. "You're right to want to stay. I just—"

"Worry. I know. I didn't think..." Elizabeth's eye filled with concern. "Why didn't you tell me how you felt?"

Simon started to answer, but fell silent. She knew the answer. Unlike her, he'd put her feelings in front of his own. He wanted to take her home and keep the world the away, but he hadn't because it wasn't what she wanted. He'd met her selfishness with selflessness. Worst of all, he'd kept his pain to himself.

"Do you remember when we were in London," she asked, "and I reached a point where I was just overwhelmed with what we had to do, what we had to face?"

"I remember."

Elizabeth smiled at the memory. "I fled into the bathroom for a good cry, and you came in. Do you remember what you told me?"

"You said," Elizabeth continued, "that I didn't ever have to hide from you." She touched his cheek and her voice began to tremble with emotion. "Simon, don't you know that you can always be honest with me? Always."

Simon closed his eyes and a let out a shaky breath. He clenched his jaw and covered her hand with his before easing it to his lips and gently kissing her palm. "Yes," he said in a voice rough with emotion.

"I want to stay," he said finally and then shook his head ruefully, "But I won't ever stop worrying about you."

"I'm sorry—"

Simon shook his head and pressed a finger to her lips. He leaned down and kissed her. She wrapped her arms around his neck as she pulled him closer.

"She'll be here soon," Christina assured him and then looked anxiously down the long corridor of the lobby.

Jack smiled. Christina might be in a hurry, but he wasn't. He'd been a nut to rush headlong into babysitting last night. Now, in the bright light of morning, he was regretting it. Elizabeth would have been better suited to the task. But there was nothing to do about it now. He'd volunteered, like an idiot, for the assignment.

He didn't really mind waiting for whoever this Diana was— probably a spinster draped in pearls and judgment—it gave him time to mull over what he'd found in Mason's room last night. He'd waited until the hotel was quiet and picked the lock. Too easy. A place like this should have better security. Although, in this case, their lapse worked in his favor.

He hadn't been surprised to see he wasn't the first to be there. The room had already been tossed. Clothes and books strewn about the floor. He gave it a quick going over, but if there had been anything worthwhile there, it was gone now.

He let out a sigh.

"She's always a little late," Christina said with a small smile and then returned to fiddling with the lace cuff of her dress. She was really quite attractive and the sort who had no idea. He knew the type, too busy hiding behind her glasses and books to notice people noticing her.

She kept looking expectantly toward the front door, but so far the half of Cairo that had come and gone didn't include the mythical Diana.

Jack settled into his chair and decided to pass the time doing one of the things he did best, watch people. There was nothing quite like the lobby of a hotel for people watching. In his business, observing people was more than half the game. He leaned back in his rattan chair and watched a young couple descend the grand staircase. Their clothes gave them away immediately as English and from money. The man's cream suit was freshly pressed, although he was not. From the small round sunglasses he wore indoors to the gingerly way he walked, the man was obviously suffering from one hell of a hangover. His wife looked only a little bit less nauseated.

She waved toward him. For a moment, Jack wondered if he'd been caught staring.

"The Everetts," Christina said, not bothering to hide her disdain.

Ah, the missing couple from last night's dinner, Jack thought. No wonder they hadn't shown up. They must have been plenty soused to be that deep in the bag this morning.

The couple slowly made their way over to them. The man grabbed a bellboy and barked an order. "Coffee with Fernet," he said.

"Times two," his wife added.

The bellboy bowed deeply.

"Yes, yes," Everett said, impatiently. "Just get on with it."

The boy scurried away and the man turned back to Christina and lowered his glasses. His squinting eyes shifted to Jack and then back. Jack's presence barely registered and what had, was filed as unimportant. "About dinner last night," Everett drawled in a tired, insincere way.

"We found ourselves at the most wonderful party," his wife chimed in. "We simply couldn't pull ourselves away. It would have been so rude."

Christina opened her mouth to speak, no doubt to remind them that not showing up for dinner was rude, but thought better of it. "Terribly," she said instead.

The woman leaned forward conspiratorially. "You're such a dear child."

Christina's face wrinkled in restrained irritation.

Everett offered Christina a false smile and hooked his wife by the arm. "Catch you later?" he asked, not bothering to wait for an answer before pulling his wife away and heading toward the dining room.

"Child," Christina ground out, showing a bit of fire and temper. "She's only seven years older than I am."

"Weren't they charming," Jack said, winning a small laugh from Christina. "Who exactly are they?"

"Constance and Trevor Everett. Of the Everetts of Leeds," she added meaningfully.

Jack shrugged. "Is that impressive?"

Christina smiled and shrugged. "They think so."

Jack's laugh was interrupted by a woman's voice calling out near the front door.

"*Chud baulk!*"

Their attention, along with everyone else's in the lobby was pulled toward the commotion. Two men carried a large crate suspended between two poles. The sea of people parted before them.

"*Taht! Byshwysh!*" the woman said again.

When the men stopped and put the large crate down, Jack could finally see her.

She took off her large brimmed hat and waved to the men. She was beautiful. Brown shoulder length hair, and a figure that even a men's white shirt and boxy, tan riding skirt could not hide. Her boots clicked on the tile floor for a moment in the silence that had followed her entrance. She spoke to the two men in Arabic, giving orders and looking used to doing so.

The men picked up the crate again and she watched them go with a frown before turning toward Christina smiling.

"Diana," Christina said. "I told you she'd be here."

Christina hurried over to the woman and gripped her by the hand. Together, they walked back over to Jack. Diana eyed him up and down, and smiled, happy with what she saw. Jack returned the favor. This woman was going to be a challenge, he thought. A welcome one.

"Diana Trent, this is Jack Wells. The one I mentioned in the note."

She stuck out her hand and Jack shook it. Firm grip, and soft hands. Of all of the Dianas he'd imagined, this was not one of them. A chaperone was a dowager. A plump, cross woman with an umbrella to whack young would-be suitors with. This woman was far from that.

"Miss Trent," he said with one of his most disarming smiles.

She laughed, not quite making fun of him, but amused nonetheless, before turning to Christina. "I am sorry I'm late," she said. "The men at the depot 'misplaced' my shipment. I had to spend the morning straightening it out. You can see what that led to."

"It's all right," Christina said, fondly. She might be on the shy side with everyone else, but the girl definitely had a special affection and admiration for Diana.

Jack was inclined to feel the same way. She was beautiful, confident and did he mention beautiful? That was a combination he found hard to resist.

"I have a carriage out front, unless you'd like to walk," Diana said with a wry smile.

Christina fought down her own smile and slipped her arm through Diana's and started for the front door.

Jack stood watching them for a moment, before Diana looked over her shoulder. "Aren't you coming?"

Jack grinned, put on his fedora and started after them.

CHAPTER ELEVEN

I F YOU SAT ON the terrace at Shepheard's Hotel long enough, you could see the world walk by. At least, that's how the saying went. Judging from the endless parade of everything from men wearing stuffed crocodiles on their heads—for sale, of course—to boys leading tourists balanced precariously on the backs of small donkeys, Elizabeth was inclined to agree. From large pythons wrapped around men's shoulders like feathered boas, to curiously dressed monkeys, the animal population was almost as diverse as the human one. Peddlers with every imaginable ware walked back and forth in front of Shepheard's Hotel. Every time an unsuspecting guest left or arrived, they were besieged by offers of hats, fly-switches, picture frames and ostrich feathers.

Elizabeth sat back in her chair and enjoyed the spectacle as they waited for Whiteside to arrive. The large front terrace was elevated from the street by about six feet, so the guests could watch the pageant without being unduly bothered by it.

She sipped her tea, grateful for the caffeine. She and Simon had been awakened before dawn by the Muslim call to prayer. Some time around 5:00 a.m., the loud, undulating call roused them from a sound sleep. Simon rolled over, but Elizabeth padded over to the window. In the distance she could see the silhouette of a muezzin standing at the top of a minaret reciting the call to prayer to the sleeping city. She could almost make out the sound of others, just a bit farther away standing atop the many minarets that dotted the city's skyline. It would take some getting used to, but considering the call came five times a day, she was sure it would seem a normal part of every day before long.

But for now, she was a little on the sleepy side and tried to hide her yawn behind her hand.

Simon smiled slyly. He'd done his part to keep her up late last night. She shook her head, amused, and he went back to reading his copy of the Egyptian Gazette, one of the two major English language newspapers available.

Elizabeth was just contemplating another cup of tea or maybe some Turkish coffee, or would that be Egyptian coffee here, when she saw Whiteside step out onto the terrace.

She waved and they met him at the top of the wide staircase leading down to the street. Whiteside gripped his cane as they headed down the stairs and into the gauntlet of hucksters, beggars and tradesmen. As soon as their feet hit the bottom stair, they were surrounded on all sides. Despite Simon's barked commands and Whiteside's pleas, the men were unrelenting, each shouting louder than the next to be heard over the din.

Elizabeth and Simon were shuffling their way through the crowd and toward a waiting carriage when she felt a hand slip into hers. She turned to look, expecting a child, only to find a baboon grinning up at her. She gasped in shock. At least she hoped that was a grin.

"What's wrong?" Simon asked.

Elizabeth didn't want to scare the animal and so she remained frozen in place, it's hand lightly holding hers. It sat on its haunches grinning up at her, baring his teeth in a frightening smile. His owner said something in excited Arabic and gestured toward her. No doubt he wanted a *baksheesh*, a sort of gratuity, for the experience.

"Oh dear," exclaimed Whiteside. "Filthy creatures."

Simon was about to step forward when a voice rang out from the crowd. It was commanding and seemed to be berating the baboon owner, who gently pulled his animal away and disappeared into the throng. Elizabeth looked over to see her savior.

"Hassan!"

She stepped forward and hugged him, before realizing how inappropriate that was.

His broad grin was a welcome sight. "Mister Cross. Miss Elizabeth. It is good to see you both."

Simon stuck out his hand and shook Hassan's heartily. "It is good to see you, my friend."

"We were worried about you," Elizabeth said.

He tilted his head back and puffed out his chest. "I am Hassan." He laughed and then nodded toward the carriage at the curb. "This is for you?"

"Yes, we're off to the museum."

Hassan nodded and then cut a swath through the crowd and helped Elizabeth up into the fancy carriage where Whiteside sat waiting for them.

"We'll be back this afternoon," Simon said.

"Hassan will be here," he said and then rapped on the carriage signaling to the driver their readiness.

Elizabeth watched Hassan stand on the sidewalk and wave to them. When traffic from other carriages and horses blocked her view she sat back in her seat.

The broad avenue took them down past the Grand Continental hotel and Opera Square before they turned to the west and headed toward the Nile. The Egyptian Museum sat just along the eastern bank near the southern tip of Gezira Island and its famed sports club and botanical garden.

The museum itself was large and well stocked thanks to the Department of Antiquities and the international digs that gave up half of their proceeds to the museum.

They paid the five piastres admission fee, about a shilling, and enjoyed the expansive museum while Whiteside conducted his business. They strolled through the large rotunda and into the central atrium where colossal statues of Pharaohs Ramses II and III and Imhotep and their queens sat. Sarcophagi and large door-shaped steles rested in niches inside the main gallery. Smaller burial displays with canopic jars and ushabti lined the walls

They wandered from room to room filled with statues and parts of tomb walls and every sort of antiquity imaginable. Each focused on a particular dynasty or empire. If you traveled clockwise around the ground floor, you could travel from 3000 BC to 700 AD in just under an hour.

The upper floor held the smaller items including the mummies, jewelry and papyri. One room even had mummies of crocodiles, apes and jackals.

Elizabeth leaned in closer to the glass case that held King Merenre. It wasn't the Boris Karloff type mummy at all. He'd been unwrapped and was only covered from chest to knees in some sort of gauzy material that looked unnervingly ghosty. His lower jaw was missing and his feet looked enormous next to his skinny desiccated legs. It hardly seemed a fitting end for a king.

"Can you imagine the parties?" Simon said at her side and then added, sensing her question, "The unwrapping parties."

Victorians and their obsession with death. In addition to those "I wish I hadn't Googled that" post-mortem portraits, Victorians loved to import mummies and have unwrapping parties. They might even give you a hand, literally, as a souvenir.

Elizabeth shuddered.

"Agreed," Simon said. He checked his watch. "Time to meet Whiteside."

Reluctantly, she allowed him to pull her away from the exhibit. She could have spent hours and hours in the museum, but this wasn't a vacation. They went downstairs to the rotunda where they'd arranged to meet the Professor.

They found him standing near the front door talking to a tall, dark haired man in an impeccable and very expensive suit. He was handsome by any standards and a hot-damn by hers. Not that she noticed that sort of stuff. Whiteside waved them over.

"I was just finishing up with Henri here," he said. "I hope we can come to agreeable terms."

Henri bowed his head in acknowledgement to Simon and when his eyes shifted to Elizabeth, a smile lit his face. He waited patiently for an introduction.

"Your manners, Arthur," Henri said in a sublime French accent.

"Oh, of course, head in the clouds," Whiteside said. "Mr. and Mrs. Cross, may I present, Henri Jouvet."

Henri ignored Simon and took Elizabeth's hand and raised it to his lips. "*Enchanté.*"

Elizabeth barely repressed her giggle. He was so movie star suave, genuinely so, she felt like a schoolgirl. Her husband was less amused.

"Yes," Simon said, his displeasure clear in his clipped tone, "Well...."

"The Crosses are friends of George Mason," Whiteside said, oblivious to Simon's crankiness.

"George?" Henri said, but it sounded like "Zhorzh."

Elizabeth repeated it without thinking, then added quickly, "Yes, we're friends. You knew him? I mean know him?"

Faux pas committed, she cast a quick nervous glance at Simon, who was apparently too busy glaring at Henri to notice.

"Yes. We were not well-acquainted," Henri said and his eyes shifted almost imperceptibly to Whiteside. "But rather business associates."

"What business exactly are you in?" Simon asked.

Henri was not the least bit cowed by Simon's tone. "What else?" he said, raising his hands and gesturing around the museum. "These things, they do not pop into the museum by themselves."

"An archaeologist?" Elizabeth asked.

He bowed in acknowledgment.

Well, that was interesting. What would Mason want with an archaeologist?

"They may not pop in, but they do seem to be popping out," Whiteside said. "A very rare aegis, a sort of broad collar, for the goddess Bastet disappeared last month."

"And a mirror of Hathor this week as well," Henri said with a shrug. "It is not the first time. Items sometimes have a way of walking out in the night," he said and then added with a look to Whiteside, "Do they not?"

Whiteside cleared his throat. "Yes, well. Why don't we circle back through, unless you've had your fill and would like to go somewhere else?"

"Well," Elizabeth said. "Maybe you can show us some of George's favorites and we can surprise him with our exhaustive knowledge when he returns?"

Whiteside beamed at the idea.

"I shall not keep you then," Henri said with a bow. "Perhaps we will see each other again?"

Whiteside turned to Henri. "Why not tonight? Drinks at Shepheard's? I hear Diana's talked the Long Bar into allowing women for the week. That should make it more enticing for a man like you, eh, Henri?" he added with a chuckle.

Elizabeth could hear Simon grinding his teeth.

Henri demurred the comment. "If you will be there," he said to Elizabeth, before turning to include Simon. "Both of you, of course."

Before Simon could say no, she said they would.

"Enjoy your day," Henri said with a final small bow. "I shall see what I can do regarding your papyrus, Arthur. It is no small task."

Whiteside spluttered his grateful understanding. "Yes, needle in a haystack and all that."

"Until tonight." Henri smiled at Elizabeth once more and then left.

"Well," Whiteside said rubbing his hands together. "How does a little stroll through Middle Kingdom canopic jars sound?"

"Perfect," Elizabeth said. "After you."

Whiteside started ahead while she and Simon lingered a little way behind.

"You can roll your tongue back into your head now," Simon said tartly.

"Oh, come on. It wasn't that bad and besides, I was just playing my part."

"Of my soon-to-be ex-wife?"

She looked up and could see the humor behind the jibe, but also the worry. "We need to know what he knows. And, anyway, he's just flirty."

"He's *French*," Simon said the word with distaste.

Simon had an unreasonable dislike for the French, which was balanced by her adoration for them. She slipped her arm into his. "You don't have anything to worry to about. I belong to one man... Hassan."

In spite of himself, Simon laughed and struggled to make his frown reappear, but he was Simon and managed.

She looked at him sympathetically, but held firm. "We knew we might have to do or say things we wouldn't normally do."

"Within reason," he reminded her.

"If I didn't know any better, I'd think you didn't trust me."

She meant it as a joke, but Simon was quite serious when he looked down at her. "Of course, I do. It's just... You are my wife," he said simply. "I will never like it when I see another man want you."

Elizabeth felt a warmth in her chest. "Even when we're old and gray, and living in the senior center?"

"Walkers at dawn if one of them so much as looks at you," he said with a smile. Finally, he sighed. "Just don't get carried away with your role, Ms. Garbo."

She squeezed his arm and gave him a reassuring smile.

"Come along," Whiteside called from across the room. "This one held the intestines!"

CHAPTER TWELVE

THE GRAND BAZAAR AT Khan El-Khahili may have been less than a mile away from Shepheard's Hotel, but it was worlds away. The hotel was an oasis of European civility for the weary and wealthy traveler. This, Jack thought, was Cairo—both grand and bizarre.

Once they left the enormous courtyard, they entered the main bazaar which was made up of confusing and intersecting narrow streets and alleys.

Christina didn't hesitate and made a beeline for the entrance to the left. Jack made sure not to let her get too far ahead. He had an obligation to look after her. Although, judging from the way she maneuvered through the crowd, she was an old hand at this. For the bookish sort, she deftly waved aside the over-eager shopkeeper or beggar. Occasionally, she'd stop to admire things, leaving compliments and a small *baksheesh* in her wake.

She skimmed along the stalls, each piled high from ground to awning with whatever they had for sale. Fruits, cushions, paintings, hats, jewelry...if it was in Egypt, it was for sale in the bazaar.

Following behind her, Jack was more than content to linger with Diana. She was a puzzle, and one he'd like to spend a few evenings trying to solve.

She must have felt him watching her, and turned to meet his gaze steadily. Instead of being embarrassed by his attention, she just arched an amused eyebrow and offered him a confident smile.

"So," she said. "This is your first time in Egypt?"

"Yup."

She slipped her arm through his. "Well, let's see if I can't make it a memorable stay, Mr. Wells."

That sounded like innuendo. He liked innuendo.

"I have little doubt of that."

She laughed lightly and easily.

Jack could definitely get used to this.

As they turned from one alley to another, the stalls shifted from copper to textiles. It was chaos, but there was a sort of organization to it if you squinted. No matter what the wares were, the shopkeepers stepped into your path to try to lure you to their stall. No one in Egypt had apparently ever heard the term soft sell.

It was loud and noisy, and filled with exotic sounds and aromas. One corridor would smell of spices and incense, the next, meats cooking and freshly brewed coffee. The smell of smoke from the water pipes men puffed on was all along the route. They passed a man sitting cross-legged near the doorway to his shop. The tip of a long hose rested in his mouth. He took a few draws and a cloud of smoke rose up to meet them as they passed. Jack inhaled the surprisingly sweet scent of the smoke and raised a brow.

"The *mu'assel*, the tobacco, it's mixed with honey or fruit," Diana explained. "Smoking a shisha is as common as breathing here. Not bad, really. You can try some at a little cafe I know."

"You certainly know the lay of the land."

"My business takes me many places," she said noncommittally. "Although, I do have a soft spot for Egypt."

Not one to be put off, Jack pressed the issue. "And what is your business?"

She just smiled at him and left his side to see the small statuette Christina was holding up. Jack joined them in front of a stall piled high with "genuine" relics.

"Are they all fakes?" Christina asked as she put the statuette of a cat back in its place.

"These? Yes," Diana said as she picked up one of the pieces. "And not very good ones. See the seam here?"

Jack leaned in to get a closer look. The seam was there, but very, very fine. Diana knew her stuff.

"These are for the tourists," she said. "The good stuff's probably in back. If you know just how to ask for it."

"Black market?"

Diana grinned.

The shop owner came outside to greet them and promptly got into an argument with Diana. He was quite insulted, apparently, took the piece from Diana's hand and waved them away from his shop before laying siege to a new, unsuspecting group of tourists.

"And what is your business in Cairo, Mr. Wells?" Diana asked as they fell back into step behind Christina again.

"Jack, please," he said.

Diana smiled. "You know, you remind me a little of George. Cagey."

"Mason?"

Diana nodded. "Don't tell me you're obsessed with Arthur's papyrus, too?"

Before he could ask her what she meant, he felt the familiar prickle of what Elizabeth had called his Spidey-sense. They were being followed. "Just a tourist," he added distractedly.

He walked another twenty feet before easing over to a booth selling tarbooshes. He slipped one onto his head and turned to show Diana, but his eyes were busy scanning the crowd. There, leaning against a wall, making a show of inspecting a small pot. Small, jet-black hair, pencil mustache and dark gray fedora. He'd seen that man twice before, once near the gates and again near a rug shop. Considering the twists and turns they'd taken so far, twice would be a helluva coincidence, but three times was trouble.

Jack put the tarboosh back into the pile and thanked the store owner, ignoring his pleas.

He put his hand on the small of Diana's back and urged her to close the gap between them and Christina. He quickly scanned the area ahead and formulated a plan. When they caught up with Christina, Jack grabbed her arm and said, "This way."

"But, he—" Christina protested. "The shop I'm looking for isn't—"

Jack ignored her and tugged her back a few steps and into a nearby shop.

Diana followed. "What's going on?"

"This way," Jack said. He'd noticed that the shop was on a corner and had two doors. He led them quickly through it and out into the other alley and then into another shop just as quickly.

He brought them to what he hoped was a safe spot and peered through the doorway. Sure enough, the little man appeared in the alley.

"Wait here," Jack said firmly. "Don't leave."

Christina looked up nervously at Diana, who put a comforting arm around her shoulders.

Jack edged his way back to the doorway. He could have just given him the slip and taken the girls somewhere safe, but he doubted he'd get a more secure chance to find out just what the hell was going on.

He waited until the man had turned his back and then stepped out of the doorway, grabbed him by the shoulders and shoved him face-first up against a wall.

"What are you doing?" the man cried out with a thick Italian accent.

Jack spun him around and grabbed him by the lapels. He pressed him back up against the stone wall. "Why are you following us?"

The man shook his head. "I am not," he said, trying to wriggle out of Jack's grasp. "You are mistaken."

He held out his hands in surrender and looked plaintively to the few passersby who gave them any notice.

"Who are you?"

"Nico," Diana said in mild disgust from over Jack's shoulder.

The man smiled weakly. "Miss Trent." He nodded his head at Jack. "Would you please..."

"You can let him go," Diana said. "He's mostly harmless."

Jack hesitated, but eased back and finally let go of the little man who tried to smooth out his crumpled lapels.

"You know this guy?" Jack asked.

Diana ignored Jack and stepped closer to the little man. "Nico," she said in a voice rich with disappointment as though she were scolding a small child.

He smiled nervously and shrugged. "You cannot blame a man for trying."

Diana shook her head. "This isn't Palermo."

He straightened his hat and shrugged.

"And besides," she continued, "you're getting clumsy in your old age."

"I was not expecting your brute," he said with a nod toward Jack.

Jack looked back and forth between them. "Would someone mind telling me what the heck is going on?"

Diana smiled. "Nico Tortetti, Jack Wells."

Nico stuck out his thin hand, but Jack had no intention of shaking it. The man let it hang in the air before slipping it into his pocket.

"Who is he?" Jack asked her.

"Nico is a common thief."

"Ohhh," Nico protested at the characterization. "I am an excellent thief."

Diana's lips curved into an amused smile. "Debatable."

Nico held up Jack's pocket watch, formerly Mason's, with a grin. Jack felt his neck burn with embarrassment. He should have caught that. Dear God, he had to be more careful with that thing. He snatched the watch from Nico's hand and quickly patted the man down in search of anything else he might have pickpocketed.

"That is all," Nico said with a grin. "Today."

Jack frowned and stepped away. "Why was he following us?"

"Because he's lazy," Diana said and Nico acted wounded. "Now, run along, Nico. You might as well go back to Rome."

Nico smiled and took a few steps away. "I think I shall stay. You have not found it yet. Perhaps I will find the prize first this time."

With that he tipped his hat to Diana, sneered as best he could at Jack and left.

"What the hell was all that?" Jack asked.

Diana sighed, resigned to something. "We are both looking for the same...valuable."

Jack stuffed Mason's watch deep into the inner pocket of his jacket. For a brief moment, he wondered if she were after the missing watch too, but neither of them had batted an eyelash when Nico had held up Mason's.

"What sort of valuable?"

Diana smiled. "The sort you can retire to the Riveria on."

Jack didn't know what to make of that, or make of her. The entire thing had left him with more questions than answers. But he would have to pursue them later. He stepped into the shop to find Christina and convince her they needed to go back to the Hotel.

Christina, however, wasn't where he left her.

"Damn."

He felt his adrenaline begin to pump again and looked hurriedly around the shop. Diana appeared at his side.

"She's gone," he said, his mind racing. He really was off his game. If this girl suffered for it...

"Don't worry," Diana assured him. "I know where she is."

Of course, he thought. What the hell had he gotten himself into?

His heart still pounding, he followed Diana out of the side door and down a block until they saw a store with silk scarves. Standing at the entrance, admiring one with hieroglyphics printed on it, was Christina. Unharmed.

Jack let out a sigh of relief. "Thank God."

He started toward her, but Diana's hand on his arm stopped him. He turned and then followed her gaze. A young man appeared next to Christina and said something to her. She turned and threw her arms around his neck. He hugged her briefly before pulling away and looking around nervously.

Christina tossed the scarf back onto the pile and the young couple secreted away to a semi-secluded doorway.

"Her boyfriend," Diana said. "They've been meeting here for over a year."

"You knew?"

"Poor girl doesn't have many confidants," Diana said with a sad smile and then added, "And...young love."

"Who is he?" Jack asked as he quickly took stock of the young man. He looked to be in his early twenties, handsome and well-dressed. Although he appeared to be Egyptian, his clothes were western.

"Ahmed Kassem," Diana said. "He's an attaché with the Cairo museum. And despite being handsome, wealthy and well-educated, her father would not approve."

Jack nodded. From the little he'd seen of Whiteside, that wasn't a surprise. Even though it wasn't any of his business, Jack still felt responsible for the girl and kept a close eye on the couple as they talked.

Jack pretended to be admiring the same scarves Christina had, but kept his focus on the doorway. After the business with Nico, his guard would remain up.

"Don't worry," Diana said.

Jack grunted and turned back to her. "This wasn't the way I saw this day going."

Diana laughed. "Nothing ever goes according to plan in Cairo." Her smile faded. "And speaking of..."

She walked toward Christina, who was alone now and crying. The young man looked back over his shoulder as he walked away. His expression resolute, but glum.

Jack walked over to Diana and Christina.

The poor kid cried on Diana's shoulder. Jack could barely make out what she was saying, but it wasn't hard to guess. Romeo gave her a pink slip.

Diana looked at Jack with a melancholy frown. "Young love."

CHAPTER THIRTEEN

"Cursed."

Henri Jouvet looked around at the people seated with him at their table in the Long Bar of Shepheard's and smiled. "Or, at least, so the story goes."

Jack stared at the small stone scarab Henri had placed at the center of the table. It looked harmless enough. But then Jack had spent his last few weeks in WWII looking for a piece of a magical sword, before discovering two time travelers, so...

Elizabeth reached forward, but Henri grabbed her arm. Jack saw Simon's hand tighten its grip around his second scotch of the night. Something had happened at the museum, but they'd barely had a chance to talk about their days before Whiteside had shanghai'd them for his cocktail party.

"Be careful, *ma cherie*," Henri said. "Anyone who touches the scarab will fall under the curse."

Her eyes went wide in amused surprise. "Good to know."

Henri smiled at her, his gaze lingering longer than a man's should at another man's wife. And he sure took his time letting go of her. No wonder Simon was being such a bundle of fun tonight.

"Is it really cursed?" Constance Everett asked.

Henri frowned and shrugged with his mouth in that way the French do.

"Oh, it's quite possible," Whiteside said as he reached for the stone and elicited gasps from Constance and a "Good God, man!" from her idiot husband, Trevor.

Whiteside chuckled as he examined the scarab. "I was going to say, that it is quite possible that the ancient Egyptians believed so anyway."

"What's that writing there?" Elizabeth asked leaning in for a closer look. "Is that the curse?"

Whiteside held it out for her inspection. "No, the hieroglyphics here in this oval area are the cartouche, or the royal name, Akhenaten in this case. And these here are something about the divine manifestation of the king. Multiplicity and such."

"So how do you know it's cursed?" Elizabeth asked.

Whiteside grinned like a small boy. "Ancient legend."

"Akhenaten, you see," Henri said, joining in, "was a heretic. He took the many gods they worshipped and tossed them away to create one true god, Aten. His god."

Whiteside practically glowed with excitement. "As you can imagine, that didn't go over quite so well. He was the pharaoh, but he was not exactly well-loved. After his death, nearly everything bearing his name was destroyed or defaced."

Henri took the scarab from Whiteside and turned it over in his hand. "He probably feared that his tomb would be desecrated and the curse was a means to protect it and his journey to the afterlife."

Whiteside leaned back in his chair and squinted at the ceiling as he recalled the words. "All people who disturb this tomb, who make evil against it, may the crocodile and the hippopotamus be against them in water, and snakes and the scorpions against them on land. And may the evil they bring swallow them…something something in sand. I can't remember the ending."

"Hippopotamus!" Trevor said, scoffing at the idea.

"They are not to be trifled with," Henri said. He slipped the scarab back into his pocket.

"You're not afraid of the curse?" Constance asked.

Henri smiled and raised his glass. "So far, dear Akhenaten has been anything but a curse for me."

"Henri has quite a dig going in the Valley of the Kings," Whiteside said. "I still don't know how you got the permit. Carter's the only one who's been able to wrangle one out of Lacau and that damned, you'll pardon me, antiquities department."

Henri smiled and finished what was left of his drink. "My patron is…convincing."

Whiteside laughed. "Oh, yes, the mysterious patron. Are you sure you can't say who it is? It's not Charles Sitwell, is it?"

Henri stood. "I am well paid for my silence." He held up his empty glass, silently asking if anyone needed another. To no one's surprise, Trevor did.

Once Henri had left the table, Whiteside leaned in and spoke in a conspiratorial whisper. "Between us, I think it's a fool's errand."

"Why?" Jack asked.

"Because Akhenaten's tomb has already been found. All of the royal tombs that can be found have been found. Of course, there's some debate, but…"

Simon leaned back in his chair, his eyes seeking out Henri as he leaned against the bar. "Aren't archaeologist usually *at* their digs?"

Whiteside laughed. "Yes, quite. Now, don't get me wrong, Henri is a talented man, dedicated, but I think this venture is a bit of a lark. I'm not sure he even believes they'll find anything of significance."

Jack didn't get it. "Then why do it?"

"Money," Simon said, his distaste for the idea as well as the man painfully apparent.

That Jack understood.

"Perhaps, I am wrong," Whiteside said. "Egypt has a way of surprising you."

Simon pulled his glare away from Henri and forced a smile to his face. "I'm sure. And I suppose his being here in Cairo isn't a total loss."

It was all Jack could do not to laugh at that, but he had to admire Simon's acting ability.

"After all," Simon continued. "He wouldn't be able to help you with your papyrus."

Whiteside's eyebrows shot up. "How did you—"

"You mentioned it at the museum this afternoon," Simon said.

And, Jack thought, Diana had mentioned it as well. And Mason's obsession with it. He'd tried to press Diana for more information on their trip back from the bazaar, but she'd said he should ask Whiteside. Papyri weren't her game.

That, of course, begged the question of just what was her game. Was she a thief like her friend Nico. Or something else?

"Oh, that's right," Whiteside said. "It's just a trifle really. More of a curiosity."

"I'd love to see it," Simon said. "I've always found that the best window to a civilization are its writings."

"Well said!" Whiteside agreed. "I am rather proud of it. Truth be told. Tomorrow then, perhaps after breakfast, if that suits you?"

Jack knew Simon would have preferred *right now*, as he did with everything he wanted, but he smiled and accepted graciously enough.

Their little party grew and contracted as new people joined and then left the table, shifting into smaller groups by the bar or other tables. The social scene at Shepheard's was alive and well. By eleven o'clock the bar was filled to capacity. Everyone in the hotel seemed to be there. Except Diana.

She was probably off outmaneuvering Gutman for the Maltese Falcon. He smiled at the thought, happy to let that daydream progress until Simon ruined it with a loud grunt.

Jack followed his gaze. Elizabeth must have gone to get another glass of wine because she was standing at the bar chatting with one of the people waiting for their drinks. Henri insinuated himself behind her and said something Jack couldn't hear. Elizabeth turned around and must have said something charming because Henri smiled and leaned in a little closer.

Simon put his glass down on the table a little too hard.

Henri nodded and then reached out and touched Elizabeth's arm.

Jack moved his chair a little closer to Simon's. The rest of the table was busy with their own conversations. "I'm confused."

Simon grunted. "By what?"

"Why exactly aren't you punching him in the face?"

Simon laughed. "Oh, I'd very much like to."

"But?"

With a deep sigh, Simon turned to face Jack. "We need to know what Mason was up to," he said quietly. "Jouvet is part of the puzzle."

Jack watched Henri with Elizabeth. He'd known men like him before. They weren't just looking for a good time, but a good time that was hard to get. It was the challenge that excited them. Forbidden fruit. Married women.

Not that Jack was exactly a boy scout when it came to women, but there were lines he wouldn't cross and that was one of them.

Jouvet touched Elizabeth's arm again.

"Maybe I can hit him for you?" Jack offered.

"Don't tempt me," Simon said and excused himself. He made his way over to Elizabeth and slid his arm around her waist, logistically preventing any more runs across the British version of the Maginot line. Jack chuckled and raised his glass in salute. But he couldn't help but feel a pang of loneliness.

He'd spent the last few months recovering from losing Betty. He'd finally come out of the deepest part of his depression, but bits lingered. They always would.

"Isn't Egypt wonderful?" Whiteside, his cheeks rosy from drinking, said to no one in particular. "The bosom of civilization."

Whiteside's eyes lit and his smile broadened. "Diana, my dear! Where have you been?"

Jack turned around and quickly stood.

She smiled at him, but there was a sadness to her eyes. "Hello, Jack."

"What's wrong?" Whiteside asked.

Diana slipped into the empty chair between them. "I have some bad news, I'm afraid. George Mason is dead."

"What?!" Whiteside exclaimed loudly enough to get the attention of the tables nearest to them and a few people at the bar including the Crosses and Jouvet. They left their spots and came over to the table.

Jack carefully watched everyone's reaction. If one of them had anything to do with Mason's murder, their expressions at hearing the news might give them away.

"That's impossible," Whiteside said.

Diana shook her head sadly. "I'm afraid not."

"What has happened?" Henri asked.

"George Mason was killed yesterday," Diana explained. "Shot on a train or something near Fayoum."

Elizabeth's eyes shifted nervously to Jack. He silently told her to stay calm. She looked at Simon briefly, whose poker face was impeccable, and then said, "That's awful. I...I can't believe it."

Good girl.

"Are you sure?" Whiteside asked Diana.

Diana nodded.

Jack couldn't be sure of course, but none of them gave any signs of the news being anything other than a complete and unwelcome surprise.

The table fell into thoughtful silence until Trevor spoke.

"That's one way to kill a party."

"Trev," his wife chided him.

He merely arched an eyebrow and shrugged.

"Well..." Whiteside said, unsure how to segue from that. "I don't know what to say."

"It's a shock," Simon said. "Perhaps it would be best if we called it a night."

"Yes," Whiteside agreed. "I think that might be best."

Slowly, their group disbanded and said their goodnights. Jack and Diana stayed at the table as the others left.

"Are you going up too?" Diana asked.

Jack shook his head.

"Well, then," she said, laying a hand on his forearm. "Buy me a drink?"

CHAPTER FOURTEEN

SIMON WOKE FROM HIS nightmare with a start. His breath caught in his throat as he jerked awake. It took him a moment to orient himself. The room was cast in oranges and reds from the sunrise filtering through the window sheers. He glanced at Elizabeth beside him, still sleeping.

He pushed out a long bracing breath and let the sight of her, alive and safe by his side, calm him. Unperturbed by his sudden waking, she slept on peacefully. Simon gently caressed her cheek and then slipped out of bed.

It had been months since he'd had a nightmare and he'd foolishly thought they might never return. He pulled on his robe and let the quiet of the early morning soothe his jangled nerves. Whatever the nightmare had been about fled from his mind. Not even a vague glimmer remained behind, except the feeling of foreboding he couldn't quite shake.

Glancing back at the bed once more, he walked quietly over to the window and pulled the sheers back. Cairo was stirring to life.

Although the view from their hotel room offered little more than a view of the rear garden he could sense the city waking. The rooftops and spires on the horizon stretched out in the dusty morning haze as far as he could see. Just beneath them the tranquil morning would transform into the chaos that was Cairo.

Elizabeth mumbled something in her sleep and then smiled. He hoped whatever was happening in her dream, he was the reason for that smile.

Since their arrival in Egypt, smiles had been few and far between for him. Somehow hers had always made up for it though. And as he felt the tightening in his chest ease, they still did.

Resigned now to being awake, Simon walked over to the front door. Gently, he unlocked it and eased it open. The day's newspaper and his freshly polished shoes sat waiting for him. As he leaned over to pick them up, a door down the hallway opened and a woman tiptoed out of a room. Jack's room.

The woman shifted her shoes into her other hand and eased the door shut. Simon sighed and she turned at the sound.

Diana. That was quick work even by Jack's standards.

Instead of being embarrassed at being caught in what Elizabeth called the walk of shame, Diana smiled pleasantly and nodded her head in greeting. Too surprised to do anything else, Simon reciprocated and Diana took a few steps down the hall before slipping on her shoes and tucking in her blouse.

He was going to have to have a talk with Mr. Wells. The last time Jack had traveled back in time with them, he'd nearly let his feelings for a woman destroy the bloody timeline. Simon's mood curdled again as he picked up the paper and his shoes and went back inside.

He spent the better part of the next hour reading the news and brooding only to be leavened again by a sleepy-headed Elizabeth as she walked drowsily over to him. He pulled her onto his lap, and much to his disappointment, she picked up the paper.

"Anything interesting?" she asked, blinking her eyes to try to focus.

"Yes."

She turned to ask him what and Simon gently pulled the paper from her hands.

"Oh," she said with a smile as he leaned in to kiss her.

An hour later, they were dressed and ready for breakfast with Whiteside and, hopefully, a clue as to why Mason was so interested in his bit of papyrus.

Simon locked the door behind them and they started down the long, wide corridor to the stairs.

They'd nearly reached them, when Elizabeth stopped. "I forgot my purse."

Simon sighed as she turned back. "I have money."

"It has my lipstick and things."

It was a pointless argument and one they'd had many times. She claimed she couldn't live without it, and yet, was forever forgetting it. In the end, he'd learned simply acquiescing was easier than explaining her faulty logic to her. And so, he lengthened his stride to catch up with her.

Opening the door for her, he let her precede him into their room. He nearly crashed into her as she'd come to an abrupt halt barely a few paces inside the door. It didn't take him long to see why.

The French doors to their balcony were open, the sheers blowing in the breeze. Standing in front of one of their trunks, a drawer left open, was a man in black robes.

They all stared at each other in equal shock.

Simon reached out for Elizabeth and tried to ease her behind him. The movement broke the man out of his fugue and he ran toward the balcony. Simon gave chase, but the man flung himself over the railing. For a brief moment Simon thought he'd plunged to his death. They were on the third floor after all. But as soon as he leaned over, he saw that the man had swung himself to a lower balcony and was scrambling down to the ground with frightening agility.

Elizabeth arrived at his side and they watched the man jump the last ten feet to the ground and run off into the garden. He easily leapt up and flipped himself over the eight foot back wall and disappeared.

"Okay, that was impressive," Elizabeth said.

Simon grunted and went back inside. He quickly surveyed their belongings, pausing as the reality of what could have happened here sunk in. He'd nearly let her come back to the room alone. It was damn lucky he hadn't. Who knows what Elizabeth might have done on her own.

He glanced back and saw her leaning over the balcony, gauging how hard it would be to duplicate what she'd seen.

Simon let out a breath and shook his head. She probably would have followed him.

And if he'd been armed? It didn't bear thinking about. They'd been damned lucky. One day that luck would run out though.

"I don't know how he did that in those robes," Elizabeth said.

Simon nodded and tried to refocus. Nothing seemed to be missing, but then he hadn't had long to go through things.

"I was kind of hoping we wouldn't see him again," Elizabeth said as she joined him and closed the open drawer.

"Again?"

"The man from the train."

It suddenly clicked. He'd sensed it, but his mind had been too busy trying to find something to use as a weapon that it hadn't gelled yet. Although, they hadn't seen the man's face, his body shape, his height, his eyes, and a thousand other tiny pieces of information were indelibly etched in Simon's memory. And the marking on the inside of his wrist. Simon hadn't been sure he'd seen it on the train. It could have been a shadow, a trick of light. But as he replayed the last few minutes in his head, he forced himself to slow down the images that had raced past in a panic. He could see the marking again. The long sleeves of the man's robe obscured most of it, but there was something there. All he could make out or remember were two curved lines.

"Dammit," Simon said. He couldn't get a clear image in his mind. He looked around their room helplessly.

It had been foolish of them to think even for a moment that their presence at Mason's murder would go unnoticed or neglected. He should have seen this coming. Despite Elizabeth's feelings on the matter, they were too vulnerable and every moment spent here was more dangerous than the next. Still, he knew his wife and there was no possible way of convincing her to return home. Despite his misgivings, they were there for the duration.

"Everything's here, I think," Elizabeth said as she took a quick inventory.

Simon walked over to the French doors and closed them. The lock was entirely inadequate. If they were to stay in this room, hell, if they were going to stay in this city, this would have to change.

"What do you think he was looking for?" she asked.

"I don't know," Simon said. "Maybe that envelope we took from Mason. Or his watch."

Elizabeth's eyes went wide. "Jack!"

She hurried to the door and ran down the hallway. Simon caught up to her just as she was pounding on Jack's door.

There was no answer, but Simon thought he heard something coming from inside.

Elizabeth shrugged. "Maybe he's already gone down—"

Simon held up a finger to silence her. There he heard it again, the muffled sounds of a struggle.

"Jack!" Simon pounded on the door. He stopped only long enough to hear a crashing sound inside. Simon thrust his shoulder against the door, but it didn't move.

"Jack!" Elizabeth cried.

A few people came out of their suites and she told them to get help.

Simon took a step back and kicked at the door as hard as he could. He felt the door frame give a little. He kicked again and again. On the third try the frame splintered and the door crashed open.

Simon hurried inside. Jack was on the floor near the balcony, the remnants of a coffee table crushed beneath him. Above him loomed another man in black robes. He'd been startled by the door flying open, enough to give Jack a small window through which he threw a solid punch. The man staggered off him, turned toward Simon and ran for the balcony.

The French doors were already open and like his partner, the man leapt over the railing and scaled down the building with frightening ease. Simon watched the assailant run through the garden and disappear. When he turned back, Elizabeth was kneeling at Jack's side.

"Are you okay?" she asked.

Jack grunted and, with her help, pushed himself into a sitting position. Bits of table clung to his bare back and the knee of his pajama bottoms was torn.

"I'm all right," Jack said, shaking his head and working his jaw. He jerked his head toward the door and the growing gathering of onlookers.

"It's under control now," Simon said as he strode over to the door. "Thank you for your concern."

The shocked expressions of the crowd disappeared behind the door as he unceremoniously closed it in their faces.

Elizabeth helped Jack stand.

"Thanks," Jack said. "Good timing."

The room was a shambles. Chairs were overturned and what had been a coffee table was only kindling now.

"We had a visitor ourselves," Simon said.

"You what?" Jack exclaimed, his senses fully returned. "Are you all right?"

Elizabeth smiled. "We're fine."

Jack nodded and smiled. He paced over to the balcony and ran a hand through his hair. "I was half asleep, and I heard something."

He shook his head, trying to get the contents of his memory to settle. "He was already inside...I didn't even hear him come in."

Simon nodded. These were hardly amateurs.

Abruptly, Jack hurried over to the table and picked up his jacket. He rifled through the pockets and closed his eyes. "Damn it."

Simon knew what he was going to say and steeled himself for the news.

"The watch," Jack bit out. "He got it."

Simon and Elizabeth shared a nervous glance, both thinking the same thing. If the intruders got his, they could have easily gotten theirs.

Elizabeth pushed out a breath. "At least you're okay."

Jack clenched his jaw and shook his head, ignoring her comforting words. "I'm sorry."

Simon wanted to be angry with him, but he knew their roles could easily have been reversed. Under the same circumstances, there was no guarantee Simon could have done any better to protect the watch than Jack had.

Simon nodded, accepting Jack's apology and accepting his own portion of blame for the situation. "I should have anticipated something like this."

"*We* should have," Jack said.

"Did he get the letter too?" Elizabeth asked.

Jack looked surprised, like he'd briefly forgotten about that. He moved over to the end table by the bed and opened the drawer. "No," he said, pulling out the letter. "Thank God for that anyway."

"The sooner we can find out what's in that, the better," Simon said. "I don't like being one step behind."

A tentative knock on the door came. "Hello?"

The door slowly opened and one of the hotel staff poked his head through the gap. His eyes went wide at the state of things. "Oh my goodness."

"Yes," Simon said. "As you can see we've had a bit of a problem."

The man nodded, his eyes still wide and taking in the extent of the damage as he hesitantly entered the room. "Yes."

"I'd like to speak to the management about it," Simon said. When the man remained fixated on the broken table, Simon added a firm, "Now."

AFTER SPEAKING WITH THE management about the break-ins and receiving their assurance that not only would the locks to their rooms be upgraded, but security for the grounds would be as well, they'd met Whiteside for breakfast in the smaller, casual dining room. Simon tried to shed his frustration and anger over his inexcusable lapse in preparedness and focus on Whiteside and what they could learn about his mysterious papyrus.

While Whiteside spoke excitedly about his collection back home in England, which was quite impressive, it was clear to Simon that the man was bothered by his daughter's mood. Jack had told Simon and Elizabeth about the poor girl's heartbreak.

She'd stayed in their rooms last night and remained there this morning. And she hadn't told him why she was upset, but it was easy to see that her hurt bothered him deeply.

Simon did his best to keep Whiteside's mind off his daughter and his sadness over Mason's death. It wasn't easy. Uncommonly for an Englishman, Whiteside's emotions were readily expressed. Although, Simon was hard pressed to blame him under the circumstances.

Elizabeth came to both their rescues and kept them entertained with outrageously preposterous stories Simon was fairly certain were the plots of one of the Indiana Jones movies and a few episodes of *Dr. Who*.

As the meal came to a close, both Whiteside and Simon were both eager to head back upstairs and take a look at the papyrus. Only Elizabeth lingered as she made her way through an enormous omelette. For such a small, slim thing, she ate like a rugby player. If she ever were eating for two, she'd eat them right out of house and home.

The thought caught him by surprise. Ever since their discussion about having children and Old Nan's portentous prophecy, the idea of children wriggled its way into his mind with increasing frequency. He'd done his best to shove it away. Neither of them were quite ready to start a family just yet. The thought, however, had been planted and surfaced in the unlikeliest of moments.

Elizabeth caught him staring at her. "Do I...?" she asked as she held her napkin near her face.

Simon hadn't even realized he'd been staring. "No," he said, recovering. "Nearly finished?"

Finally, she was, and the three of them made their way up to Whiteside's suite.

"It's really quite remarkable," Whiteside said as he retrieved the leather tube and carefully removed the ancient scroll onto a table. The lower half of the papyrus was ragged and torn. "Some fascinating details and a few inconsistencies that are delicious little mysteries."

He gently placed four stones at the corners to keep it flat. Simon stared down at it. While he recognized some of the symbols, he had no idea what any of it meant.

Whiteside put on a pair of glasses and leaned over the table.

"Hieroglyphics is a terribly clever and complex language. It uses phonetic glyphs, logograms, where the whole word is in the symbol, and something called derivatives. They're sort of signposts that tell you what the word you've just read really means."

"That does sound complicated," Elizabeth said, looking over Whiteside's shoulder with a sinking expression.

"You see, most of the symbols are phonetic, " Whiteside said pointing to what looked like a leg. "This might represent a single sound. The 'bah' sound in B words. Barge, banana and so on. Sometimes they represent two or even three letters together. And of course, with no vowels to speak of..."

Simon knew he'd need to direct Whiteside's enthusiasm if they were ever going to find out what the darn thing said.

"But you *can* read this?" he asked.

Whiteside straightened and took off his glasses. His chest puffed out and he polished his glasses. "I can."

"Well, I'm dying here," Elizabeth said. "What does it say?"

Whiteside chuckled and put his glasses back on. His finger hovered just above the delicate papyrus as he translated. "Let's see... Behold the gift from Ra, from Amun, from Aten," he read. "Those are all variations of the sun god, unusual to see them all together like that...from eternity. Heka, the god of magic, appeared to the king, in the temple and bestowed upon him a piece of the sun."

Whiteside scratched his chin. "This part is a little more difficult, some of the..." he waved his hand over the writings, "well, I'm just not sure."

"Go on, Professor," Elizabeth urged him. "It's fascinating."

Pleased, Whiteside read on. "Heka, with white skin, I'm not sure what that means, gave the king...and this could be wheels or gears of gold, that moved and lived in his hand. Not sure quite what this word is, lever, device? Sounds odd, held the key to eternity."

Simon felt his mouth go dry. Gears of gold that moved in his hand. The watch. He glanced over at Elizabeth. Her wide-eyed expression mirrored what he felt.

Whiteside continued, "The gift was a sign from the gods of his divinity above all others."

"Whose divinity?" Simon asked.

Whiteside shook his head. "That's the thing of it. The rest of it's torn off there you can see." He read the last line. "It says that the gift was given to the king, but the part that starts to identify which king is missing. Quite the mystery, isn't it?"

"Yes," Simon managed, his mind racing with the possibilities. Dear God, was the watch in ancient Egypt? Like hell they were going there!

"Have you seen any other references to these gears of gold?" Elizabeth asked. He marveled at how calm she appeared.

Whiteside shook his head. "No, it's most unusual in that respect." He began to carefully re-roll the scroll. "I'm afraid it will all remain an unsolved puzzle until we find the missing half."

CHAPTER FIFTEEN

"**B**LOODY HELL," SIMON GRUMBLED as they went back to Jack's room to bring him up to date.

"It might not be so bad," Elizabeth said.

She knocked on Jack's door.

"I draw the line at Before Christ."

Elizabeth laughed and Jack opened the door.

"What's so funny?" he asked.

"Nothing," Simon said as he pushed his way into the room.

"You must have lit a hell of a fire under the manager," Jack said, gesturing to the door as he closed it as best he could given its splintered frame. "They've been up twice already to see about that and the locks."

Simon grunted.

"Simon," Elizabeth said. "Just because the watch might have been in ancient Egypt doesn't mean it still is. It—"

"Hold the phone," Jack interrupted. "The watch is in *ancient* Egypt? Building the pyramids kind of Egypt?"

"Perhaps," Simon said. "It might be, might have been."

"Well, that clears things right up."

Simon glared at him and then gestured to a chair and waited for Elizabeth to take a seat before joining her at the small table. They told Jack everything they'd learned from the meeting with Whiteside.

"So," Jack said. "If it is the watch, we still don't have any idea exactly where it is."

"Or when," Simon said.

"I've been thinking about that." Elizabeth chewed on her bottom lip for a moment. "If it was lost in the past. We can't exactly go wandering around a thousand years of history."

"Several thousand," Simon corrected.

"But, all those centuries have one thing in common," she continued.

Simon waited, intrigued.

"Today."

"I don't follow," Jack said, taking a seat on the end of the bed.

"All this stuff, all the things buried in those ancient tombs are here today. Right now. In some museum or a collection. Those thousands of years of history all converge here, now."

"True," Simon said, mulling it over. "Assuming the watch was buried with the king or buried somewhere at all and not destroyed."

"The key to eternity or whatever it was," she said. "That sounds like the sort of thing I'd want to take with me."

It was logical. Despite that, it still got them no closer to knowing where the watch actually was. "Whiteside did say that all of the royal tombs that could be found have been found. Which is only partly true, of course, because we know Carter finds Tutankhamen's tomb two years from now."

"But most of them have been found," Elizabeth reasoned. "That means it's most likely that the tomb with the watch has already been discovered."

"You'd think it would have stood out a little, don't ya?" Jack asked. "Surely someone would have mentioned finding a modern watch in an ancient tomb."

Simon frowned at that. "Yes."

"We'll just have to hope we can find the other half of the papyrus," Elizabeth said. "That must have been what Mason was after."

Simon noticed Mason's letter and a pad of paper on the table. He pulled it over and read what looked like gibberish. "Any luck with this?"

"Not yet."

Simon sighed and pushed the pad away. "Well then, all we can do is look for the other half of that papyrus and hope it answers some of our questions."

"And hope," Elizabeth said, "that no one else has found it first."

"Why couldn't Jack talk to Jouvet?" Simon said as held the door open for her and they entered the museum.

Elizabeth knew this wasn't easy for him and offered him a comforting smile which he did not return. Instead, his eyes sought out Henri so he could start the flow of unrestrained disdain for him as soon as possible.

They enquired of one of the staff who told them that Monsieur Jouvet was in the "sale room," which ended up being a cross between a kitschy museum shop with hieroglyphic print scarves and post-cards and a high-roller store with genuine artifacts for sale. If you wanted an ashtray with the pyramids on it or an original ushabti burial figure, this was the place. It was called the sale room, but it was actually a fairly large pavilion in the front corner of the museum. They found Henri inside arguing with a man over a pair of bracelets and an amulet. Elizabeth's French was rusty, but she was pretty sure Henri called the man a thief or maybe a steering wheel.

The man grunted and gathered up his belongings, snatching the amulet from Henri's hands and stormed out.

Henri's shrug of indifference turned into a broad smile as he saw them. He strode across the room, hands held out, head cocked to the side as if to say, "Of course, you have come back to me."

He reached out and took hold of Elizabeth's hand and kissed it before covering it with his other hand and smiling down at her. *"Cherie.* I hoped you would come." His gaze shifted to Simon. "I had hoped you would come alone, but—"

"Now, see here," Simon started and Elizabeth knew she had to intervene quickly.

"We were hoping you could help us."

Henri's eyebrow arched and he released her hand, clearly disappointed, but he was still a gentleman, albeit a debauched one. "How may I be of service to you?"

"Arthur showed us his papyrus this morning," Elizabeth said.

Henri laughed. "Not that again."

"Yes," Simon said through clenched teeth.

Henri raised his hands palms up. "Do not mistake me. It is an interesting piece, I suppose, but it's value is...minor."

"It's more the mystery for us," Elizabeth said.

Henri smiled. "Oh, you like the intrigue?"

"Something like that. It's interesting, I think," Elizabeth said, "And, well, George Mason thought so too and it seems like a decent way to honor his memory, don't you think? Solve that last riddle for him. And for Arthur."

Henri nodded thoughtfully. "Arthur is a good man. I was not close to your friend, George, but I appreciate your sentiment."

Elizabeth beamed. "Then you'll help us."

He shrugged. "I will do what I can. I have told Arthur before that it is unlikely we will find the other half. The provenance of the piece he has is..." Henri puffed out a breath.

"Oh." Elizabeth had hoped for more than that.

Henri frowned and held up a finger. "I have asked one of the museum liaisons if he has any idea. Let me see what he has come up with, no?"

With that he disappeared into one of the back rooms.

"I had hoped you would come alone," Simon said in a fairly hilarious and mocking impression of Henri.

Elizabeth barely had time to stifle her giggle as Henri returned with a young man in tow. He was handsome and well-dressed in a smart dark gray suit.

"Mr. and Mrs. Cross," Henri said, "This is Ahmed Kassem. He is an attaché with the department of antiquities."

The young man's charming smile fizzled. He forced it back on, but could only numbly shake Simon's hand. His face paled as he inclined his head toward Elizabeth. Looking suddenly unwell, he kept his eyes down. Or tried to. He couldn't help but sneak a peak at Elizabeth again and when he did, she saw his eyes clearly, and slowly, it dawned on her just why he was acting so strangely.

Ahmed was one of the bandits.

CHAPTER SIXTEEN

Jack scratched out another failed attempt at solving the cipher in Mason's letter. He looked down at the pad in front of him and shoved it away in disgust. The little experience he had with codes was proving to be pathetically inadequate. It was one thing to read a coded message when you knew what kind of code it was and knew the key. Without that, without a key... This wasn't exactly Enigma, but it might as well have been.

101247.330523.550198.36533.451225.03244526...

A line of numbers like that could represent anything—dates, coordinates, or it could be a substitution cipher where each number or set of numbers, or every third number, represented a letter or a phonetic sound or God knows what. The whole thing was starting to make his brain ache.

There was a reason he had been a field operative and not stuck behind a desk. He was far better with people than paper. But Mason's letter was the best clue they had so far. Other than Whiteside's half papyrus, it was the only clue.

As much as he wanted to be out there with Simon and Elizabeth, breaking this cipher was more important. He was beginning to wonder though, if he ever would. Judging from the heaping pile of crumpled paper in the trash bin waiting to be burned, and the fact that he'd made absolutely zero progress and had even fewer ideas, he might be right. He had a newfound respect for the men and women who broke Enigma and Purple.

He reached for his coffee, but it had gone cold. Just as he was about to ring the bell to check on his order for a fresh pot there was a knock on the door.

"I was just about to come looking—" he said, as he yanked the door open.

Diana smiled. "Were you?"

"Sorry, I was..." Jack, stepping back, waved her in. "Thought you were room service."

Diana stepped inside and fingered the splintered door jamb. "What happened here?"

"A little misunderstanding," Jack said hoping she wouldn't press him.

He closed the door and went to the table and flipped his pad over to cover Mason's letter. The room was still in a shambles and he started to tidy things up. "Sorry about the mess."

"Don't worry," Diana said as she sat down in one of the chairs at the small table by the window. "I had fun making it."

Last night had definitely been fun. "Right."

Relieved, she put it all up to their...robust evening, he tossed aside the shirt that dangled in his hand and smiled.

He'd needed last night. Needed to be with a woman. The fractures in his heart were finally mending, but he wasn't ready for more. He wasn't sure he ever would be. "About that, I hope I didn't do anything—"

Diana raised her hand to stop him. "There was nothing wrong with anything you did last night," she said with a wry smile. "Trust me." Then she grew more serious. "I just hope that I didn't mislead you."

"Mislead me?"

"I like you, Jack. I enjoy being with you, but I'm not looking for anything more than this right now," she said carefully. "I hope we can—"

He burst out laughing.

She frowned and he tried to control himself. "I'm sorry. It's just that I was about to say the same thing."

Then the light dawned on her. "You mean...you were going to let me down easy?"

He nodded and she joined in his laughter.

"Well, aren't we a pair?" she said.

Jack smiled. "Well matched. Did you come here just to break the news or...?"

"Oh! My necklace." Her hand went to her throat and she looked about the room. "You didn't find it, did you?"

"You're in luck!" Jack went over to the nightstand and opened the small top drawer. He'd found it when he'd started and immediately given up cleaning his room. He pulled out the necklace. "Found it this morning."

"You're a life saver!" She walked over to him and took it from his hand. Her relief was palpable.

She saw his unspoken question. "It was my mother's," she said simply and he didn't press the point.

Diana put it back around her neck and slipped the small gold cross beneath her blouse. She patted her chest between her breasts and then seemed to realize she was giving too much away.

"So," she said, easing seamlessly back into her less vulnerable persona. "Are you going to spend the day inside writing letters or look for Arthur's missing papyrus?"

Jack managed to hide his surprise at her question. Just as soon as he was back on sure footing with this woman, she pushed him off kilter again.

"His papyrus?" While it wasn't exactly a state secret, they didn't want to broadcast what they were doing either.

"I stopped by this morning to see how Christina was getting along, not well, by the way, and she mentioned that the Crosses were keen to find it. I just assumed."

"I'd like to, but..." he said looking at his pad of paper.

"Is it anything I can help with?"

"No," Jack said quickly. "I've just got to stick with it."

"You sound frustrated," she said. "Maybe some fresh air and time away would help?"

Jack liked the sound of that. "It might."

"I have a quick errand to run, but if you come with me, I might know a few places we can check for leads on the papyrus and you can be back at," she waved her hand toward the table, "whatever it is, in a few hours."

Her eyes lit up with mischief and he found it hard to resist. Besides, time away was probably the best thing. He was just spinning his wheels sitting here.

"All right," he said. "I'll meet you downstairs in ten?" He had to burn the papers that contained his fruitless morning labors. He trusted her, but there were limits.

"Perfect."

"What is this errand of yours?" he asked as she reached the door.

She gripped the door handle. "Just have to pick something up."

Elizabeth saw the fear in Ahmed's eyes the moment he realized she recognized him. Panic and fear and shame raced across them and he looked quickly at Simon. For his part, Simon seemed none the wiser. If he had recognized the boy, Elizabeth doubted he'd be asking him a question with anything other than his fists.

The boy nodded at something and cleared his throat.

"Elizabeth?" Simon asked, touching her arm and bringing her back to the conversation. "Are you all right?"

"Yes? Yes, I'm sorry."

She glanced back at Ahmed, who swallowed hard as Simon addressed him. "Do you think you might have a lead for us?"

Ahmed cleared his throat again. "I'm..." he coughed. "Bit of a cold," he said, clearly trying to disguise his voice. "Perhaps. I will write it down."

Simon's eyes narrowed. Elizabeth knew she should have said something. Why she felt compelled to protect this man, she didn't know. He'd been part of a marauding band of criminals who'd kidnapped them for heaven's sake. Sure, he'd promised to come back and help, but he'd ended up being a complete no-show.

But now, looking at this clean-cut, handsome young man, it hardly made any sense even though she wanted it to. And he had been kind to her. He'd seen to her comfort and clearly, he was not a fan of the whole hostage taking part of the operation. Maybe he hadn't had a chance to help them when Jack arrived.

"You are in good hands," Henri said. "I am afraid I must tend to other things."

He bowed to Elizabeth. "I hope to see you again soon."

With a more than slightly smug smile for Simon, he left.

Ahmed quickly excused himself and hurried nervously over to a glass counter near the register.

"Wait here?" Elizabeth asked Simon and despite his curious look, left him alone to join Ahmed.

He looked up from unscrewing the cap to a fountain pen and cast a furtive glance back toward Simon.

"Funny meeting you here," Elizabeth said.

Ahmed gave a small laugh, but grew serious again quickly. "I am so pleased to see you are unharmed."

"Yeah, about that…"

"I am sorry," he said in a rough whisper. "I could not come to you and by the time the alarm had sounded all I could do was delay them, but it was not long."

Elizabeth's heart went out to him. He sounded so worried and sincere. "You helped us get away?"

He nodded. "It was not much, but I'm relieved it was enough. I had to leave the camp the next day and your fate was unknown to me."

"What's a nice kid like you doing with bunch of Hell's Angels?"

"Hells Angels?"

She waved it off. "What I mean is you don't seem like the marauding type."

He smiled and shook his head. "I want to help the revolution, but…" He looked at her, sincerity dripping from his light brown boy-band eyes with long dark lashes she would have killed for. "I had no idea things would go so far. You must believe me."

"I do," she said and then glanced over to where Simon stood examining some of the museum's artifacts. Her husband might be a different matter though.

He followed her gaze and blanched.

"I can handle him," Elizabeth assured him, although in this case, it would not be easy. He tended to take umbrage at things like being kidnapped.

"If my parents were ever to find out. The shame I would bring..."

"I'll keep your secret," she said. "On one condition."

"Anything."

"No more hostages."

He laughed lightly and smiled. "Yes. Thank you. If there is anyway I can repay you. I have money—"

She held up her hand to stop him. "Help us find the papyrus. All right?"

"Yes, of course," he promised. "If I can. This might not lead anywhere," he said as he jotted down an address. "But I shall keep looking."

Simon, who'd grown impatient with waiting, came over to the counter. "Almost ready?"

"Yes," Ahmed said and slid the paper toward Elizabeth.

Simon's eyes narrowed, the wheels turning and catching on something.

Elizabeth slipped her arm through his and raised the slip of paper in the air as she started to lead him out. "Thank you, Ahmed. Let us know if you find anything else that might be helpful."

Ahmed nodded quickly.

Simon craned his neck back to get another look as Elizabeth forcefully escorted him from the room.

"What are you doing?" he asked testily.

"There's something important I have to tell you," Elizabeth whispered.

Simon looked again at Ahmed, his frown deepening, but he let Elizabeth pull him away.

Finally, she managed to get him outside where he decided he'd had enough and brought them both to an unceremonious stop. "Well?"

"What?" she asked innocently.

Simon scowled. "I'm in no mood." His eyes shifted back to the museum door, those wheels turning again.

"All right," she said, giving up the pretense. "But try not to get angry."

Simon's eyes narrowed. "Elizabeth…"

She slipped her arm into his and started to walk them casually away from the museum. "You remember when we were out in the desert near Fayoum…"

"JUST HAVE TO PICK something up?" Jack asked under his breath as two more men stepped out from the shadows and into the light that filtered into the small upstairs apartment.

Diana shifted her gaze from the sweaty fat man with the broad smile sitting at the table just long enough to apologize. "Sorry. This wasn't exactly what I had planned."

Her eyes fell on a small man with a white turban that was starting to unravel. Amir had been her contact until he'd been forced to betray her. He clasped his hands in front of himself, in prayer or begging for forgiveness, Jack couldn't tell.

Amir looked at Diana and shook his head sadly. Maybe a little of both. Jack kept his hands up in surrender and took stock of their situation. It wasn't pretty.

They'd come to Old Cairo to meet with Amir. He'd found a small piece Diana had been searching for. Sounded simple enough. She'd dealt with Amir before, even visited his home, where they were now standing. Except it hadn't been a quick pick-up at all. The heavy-set man, Reza, and his band of not-so-merry men had crashed the party. Which might not have been so bad if one of them hadn't had a gun and the room only one way out.

Amir wiped his sweaty forehead with the back of his sleeve. Reza said something to Diana in Arabic.

"*Ingilicze*," she said. "English."

Reza frowned, but nodded. "Very well. For your partner?" He grinned at Jack.

"I'm homesick," she said.

He laughed. "Then you should go home, Diana. This is no business for a woman."

There was a subtle shift in the way she held her jaw, but she didn't rise to the bait. Reza smiled anyway and unfolded the velvet cloth on the dining table in front of him.

"That doesn't belong to you," Diana said.

Reza admired the jeweled necklace. "It does now." He wrapped the velvet covering back over it and handed it back to one of his men. "Now, the question is what to do with you."

Diana smiled and took a step forward. The man with the gun raised it from his lazy half-hearted position to one that would stop her in her tracks.

"Reza," she said, drawling out his name like a purr. "We're old friends."

His smile dropped and Jack tensed.

"We are not friends," Reza said.

"Business associates," she tried.

He laughed and turned to share his amusement with his men. In that split moment when they were busy laughing, she grabbed the edge of the table in front of him and flipped it over. It caught everyone, including Jack, by complete surprise. Reza and his men fell into a tangle behind it.

Diana turned on her heels and grabbed Jack by the arm. "Run!"

They were out the door in seconds. She turned left to go down the stairs, but the noise had alerted one of Reza's men who'd been waiting downstairs. He was already nearly at the top of the short stairwell, and reached out to grab them. He would have if Jack hadn't landed a quick right.

It wasn't flush, but it was enough to knock him off balance and send him tumbling down the stairs.

"The roof!" Diana said and grabbed Jack's hand again, pulling them back the way they'd come.

They climbed a narrow, dark staircase and emerged into the bright Egyptian sun. Jack blinked against the bright light, then looked over his shoulder as the sound of the men coming up the stairs behind them grew louder.

They were standing on a flat rooftop that Amir must have used as a makeshift patio. There were two small wooden chairs and a table. He grabbed one of the chairs and shoved it under the door handle. It would hold, but not for long.

When he looked back Diana was at the edge. "Over here."

Jack joined her, but made sure to keep back from the edge. He could feel the world starting to spin the closer he got.

She nodded toward the roof across the alley. "We can make that, right?"

Jack eyed the gap between the buildings. It wasn't that far. Six or seven feet, but it wasn't the across that killed you. It was the down.

"Come on," Diana said and took several steps back.

The men pounded on the door. The chair would give way any minute. Before Jack could suggest maybe there was another way, Diana took a running start and leapt. She swung her arms wildly in the air, before landing and stumbling on the other side. She quickly got to her feet and waved him across.

Jack hesitated. He could face a dozen armed Nazi and not break a sweat, but this....He looked down over the edge despite telling himself not to. The ground telescoped away from him. Twenty-five feet looked like fifty, a hundred. His mouth went dry and his palms were instantly slick with sweat.

He panted out a few quick breaths to try to control himself. No problem. All he had to do was defy gravity.

"Hurry!" Diana yelled and reached out as if she could catch him.

Behind him the doorframe began to split as yet another shoulder was thrown against it.

Jack took a deep breath and a few steps back. He had no choice. Jump or die. Or both, the wicked part of him echoed.

He ignored it and the pounding of his heart and ran toward the edge. He jumped out and up as high and as far as he could. It felt like he hung in the air suspended until time caught up with him and he landed hard on the far side. He barely managed to, but he kept his feet.

Diana ran over to him. The men broke through and spilled out of the stairwell and onto the other roof.

Diana grabbed Jack's hand. "Come on."

She pulled him away just as a gun shot pinged into the masonry of the stairwell enclosure near where he'd just been standing. They ran to the far edge of the roof and leapt again. This one wasn't as far and, thankfully, Jack didn't have time to look down.

From here, he lowered Diana down onto the roof of a lower level room and then jumped down himself. They moved quickly to the next ledge. The ground was only about ten feet down now. Jack grabbed Diana's hand and lowered her as far down as he could and let go. He clambered over the edge and dropped to the ground beside her, ignoring the rebellion in his stomach as he did.

"This way," she said, and they ran down the narrow alley, turning from one into another. They zigzagged their way through the old cobblestone streets. Finally, they turned hard to the right again and fell in with the crowd at a large, busy market.

Jack looked back over his shoulder as they meshed with the surging foot traffic. No one seemed to be following them. They walked for another few minutes before he felt safe. Finally, he glared over at her. She smiled innocently back.

"Ya know, I love a good run for your life as much as the next man, I just prefer to know what I'm getting myself into before I start running."

Diana stopped at a fruit vendor and picked out a pair of oranges. "I'm sorry about that." She handed the vendor a few small coins. "It really was supposed to be a simple pick-up. Poor Amir."

She handed Jack one of the oranges and tore into the peel of hers as they continued along with the crowd, as if they hadn't just leapt across buildings to escape being shot.

Jack shook his head. This woman was insane. "Who are you? Are you some kind of thief?"

She looked at him askance. "Is that what you think?"

He shrugged. What else was he supposed to think?

Diana chewed thoughtfully for a moment. "I...repossess things. I reclaim objects for their rightful owners," she said as she popped a piece of orange into her mouth. "Things turn up missing and I find them."

"Isn't that the police's job?"

"It is, but some of my clients would rather not involve the authorities."

Jack frowned. "Riiight."

She arched an eyebrow. "They're either inept or corrupt. And some people would rather keep a low-profile about these things."

Jack shook his head. "And running over rooftops and getting shot at is your idea of a low-profile?"

Diana frowned and ate another slice of her orange. "That wasn't part of the plan."

"And throwing the table at them. I think you're probably insane."

She laughed and wiped some juice from her chin. "Probably. But Reza definitely is. Nico's harmless, but Reza, he's...better avoided."

Jack looked back over his shoulder. Still clear. "I'm all for that."

Diana finished her orange and took Jack's from his hand. "Right," she said. "Now, about that papyrus...."

CHAPTER SEVENTEEN

THERE WAS JUST SOMETHING about a man in a tuxedo, Elizabeth thought as she looked from Simon to the rest of the men in the main hall of Shepheard's. From dress uniforms to black tie attire, the weekly party at the hotel was a high-class affair. Champagne flowed freely, silver trays filled with canapés never seemed to deplete, and music from popular standards to classical waltzes drifted down from the orchestra in the gallery above.

Smoke from Virginia tobacco, imported to Europe and brought on steamers to Egypt rose from every corner of the room. White-gloved hands gently gripped tortoise-shell cigarette holders; the ivory tips never straying more than a few inches from their owners' ruby red lips.

Even in what she thought was a pretty posh green silk evening gown, Elizabeth felt underdressed. Maybe it was because she'd left the matching evening gloves upstairs, but she didn't regret it. They made her hands sweaty.

She held on to Simon's arm as they reached the bottom of the grand staircase and tried to forget how much this trip had cost. Travers had offered to fund their expedition, but Simon had steadfastly refused to accept more than a few hundred pounds in period currency. He insisted they pay for everything else themselves. The last thing on Earth he wanted was to be beholden to the Council. It was much more comfortable the other way around.

Arthur and Christina Whiteside sat at one of the white-linen covered tables that ringed the impromptu dance floor that had previously been the main hall and lobby. Simon inclined his head in their direction, silently asking if Elizabeth wanted to join them. She nodded and he led her toward their table.

Arthur looked tired and drawn and, looking at Christina, it was no wonder. She brought sullen to new depths. Not that Elizabeth could blame her. She'd had her heart broken. A girl was allowed to mope after that.

Arthur rose to greet them and gestured for them to join them.

"That's a beautiful dress, Christina," Elizabeth said as Simon helped her into her chair.

Christina smiled, but it faltered and fell quickly. Her father looked sadly at her, clearly wishing to help her, but having no idea how. Elizabeth offered him what she hoped was an encouraging smile. Caught with his emotional pants down, Whiteside cleared his throat and blushed.

"Henri tells me you stopped by the museum today?" Whiteside said hopefully.

The man Ahmed had sent them to see was very knowledgeable about ancient writings, but he hadn't come across anything like what they were looking for. Jack hadn't made progress on the cipher and the lead he'd followed ended in a total of bupkis.

"Yes," Simon said. "But nothing's come of it yet, I'm afraid."

"Well," Whiteside said and then briefly clamped his hand on Simon's forearm. "You're keen for trying. Both of you. And I hope you'll let me repay your kindness and accept my invitation to Giza the day after tomorrow."

Simon and Elizabeth exchanged a quick glance. "Giza?" Simon asked.

"Yes, a fundraiser for the museum. A bit of fun," Whiteside said, with an infectious grin. "We stomp around the area for a bit, being suitably impressed, and have tea at Mena House. George, God rest his soul, was quite looking forward to it."

Whiteside's enthusiasm dimmed.

"Was he?" Elizabeth asked, both out of a need to comfort Whiteside and to find out what Mason would have wanted there.

"Oh, yes," Whiteside said. "Quite the social event. We finish it all off with *Aida* at the foot of the Great Pyramid. Bedouins and their camels, hundreds of horsemen ride over the hill at the climax. It's quite spectacular."

"*Aida*?" Simon asked with a hint of enthusiasm.

"In its full glory," Whiteside assured him.

Going to the opera wasn't exactly at the top of Elizabeth's Top Ten Things I Simply Absolutely Positively Have To Do in Egypt list. And even though Simon loved it, he seldom indulged. Her falling asleep and drooling on his shoulder the last time they went might have had something to do with that, she thought guiltily.

"We'd love to," Elizabeth said before Simon could be noble and offer their apologies. And, honestly, if she left Egypt without going to see the Great Pyramids she'd have to have her head examined. A night at the opera was a small price to pay. And she would have paid it ten times over just to see the surprised smile that spread across Simon's face.

Sadly, it was short-lived and a deep scowl soon took its place. Elizabeth knew who had caused it before she heard his voice.

"Good evening," Henri said. "You look quite beautiful," he said taking in both Elizabeth and Christina, "both of you. My heart is in my throat in the presence of such loveliness."

Whiteside chortled. "Frenchmen."

Henri smiled unfazed. "We have a passion for beauty. It makes our blood warm."

He gazed at Elizabeth so long she shifted in her seat and Simon threw back half a glass of champagne with one swig. Henri seemed to enjoy making them both uncomfortable, but finally shifted his attention to Christina.

"Beautiful things need to be seen to be admired. You should not deprive the world by sitting here all night, Christina. Hmm?" He held out his hand. "Dance with old Jouvet, huh?"

Apparently, Henri could use his super powers for good when he wanted to. In the end though, she shook her head, unable to rise out of her funk. "Not tonight, Henri. Thank you though. It was very kind of you to ask."

Henri nodded sadly, as if he seemed to know what she was going through. Elizabeth doubted Whiteside had told him. She was fairly certain Christina's father was completely in the dark about her heartbreak. Maybe it was some sort of French affairs of the heart ESP.

"I am bereft." Henri smiled down at Elizabeth. "Unless you would like to dance, Mrs. Cross?"

She glanced at Simon, whose expression was as hard as stone.

"With your permission, of course?" Henri asked him. "Unless you mind?"

Simon paused and finally inclined his head. "Not at all."

"*Merveilleux!*"

133

Elizabeth hesitated, but took Henri's outstretched hand and let him help her up. She glanced back at Simon who was watching them both coolly.

She knew he wasn't a fan of Henri's, but Jouvet's contacts through the museum and the rest of the world of archaeology might be the key to finding the missing half of the papyrus. And, after all, it was just a dance.

Henri led her out to the dance floor. Thankfully, the song was a slow waltz and she wouldn't embarrass herself too badly. She hoped.

Henri put his hand on her waist, raised their joined hands, and started them easily into the flow of dancers.

"How are you finding Egypt?" he asked.

"I love it," she said honestly and despite the dangers they'd faced and the seriousness of why they'd come. "It's an amazing country."

Henri smiled, pleased. "Yes, it is." The hand on her hip pulled her just a bit closer.

Elizabeth narrowed her eyes and smiled. "You do realize that the ring on my finger isn't just for show?"

Henri's smile widened. "Where would the challenge be if it were?"

In spite of herself, Elizabeth laughed and shook her head. "I don't want you to get the wrong impression. I love my husband very much and I would never—"

"Never is quite a long time," Henri said and spun them around.

Elizabeth studied Henri for a moment. "Have you ever been in love, Henri?"

"I am always in love."

Elizabeth pursed her lips in impatience and Henri sighed. "Once, but it was long ago and better forgotten."

His words might have been casual, but she heard the emotion in them. "I'm sorry."

Henri shook his head. "Please, no pity. It makes it very difficult to seduce you."

Elizabeth laughed and Henri smiled. He was handsome and genuinely charming when he wanted to be.

"Well, we do have to keep it challenging, don't we?" she said.

Henri grinned broadly. "We do."

Jack sat in the near dark of his hotel room and stared down at Mason's letter. The light from the moon was bright enough to read by, but wouldn't disturb Diana's sleep.

He sighed and let his hand fall into his lap. He glanced over at the bed. Disturbing Diana sounded like hell of a better idea than sitting here staring at numbers that only stared back.

He'd woken with half a thought of how to solve the cipher, but by the time he'd slipped out of bed and unfolded the paper, the idea had disintegrated. He'd pulled on his pants, sat down in a chair by the window and squinted down at the rows of numbers, hoping somehow his dream revelation would come back to life.

It hadn't.

With another sigh he started to refold the paper when he heard a rustle of sheets. Diana pushed herself up sleepily onto her elbow. "Can't sleep?"

Jack shook his head and looked back down at the letter. It was a risk trusting her, but his gut hadn't let him down before. Except for Blake, a little traitorous voice whispered.

He looked over at Diana. She'd risked hers and saved his life earlier. She'd brought him into her world, maybe he could afford to do the same? After all, she already knew about the papyrus.

"Anything I can do?" she asked.

Normally, he wouldn't have let an invitation like that go, but this was too important. "Maybe."

He walked over to the bed and handed Diana the letter. She turned on the bedside lamp and sat up. Keeping the sheet wrapped around her, she leaned back against the headboard.

Jack stretched out next to her on top of the covers. He planted one foot on the bed and leaned on his elbow as he watched her eyes dance over the numbers.

"What is this?" she asked.

Jack hesitated. "A code."

She smiled, but didn't press him. He loved that about her. She didn't mind secrets. She had plenty of her own.

"There was a client," she said after a moment of studying it. "Strange little man from Philadelphia. Had a glass eye he could pop out on command. Anyway, he was a bit paranoid and insisted every communication be encoded. It was silly. The painting that had been stolen wasn't worth very much, but I always humor rich men's eccentricities."

Jack chuckled.

"Every note he sent or I sent him," she continued, "used The Wizard of Oz as the key. The messages looked a great deal like these."

As soon as she said it, the image from his dream coalesced. He sat up and took the paper from her. A book cipher. He shook his head. Why hadn't he seen that possibility sooner? Each number could represent a page number, a line and word or letter. It was a simple, but incredibly effective code.

"I could kiss you right now!" he said.

Diana smiled. "I think you should."

Jack laughed and looked back at the letter.

"Any idea what the key might be?" Diana asked.

The excitement from the realization ebbed. Without the right key, he was still only at square one. There had been books in Mason's room though. Surely, one of them had to be the key.

"Maybe," he said. Mason's room had been searched by the police. His belongings were probably locked away somewhere. "I'll have to do some checking tomorrow."

"Good," Diana said as she gently took the letter from his hand and set it on the nightstand. "Now about that kiss..."

Jack grinned and leaned in, more than happy to oblige.

CHAPTER EIGHTEEN

$\int$ IMON HAD NO IDEA the basement beneath Shepheard's was so cavernous. Dozens and dozens of trunks and suitcases filled several large rooms that ran along the main underground corridor. From abandoned items to those left in long-term storage, the basement was a maze of crates, steamer trunks and valises.

Simon had been relieved to find out the police hadn't held Mason's belongings as evidence and instead stored them at the hotel until the next of kin could be contacted. Which, he thought sadly, would be a very, very long time. Another well-placed monetary inducement had given them the location of Mason's belongings.

Simon bumped into a tall stack of boxes and nearly dislodged a large hatbox perched precariously at the top. He reached up to steady it and a cascade of dust fell into his eyes.

He coughed and blinked it away, wishing and he and Elizabeth had traded places with Jack and Diana. He'd much rather be out looking for the papyrus than digging around the bowels of the hotel, but Diana's contact was apparently "skittish."

Simon brushed the dust from his shoulders and pressed on. Somewhere in the mass of things forgotten was Mason's trunk. Squinting in the faint light cast by the single overhead lightbulb, he checked the tags as he went, looking for the brown leather steamer trunk Jack had described. That, unfortunately, narrowed it down to just over half of the contents of the room.

He picked his way through the haphazard stacks, winding down a crooked path from the door around the perimeter of the room, checking both the things along the wall and those piled into the center of the room. When he'd reached the far end and turned back toward the door to complete the circuit, he heard a sound. "Elizabeth?"

They'd been the only people in this section of the large basement. To cover more ground they'd split up, Elizabeth started at one end of the corridor with him at the other, each working their way toward the center.

When no answer came, he paused and listened. Nothing.

Simon waited another moment before continuing on. He was nearly at the end of his circuit. Mrs. Swanson of New Brunswick, Mr. & Mrs. Atherton of New York, Mr. George Mason, San Francisco.

"Finally," Simon breathed. He moved a crate of candlesticks and lamps aside and reached for the latch to Mason's trunk. He'd half expected it to be locked, but it wasn't. In fact, the lock had clearly been broken. There was no doubt in his mind it happened when whoever it was had searched Mason's room.

Simon lifted the lid, letting it rest against the wall. Moving aside neatly folded clothes, he quickly found what he was looking for. Sitting at the bottom of the trunk were four large leather-bound books. He picked one up and flipped through the pages. He put the book aside and reached for the others. Somewhere in all of that, he hoped, were the clues they needed.

He bent over to retrieve the others when he heard a sound again. Slowly, he stood back up and turned around.

An enormous man in black robes stood just feet from him. Simon's heart raced and he clenched his fists. Where was Elizabeth? Had he found her first?

"Elizabeth?" Simon called out.

When there was no answer, Simon's breath caught.

Beneath the man's *keffiyeh*, his eyes began to wrinkle into a smile. He started to say something, but Simon didn't let him finish. His fist collided with the man's jaw.

The man grunted, but shook off the solid blow easily. Simon felt his heart sink at that. His best punch had almost no effect.

Simon looked for something to use as a weapon and his moment's hesitation cost him. The other man lunged forward with shocking speed. One hand shot out like a striking snake and grabbed a fistful of Simon's shirt. The other was a blur until it crashed into Simon's face.

A spike of pain radiated through Simon's temple and a vague sense of nausea choked his throat. Dazed, Simon stumbled back against a teetering pile of crates. The man held onto his shirt and punched him once, hard in the gut. Simon gasped for air. The blow seemed to have forced every last ounce out of him. The stinging panic of not being able to breathe sent a shot of adrenaline through Simon's veins.

Almost casually, the man threw Simon to the ground. He struggled for breath as the man in black loomed over him. Small gulps of air took the edge off the panic that gripped him. He blinked against the red and black splotches that colored his vision and tried to think.

The bottom crate in the wobbly stack was to his right. As quickly as he could, Simon rolled over onto his back, braced himself with his arms and kicked. The bottom crate slid out from beneath and the stack toppled, crashing into the man. He stumbled in surprise, the weight of them pushing him aside.

Simon tried to stand, but he was too slow and the other man too quick. Before he could get to his feet, the man in black was on him again. With disturbing ease, the man flipped Simon over and leapt on top of him. It felt like a lead weight pressing down onto his chest. Simon swung wildly and earned a wicked backhand for his trouble.

Then, faster than any big man had a right to, the man's hand shot out again and his fingers wrapped around Simon's throat. Simon tried to throw him off, but the man had fifty pounds on him and arms like iron. Simon's hands gripped the man's wrists trying vainly to pry his hands away.

Simon coughed and gasped as the hands tightened over his throat, slowly squeezing the life out of him. The more he struggled, the weaker he felt. The world outside of his body became muffled as if someone had a laid a thick cloak over everything. All he could see now was the hulking black figure of the man above him.

Simon felt himself start to slip away and clawed for a handhold, but he was fading. "Eliza—" Simon said in a rasping whisper, but the word wouldn't form. Simon closed his eyes and felt the dark begin to take him.

"Simon? Simon!"

Was it a dream? Was he dead?

"Simon!"

He opened his eyes and the black figure was gone. Standing in its place was Elizabeth.

"Thank God," she said breathlessly.

Simon gasped for air and it took him a moment to regain his senses. Where had she come from?

As if reading his mind, she held up her right hand. A large silver candlestick clenched in her fist. She nodded down toward the man in black who was out cold. "It's a little Clue, but..."

Simon blinked in confusion.

"Come on," Elizabeth said, reaching out to him. "Before he comes to."

Simon untangled his legs from the man's and stood. He was shaky, but so damn relieved they were both alive. He swallowed a few times, trying to get his throat to work.

Elizabeth touched his cheek and frowned in worry. "Okay?"

He nodded and glanced back down at the man in black. Elizabeth put down her candlestick and gathered Mason's books and they hurried out of the basement. They found hotel security and told them about what had happened. Somehow, Simon wasn't surprised that the man was gone by the time they got there. At least, he thought, they'd escaped with their lives...and the books.

SIMON SET ASIDE THE sodden rag that had once been an icepack. His throat was sore, his body bruised, but he was otherwise damn lucky to be alive. He gazed across the table at his wife.

Elizabeth must have felt him staring at her and looked up from her book and pad of paper. "How do you feel?"

Simon put down his pen. "Damn lucky."

Elizabeth quirked an eyebrow and smiled. "Might have been more than luck."

"I meant having you."

A charming blush blossomed across her cheeks. He adored that she still did that with him.

It had been more than luck, he thought. And not just because she'd come to his rescue, but that he'd been alive for her to rescue at all. The man he'd fought could have killed him. Easily, if Simon were honest with himself, but he hadn't. Simon had thought it when they'd fought, but it was even clearer now. The man had simply been toying with him. But why?

Elizabeth sighed and tore off the sheet of paper she'd been working on. "I wish we'd get lucky with this."

Putting aside his thoughts about the man in the basement, Simon refocused on the code. Jack had explained the basics of book ciphers to them, and Simon and Elizabeth had started work with the four books to start trying to decode the message. It was tedious work. Assuming it was indeed a book cipher, they still had no idea which number in the sequence identified the page, word or letter, or if there were dummy numbers mixed in. The code could have used multiple books in multiple variations.

They'd been at it for several hours so far, trying to find patterns that created something resembling a sentence. So far, with no luck whatsoever.

Simon gently probed his neck and with one last thought to his good fortune, redoubled his efforts. It wasn't until sometime after lunch that the pieces of the puzzle started to fall into place.

Simon had moved on from *Anna Karenina* to Samuel Richardson's *Clarissa*. They'd formulated a strategy, moving from the simplest cipher—page number, line number, word on each line—to those that became progressively more convoluted.

Simon's heart beat faster as the first two words fell into place. *Now is*. He'd been down that path before though, only to be tripped up by the third word. It was no different this time. *Having. Now is having...* He sighed and moved on to the fourth word, hoping the third was a decoy. *The*. That had promise. *Now is having the.*

He felt the tingle of anticipation as he ran his finger down the next page in sequence. *The. Now is having the the.* That couldn't be right. He moved onto the next.

Winter. Now is having the the winter. He moved on to the next word and the pattern became clear. The third word, then the second, then the first should be skipped. That left him with…*Now is the winter.*

He hurried on, the heady feeling of knowing what was coming, making his pulse race.

"Now is the winter of our discontent," Simon read aloud.

Elizabeth looked up from her work, her expression confused. "Wait. What?" she said. "You've got it?"

"I think so," Simon said.

Elizabeth moved her chair next to his. The rest of the sentence came easily. He knew it by heart.

Elizabeth leaned forward and read it out loud. "Now is the winter of our discontent made glorious summer by this sun." She straightened. "Shakespeare."

"Richard the Third," Simon said. "But, what does it mean?"

Elizabeth leaned back heavily in her chair. "Crud."

Simon chuckled.

She shrugged. "I know. I was just hoping for a big flashing pointy finger. The watch is here!"

Simon put down his pen. He was disappointed, too. "It's hardly that, is it?"

"No, but we solved it," Elizabeth said raising her hand in the air. "Yay us!"

Simon sighed. He was pleased that they'd managed to solve the cipher, but what good had it done? They were no closer to the watch and had nearly been killed in the bargain. Worse yet, maybe it had nothing to do with the watch at all.

"One thing at a time," she said, throwing back the words of wisdom he'd dispensed when she grew impatient earlier. "I think we've had a pretty good day. Super secret code? Ass kicked."

"Need I remind you—Simon Cross. Ass also kicked."

Elizabeth grew serious and shook her head somberly. "No, you don't have to remind me."

He nodded. Neither of them needed a reminder of how dangerous their situation was.

He pulled her toward him and she leaned into his side.

She was right. They were one step closer. But Simon could not shake the feeling that they may be closer to something they'd wish they hadn't found.

CHAPTER NINETEEN

SIMON TURNED DOWN THE offer of champagne and watched with some trepidation as Elizabeth accepted a glass from the in-car steward. It was, after all, barely past one in the afternoon.

Elizabeth sensed his concern and shrugged. "Half a glass." She gestured to the rest of the first class tram car filled with wealthy tourists doing what they do best, indulging themselves. The Everetts were already on their second glass. "When in Rome, or Cairo..."

Simon sighed and took her glass. She frowned at him until he took a sip and handed it back. Smiling, she leaned back into her seat and gazed across the car at the Whitesides.

"Poor thing."

Christina gazed wistfully out the window of their little electric tramcar as Cairo passed by. "Perhaps a day out at Giza will do her good?"

"Maybe," Elizabeth said half-heartedly. "But nothing heals a broken heart except time."

"She's young," he said. "She has plenty of that."

Elizabeth hmm'd in reply and took another sip of champagne. "I wish we could find that papyrus."

Simon looked down at her confused by the apparent non-sequitur.

"Well, obviously, we need to find it to understand what Mason wanted with it, but it would also go a long way to cheering up Arthur."

It would, although at this point, Simon was wondering if it even still existed. Granted, they'd only been searching for a few days, but there was a very real possibility the other half had long been destroyed.

That morning, they'd asked Hassan if he knew of any traders in ancient papyrus and to no one's surprise, he knew several and was more than happy to escort them. They'd only had time to visit two before they had to depart for Whiteside's Giza afternoon adventure. Both had come up empty.

Jack and Diana had promised to see about the others, but Simon didn't hold out much hope. Whiteside had acquired his half barely a week before they'd arrived. Even with such a fresh trail to follow, they'd turned up no trace of the other half. The provenance was vague and tracing it back to its sister had proven fruitless so far. The decoded letter had left them with nothing. Without the other half of the papyrus, they had no leads to follow to find the watch.

Elizabeth nudged him in the side and held out her glass. "You look like you could use another sip."

Simon smiled and shook his head. There was no point in worrying about all that right now, nothing to be done for it today. Not to mention that they were off to see something wonderful, and it was just appearing in the distance. Simon nodded his head toward the window and Elizabeth turned to look.

Emerging from the haze were the peaks of the great pyramids. Their tram crossed another canal and turned toward them. On the left side of the tram a broad avenue lined with tall sycamores was busy with cars and carriages and foot traffic as an endless parade of people made their way to and from the pyramids. Their little two car tram trundled along the tracks, marshy water from the canals to the right and the ancient past just ahead on the horizon.

The tram terminus was at a grand hotel called Mena House. It had once been the hunting lodge of the Khedive, the ruler of Egypt under the Turks in the mid-to-late nineteenth century. Like so much of Egypt it was purchased by an English couple and eventually turned into a hotel. Enormous and elaborate, the hotel complex included tennis courts, croquet lawns, a large swimming pool and a golf course that expanded out into the arid desert.

Whiteside had made all of the arrangements. He retrieved their tickets from a small office and led them to where their transportation to the pyramids awaited.

An all too familiar odor wafted its way toward him and Simon sighed. "Camels."

Undaunted, Elizabeth climbed atop hers with a grin and confidently gave it the command to stand. Simon was secretly and peevishly pleased when it ignored her and only moved when its master ordered it to.

Their little group cut their way through the ubiquitous beggars and vendors of dubious antiquities and lumbered off toward the pyramids as Whiteside began his running commentary on all points of interest, great and small.

Simon grunted in assent or asked the occasional question, but his focus was on the massive pyramids looming before him. Whether Petrie or Herodotus was right about the methods of construction faded away in the face of the sheer magnificence of them.

The Great Pyramid of Khufu towered 450 feet above the plateau. Only small sections of the polished white limestone casing that had covered and smoothed the now-jagged sides remained. As amazing as it was now, seeing it gleaming white in the sun, smooth to the touch, would have been breathtaking.

"The whole thing covers about thirteen acres," Whiteside said. "Over two million individual stones each weighing over two and half tons. Some ten times that. Can you imagine?"

He could not. The Bedouin guides brought the camels to a stop. Thank God. And they all dismounted.

"Now," Whiteside said, holding out small ticket stubs. "You can ascend if you'd like. It's all paid for. Quite the view if you can see around those scoundrel vendors lying in wait."

"There are vendors at the top?" Elizabeth asked, tilting her head back and peering up into the bright sun.

"They're everywhere, the buggers."

Simon hadn't noticed the climbers at first, but now he saw small groups of tourists at the northeast edge making their way to the top of the pyramid. Two men stood on a level above and pulled each person up by the arms while a third got behind and pushed. It looked like a cross between an awkward ballet and torture on the rack.

Simon could tell from Elizabeth's expression that she was dying to see what it was like at the top, but she shook her head. The Everetts happily took their tickets.

"Right!" Trevor said, raising his golf club into the air. "You brought extra balls this time?" he asked his wife.

She patted her purse.

Good God in Heaven, what an ass. He was going to hit golf balls from the top of the Great Pyramid.

"Up we go, old girl!" Trevor said as he pulled his wife away. "See you at the hotel later. Ta!"

Simon watched them go with disgust. Finally, he turned to Elizabeth and could see the longing for adventure in her eyes. "Are you sure? Don't mind them."

She nodded, but it was regretful. "I hate not to do it, but I can't bring myself to, knowing how much damage it does."

Simon, although not tempted to climb it, had the same thoughts. It was a shame so little care had been taken in these early days. God only knows how much destruction reckless tourists had done over the years. As two nearby sightseers chipped off pieces from one of the giant stone blocks, he had an idea how much. He'd even heard that most would carve their initials at the summit. Carved them into the last standing of the Seven Wonders of the Ancient World. He was glad he wouldn't, at least, have to see that for himself.

"Well," Whiteside said, "There's always the interior."

"We can go inside it?" Elizabeth asked in shock.

"Of course, but it is close quarters in there. It's a bit dodgy, but safe enough. Although," he said as he took in her white frock, "I'm not sure you're exactly dressed for it."

"It's very cramped," Christina said. "You have to crawl in some parts. And it smells like bats anyway," she finished, wrinkling her nose.

The temptation to see the great chambers and halls was strong, but Simon was saved by a long line of tourists waiting their turn. Instead, they walked along the base of the massive pyramid past blocks taller than a man, before moving on to the Sphinx.

"Wow," Elizabeth said softly. He knew this was one of the things she'd most wanted to see and it did not disappoint.

There was something incredibly powerful and majestic about it. Over 60 feet tall and over 200 feet long, it was hard to imagine it had been carved out of a single piece of stone. Whoever built it remained a riddle worthy of the Sphinx itself.

The face was battered from weather and man. Supposedly, Napoleon's troops had used it for target practice. Whoever it had been, they were hardly the first or the last, he thought as several men stood on the shoulders and posed for pictures.

The sand itself had buried the forepaws as it had the entire thing many times through the ages and worn away the edges. Time and man had taken their toll. The long narrow pharoanic beard and the six-foot wide nose were broken off.

He was about to say as much to Elizabeth, but as he looked down at her he knew that wasn't what she was seeing. Her eyes had that far off look in them and a gentle smile played around the corners of her mouth.

He knew in her mind, she'd cleared away the sand, repaired the damage, and swept the men off its shoulders. While he saw simply what was, she saw what could have, should have been. It was one of her gifts. She could see the best in everything, living or not.

She glanced up at him and slipped her hand into his as if their touch could make him see what she saw before she turned back to the Sphinx.

"This is amazing," Elizabeth whispered.

"Shall we?" Whiteside asked from behind.

They lingered a moment and then turned to leave. Simon heard Elizabeth sigh. He followed her gaze. Christina. The girl sat on the edge of a stone, drawing into a small sketchbook before closing it and staring off into space.

"Poor thing," Elizabeth said with a concerned pout. "I wish there was something we could do."

Simon knew that look in her eyes and sighed as he released her hand. Honestly, he was surprised it had taken her this long to stick her oar in.

"Go on," he said, nodding toward the forlorn girl. "Work your magic."

Elizabeth's eyes twinkled with a smile. She kissed his cheek before walking over to Christina. The girl was like an injured bird and Elizabeth never could resist helping anything or anyone in need. Knowing he would only get in the way, Simon lengthened his step and caught up with Whiteside, who forged ahead like Stanley looking for Livingstone.

After the Valley Temple, they walked up the long, 500-meter causeway carved from bedrock that lead to Khafre's mortuary temple and pyramid. Whiteside, happy to have an audience again, picked up where he'd left off and spared no detail.

Despite his initial misgivings, the company suited Simon well. Whiteside was incredibly knowledgeable and even Simon had to admit his enthusiasm was catching. By the end of their three hour tour, Simon had learned more about Giza and the necropolis than he would have in reading a dozen books.

SIMON LET HIMSELF ENJOY the respite as the sun began to set behind the pyramids just beyond the lush front garden of Mena House. Elizabeth had managed to pull Christina out of her shell. The girl was still clearly upset, but bucking up and making the best of things. Despite Whiteside's general bewilderment at nearly everything Christina said or did, it was clear how much he loved her, and how much she loved him. He chatted amiably of his time with the Ashmolean museum and his travels with his daughter.

"Do you remember in Switzerland, Christina," Whiteside said, "when you found that Neolithic axe made from deer antler. Quite clever."

Simon smiled over at Elizabeth, enjoying Whiteside's obvious fatherly pride.

"If I recall, father, I found it by literally tripping over it."

He smiled. "Well, you still found it, didn't you?"

"It was quite by accident. I was only seven."

"Such a precocious child!" he said proudly.

Christina shook her head, but smiled fondly at her father.

"I used to travel with my father," Elizabeth said. "Although," she added with a small smile for Simon, "we didn't go to such exciting places as Switzerland."

To anyone else, she would have sounded like the usual Elizabeth—charming and self-effacing. However, Simon knew her too well and heard the sadness in her voice that always accompanied thoughts of her father.

Eddie West had been an itinerant gambler. He'd taken Elizabeth with him on his travels much the same way Whiteside had with Christina. Except, of course, Elizabeth stayed in shabby motels in Texas and not the four-star elegance of Europe and beyond that the Whitesides were accustomed to.

Arthur was about to ask Elizabeth about her father when a man announced that dinner was being served. Their foursome followed the rest of the crowd into the main hotel and toward the special dining area designated for the Cairo museum benefit.

Simon's good mood evaporated as they rounded the corner. Standing just inside the main hall leading to the dining room were the last two men on earth Simon wanted to see. Henri Jouvet and Ahmed Kassem stood talking with a well-dressed woman he'd seen around Shepheard's.

Jouvet called out to them and Ahmed blanched as he saw Simon. Or had he? It took Simon a moment to realize that he didn't appear to be the cause of Ahmed's discomfort. The boy was looking right past him and at Christina.

The small amount of color her cheeks had had a moment earlier paled, and her large eyes widened behind her glasses. "Ahmed."

Oblivious to it all, Whiteside greeted Jouvet with an enthusiastic handshake. The boy stared at Christina, a moment of joy at seeing her vanished and was replaced by embarrassment. Simon's jaw tightened as the realization set in. Their erstwhile kidnapper had been the one who'd broken Christina's heart.

That was strike two against the young man. Simon narrowed his eyes at Ahmed, who tugged uncomfortably at his collar.

"Aren't you going to introduce me?" the woman by his side said as she slipped her arm possessively through his.

She was attractive in a forced beauty pageant sort of way, mid-twenties, wealthy from the look of her clothing, and, from the look of annoyance on her face, the sort who expected to be the center of attention At. All. Times.

"Awkward," Elizabeth whispered under her breath, before giving Christina a "courage Camille" smile.

Ahmed started to speak, but had to clear his throat. "I'm sorry. This is Annabelle..."

"Douglas," she finished with an impatient edge that was hardly softened by a Southern accent and a ridiculous amount of eyelash batting. "Of the Savannah Douglases."

"Oh, of course, pleasure," Whiteside said. "I'm sure I've seen you around the hotel, haven't I? Are you a patron of the museum?"

She laughed and her eyes slid to Ahmed, clearly enjoying his good looks and oblivious to his discomfort. Simon rolled his eyes. He'd met this type before and they never failed to set his teeth on edge. "I am now," she said as she pulled Ahmed closer.

Ahmed obviously wanted to edge away, but was forced to smile politely and endure her advances. Simon took a moment to enjoy his discomfiture.

"Yes," Jouvet said. "Miss Douglas has been quite generous."

"I just love old things," the woman said. "They're just so..."

"Old?" Simon finished for her, politely ignoring Elizabeth's snort of laughter.

"Yes!" she said enthusiastically.

"Well," Whiteside said, trying to fill the awkward silence that followed. He glanced around the small group and finally noticed his daughter's expression. "Are you all right, my dear?"

Christina looked at Ahmed for a moment and then straightened her shoulders and turned away from the man who had obviously broken her heart. Good for her, Simon thought. "I'm fine, father."

He frowned and looked between her and Ahmed, but before he could say anything more, Elizabeth stepped in to save her.

"I think Christina and I are going to wash up. Will you excuse us?"

"Are you going to the little girls' room?" Annabelle said, as she moved to follow.

Simon abruptly stepped in her way. "I think your table is ready." He glared meaningfully at Ahmed who spluttered in agreement.

"Good seeing you again," he said as he pulled a confused Annabelle away.

Jouvet, arched an eyebrow. He'd clearly seen the undercurrents, but appeared to have no idea what they were about. He bowed slightly. "Arthur. Cross."

Whiteside watched him follow Ahmed and Annabelle into the dining room and Simon could see the dawn breaking as he realized why his daughter had been upset.

Simon cleared his throat. "Perhaps we should wait for the ladies over there?"

Christina's eyes were red-rimmed when they returned, and he half expected the girl to beg off for the evening, but she stayed, soldiering through dinner and conversation. She commented occasionally throughout their meal, but the bright, charming girl he'd had a glimpse of earlier had dimmed.

When the last plate had been cleared, the men were invited into the billiard room for cognac and cigars. Simon would have preferred to have gone with Elizabeth to sit on the veranda, but he dutifully played his role.

Men sat in large leather club chairs clustered together in a comfortable salon. Simon and Whiteside found a pair of chairs in a corner near the windows. It was dusk now and hotel workers traversed the perimeter of the grounds lighting torches as they went.

Whiteside watched them move from right to left and puffed thoughtfully on his pipe. Simon took a sip of what turned out to be a rather fine glass of Martell.

"I wish she'd told me," Whiteside said at last. When Simon didn't respond, he glanced over at him and smiled. "I'm old, but I'm not blind. Or perhaps I am. I had no idea until today."

Simon shook his head in confusion, pretending not to know what Whiteside was talking about, but the other man just smiled sadly. "It's all right. I suppose the father's always the last to know."

Having never been on this side of events, Simon didn't know what to say and found himself offering vague platitudes. "I'm sure she'll be fine."

Whiteside nodded, although the crease between his eyes and the worried set of his mouth betrayed his true thoughts. "Of course."

He took a pull on his pipe and let the smoke drift of its own accord before blowing it out in a long smooth stream. "You don't have children, do you, Cross?"

156

"Not yet," Simon said. The confidence in his voice caught him by surprise, as though it were a certitude. Perhaps, in his heart it was.

"Hmm." Whiteside settled back in his chair. "You know, I was about your age when Christina was born."

It was a simple truth, but it hit Simon squarely in the gut.

Whiteside shook his head and looked every year of his sixty. "I didn't think anything of it at the time. I never realized how old I'd feel even though she's still so young. Now she's growing up and I feel like one of those antiquities half buried in the sand. Bound to be forgotten."

The realization that he would be in his sixties when his child was Christina's age caused Simon's head to spin and his chest to tighten.

"Of course, if her mother were still alive, I..." Whiteside inspected the bowl of his pipe and frowned. "I don't mean to be so maudlin, but it's times like these when I feel her loss most acutely. Most acutely indeed."

Simon could only imagine. Just the merest thought of losing Elizabeth made his blood run cold. "How long has it been?"

"Ten years. Christina was just eight when...her mother passed. I was at a total loss, as you can well imagine." Whiteside took in a deep breath and let it out slowly. "I'm afraid I've not done a very good job of it. Dragging the poor girl all over the world."

He sat forward in his chair and tapped his pipe against a crystal ashtray. "I just couldn't bring myself to pack her off to boarding school or leave her in London. Told her we were a matched-set, couldn't be broken up. I suppose it was selfish of me."

"I don't think so." Simon knew all too well what it was like to be packed off to boarding school. "She's a lovely young woman. Broken hearts are part of growing up, I'm afraid."

Whiteside grunted and drank down the last of his cognac. "An Egyptian boy no less. "

Simon wanted to argue that point, but what could he say? Don't be prejudiced against him because he's Egyptian, be prejudiced against him because he's a thief and liar.

"Perhaps, she's better off."

"No doubt," Whiteside agreed as he pulled out a leather tobacco pouch and dug his pipe deep into it. He tamped down the fresh tobacco and stared at it for a moment before slipping both the pipe and the case back into his pocket. He reached for his glass and realized it was empty. "Damn."

"I'll get us both another," Simon said and turned to flag down a waiter, but they seemed to have all disappeared. "Excuse me."

Simon left Whiteside and walked over to the short wet bar at the end of the room. He placed his order and leaned back on the bar while he waited.

Ahmed clearly could not be trusted. Not that Simon ever did, but Elizabeth had. But then she'd trust the Devil himself. In fact, Simon remembered, she had. He would have laughed if it hadn't been so damn foolish and dangerous. And now, their kidnapper was mixed up with Whiteside's daughter. Nothing good could come from any of this.

"Your drinks, sir."

Simon turned to retrieve them when a waiter who had just come in with a tray caught his attention. They stared at each other for a moment before the man lowered his eyes. Simon couldn't shake the feeling that he knew him and took a step toward him.

The man shifted the tray in his hands and reached to open the door he'd just come through. As he did, his sleeve rode up and Simon saw the tattoo on his inner wrist.

"You!" Simon called out. It was the same as the marking on the man who'd broken into their room.

The waiter hurried through the door and quickly shut it behind him. Simon raced after him and yanked it open. The hallway was crowded with people. Simon shouldered past a few, ignoring their indignant protests. His heart pounding with adrenaline, he spun around, looking in every direction, but the man was simply gone.

He grabbed another of the hotel staff. "A man just came out of this room. A waiter. Which way did he go?"

The man shook his head.

Simon clenched his jaw. "He had a marking, a tattoo, just here." Simon shoved up his sleeve and pointed to the inner part of his wrist, but the other man just shook his head.

Simon let him go with a grunt. Dammit. He'd almost had him.

"Is everything all right?" Whiteside said, appearing at his side, slightly winded. "I saw you rush out."

"No," Simon said, keeping his eyes on the crowd. Finally, he spared Whiteside a glance. "Everything is not all right. I need to find Elizabeth."

"Oh," Whiteside said. "Well, I'm sure she's not—"

Simon ignored Whiteside's protest and set off to find her. They found Christina and Elizabeth on one of the verandas, unharmed and unaware that anything had happened. Simon let out a sigh of relief.

Elizabeth's smile faded as her eyes danced over his face and she started to stand, her own expression now alarmed. "What happened? Are you all right?"

Simon nodded and waved her back into her seat, but she wasn't fooled. "I'm fine."

Whiteside put his hands to his hips and frowned. "I think you'd better tell me what's going on here."

Simon glanced at Elizabeth, who frowned and said, "That makes two of us."

He obviously couldn't tell the Whitesides the entire truth, but perhaps some of it.

"Not here," Simon said. He looked over his shoulder at the milling crowd, still feeling far too exposed. "We should go."

"But what about the opera?" Elizabeth asked. "You've got me all worked up for it."

Simon held out her chair and as she stood, he turned her to face him. "The hero and the heroine die, buried alive."

Her face fell. "How 'bout we go back to the hotel?"

CHAPTER TWENTY

Elizabeth hadn't been able to get much out of Simon on the ride home with the Whitesides. Something had spooked him, but whatever it was, he didn't want to talk about it openly.

They'd barely set foot inside Shepheard's when the manager appeared and stopped them in the lobby. "Professor Whiteside!"

The tall, slender man mopped his brow and stuffed his handkerchief into his pocket as he hurried toward them. "Professor, I am most sorry to be the bearer of such news, but it seems that we have had another," he lowered his voice, "break-in."

Elizabeth cast a quick glance at Simon.

Whiteside squinted at him in confusion. "What do you mean? Break-in?"

The man clasped his hands in front him and looked furtively around to see if other guests had heard. "Please, will you come to my office?" His eyes shifted to Simon. "All of you."

He hastened them into his office adjacent to the front desk.

"Now, what's all this about a break-in, Salim?"

The man shook his head. "I am sorry. After the recent incidents," Salim said as he looked at Simon and Elizabeth. "We increased security on the grounds. You will find, new, much stronger locks on your balcony doors, but even our precautions could not prepare us for such a bold thief."

"Thief?" Whiteside said, his voice rising in an uncharacteristic show of anger. "By God man, if—"

Salim raised his hand to stop the coming tirade. "We caught him."

"Oh," Whiteside said, the wind taken right out of his bluster. "Well done."

Elizabeth saw the "however" on Salim's face before the word came out of his mouth. "However, there was a bit of damage, I am afraid. Not much," he added hastily. "Our men were there within moments, but..."

WHITESIDE SAT DOWN HEAVILY at the small, round table in his room and let the hand that held the tiny remaining bit of charred papyrus fall to the table. "Oh, dear."

Christina went to her father's side and laid her hands on his shoulders. "I'm sorry, papa."

He reached back and patted one of her hands. "It's all right, my girl. Nothing we can't live without."

"I don't understand," Christina said. "There are far wealthier guests here if they wanted to rob someone. Why target us?"

"I had hoped this wouldn't involve you," Simon said and looked sadly at Elizabeth. "I'm afraid this might be our fault."

Whiteside put down the remnant and turned in his seat. "I beg your pardon?"

Simon gestured to Christina to take a seat next to her father. While she did, Simon looked to Elizabeth, silently asking permission to share some of what they knew. She nodded. The Whitesides were mixed up in it now and had a right to know. Elizabeth joined them at the table.

Simon took a deep breath and began. "Two days ago, a man broke into our room. And another into Jack Wells'."

Whiteside arched an eyebrow in surprise, his eyes shifted uneasily to his daughter.

"We weren't sure what they were looking for," Simon continued, "but I'm afraid it might have something to do with George Mason."

Whiteside frowned as the seriousness of what Simon was saying began to sink in. He put both hands on the top of his thighs and sat back in his chair, seeming to be lost in his own thoughts. "I see."

Simon scratched the back of his neck. "We knew he was looking for something, but he never told us what it was. But I think two things are clear now. Whatever it is, it's related to your papyrus and secondly, he wasn't the only one looking for it."

"What would anyone want with a bit of old papyrus. It's not exactly a treasure map, now, is it?"

Simon tilted his head to the side. "Perhaps it's part of one or leads to one."

Whiteside's forehead wrinkled in thought.

"But then why burn it?" Christina asked. "If it's so valuable, why not steal it?"

"Maybe they were going to and when the guards came, they did the only thing they could," Elizabeth said. "Destroyed it so no one else could have it."

Whiteside shook his head. He looked up at Simon, doubt still etched in his creased forehead. "And George was involved in this?"

Simon nodded. "We think so."

"And someone killed him because he was getting close to finding the answers he sought?" Whiteside reasoned.

"Possibly," Simon said, pausing for a moment and Elizabeth could see him weighing how to continue. "We have reason to believe that the man who shot him and the man who broke into our rooms, and yours, are connected."

Whiteside turned to his daughter. "We'll make arrangements tomorrow for you to return to London."

Christina sat up defiantly. "Only if you come with me."

"No," Whiteside said and the absent-minded professor fell away and the man he had once been, many years ago reasserted himself. "I'm going to stay. I don't like being run out of places. And I think I'd like to have a few words with the man who did this." He pushed the scorched bit of papyrus across the table.

"Then I'm staying, too," Christina said. He started to protest, but she shook her head. "You always said we were better off together than apart. We're a matched-set, remember?"

Whiteside started to argue, but then reached out and squeezed his daughter's hand before turning his attention back to Simon. "And this evening? In the salon?"

Simon nodded. "I recognized one of the waiters. He had the same marking on his wrist as the man who broke into our room."

And shot Mason, Elizabeth added silently. "What happened back there?"

"After I saw him," Simon said, "I tried to follow him, but he disappeared into the crowd."

"This marking," Whiteside said. "What exactly is it?"

Simon thought for a moment. "It was a symbol of some sort. I never did get a good look at the whole thing. All I could make out were two arching lines and a circle, a dot, touching the lower line. Centered on it almost."

"Can you draw it?" Whiteside asked.

Simon nodded and Christina handed him her small notepad and pencil. He sketched what he'd described—two arching lines with a black circle touching one.

Whiteside studied it for a moment before a smile came to his face and he laughed in delight.

He took up the pencil and added to Simon's sketch.

"Could it have been this?" he asked, turning the sketch pad so Simon could have a better look.

"Yes," Simon said. Elizabeth could see the light of recognition in his eyes, hear it in his voice. "Yes, I think that was it."

He lifted the sketch and showed it to her. Clearly it was an eye, ornate and iconic. She'd seen the symbol many times before. Variations of it had been used and abused for centuries by everyone from the Illuminati to the Alan Parsons Project. "The Eye of Ra?" she said.

"Precisely!" Whiteside said. "It's also called the Eye of Horus. It sometimes symbolizes the goddess Wadjet."

"Wadjet?" Simon asked.

"Yes, she's a very old goddess, although the symbol is also associated with several later goddesses you might have heard of— Mut, Hathor, Sekhmet, and Bast."

Elizabeth had heard of them, but she knew a total of diddly-squat about them.

"They're all mother goddesses of some sort, aren't they?" Simon asked.

Whiteside smiled. "Yes. This...this marking it was on their wrists, you say?"

"Yes." Simon held up his arm. "The inner part, just here."

Whiteside hmm'd in a way that made Elizabeth uneasy. "Does that mean something?"

Whiteside tugged on his ear. "Well, it's just that some of the ancient cults used to tattoo various symbols on their bodies."

"Cults?" Elizabeth gulped. Cults conjured images of dark ceremonies and daggers and sacrifices. Cults didn't throw jamborees.

Whiteside frowned as he answered. "Nearly every god or goddess had a cult of their own. But I haven't heard of anything of this sort in...well, over a thousand years or more."

Simon and Elizabeth shared uneasy glances. Elizabeth felt her pulse pick up speed as her imagination took hold. Thousand year old cults didn't exactly conjure images of puppy-dogs and butterflies, more like beating hearts ripped out of chests and desiccated mummies that turned into vengeful, murderous lovers.

"Maybe some cult has been reformed?" Simon suggested.

"Take the band on tour one more time?" Elizabeth said, winning a sour look from Simon.

"It's possible," Whiteside said. "But why?"

Elizabeth knew it had to have something to do with the watch, but what?

"Do you have any books on these cults?" Simon asked.

Whiteside shook his head. "No, I'm afraid not."

He held up a finger, pushed back his chair and stood. "Although," he said as he retrieved a book from the sideboard. "This one might have some detail about the goddess—Mut, Hathor and the others."

Simon took the book. "Thank you."

Whiteside still looked perplexed, almost wounded. "I just don't understand. What could they possibly want with my papyrus?"

"You translated it; you know what it said," Elizabeth said. "There must be some connection."

"Well, yes, but I don't remember it all exactly. And there were partial symbols at the bottom, where it was torn...I can't be sure what those were without the whole of it and now, that seems quite impossible."

"Maybe not," Christina said. She smiled and hurried into an adjoining room, returning with a large sketchpad. With an even larger grin, she put it down on the table and flipped through the sheets. "I wanted to practice in case Henri let me sketch in the tomb. Here!"

She flipped over the last large sheet and revealed an exact rendering of the papyrus. "I know it's not the same as the real thing, but..."

Whiteside kissed her forehead. "It's far better than that, my girl." He looked at Simon and Elizabeth proudly. "Now if we can just find the other half we might have some clue as to what in blazes is going on. There's just no other way."

Simon tucked the book under his arm and straightened his shoulders. "There might be one more way."

TWENTY POUNDS. APPARENTLY, THAT was the going-rate for bribing a police officer in Cairo. A bargain. In 1906 she and Maxwell had paid San Francisco's finest a lot more than that.

"Think they're included in Egypt's Consumer Price Index?" she murmured to Simon as their little entourage, including Jack and Hassan, was escorted into the back holding cell area.

He narrowed his brow in question.

"Bribes," she mouthed, and his narrowed brow turned into a full blown warning glare turned eye roll.

She shrugged. It seemed a fair question. From what she'd seen it was part and parcel of every day life here. They seemed to have had their pick of officers ready to take a payoff to see the man who'd been caught breaking into Whiteside's room. Maybe high supply kept prices low.

"You understand the need to keep whatever happens here between us," Simon said.

Hassan grinned.

Simon held up his hand. "Yes, yes, I know. But do you understand?"

Hassan nodded. "Hassan is nothing if not discrete, Mister Cross. I have told no one about New Year's Eve 1918. What happened between Her Royal Highness and that busboy in the kitchens is their own business."

Jack laughed while Simon looked at Hassan blankly before Elizabeth stepped in. "He understands."

"Good," Simon said. "And thank you for translating."

Hassan inclined his head.

Jack closed the door to the small jail area in the back of the station as the officer left them alone with the man in the cell. "We only have five minutes."

Simon walked over to the iron bars and stared at the man inside. He had on the same jet black robes as the man who'd broken into their rooms, but his *keffiyeh* was gone. His complexion was dark and his beard as black as his robes.

"Who are you?" Simon asked. Hassan quickly translated.

The man looked over at Simon, his expression flat, and he slowly stood from his spot on a wooden cot. He walked over and stood near Simon, the bars the only barrier between them. His eyes, nearly black, shifted from Simon to Jack to Elizabeth and back again.

He leaned forward and said a single word in Arabic.

Hassan looked surprised, but translated. "Vengeance."

Elizabeth and Jack shared a nervous look.

Unperturbed, Simon pressed on. "Who do you work for?"

The man listened to Hassan, but his eyes never left Simon's.

"I am an arrow of the Goddess," Hassan translated quickly. "Hovering in the air, waiting to pierce your heart."

There was so much conviction in his eyes, so much hatred. Elizabeth couldn't stop the shiver that made her wriggle in place.

"Who do you work for?" Simon asked calmly.

Simon must have heard and felt the Charles Manson crazy that practically dripped from every word the man spoke, but somehow he managed not to let it show.

Hassan relayed the question.

"It has been foretold," the man said. "The fate of the evil ones is sealed in the earth."

The man lifted his eyes upward in devotion. His arms outstretched and the rest of them took a small step backward. His robe sleeves fell back slightly and Elizabeth could see the tattoo on his wrist clearly now. It was definitely the Eye of Ra.

"The Mighty One, Lady of the Flame, One Before Whom Evil Trembles," Hassan translated. The man spoke with growing passion. "Mine is a heart of carnelian, crimson as murder on a holy day. Mine is a heart of cornmeal, the gnarled roots of dogwood and the bursting..."

The man's religious zeal grew louder and faster. Hassan struggled to keep up with the rantings.

"I will what I will. Mine is a heart of carnelian, blood red as the crest of a phoenix!"

Then, just as suddenly as he'd started, the ravings stopped.

"I told you we weren't going to get anything useful out of him," Jack said. "Guy's a nutcase."

The man smiled and whispered in English, "Betrayers."

And then, suddenly, everything went black. The darkness was so complete and so abrupt Elizabeth wasn't sure if the lights had gone out or she'd simply ceased to be.

She felt a hand grip her arm and pull at her, and she gasped in alarm.

"Elizabeth?" Simon said.

"Sorry, that's just me," Jack said, as he squeezed her arm.

Elizabeth pushed out a relieved breath. "Simon?"

"Here," he said, his voice not far.

She couldn't make him out in the total darkness. The room was in the center of the building and had no windows at all.

"Everyone all right?" Simon asked.

Elizabeth felt Simon's hand touch her shoulder and pull her closer to him.

"The power grid," Hassan said. "It is...unreliable. But," he added and Elizabeth heard the snap and whoosh of a match being lit, "Everything will be all right."

He touched the tip of his match to two taper candles.

"Where did you get those?" Elizabeth asked.

Hassan patted his cloth belt. "Trust in Hassan."

Simon took one of the candles and held it out toward the cell. The pool of light it gave off was weak, but there was enough to see inside the small cell. And it was empty.

CHAPTER TWENTY-ONE

Elizabeth brushed a few strands of hair from her eyes. The wind was beginning to pick up, but she didn't mind. The sun and the warm wind felt good. Anything warm would feel good after the chill that had taken up lease in her guts.

Fate. Prophecies. Were they ever good? Just once she'd like to hear, "You will lose two pounds without trying!" or "You will hit only green lights on the way to the market today!"

"I'm sure it was just religious claptrap," Simon said.

"Could be," Jack said, as he took a drag off his cigarette, "but betrayers is kind of specific."

Simon took a drink of his lemonade. "I'm sure anyone who isn't a true believer is a betrayer of some sort in the cult's eyes."

"And his little disappearing act?" Jack said.

Simon lifted his chin in silent defiance. "Just that, an act. Rather coincidental, wasn't it for the lights to go out just then?" He shook his head. "Theatrics."

Jack frowned and tapped his cigarette on the edge of the ashtray on the table. "Pretty good ones. I didn't see any way out of that cell."

"Just because you couldn't see it, doesn't mean it wasn't there," Simon countered and then frowned deeply at Jack's cigarette. "And must you do that?"

Jack took a long defiant drag before snubbing it out.

"Thank you," Simon said tersely.

While they argued about what they'd seen or not seen and the little they'd learned at the police station, Elizabeth tried to clear her mind. She'd let her fears get the better of her back there and she seriously needed to find something and grip it.

Okay, so they were up against an ancient cult that wanted them dead; they'd faced worse. Hadn't they? She frowned at that rather unpleasant thought and decided to focus on something tangible instead.

If they could just find the other half of the papyrus, they might know what this was all about. The cult member hadn't torched it just for giggles. That meant it mattered. But without the second part, it was useless.

Another dead end. She took a deep breath and tried to let the warmth of the sun that shone down onto Shepheard's veranda soothe her. She closed her eyes and just as she did a strong gust of wind came.

Someone's hat flew past and napkins and papers swirled in the wind. A woman near the next table gripped the wide brim of her sun hat, but forgot her scarf. The silk began to float off her shoulders, but an edge snagged and it rippled in the air. It streamed out behind the woman like a flag before slipping away.

The scarf danced on the wind, fluttering like some living creature before taking a sudden nosedive and wrapping itself around the leg of a nearby chair. The woman was too busy readjusting her hat to notice she'd lost her scarf and Elizabeth hurried to pick it up before it worked itself free and was caught in another gust.

She saved it just in time and ran the silken material between her hands to loosen any sand that might have found its way onto it. Glad for the distraction from the doom and gloom, Elizabeth paused for a moment to admire the pattern on the scarf. What she saw brought her up short.

The lightbulb that went off in her head was so bright it nearly blew a fuse. She quickly studied it, her heart racing and ran over to the woman.

"Elizabeth?" she heard Simon say in alarm.

"Where did you get this?" Elizabeth asked the woman as she held the scarf out.

The woman stared at her dumbly.

"Where did you get it?" Elizabeth repeated, more urgently.

The woman looked at Elizabeth warily and pointed to a vendor's cart on the street in front of the hotel.

Forgetting her manners in what she thought just might be the break they needed, Elizabeth tossed the scarf back to the woman and turned back toward her table, but Simon and Jack were already standing and coming over to her. "What's the matter?"

Elizabeth stuck out her hand. "I need money." How could they have missed it? How many times had she seen this scarf walk by wrapped around the neck of a tourist, sitting in a shop window or on a vendor's cart?

Simon frowned, but dug into his wallet.

Before he could choose a bill, Elizabeth snatched the whole thing and hurried down the broad steps of the hotel. She ignored the peddlers and beggars and headed straight for the cart with the scarves. Simon and Jack trailed close behind.

"How much?" she asked, pointing to one of the scarves. "*Bikeam?*"

The man replied; she shoved a bill at him and snatched up one of the scarves.

"What on earth's gotten into you?" Simon said.

"This," Elizabeth said as she held out the scarf.

Simon and Jack exchanged worried glances.

"This is the other half of the papyrus." She unfurled the scarf to reveal rows of hieroglyphics, the top row only half there, the remaining silk screened image was the missing bottom half of Whiteside's papyrus. "It's been right in front of us the whole time."

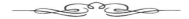

"REMARKABLE," WHITESIDE SAID AS he studied the scarf.

Christina flipped through her sketchpad and then laid it out on the table above the scarf, lining up the two edges.

Elizabeth could barely believe it. It was a perfect match. The anticipation in the room was electric.

"What does it say?" Jack asked.

Whiteside brought a finger to his mouth and pursed his lips. "Well, let's see. The gift was given to the pharaoh of the New Kingdom."

"Who would that be?" Elizabeth asked excitedly. They were so close now.

Whiteside stood up straight and tugged on his ear. "Oh, that covers quite a few. The New Kingdom, well that's the 16th Century to the 11th Century. It could be anyone from Amhosis the First to Ramesses the Eleventh. Or it could refer to something else entirely."

Elizabeth didn't bother to hide her frustration and looked to Simon. Where was that darned Easy Button? He held up a hand urging patience.

Whiteside leaned back over the scarf. "It speaks of the glory and the power of the gift...Hail his majesty, the sun disk shining from his palm, glittering above the sky second to no other. The gods bowed down. All pay adoration to the one, the glorious being who rises above all. The Aten, that's the sun or Ra or sometimes more generic for God...the Aten, the living one who rejoices on the horizon and is the throne of the Lord of Heaven."

Whiteside leaned back and silence followed.

"Is that it?" Jack asked, the disappointment in his voice echoing Elizabeth's.

"Yes," Whiteside said thoughtfully.

Elizabeth looked down at the scarf, that sinking, disappointed feeling heavy in her stomach. She'd been so sure. Maybe he'd missed something? "What does all that mean? Can you tell which Pharaoh it's talking about?"

Whiteside took off his reading glasses. "It's fairly typical of the period, I'm afraid. I wish I had more."

"If it doesn't really tell us anything," Jack said. "Why would the cult want to destroy it?"

Whiteside looked at the scarf for a moment before shaking his head. "Have you learned anything more about that? The cult, I mean."

Simon told them the abridged version of events, leaving out the surprise ending.

Whiteside pursed his lips and then chewed thoughtfully on the end of his glasses. "Sekhmet."

Simon nodded. He'd read the book Whiteside had given him and recognized the names the cult member had recited. "The Lady of the Flame."

"She has well over a hundred names. The Eye of Ra, the Devouring One, Mistress of Dread. And so on."

175

"She appears in the form of a woman with the head lioness, doesn't she?" Christina asked.

"Yes," Whiteside said. "She's the goddess of conquest and vengeance."

Betrayers, Elizabeth thought.

"What's her connection, or her cult's, to the papyrus?" Jack asked.

Whiteside leaned back in his chair. "Amenhotep III was quite taken with Sekhmet. He had hundreds of statues built in her honor."

"And he was a pharaoh of the New Kingdom," Christina supplied.

Elizabeth plopped down into the nearest chair and chewed the inside of her lip. That sounded logical enough, but what did the watch have to do with it? What did *they* have to do with it?

Whiteside tucked his glasses into his pocket. "Perhaps we'll find something else to help us be sure."

Simon pushed out a breath and paced to the far side of the room. He stopped, pivoted and looked at Elizabeth. "There is something else," he said and looked to Jack and Elizabeth for permission. "The letter?"

She nodded and Jack did the same. In for a penny, in for a pound.

"It's probably nothing," Simon continued, "but there was a note. It could be unrelated but...it said, 'Now is the winter of our discontent, made glorious summer by this sun.'"

Christina chewed on her thumbnail in thought. "Richard III."

"Yes," Simon said. "Other than in this case, ironic, references to the glory of a king and the sun, of course, that's a play on words though..."

Christina looked up at him, a thoughtful scowl on her face. "He was a hunchback, wasn't he?"

"Yes, in the play, he was," Simon said. "'Deformed, unfinished, sent before his time into this breathing world, scarce half made up.'"

A slow broad smile stretched across Christina's face and she turned to her father.

Whiteside laughed. "Very good, my dear."

Elizabeth felt that prickle of excitement again. "What?"

Whiteside stood to his full height, like a professor at his podium. "There was a pharaoh not unlike our dear King Richard. Deformed, a hunchback by many accounts, cast as the villain by history. And he reigned during the New Kingdom. In fact, he was the son of Amenhotep."

"Akhenaten," Christina supplied.

"It all fits," Whiteside said. "The sun disk in his hand, the description of the Aten, I'm certain of it."

He tapped the scarf. "It must be Akhenaten."

Elizabeth felt the shiver of the joy of discovery run through her body. She looked at Simon and then Jack. Both wore the same exhilarated expression, triumph and relief.

Whiteside shook his head and looked back at the sketch of the papyrus and the scarf. "Fascinating."

"And lucky," Christina added. "We just happen to know one of the foremost experts on that particular pharaoh."

CHAPTER TWENTY-TWO

Henri held out his hand for Elizabeth as she boarded the steamer. "I am so pleased you could join us on our little adventure."

He helped her off the boarding plank and onto the ship's deck. Casting a glance over her shoulder at Simon, he smiled. "Both of you, of course."

Simon smiled tightly and inclined his head.

This was going to be an adventure all right, Elizabeth thought. Simon and Henri in close quarters for a four day cruise up the Nile. As Henri's eyes lingered on her, she wondered if Simon's suggestion of taking the train and meeting them in Luxor might not have been the better one.

"Arthur!" Henri said, turning his attention to more of his guests.

Although, Elizabeth had to admit, she was looking forward to the cruise. Henri had chartered one of Cook's finer ships and arranged the entire journey. What would normally be a cruise of several weeks, he'd cut down to just four days. They would sail with only a few stops along the way. It wasn't the usual tourist pilgrimage up the Nile, but far more pleasant than the train.

They'd get to relax a little, see some of the country and hopefully leave the Cult of Sekhmet back in Cairo. Not to mention they needed to stay in Henri's good graces. The last thing they needed was for him to kick them out of his inner circle. Without Henri, they wouldn't have a chance at getting into Akhenaten's tomb, and finding the watch they hoped was inside it.

The clues weren't exactly ironclad evidence, but it all made sense. It certainly explained why Mason had befriended this particular group of people and ingratiated himself with Henri. After all, if they'd been off course, those pesky cult members wouldn't keep showing up. All signs pointed to Henri's dig in the Valley of the Kings and that's where they had to go.

She glanced over at Simon. The marks had faded from his neck, leaving only faint bruises, but the memory of seeing that man trying to kill him had not. She shivered and Simon looked down at her in concern.

"Just a tickle," she said vaguely and took off her sun hat, and began fanning herself with it. So far, the weather had been very mild, but today felt like it was shaping up to be a scorcher.

She and Simon stood on the deck as Henri greeted the Whitesides and Jack and Diana.

"*Parfait!*" he said. "Everyone is here."

He waved to one of the crew who hurried down the plank to finish seeing to the stowing of the piles of luggage still resting on the shore.

"The stewards will see you all to your cabins," Henri said with a pleased smile. "I hope you will find the accommodations to your liking. In an hour, please join me on the upper deck for a toast to our voyage?"

Several stewards in crisp white robes ushered the group toward their rooms on the upper deck. Instead of the two-sailed dahabeah most wealthy travelers hired to explore the Nile, Henri had chartered a small steamer. It was a bit like a miniature cruise ship. Long broad promenade areas with large, white-cushioned chaise lounges, and small clusters of rattan tables and chairs lined nearly the full 200 foot length of the ship.

After having left the rest of the group at their cabins, Simon and Elizabeth finally reached theirs at the rear of the upper deck.

"Wow," Elizabeth said. The suite was incredible. Complete with a sitting area and vanity, it was larger than any of the other cabins they'd passed on the way. The dark mahogany panelling and varnished oak floors might have made the room feel dark if it weren't for the enormous, panoramic bay windows that gave them the perfect view of the Nile.

"Was awfully kind of Henri to give us this and on such short notice too," she said.

Simon humphed and tossed his hat onto the vanity. What could he possibly find wrong with this?

He glared at the two twin brass beds separated by a nightstand. "Yes, very thoughtful."

While most of the other suites did have queen size beds, she was sure it was merely coincidence and not some plan to keep them apart. She slipped her arms around Simon's waist.

His expression softened as he looked down at her. He tucked a stray curl behind her ear. "If he thinks that's going to stop me, he's more of a fool than I thought."

Elizabeth smiled and kissed him. "Something to look forward to." She started to slip away, but Simon held her to him.

"We have an hour," he suggested.

Elizabeth laughed and shook her head. "Later. I promised Christina I'd meet her on deck."

Simon sighed and let her go. "All right. In that case, I suppose I should go introduce myself to the captain and meet the crew."

Which was code for "make sure none of them are cult members."

"I'll meet you later then," she said.

Simon picked up his hat and took one step toward the door before turning back.

"I'll be careful," she said, before he could remind her.

"Good." He put on his fedora and pulled the brim down. He nodded toward the beds, a sly smile on his lips. "Until later."

A thrill ran through her at his silent promise and she smiled. Score one for the cruise.

SIMON SIPPED HIS CHAMPAGNE and leaned back in his chair, watching as Elizabeth, and Jack and Diana chatted with each other around their small table. Jouvet had toasted them all and welcomed them to his adventure, as he put it. He was jovial and a consummate host, and completely irritating. His gaze always lingered a little too long on Elizabeth, and he offered her all too frequent, what Simon supposed were, charming smiles.

Simon narrowed his eyes and kept a close watch on the smug Frenchman. He seemed to delight in finding ways to spend his benefactor's money. A luxury cruise for a dozen of his closest friends was pushing the edge of decency though.

If Simon hadn't known any better, he'd almost think Jouvet was stalling the opening of the chamber at his dig. Maybe he was. He seemed to spend more time in Cairo than on-site and had planned a four-day luxury party instead of overseeing his work. He didn't seem at all enthusiastic about it, beyond a bit of showmanship for the crowd. He was competent enough, Simon supposed. Christina hadn't been overstating it when she said he was an expert on Akhenaten, but for some reason he didn't seem to be actually looking forward to getting to Luxor and opening the chamber. It was puzzling.

"More?" Simon asked as he lifted a champagne bottle from its silver ice bucket.

Elizabeth shook her head. It was just as well. Between the champagne and the heat she was looking very sleepy. One more, and she might just slide under the table.

Not that he could have blamed her. Even without the drink, the atmosphere was rather peaceful and hypnotic.

Even under the shade of the tarpaulin on the upper deck, the sun was strong. The smooth water of the Nile slipped beneath them. If it weren't for the slight hum of the deck from the engines and the churning sound of the paddlewheel, Simon would have thought they were standing still and the shore was moving.

The occasional wooden feluccas with their pointed, triangular arching sails moved past them up the river just as they had for thousands of years. The mud villages and bits of ruin along the shore felt as timeless as the Nile itself.

He rarely gave into thoughts of a spiritual nature, but this experience was surprisingly so. Or it was until Trevor Everett started driving golf balls from the stern of the ship.

"Dammit! Another slice."

"Idiot," Simon grumbled between sips.

"Maybe he'll fall in," Diana suggested.

Simon grinned. He liked Diana. What was not to like? She was smart, funny, independent. A good match for Jack. A good *temporary* match. After the unfortunate Betty disaster in Hollywood, Simon hoped to God Jack had learned his lesson. He didn't think the three of them could survive another three-month funk. He'd been content to let the man lick his wounds in peace, but Elizabeth had worried.

Jack had promised he was fine when he wasn't, and Simon told her to mind her own business and she hadn't. Eventually, Jack had climbed out of his depression and they'd seen the spark of the man they'd met in London.

As if Jack heard Simon's thoughts, he turned and caught his eye. Jack smiled, happy, thankful, and then he winked and gave a dramatic stretch. "Well, I think I'm gonna take a nap before dinner."

He excused himself and unsurprisingly Diana followed a few minutes later. Lucky bastard. Simon was about to suggest he and Elizabeth do the same when Whiteside and Christina appeared.

Simon sighed, but stood and invited them to join his table. Later would have to wait until later.

The rest of the afternoon and evening passed by quietly and inconspicuously. Simon enjoyed the respite. Not that he let himself completely relax, not here, not ever. However, sharing fine meals and finer brandy aboard a luxury ship moving slowly up the Nile wasn't the worst mission they'd ever had, as long as the men that plagued them had stayed behind in Cairo.

After an excellent dinner of roast lamb, the group retired to the salon and, naturally, Elizabeth found herself a poker game to join.

"You must be cheating somehow," Trevor Everett said as Elizabeth raked in another impressive stack of chips. "No woman is that good a poker player."

Simon laughed, too happy and, perhaps a little too tipsy to bother taking umbrage at Everett's absurd insults.

Elizabeth smiled and happily stacked her chips, most of which had belonged to Everett at the start of the game. "I'm really not that good. You're just that bad."

Offended, Everett stuck his cigarette into his mouth and pushed away from the table. Simon barely remembered to suppress his laughter as the man walked away. God, how he loved his wife.

Jouvet, who'd been standing watching the game unfold, gestured to the empty seat. "May I?"

Elizabeth shrugged and shuffled the cards ending with a long cascading flourish.

Jouvet grinned. "You have many talents."

Simon turned away. He'd be certain to lose his good mood if he watched Jouvet attempt to seduce his wife all night. He was feeling too good to let that damn Frenchman ruin it.

Simon sipped his scotch and looked for something else to occupy his attention. Everett's wife and a woman whose name he couldn't remember were deep in conversation, no doubt something important like the value of their portfolios or the ghastly spring ball at Highclere last season. Whiteside spoke animatedly to an American merchant named Sanford who'd made his fortune selling women's brassieres. Jack and Diana danced haphazardly to the ragtime jazz coming from a Victrola in the corner. The rest of the passengers had either retired or were busy being fleeced by Elizabeth. That left only Christina.

She sat alone in the corner, glum, on the periphery, watching the rest of them enjoying the party. The book she'd been reading lay forgotten on her lap.

He felt for the girl. She was bright and engaging, or would be, if she weren't busy nursing a broken heart.

A little voice inside his head, that sounded remarkably like Elizabeth, urged him to go to her. Despite feeling unsure what he could possibly do to help the girl, Simon lifted himself from the comfort of his leather club chair and walked the short distance across the room.

"May I join you?"

Startled, Christina looked up at him and then lowered her eyes as if she'd been caught doing something she oughtn't. "Of course."

Simon sat down in the chair next to hers. "*The Mill on the Floss,*" he said nodding toward her forgotten book. "I think I preferred *Silas Marner.*"

"You've read them?"

"I used to read quite a lot," Simon said. "I find that I don't have quite so much time for it anymore." He carefully left out the reason for that as his eyes drifted to her across the room, as she dealt the next hand.

"Sometimes I think I'd be happier if I could live in a book."

Simon nodded. "I spent a great deal of my youth doing just that. I could control the world just by turning the page."

Christina looked at him with empathy. "Yes," she said and pushed her glasses back up onto her nose. "Exactly." She folded her hands and studied them. "Everything else is so unpredictable."

That was an understatement. "Eventually," Simon said, "you'll find that's what makes it all worthwhile."

She nodded politely, but looked far from convinced.

Simon hesitated only a moment before letting his guard down. Perhaps he could say something to cheer her up. "When I was sixteen, I fell madly in love with a girl in Sussex. She had fiery red hair. It was a glorious summer; we spent every moment together until she tore out my heart and crushed it like a walnut."

Christina laughed and then covered her mouth and apologized, but he could still see the slight humor in her eyes.

"I thought I'd never get over her," he said, "but another summer came and another. And eventually I found Elizabeth." He failed to mention the twenty lonely years in between.

185

Christina looked over at the poker table. Elizabeth held up her cards to cover a smile. Her eyes flashed and she said something that elicited whoops of laughter from the table.

"Now, I can't even remember that girl's name."

Christina ran her fingers over the leather bound edges of the book in her lap as she thought about what he said.

"It might not seem so now," Simon continued. "But the hurt will fade."

She nodded quickly and worried her lower lip.

"You're a lovely, bright girl, Christina. I think, if anything, you'll be spoilt for choice before long."

She blushed and shook her head, but a small smile curved her lips.

"Christina," Jack said suddenly appearing in front of them. "Just the girl I was looking for." He jerked his head toward the impromptu dance floor. "Diana's given up on me. How about a go?"

He held out his hand and Christina looked at it unsure. Simon gave her an encouraging nod and she took it.

"He's got two left feet," Simon called after them. "Don't let him trample you."

Quite satisfied with himself, Simon finished his scotch and set the empty glass on a table. He watched Jack and Christina for a moment before stepping outside to get some air.

He walked toward the bow to a quiet spot away from the music and the mayhem of the salon. The sound of the boat as it cut through the water was soothing and entrancing and Simon enjoyed the solitude for a few minutes, watching the distant shore slide past in the night.

He felt Elizabeth's approach before he heard her footsteps on the wooden deck. It was strange and wonderful, this connection to someone—this subtle sense of her, a gentle hum in his soul.

"There you are," she said.

Simon smiled to himself. He could see her in his mind's eye, standing behind him, wearing that dress, the diaphanous fabric flowing in the slight evening breeze. Waves of auburn hair falling about her face and caressing her bare shoulders. The curious look on her face that he would kiss away.

He turned and watched her walk toward him. She stopped in front of him and tilted her head to the side. The flush in her cheeks ran down her neck into the décolletage of her dress and Simon's eyes followed it.

She smiled then and leaned forward against the railing and took a deep breath of the cool night air. The breeze moulded her dress to her body and Simon stood for a moment content to appreciate the shape of her calves, the curve of her back, the supple skin of her shoulders.

"Beautiful, isn't it?" she said.

The evening, he had to admit, was beautiful, too. The sky was clear and the moon shone brightly, reflecting in the glassy surface of the river. Palm trees stood in silhouette on the shores as they slipped silently by and into the night. But it all paled next to his wife.

Simon stepped behind Elizabeth and put his hands on the railing on either side of her. For once, a mission seemed to be going their way. The clues had fallen into place and he forgot what he was thinking about as Elizabeth leaned back into him.

He swept her hair from her shoulder and kissed the hollow of her neck. She sighed softly and leaned her head to the side to give him better access. He happily took it.

Simon kissed her again and again, slowly moving his way up her neck. Elizabeth put her hand on his and silently urged him to wrap his arm around her waist. He did and pulled her more tightly against him.

He groaned and she turned around in his arms. She tiptoed up and kissed him.

The next thing he knew they were on their way upstairs and could not get there soon enough. He was already unzipping her dress before they were even inside their stateroom. She slid his dinner jacket to the floor as she kissed him and he eased the straps of her dress over her shoulders and heard the fabric hit the floor at their feet.

He kissed his way up along her neck as her hands went to his belt.

"What about the beds?" she said, her voice slightly breathless.

Simon pulled back and saw the wicked grin on her face. He matched it with one of his own and then lifted her up until her legs wrapped around him.

"Who needs a bed?"

CHAPTER TWENTY-THREE

B REAKFAST WAS A FOUR course affair that left Elizabeth with barely enough strength to find a deckchair to lie down in. The entire trip was an indulgence and she was enjoying every luxurious minute of it. Although, she thought, she probably should have skipped the éclair.

She sat down on her rattan lounger and let herself relax. They were away from the unknowns of Cairo, and safe, relatively anyway, on board a beautiful boat, serenely floating up the Nile to Luxor. Where, if they were right, the watch was waiting for them.

Simon was off being academic with Arthur and so Elizabeth stretched out and watched the lush banks of the Nile drift past. The low lying farmland gave way to hills and steep cliffs before flattening out again into tracts of wheat, cotton and sugar cane. A small herd of water buffalo waded in for a drink and a bath.

The river was sometimes narrow and sometimes wide. They passed islands big and small. It was no wonder life in Egypt centered around the Nile. It literally gave sustenance to the desert and its people. It grew and contracted, flooded and receded and left the seeds of life in its place.

Thick growths of pampas grass lined the shore, a jungle of date palms standing behind them. Tawny rocks and nearly inhospitable desert beyond that. A man standing in a green and red rowboat, poled himself along near the shore toward a village.

She could just see Cleopatra arriving on her barge to seduce Mark Antony. Now, *that* was the original party barge. If she closed her eyes, she could...

"Elizabeth."

She sat up with a start and found herself looking into the bemused face of her husband.

"I didn't mean to startle you," Simon said, but there was laughter in his eyes. "You fell asleep."

"Just closed my eyes," she said, stifling a yawn.

Simon pointed to the corner of his mouth. "You drooled a little."

Elizabeth wiped her chin and blushed.

Simon's rare, rich laugh eased her embarrassment and she took the hand he offered without question. "Come on," he said as she let him pull her up. "We're going on an excursion."

Elizabeth glanced out at the still moving water. "Are we going swimming?"

Simon gently combed his fingers through her hair to tame it. "We're about to dock and I thought..."

"I should walk off that éclair?"

He was too polite to agree, but he did smile and hold out his arm for her.

She slipped her arm through his. "Maybe we can bring a picnic."

"Elizabeth."

The boat docked at a small landing at the bottom of a big hill. The rock tombs of Beni Hassan were somewhere near the top.

Luckily, they didn't have to hoof it, not personally anyway. Donkeys were provided for five piastres. As they made their slow and swaying way up the long slope, Elizabeth decided that you could learn a lot about a person from the way they rode a donkey.

Christina was gentle with hers, occasionally patting its neck and offering encouragement. Jack and Diana carried on an animated, good-natured argument about something as they rode. Neither seemed the least bit aware of the beast beneath them.

Arthur swayed back and forth, his head up and back straight like the captain of a great ship making a crossing to the new world. He took in every inch of the hills and the rocks, ready to spot potential bits of pottery sticking out of the dry soil.

Trevor Everett seemed to have found a beast as unpleasant as he was. Despite the donkey boy's putting his entire weight into pulling the rope attached to the donkey's muzzle, it refused to budge. Everett cursed and hit it with his walking stick while his wife pouted and Henri nearly fell off his own from laughing.

And poor Simon. His legs were so long they'd scrape on the ground if he didn't hold them up. He rode with as much dignity as anyone could on a donkey, and made the best of it. But, clearly, he would have rather walked.

The slope leveled off for a jog across to the next zigzagging path and Elizabeth spurred her little donkey on. It picked up the pace and she bounced atop the saddle. Finally, she caught up with Simon and began to overtake him. As she did, she leaned forward, gripping the reins to her chest as if she were on the last leg at Pimlico.

"On Bucephalus!" she cried, as she and her little mount bounced past Simon.

She could hear Simon's bark of laughter as she passed him. Turning around, she saw him shake his head and smile fondly after her.

After a forty minute ride, they spent the next few hours exploring the rock tombs of Beni Hassan. Embedded into limestone cliffs above the east bank of the Nile, dozens of Middle Empire tombs lined the rock face. Modern iron gates protected some of the entrances.

The first tomb they entered had a simple facade, while wonderfully detailed paintings of domestic life in early Egypt covered the interiors. Some of them were faded and chipping, but others were still vivid, bright colored scenes on the stucco walls.

Tall lotus columns, the few that were left, still had their bright colorings.

"You'll notice," Henri said. "That the capital, the head of the column, is a lotus bud, but as you go deeper into the tomb, the buds open to become a flower."

He looked at the room with undisguised admiration. "Every nuance, every image has meaning. The Egyptians, they combined purpose with art in ways we have long since forgotten. *C'est dommage.*"

He led them into another chamber and made sure to point out that mixed in with the scenes of everyday life were the deceased and his wife, hunting fowl, fishing, or watching as men built their funeral shrines. The drawings signified their life together after death.

Henri happily answered the most ridiculous questions and spoke passionately and knowledgeably about each tomb. He was a different man out here. Gone was all of the pretense, all of the posturing and a brilliant, earnest man took his place. He lingered at the fresco of the couple.

"*L'amour fait les plus grandes douceurs et les plus sensibles infortunes de la vie,*" he said softly.

Elizabeth stayed back with Simon as Henri and the others moved on. Simon looked after Henri with an expression she hadn't seen before. Sympathy.

Without her having to ask, Simon translated. "Love makes life's sweetest pleasures and worst misfortunes."

They quietly wandered through the cool, quiet interiors of the rock tombs until another group of visitors arrived. The braying donkeys and the blustering tourists stole the peace of the moment and they hurried through the final tombs before beginning the long journey back down to the landing.

Cocktails were waiting for them. The ship pulled away from the shore and continued its journey up river as they all slipped into a dry martini and left the ancient world behind again.

IT WAS REMARKABLE HOW quickly things changed. For years, decades, if he were honest, Simon had never slept well with another person in his bed. And now, he couldn't sleep without one. One in particular.

Elizabeth lay sprawled out across most of her twin bed. They'd started the night sharing his, but Elizabeth was as active in sleep as was she was in waking and had unceremoniously fallen out of bed at about three o'clock in the morning.

She'd crawled into her own bed after that and had fallen back to sleep within minutes. Simon wasn't so lucky. He'd lain awake for another hour and only found sleep in fits and starts without her by his side. Now morning had come.

The sun reflected brightly off the river and cut through the window sheers. Simon considered waking Elizabeth, but ultimately decided to let her sleep in. He dressed quietly, kissed her on the temple and slipped out of the room.

As he'd expected, he found Whiteside and his daughter having tea on the upper level.

"Good morning." Whiteside gestured to an empty chair at their table. He glanced around the empty deck. "We seem to be the only early risers."

"After the amount of champagne consumed last night, I doubt we'll see anyone before noon," Simon agreed.

He took his seat and gratefully accepted a cup of tea from the steward. He'd been delighted to find they had his preference on board, Chinese Gunpowder. His grandfather Sebastian would have approved.

"Christina," Whiteside said, wiggling his fingers over her sketchpad. "Manners, my girl."

Christina nodded and quickly began to gather the colored pencils she'd scattered about the table. She bumped one and it rolled toward the edge. Simon caught it before it fell.

"I don't mind," Simon said, as he handed Christina the pencil.

She smiled gratefully and put the errant pencil back in its box.

As she did, Simon noticed her sketches. "What are those?"

"Oh." Christina looked to her father for permission who nodded. She turned the pad so Simon could see. "These are from last season. We visited Amarna. I thought it might be fun to revisit them before they open the chamber."

"May I?" Simon asked as he pulled the sketchpad closer.

"These are sketches of what's left of the palace and temple," Christina explained. "And the others are from the royal tomb of Akhenaten, what's left of it anyway."

"These are quite good," Simon said, and it wasn't a hollow compliment. She had talent. A few of the drawings were incredibly detailed and wholly realistic.

"Yes, they are," Whiteside said proudly. After enjoying Christina's blush for a moment, he pointed to the sketches. "You see, when Akhenaten ascended the throne, he wanted to move the capital, to create a new city in his image. And so he built Tell el-Amarna. Of course, being a heretic, most of it was destroyed after his death, but bits and pieces survived."

Simon flipped the page. He instantly recognized a sketch in the upper corner of the page—the beautiful queen Nefertiti. The few images of Akhenaten showed him as oddly misshapen with a long narrow skull and pot belly.

Simon continued through the sketches until he saw something that made his heart stop.

"This," he said, hoping his voice didn't betray his surprise. "What's this?"

"That's quite interesting, actually," Whiteside said. "That's an Aten disk. The icon was originally drawn with long, outstretched wings and represented the aspect of Ra. But when Akhenaten came to the throne...He changed his name, you know, from Amenhotep like his father to Akhen*aten*...the icon itself changed as well."

Simon heard what Whiteside was saying, but his eyes were fixed on the drawing of what looked exactly like his pocket watch. The shape, the crown and stem, all of them were an exact match for the watch. It was upside-down, but the resemblance was unmistakable.

"Of course, Aten replaced all of the other gods," Whiteside said. "That's undoubtedly what the papyrus was referring to with the sun disk shining in his palm and all that."

"Yes," Simon said. Whatever remaining doubts he had that the watch was truly buried with the pharaoh faded away. "Remarkable."

ON THE FOURTH DAY, their boat traversed the last bit of the long u-shaped curve in the Nile that arched to the west and ended near Luxor. Simon could see the Winter Palace standing like a white colossus on shore even from miles away.

The boat pulled up to the landing at the very foot of the hotel. A wobbly, wooden plank was draped across the space between it and the short pier. Beyond that, rows of water steps that had been carved into the rocky bank led from the landing to the forecourt of the grand hotel. From there, double marble staircases led up to a colonnade and the horseshoe-shaped terrace that ran the length of the enormous Winter Palace Hotel.

They crossed the threshold under an immense parapet emblazoned with the hotel's name and were shown to their rooms. The view from their third-story suite was spectacular. The Nile stretched out in both directions. Across the river sat the Theban Hills, hiding within them the riches of the Valley of the Kings.

Simon and Elizabeth barely had time to shower and change for the party that night. Elizabeth watched for a moment as he wrestled with his bow tie and then took pity on him and brushed his hands away. She gently pinched the knot and adjusted the wings. Satisfied, she patted his chest and turned to admire them both in the mirror.

They looked every inch the 1920 society couple they were supposed to be. His tuxedo was smart and well-pressed, but it was Elizabeth that had his attention. He'd practically had to force her to buy the vintage gown they'd found back home. It was outrageously expensive, but looking at her now, worth every penny. The pale green silk chiffon and embroidered crystals showed off the creamy skin of her shoulders and just enough of her chest to make him slightly uncomfortable. As she turned, the chiffon moved like gossamer, just brushing her knees above her bare and quite lovely legs.

"Ready?"

"Hmmm?"

She smiled, realizing she'd caught him staring. "The party," she reminded him.

"Right." Simon held out his arm and they headed downstairs for yet another round of cocktails and smalltalk. God help him.

One of the larger salons had been staged for the cocktail party celebrating Jouvet's dig, although what there was to celebrate yet eluded Simon. So far as he could tell, the man had found a scarab and willing mark in a rich patron and nothing else.

No one seemed to mind though. Any excuse for a party was welcomed with open arms and hollow legs. Nearly one hundred people mingled inside the plush salon, some in large chairs by the windows enjoying the view of the Nile. Others stood in small packs enjoying the glasses of champagne that continually circulated the room on silver trays. Small talk, gossip, general inanity. Simon was glad, not for the first time, that he'd given up this sort of life.

Elizabeth, always attuned to his moods squeezed his arm and gave him a reassuring smile. He took a bracing breath and they plunged into the fray.

They'd just freed themselves from yet another story about Mrs. Cavandish's corgis when Jouvet caught them. Simon groaned inwardly and plastered a false smile onto his face.

"Ah," he said. "There is someone I should like you to meet."

He pulled them toward a small group who was busily chatting away. At the center, with her back to them, stood a slender woman in a deep purple velvet dress with black, almost aubergine hair.

"My mysterious patroness," Jouvet said, gesturing to the woman. "Pardon?" He stepped closer to her to get her attention.

"Mrs. Katherine Vale," Jouvet said. "May I present, Mr. and Mrs. Simon Cross."

When she turned Simon's blood ran cold and he heard Elizabeth gasp softly beside him.

Eyes of pale soulless violet.

The rest of the room faded from existence. Jouvet and other partygoers blurred and the hum of voices dulled. Simon stood, frozen for a moment, stunned. All he could see was her, Madame Petrovka, the cold, heartless psychopath standing in front him, smiling.

Her grin broadened, the cat about to eat the canary. Her eyes glittered with barely bridled excitement at his shock and discomposure. Chest rising and falling quickly with excitement, her eyes danced as she tried to control her exhilaration at her moment of triumph.

"Well, hello again," she said, in a voice so hard and smooth it could have been a knife.

Simon felt an icy hand grip his heart. There was no surprise in her face, no shock. She'd *expected* this, *planned* this. And they'd walked right into it.

"You know each other?" Jouvet said in surprise.

Vale, or whatever the hell she was calling herself these days, laughed. "Yes, we met in San Francisco, wasn't it? Imagine my surprise when I found out you were here and friends of Henri's."

Simon barely found his voice. "Yes." He reached over and without looking took hold of Elizabeth's hand. She gripped his tightly.

Vale smiled again and her calculating gaze shifted from Simon to Elizabeth. "You were unmarried when last we saw each other. I suppose congratulations are in order."

"Thank you," Elizabeth said, her voice surprisingly calm.

Vale's eyes shifted to their joined hands for a moment. "Such a lovely couple. No doubt you have nurseries full of children by now?"

Simon felt Elizabeth start slightly at the mention of children. The movement wasn't lost on Vale. A small quirk of her lips gave away her pleasure at having found another vulnerability. Her eyes danced over them in delight, taking in every nuance of their clothing, their body language. Delighting in their fear. Every bit of knowledge she gained was a potential weapon in her arsenal of manipulation and cruelty. And all Simon could do was stand there.

His heart thundered in his chest as he tried to regain his feet. He'd like to start by putting one on her bloody throat.

"Mrs. Vale?" he said, hoping no one but her heard the loathing in his voice. "You've remarried. Again."

She stifled her amusement at his jibe and sighed dramatically. "Sadly, my dear husband is no longer with us."

Simon was disgusted, but hardly surprised. She'd killed her first husband, and who knew how many others.

"I'm sorry to hear that," Elizabeth said, her tone and words compassionate, and only Simon hearing the false note.

The offer of sympathy was unwelcome and her gaze shot to Elizabeth. The mask of calm composure slipped for just a moment and her pure, unadulterated hatred showed through. Elizabeth flinched, and then instinctively, Simon edged forward slightly, putting himself in front of Elizabeth.

The brief flash of anger subsided and Vale's icy self-assurance returned. She wound her arm through Jouvet's. "We really should mingle, Henri." She turned her attention back to Simon and Elizabeth. "It's *so* nice seeing you again. I do hope we have a chance to catch up later. I'm just dying to hear what you two have been up to."

Henri, if he'd been aware of any of the subtext, hid it well and blithely escorted Vale toward another group of guests.

Once they'd moved a fair distance away, Elizabeth clutched at Simon's arm, her eyes wide with the same alarm he felt. "Holy crap."

Simon watched Vale and Jouvet across the room. "Yes," he said absently, his mind racing. "Come on."

He quickly led her from the room, ignoring a greeting from Whiteside as he did. Once they reached the main hall, he turned back to make sure they hadn't been followed.

"What are you doing?" Elizabeth asked.

Simon looked around the busy vestibule. It wouldn't do. They needed somewhere they couldn't be seen. "Getting us the hell out of here."

He took Elizabeth's arm, but she resisted.

"Elizabeth," he said and pointed back into the salon. "That woman is insane."

"Believe me, I know. But we've been through this. We can't go."

They had, but that was before *she'd* come along. He gave up looking for a place downstairs. Their room would do. "The hell we can't."

"Hey," Jack said, as he hurried to their side. "What's going on? You ran out of..." His expression darkened. "Jeez. You look like you've seen a ghost." He paused and then looked anxiously around. "You didn't, did you?"

"Worse," Simon said.

"Zombies?"

Simon sighed impatiently. "We're leaving."

"No, we're not."

Simon glared down at Elizabeth and took a calming breath. It didn't work.

Jack stared at them both in confusion. "Maybe someone should tell me what's going on."

Simon sighed. "Upstairs."

Jack nodded and followed them up to their room. Once Simon had locked the door behind them, he moved to close the drapes.

"Okay," Jack said. "What the hell happened back there?"

Elizabeth sat down in a corner of the sofa in the sitting room and played nervously with the piping of one of the throw pillows. "Do you remember what I told you about San Francisco?"

Jack nodded. "Yeah, he was being a controlling jerk," he said, nodding toward Simon, "and you went alone to try to stop some Council guy from dying."

Simon scowled at Jack's interpretation, accurate though it might be, and pushed ahead. "The antecedent of a Council member."

Elizabeth nodded. "Charles Graham, a Council member from our time had abandoned his partner in 1888 London. She went a bit mad and ended up in Bedlam, the mental hospital."

"Right," Jack said, as he took a chair opposite her. "She escaped the looney bin, pretended to be a psychic and tried to kill the guy's great, great grandfather or something."

"Did kill him," Simon corrected. He walked over to the seating area, but remained standing. He stared down at Jack. "She tortured the man with the ghost of his dead child until he went mad and killed himself."

Jack nodded, his usual casual flippancy gone now. "But his wife was already pregnant so your Charles Graham lived. What was her name? Madame—"

"Petrovka," Simon finished for him. "But she's going by the name of Katherine Vale now."

Jack sat up in alarm. "Now? You mean she's here?"

"And seriously scarier than I remember," Elizabeth said. "And she was pretty scary then."

Simon had to agree. There was always an unhinged nature to the woman, there had to be considering what she'd done, but now, the way she'd looked at Elizabeth....It was absolutely terrifying.

He put that thought aside and refocused. "She's Henri Jouvet's mysterious benefactor."

"But wait," Jack said, sitting forward. "Didn't you trick her into going back to the asylum with a rigged watch?"

Elizabeth nodded. "I did."

"We did," Simon corrected her. Elizabeth had always harbored guilt about that, although he couldn't fathom why. The woman was a cold-blooded killer, and one that hated them with a passion. They'd deceived her into using a watch, but instead of granting her freedom, it had landed her back in Bedlam, her prison for twelve years.

Simon tried to put the pieces together. "Somehow she's managed to escape. Again."

"Or somebody got her out," Jack said.

Elizabeth looked up sharply. "What do you mean?"

Jack shrugged. "She was a Council member, right?"

Simon nodded and sat down next to Elizabeth.

"That Travers guy said there was a Shadow Council made up of, well, evil Council members," Jack said. "I'd say she fits the bill pretty well."

Simon's anxiety rose at the thought, but it made sense. Or it was starting to.

"If I were up to no good, working for the Shadow Council," Jack continued, "I'd recruit people who had experience with time travel and maybe a grudge or two against the good guys for added inspiration."

Elizabeth whistled softly. "She's got those. In spades."

Simon took hold of Elizabeth's hand and remembered something Travers had told them. "And not just against us. No wonder Charles Graham is running for his life."

"Do you think she tried to kill him?" Elizabeth asked and then rolled her eyes at what she saw was a silly question. "Of course, she did. She's..."

"Insane," Simon supplied.

"Well, true," Elizabeth conceded. "But clever, too."

"That's a bad combination," Jack said.

Simon's frown deepened. "She knew we were going to be at that party."

"Maybe she just found out?" Jack suggested.

"No, the look on her face, that was from a woman who'd anticipated this, savored it," Simon said. "I don't know when she knew or how she knew but...maybe Jouvet mentioned us." He turned to Elizabeth. "Speaking of whom you will not be spending any more time with."

Elizabeth didn't argue but, Simon noticed, she didn't agree either.

He was about to remind her of the dangers when she said softly, "Maybe she found out we were coming here and all of this is for us?"

"No," Simon said. "I don't think so. I think she's here for the watch. Why else would she fund Jouvet's dig?"

Elizabeth nodded thoughtfully. "And the Cult of Sekhmet? They must be working for her. They killed Mason, stole his watch from Jack and have done everything they can to keep us from finding out where Shelton's watch was." She looked at Simon curiously. "But why would they help her?"

"She can be very convincing, can't she?" Simon said, wishing he could spare her the truth of it, but knowing he couldn't. "And I'm sure the cult was not an arbitrary choice on her part. Sekhmet is the goddess of vengeance."

"Against us," Elizabeth said.

Simon arched his eyebrows and shook his head. "Perhaps."

"Well, the good news is," Jack said, scratching his chin in thought, "that you're not dead."

"Yes, I like to think that's good news," Simon said blandly.

Jack laughed. "No, I mean, if she knew you were here and she wanted you dead, there were plenty of opportunities."

Elizabeth's forehead wrinkled. "Somehow that's not as comforting as it should be."

There was nothing comforting about this situation at all. He'd been a fool to think things could run smoothly with that damned Council involved.

"She's been one step ahead of us," Simon said. "But her advantage is gone now."

"Okay," Jack said, "So, what do we do?"

Simon wanted to leave. It was insane not to. But he knew they were going to stay. Whether Vale was working for the Council or not, she wasn't here to sightsee. "Stop her."

CHAPTER TWENTY-FOUR

Elizabeth stood at the rail of the ferry. A cool morning breeze from the river blew her hair back off her shoulders as they reached the midway point of their crossing. Her fingers traced the outline of the small watch key that hung on a necklace underneath her blouse.

Last night had been a long night, but Elizabeth had faith they'd made the right choice in staying. They'd argued over what to do with the watch. If Vale was there on the same mission they were, she'd want any watch she could find, including, and maybe especially, theirs.

Elizabeth wanted to hide Simon's watch somewhere, to keep him from being a walking target, but had been outvoted. Simon was not going to let his watch out of his sight. And Jack had agreed.

That left the key Teddy had given her. If a looney tune like Vale ever got her hands on it, and could travel at will, history would never be the same.

"Try not to fiddle with it," Simon said as he joined her at the railing.

He was right, of course. There was no telling who was watching them. She patted it once more, smoothing the cotton placard of her white blouse and gripping the railing in front of her.

"She's not here. We should try to relax and enjoy that," she said looking at the western bank of the Nile and the Theban Hills beyond.

Simon grunted.

"Okay, stay tense and enjoy it."

Simon's smile didn't reach his eyes as he placed his hand over hers before looking back out at the horizon.

Their group had left the hotel shortly after breakfast for a day exploring the Valley of the Kings before meeting Jouvet at his dig for lunch. So far, Katherine Vale was nowhere in sight, thankfully, but that didn't mean they could afford to let their guard down. Looking at the set of his jaw and tension around his eyes, Elizabeth could see that Simon's guard was high and tight.

"I worry about you, too, you know," Elizabeth said.

Simon squeezed her hand and this time his smile was genuine. "I know."

After a few more minutes, the ferry reached the landing where they disembarked. Whiteside looked very much the great explorer in his khaki suit and Stanley pith helmet, a leather-cased canteen slung over one shoulder. Christina followed behind him, her sketchbook clutched tightly to her chest. They were followed by Jack and Diana and, bringing up the rear, the Everetts sloshed off the boat.

Carriages had been arranged for them and, after they'd bullied their way through another gauntlet of vendors and hucksters, they piled in for the ride to the valley. As they passed the cultivated land that edged the river, the earth went from rich and fertile to dusty and bone dry in an instant. Elizabeth squinted over the top edge of her smoked-glass spectacles. They cut the glare from the blazing sun and reflective sand, but they gave everything a green tint. She took them off and tucked them into the small front pocket of her blouse. Her broad-rimmed sunhat would have to do.

Whiteside, who'd happily assumed the role of tour guide, sighed in delight as their carriage came to a stop at Deir el-Barhari. Simon helped Elizabeth and Christina down the awkward carriage step.

Elizabeth looked toward the rocky cliff face. Long sloping ramps rose from one terraced level to the next, leading to an immense colonnade at the base of an escarpment.

"*Djeser Djeseru*. The Holy of Holies," Whiteside said. "The Mortuary Temple of Hatshepsut."

They started toward the temple. "Some say she was the first leader to break tradition and not build a pyramid for her tomb."

"She?" Elizabeth asked.

Whiteside smiled, but it was Christina who answered. "She was a Pharaoh."

"Now, there's no evidence of that," Whiteside corrected her gently. "Although, title or not, she was by all accounts a great leader for many years."

"I like that," Constance Everett said. "A woman in charge."

"Don't get any ideas, darling," her husband said as he took a swig from his hip flask.

"It might look a bit stark now," Whiteside said, ignoring the Everetts, "but imagine the temple painted with bright reds and yellows. Lush gardens spreading out on either side of the causeway. Magnificent."

As they got closer, Elizabeth noticed a series of dust clouds off to the right. "What's happening over there, Professor?"

He chuckled. "Winlock won't leave that quarry alone. Looking for temples and more tombs." He pointed to a dust cloud at the juncture of a long steep slope and a sheer cliff face. "Those are the tombs of the nobles. Not kings mind you, courtiers and priests and such."

Elizabeth could just make out the workers through the nearly endless stream of dust. Like a human conveyer belt, dozens and dozens of men moved in an endless loop up and down the slope. One after another they'd dump their baskets of debris at one end and hurry back up the slope for more. There were several groups of them on the hills, like colonies of ants moving in undulating circles.

Much larger groups of men worked in the flats beside the road that led to the valley. Gangs of men hoed the ground, while others gathered the debris into small baskets and took them to waiting carts that were pushed down a long track to a dumping ground.

"Quite an operation," Simon said, impressed.

"Yes. Over 700 workers," Whiteside said. "Sometimes it looks less like a dig for the Metropolitan Museum of Art and more like the work of a pharaoh building his tomb."

Small boys and women, dressed all in black, walked donkeys back and forth between the men and what she guessed was a well somewhere. The women dumped enormous jars of water into an even larger one, where men dipped a cup for a drink before hurrying back to their position in line.

"They're barefoot," Constance said.

Elizabeth couldn't imagine running over the sharp, rocky shale in her bare feet. Heck, she'd worried her boots wouldn't be protection enough.

"Tough as nails, these people," Whiteside said. "They'll work from sunup to sundown for just a few bob a day. Of course, the more skilled laborers might earn five or six with bonuses for anything of significance they might find."

"Slave wages," Christina said.

"Hardly," her father said. "Despite the wealth of its history, this is a poor country, my dear. Men line up for those jobs and are grateful to get them."

Christina bit her tongue and Elizabeth offered her a sympathetic smile. It wasn't the first time she'd heard the girl argue for improved conditions for the Egyptians. Ahmed and his cause had rubbed off on her.

After a tour of the temples, they began the long hike into the valley. The trail they followed had been used since ancient times. It wended its way through the cliffs and up to the top of the hills. They stopped at the summit to admire a spectacular view of the Nile Valley below as it stretched out as far as they could see before disappearing in the haze.

Elizabeth took a sip from her canteen and then began to put it over her shoulder.

"I wish you'd let me," Simon said, holding out his hand, ready to take it from her.

"It weighs like three pounds," Elizabeth said. "And besides, you might end up carrying me and the bottle at some point, so save your strength."

Simon laughed and shook his head. "Suit yourself."

"Now, that's a gentleman," Constance said, turning to her husband. "Why didn't you offer to carry mine?"

Everett held up his canteen and his flask. "I've already got two," he said and started down the path without her.

Constance sighed and started to shoulder hers.

"Let me," Jack said.

Constance smiled and held it out to him. "Aren't you a dear?"

But before Jack could say she was welcome, she'd turned heel and caught up with her husband.

Jack stood dumbly watching after her and then, with a sigh, slipped the canteen over his shoulder.

Diana put hers around his neck. "Aren't you a dear?"

A laugh bubbled up at his expression and she hurried to hook her arm through Elizabeth's in a perfect imitation of Constance Everett.

The path led them from the top of the hills down through ruts in the cliffs until they emerged into a wide and winding rocky gorge.

"The Valley of the Kings," Whiteside said.

They carefully made their way down the path. It wasn't overly steep, but the footing was precarious. Every bit of it was loose. Small chunks of shale dislodged with each step, some cascading down to the bottom in a cloud of dust.

Finally, they reached the valley floor. Of the sixty or so tombs, just over a dozen were accessible. Each was marked with a number stenciled in red above the door and many had large iron gates at the entrances.

"These are unlit," Whiteside said pointing at the sunken entrance to a few tombs. "We'll do better ahead."

The party followed him down the canyon and Elizabeth could hear the sounds of workmen again and see the small dust clouds that always surrounded their work rising into the air.

The narrow gorge widened and split off into several small ravines. In the midst of the main wadi, dozens of workers meticulously picked through the dirt and stone.

A short, stocky man in a tan seersucker suit waved his hat at a group of workers, summoning one with a loud, barked command in Arabic.

"Howard!" Whiteside called out.

The man turned at the sound of his name and waved, a little reluctantly. He finished giving orders to the worker and started toward them.

Whiteside met him halfway and stuck out his hand. "How are you?"

"Fine," Howard said, eyeing the rest of the party impatiently. "Arthur."

"Howard Carter," Whiteside said, "I'd like to introduce you to, Mr. & Mrs. Cross, and—"

"Yes, yes," Carter said cutting off any extended pleasantries. He belatedly realized how rude he'd been and tipped his hat, and offered a brief smile and a nod to Christina.

"Terribly busy, you understand?"

Elizabeth squeezed Simon's arm. This was *the* Howard Carter. The man who would discover one of the world's most amazing archaeological finds—the intact royal tomb of Tutankhamen. She looked around at the workers, knowing the magnificent tomb lay hidden just yards from where they were standing. Her fingers itched to pick up a hoe and speed history along just a little.

"Is Lord Carnarvon at the hotel?" Whiteside asked.

Carter sighed. "Yes. He's growing restless, but damn it, these things can't be rushed."

Elizabeth had read up on it and by 1920, Carter had already been looking for King Tut's tomb for five years and Lord Carnarvon had poured loads of money into the valley. In two years time, Carnarvon would give Carter one last season and it would be the one that everyone remembered. That everyone still remembered.

Carter took off his hat, wiped his forehead and barked out an order to someone who was apparently doing something not to his liking.

"We won't keep you," Whiteside said.

Carter grunted, his dark, brooding eyes already on another thought and tipped his hat.

"You'll find it," Elizabeth said, unable to stop herself. Carter paused, looked at her for a moment, before nodding curtly and going back to overseeing his workmen.

"Elizabeth," Simon whispered.

She didn't bother hiding her smile. "Well, he will."

They passed around the edges of Carter's dig and visited some of the tombs in the east valley. A few of the more impressive tombs were lit with electricity, including number 11, the tomb of Ramesses III.

Simon and Elizabeth walked down either side of the divided staircase each on one side of an inclined plane leading to the first chamber. Pilasters, a sort of column embedded deep within a wall, with rams' heads stood at the entrance. They passed through a series of gates and corridors with reliefs of the god. Small side chambers lined each corridor with more frequency the deeper they went in.

"Each served a unique purpose," Whiteside said. "An armory or a treasury. Everything the king would need in the afterlife was stored here."

Whiteside stopped and pointed to a brightly colored painting on the wall. "You see, this is a sort of guidebook for the king's journey through the underworld. They'd face twelve gates, twelve challenges."

Whiteside explained each painting and relief as they passed it. "Enemies bound to a pillar..."

"That looks like it doesn't end well," Jack said.

"The king had to vanquish someone," Diana added with a smile.

"And finally, here, is Ramesses in the presence of Osiris. And the burial chamber. Of course, the old king is sleeping somewhere else now."

Elizabeth wandered around the four pillars of the burial chamber. Even the sarcophagus was gone.

"Many of the tombs, including Ramesses', were plundered in antiquity. Tomb robbers." Whiteside looked around the empty chamber. "Although, I suppose we're a sort of modern day tomb robber, aren't we?"

Elizabeth bit her lip. She and Simon certainly were. If everything went well, they'd slip into a king's tomb and steal one of his most precious belongings.

"Some believe that the spirits of the dead can't rest because we've disturbed their journey," Christina said.

"Nonsense," Everett said. "The Egyptians themselves profit the most from these tombs. If they're not worried about the souls of their ancestors, why should we be?" He waved his hat to cool himself. "It's unbearable in here. We'll be outside."

He took his wife's arm and started back out.

"I do wonder sometimes," Christina said. "But then no one would be able to appreciate their beauty, learn about them, if it weren't for museums."

"Yes," her father said, but he sounded unconvinced.

"You're not superstitious, are you Arthur?" Simon asked.

Whiteside smiled. "Ordinarily, no. But there is something about standing here," he said, looking around the empty tomb. "It gives one pause, doesn't it?"

Elizabeth had to agree. Despite the heat, she felt a chill. The idea of sneaking into Akhenaten's tomb had excited her before. Despite even Vale being here, it was an adventure. But now, all she felt was a growing sense of dread.

CHAPTER TWENTY-FIVE

THEY LEFT THE EAST valley and began the last leg of their journey over the hills to the fairly deserted west valley where Jouvet and his dig awaited them. As they crested the last hill, Elizabeth's stomach rumbled. No one heard, or if they did, they had the grace not to say so. Judging from the looks on everyone's faces though, their stomachs had the same idea.

Elizabeth was tired and definitely in need of sustenance. It had been a long, morning and the midday sun was taking its toll. Thankfully, Henri had promised them transportation back to the ferry, so this would only be a one-way hike.

Simon took Elizabeth's hand as they descended the rocky slope toward the west valley floor. In the distance, she could see two large white tents set up for their luncheon. It was probably her imagination, but she could have sworn she smelled chicken cooking. She hurried Simon along a little bit faster.

When they reached the valley floor, Elizabeth saw the dig workers. Like the others, many of them carried baskets of debris on their shoulders and deposited them into a large dumping pile at the far end of the ravine.

Someone called out something in Arabic and everyone laid down their tools and their baskets en masse, and ran toward a pair of women and their donkeys—the Egyptian version of a lunch truck. Meals wrapped in brown paper were purchased with a few coins and then the men sat down in the shade of one of the cliffs to eat.

"Ah, you have survived," Jouvet said, turning to greet them. As he did, Elizabeth saw Katherine Vale standing there. Her appetite dwindled.

Jouvet left the shade of the tent and met them with a broad smile. "The weary travelers. Perhaps some champagne will help?"

He gestured toward one of the tents. It had been set up with a long table and fine, white linens. Ice buckets resting on tall stands at each corner of the table stood ready with chilled wine and a waiter stood by several chafing dishes filled with food.

The Everetts wasted no time and headed straight for the booze.

Katherine Vale ran her long black gloves through the circle of one hand as she gazed at Elizabeth in pity. "Oh, dear. You do look done in, don't you?"

The words were kind, but the tone was not. She relished in misery, other people's misery.

"I think she looks beautiful," Jouvet said. "So alive, uh?"

Vale smiled and it made Elizabeth's blood run cold. Looking into those pale soulless eyes was unnerving. Finally, her attention shifted away. Elizabeth was relieved not to be the focus of her scrutiny until she heard Vale say, "Christina, my dear. It's so good to see you again."

Vale drifted over to the girl like a dark specter. "I see you've brought your sketchpad! I'm sure you're very talented."

Christina smiled guilelessly at her, pleased with the compliment.

"Perhaps you'll sketch something for me?"

Elizabeth wanted to say, "over my dead body" and would have if Vale hadn't been the sort to take her up on it.

It was disturbing though, watching Vale with her black feathered hat looking like a vulture, prey on an innocent like Christina. God only knew what she might have in store for the girl.

It was one part of their missions Elizabeth didn't like to think about. Putting herself in danger was one thing, but putting the people they met in danger as well was another.

"You'll have to get in line, I'm afraid," Diana said, stepping forward and putting an arm around Christina's shoulders. "You promised to sketch me today, remember?"

Christina grinned and blushed, overwhelmed by the attention.

Vale eyed Diana carefully, displeased at having been so neatly deposed.

"Perhaps another time," Vale said.

Diana smiled sweetly, unfazed.

"Are you sure you won't stay, *cherie?*" Jouvet asked.

Vale made a show of thinking about it. She glanced around at the group, her eyes lingering uncomfortably on Simon and Elizabeth.

"That's very kind of you, or of me, since I'm paying for all this," she added softly, "but no. I have things that need attending to."

She turned back and offered one last strychnine smile. "Enjoy yourselves."

With a wave of her gloves she summoned her car, which Elizabeth hadn't even noticed was parked in the shadows. A beautiful Pierce-Arrow convertible pulled up and Jouvet gave Vale the European double-kiss and then helped her into the back seat.

As they drove away, Jack came up to stand with Simon and Elizabeth and watch the dusty trail the car left behind. "So, that's her."

"The wicked witch herself," Elizabeth said.

Diana, having left Christina at the table enjoying a cool glass of lemonade, joined them. "I don't like that woman."

Simon nodded. "Welcome to the club."

After they'd had some refreshment, Jouvet suggested they take a tour of the tomb before lunch while the workers were at rest.

Carefully, they made their way down the steep, rough-hewn steps at the mouth of the tomb. A small electric generator hummed and gave life to a string of lights that lit their path. Small, bright mechanic's lights clung to the walls like giant lightning bugs.

Henri went first, followed by Elizabeth, and then Simon and the others.

The outer corridor walls were rough and unpainted.

"Was it unfinished?" Elizabeth asked.

"Yes. We believe this tomb was originally built for Ay or perhaps another. It is difficult to say." Henri held out his hand for Elizabeth as they passed through a dark gate that led into another corridor. "Watch your step."

Elizabeth took the offered hand briefly, until she'd navigated the small gap.

"The outer walls remain incomplete. There are rough sketches, here," he said, pointing to a wall in the second corridor where the rock had been smoothed. "You see the grid, and the outlines for the reliefs that were never carved or painted."

"Why was it abandoned?"

"We do not know, but I think, I hope," he added with a smile, "that it was used later, repurposed as a safe place to harbor the body of Akhenaten."

Elizabeth exchanged a quick look with Simon. They certainly hoped so, too.

"Perhaps even Carter's Tutankhamen might have built it to shelter his father."

Elizabeth could see debris at the bottom of the shaft and a doorway. "Is that it? The burial chamber?"

Henri looked down at it. "The ante-chamber. Beyond that, there is one more small corridor and then, what I believe, I hope is the burial chamber."

"Why the support beams there?" Simon asked.

Elizabeth had noticed them, too. The first few corridors were simply rock, but now they were at the start of one that was buttressed by a large wooden framework.

"The rock has changed," Henri explained. "The limestone is very hard, very stable, but this," he said, rapping his knuckles against the stone, "is shale. It, uh, what is the word...?"

"Fractures," Simon supplied.

Henri nodded. "Yes, it is dangerous. We should not venture further until they have finished reinforcing the walls and the ceiling of this corridor and the other one below." He gestured for them to return the way they'd come.

Elizabeth turned to start back up. She'd barely taken a step when she felt her dress snag on something and heard the tell-tale ripping of fabric.

"*Arrêtes!*" Henri commanded as he gripped her shoulder. "Do not move."

To emphasize his point, bits of dust rained down from the ceiling above the crossbeam. Elizabeth held her breath as she waited for the whole thing to collapse on top of them.

Simon cautiously stepped closer and took hold of Elizabeth's arm, ready to wrench her right out of her dress, if need be.

Elizabeth looked at him nervously and turned slowly back to Henri. He reached down and unhooked the fabric of her skirt that had snagged on a sharp protrusion from one of the support columns.

She'd thought she was out of the woods with clothes trying to kill her. No corset, no petticoats and yet, they still found a way to nearly do her in.

Henri glanced up at the ceiling again. The trickle of dust slowly subsided.

"Perhaps we should..." he gestured to the outside. "Carefully."

Elizabeth nodded and started back up the corridor. She smiled sheepishly at Simon who scowled and let out a deep breath as he let her pass in front of him.

Once they were all safely outside, Henri angrily berated the foreman. Elizabeth felt guilty. She'd been the one who'd almost brought the house down, literally. But Henri would have none of it. Leaving something like that to catch on clothing was unacceptable. It could have been any one of them, he'd said.

Elizabeth wasn't so sure. Somehow the any one was always her. Even when she wasn't actively courting trouble, it turned into the boyfriend that just wouldn't go away. Henri's apologies only made her feel worse.

Finally, the furor died down and they settled in to lunch. It was catered by the hotel. Sublime coq au vin and a chilled glass of wine went a long way to making Elizabeth feel better.

With full bellies and perhaps a glass or two too many, everyone was in a fine mood, even the Everetts. Diana took a spot on a picturesque outcropping of rocks as Christina set about sketching her. Jack joined them, offering "helpful" advice.

"She seems to be recovering well," Elizabeth said to Whiteside.

Her father watched Christina for a moment and nodded. "She's a brave heart." He cleared his throat and turned his attention back to the table. "So, Jouvet. When can we expect to see the chamber?"

Henri tilted his head from side to side as he considered. "Two, perhaps three days. As you can see, there is still work to be done."

"I'm sure it will be well worth the wait." Whiteside lifted his glass in salute. "To Jouvet, and whatever treasures await us." He waited for everyone else to follow suit before he drank. Elizabeth sipped her eau de vie. The pear taste was almost overwhelming, but pleasant.

Henri arched an eyebrow, unsure, but nodded his gratitude at their confidence in him. Even if he didn't seem to share it at that moment.

"Treasure," Trevor Everett said. "I'll drink to that."

Henri smiled, a little sadly Elizabeth thought, and set his drink down. "You will excuse me?"

He left the table and spoke briefly with his foreman again.

"Three days?" Everett complained. "What are we to do in the meantime?"

"This is ancient Thebes," Whiteside said. "The capital of perhaps the greatest civilization the world has ever known. Surely, you can find some way to amuse yourself for a few days."

"Of course, we can," Constance said, laying a comforting hand on her husband's arm. "The hotel has wonderful tennis courts."

Elizabeth bit her tongue. Simon stared in awe at their stupidity, formulating a riposte and then clearly deciding they weren't worth the bother. He turned to Arthur instead. "Thebes. That's a Greek name for it, isn't it?

Whiteside glowed with the prospect of an able and willing student. "Yes! The Egyptian name is Wase, or Wo'se or Waset. Of course, most of the names we use are Greek in origin...."

As he and Simon discussed the etymology of...everything, Elizabeth slipped off to speak with Henri. Despite Simon's wishes she not speak with him more than was necessary, she had to at least apologize for almost ruining his dig.

She found him about twenty yards from his workers, leaning against a large rock, his arms crossed over his chest.

"Henri?"

He started and then looked down almost shyly.

"I didn't mean to startle you."

He shook his head and straightened. "I was miles away," he said with a smile.

"I wanted to apologize for, well," Elizabeth said. "Nearly killing all of us earlier."

He laughed. "It was not so bad as that. I am sorry you tore—"

Elizabeth waved his apology away. "It's all right." She needed to change tacks or they'd be caught in an endless loop of dueling apologies. "This is all very exciting. Thank you for letting us be a part of it."

"You are most welcome." His eyes drifted over to the tomb entrance. "If there is indeed something there, it is much more pleasurable to share the experience."

He might have been a shameless Lothario, but Elizabeth liked him. She just couldn't believe he was in league with the devil. "How did you and your mysterious benefactor, Mrs. Vale, meet?"

"She popped out of thin air," he said and it took Elizabeth a moment to realize he didn't mean that literally. "She was quite sure of what she wanted and," he added with a smile, "quite convincing."

Translation, she gave him more money than he could say no to.

"She made all of the plans, down to the last detail. She even told me where to dig." He shrugged. "I am, how do you say, merely window dressing."

"How did she know where?"

He shook his head. "She says," he said, with a wry smile, "that the dead have told her."

Elizabeth couldn't suppress her shudder. She'd really hoped that part of Madame Petrovka's schtick had been left in the past. "She talks to the dead?"

Henri grunted. "I have yet to meet a man or woman with more money than God who is not at least a little...eccentric. But please do not speak of this freely?"

She promised.

"It is bad enough with the talk of curses and people like Conan Doyle spinning their stories of death and the spirits," he continued. "If word got out that my patroness believed she was a necromancer..."

"I won't say anything."

Henri nodded his thanks. "And the strangest part of my strange story is that I am starting to believe as well."

Elizabeth felt a cold ball begin to form in the pit of her stomach.

Henri shrugged, lost. "She tells me to dig in the sand and I do, and there is a tomb. She tells me I will find a scarab with Akhenaten's cartouche in a place it should not be, and yet it is. How does she know these things that no one can know?" He leaned back against the rock. "Perhaps she can speak with the dead after all."

CHAPTER TWENTY-SIX

"THIS ISN'T EXACTLY INCONSPICUOUS," Jack said as he looked around the plush leather interior of the Rolls-Royce Silver Ghost. The shiny mustard and black paint job didn't really blend in with the landscape either.

"In this neighborhood," Diana said. "No one will notice."

She was probably right. Hopefully right. They'd parked the car on a nice tree-lined street in a small, wealthy suburb of Luxor that ambassadors, foreign nobility and business magnates called home.

Jack had promised Simon and Elizabeth that he'd find out everything he could about Katherine Vale. He'd only hesitated a moment before asking Diana for help. He might be good at what he did, or used to do, but not speaking the language was a crippling handicap. And, he thought, as he admired the way her keen eyes kept a lookout without looking like she was, this sort of work was a heck of a lot more fun with a partner. Having a pretty one didn't hurt either.

She turned and smiled. "We're supposed to be looking out there," she said with a nod toward an elaborate house across the street.

Jack grinned. "View's better in here."

Diana shook her head and picked up the binoculars from her lap. A delivery truck pulled into the semi-circular driveway.

"Another?" Jack asked as he squinted to see the logo on the truck, not that he could read it.

"Maybe she's having a party," Diana said, peering through the glasses. "Truck's blocking the door."

She slipped the binoculars back into the leather case on the seat between them.

Jack tried to see anything useful, but she was right. He shifted back into his leather seat and ran his hands over the large steering wheel. "How'd you get this thing again?"

"I told you," she said, "Lord Haversham owed me a favor."

Jack narrowed his eyes. He wanted to ask the logical question, but knew he wouldn't get a straight answer. It was odd, having the tables turned. He was usually the one keeping secrets. Not that he didn't still have a few of his own.

He'd told Diana that Vale had been trouble for the Crosses before and that they had reason to believe she was up to something, something dangerous, and he needed her help finding out what it was. She'd stared at him for a long moment, her beautiful brown eyes taking measure of his honesty, and then she nodded and said, "Where do we start?"

It had been as simple as that. Just, "Where do we start?"

They'd started poking around the Winter Palace. It hadn't taken long for them to learn that Vale had arrived in Luxor two months ago. Since then, she'd come and gone, traveling to Cairo and Alexandria. For the most part, she'd kept to herself, except for appearances at the Winter Palace.

She'd rented a house in Luxor that was owned by some Italian baron. She'd taken it for the season, although why the Baron wasn't in residence as usual no one knew.

Jack glanced over at the house as the delivery truck pulled away. He hoped the baron wasn't chained up in the basement or something. From what Simon and Elizabeth had told him about Vale, and the chill he'd felt when he'd met her, he wouldn't be surprised.

"How long do we sit here?" Diana asked. "Surely, there's something we can *do*."

Jack had to smile. Diana was a woman of action, impatient by nature, not that he blamed her. Sitting, waiting, watching—was boring as hell. But they were also some of the most important aspects of gathering intelligence. It wasn't all excitement and intrigue. In fact, very little of it was. Most of his time as an agent had been spent just waiting and not always in such plush accommodations.

"We'll give it a few more hours," he said.

She sighed. "All right," she said. "But then I think we should go nose around those delivery services and see if your man in Cairo has learned anything."

"Agreed."

Once they'd realized that Vale had traveled to Cairo several times, Jack knew they had to follow that lead. Since he couldn't go himself, he called the only man in Cairo he trusted—Hassan. The clerks at Shepheard's had thought he was mad when he'd explained who he wanted to speak to, they weren't accustomed to taking calls for a dragoman out on the streets, but they'd managed it. Before long they'd called back, and put Hassan on the line. Hopefully, he'd have better luck finding out about what Vale was up to.

"Get down," Diana whispered in a harsh voice as she scooched down in her seat.

Jack did as she ordered and carefully peered over the edge of the window. "What is it?"

Diana had the binoculars up to her eyes and had them trained on a carriage that had just passed by. She frowned and handed them to Jack.

He focused them on the back of the carriage. As it turned and stopped at Vale's front door, he realized why she was upset. "Ahmed?"

"It could just be museum business," she said hopefully.

"Yeah." Jack hoped she was right. If the kid were mixed up with Vale and whatever she was really up to, it was bad news.

Ahmed climbed out of the carriage, knocked and then disappeared inside the house.

"How long have you known him?" Jack asked.

"Two years, but not very well. I met him through Christina." Her brow wrinkled in worry. "He seemed like a fine enough young man, but recently...?"

"Recently...?" Jack let the question linger.

Diana weighed her answer before speaking. "He's developed some...political affiliations—"

"The desert bandits?"

Diana started, surprised. "Yes." She stared at Jack for a moment, but swallowed her questions and turned her attention back to the house. "I've known the Whitesides for many years, and I'd hate for Arthur to think I've betrayed his trust."

"By helping his daughter have an affair with a revolutionary?"

Diana frowned, but didn't argue. "It was all just pamphlets and meetings before last month. Harmless. And a just cause, I think."

"I'm sure that'll ease Whiteside's mind," Jack said with a sardonic smile.

"They were in love," Diana said a little fiercely and then sighed. "It was sweet and innocent."

"I'm not sure anything involving a 21 year old boy is ever all that innocent," Jack said.

"You're a cynic."

"No," he said. "It's just that I've *been* a 21 year old boy."

Diana watched the front of the house. "Well, they've broken up now, so it's all in the past."

Jack laughed. "You've never been in love, have you?"

Diana paused, shifted her eyes to him and then back to the house. "No," she said a little sadly. "I've been too busy."

Jack instinctively wanted to comfort her, but knew it would be unwelcome and unwise to try. "You've known the Whitesides for a long time?"

Diana smiled. "Yes. Arthur and I had business together."

"He hired you?"

Diana laughed at the memory. "Not exactly. He caught me breaking into his house."

Jack chuckled. "Why would you—don't tell me Whiteside stole an artifact."

"He didn't know it was stolen, of course. Came downstairs in his nightshirt, elephant gun in hand and told me to raise my hands or meet my maker."

Jack flashed on a scene from the Marx Brother's *Animal Crackers* and wished Diana could have seen it. He was fairly certain, she would adore it.

She laughed again at the memory. "I explained why I was there. He was completely unaware that his recently acquired Athenian vase was recently stolen from a collection in Berne."

"And he believed you?"

"Well, it took a little convincing, but yes," she said. "And we've been fast friends ever since."

They watched the front door of Vale's house in silence for a few moments. "I wouldn't have let anything happen to Christina, you know," she said.

Jack kept his eyes on the house. "I know."

After a few minutes had passed, Ahmed and Vale came out the front door. They lingered talking on the front landing for a moment before shaking hands. Ahmed climbed back into his carriage.

Jack and Diana slouched down in their seats again until he was well past.

"What are you up to?" Diana said to herself as she watched Vale wait for her car to be brought around front.

Jack and Diana hid again as her chauffeur drove right past them. Once the other car was far enough down the road, Diana opened her door.

Jack grabbed her arm. "What are you doing?"

"Finding out what she's got in there."

"You're just going to go up and ring the bell?"

Diana shook her head and looked at him with a kind of pity. "I'm going to break in."

"Unless you've forgotten, there's still at least one of her men in there, probably more," Jack reminded her. "And I doubt you two will become fast friends."

"Then I'll just have to avoid meeting them, won't I?" She didn't wait for another round and slipped out of the car.

She was halfway across the street before Jack caught up with her. They crept around to the back of the house and crouched in the bushes trying to find an easy way in.

"There," Diana said.

"Where?"

"The French doors."

"On the second floor?" Jack asked.

Instead of answering, Diana dashed across the back lawn. He really wished she'd stop doing that.

Jack grumbled, but followed quickly behind. They sought cover between a mulberry bush and the house. Jack edged along the outside of the house and then peered inside a window.

While he was doing that, Diana had already managed to climb onto the railing of the back porch and clung to the edge of the balcony above, struggling to lift herself up.

Jack pulled out his pen knife and slid it between the window sashes. The lock swiveled easily. Very slowly, he eased the lower window up. "Pssst."

Diana's head turned to look at him, she frowned as she hung there and then dropped to the garden. Jack refolded his knife and grinned.

"Show off," she whispered as she carefully climbed inside.

They had gotten lucky. It was the study and the door to the rest of the house was closed.

Jack hurried to the desk and rifled through the papers there. Hotel bills, rental agreements and the usual sort of thing. It wasn't until he found a separate folder that his heart started to really race. In it were four envelopes. All of them addressed to Louche, Blomster & Blackwood, the same legal firm as Mason's letter. Except these had been mailed, the stamps cancelled.

Jack knew what he'd find in them before he looked. Four more codes, just like the one he'd deciphered. That helped explain how she'd been one step ahead of them anyway. Jack put them back just as he'd found them.

"Jack," Diana whispered. She jerked her head to the side, urging him to join her.

He made sure the desk was as he'd found it and walked over the to the sideboard next to Diana. "Creepy. What are those?"

Resting in a long wooden box were four wax figures.

"They're Egyptian gods," she said.

There was a fifth figure, slightly larger than the others, perhaps ten inches, wrapped in raw cotton linen. It was made of black wax and formed into the shape of a man. A short lock of blond hair was pressed into its waxy scalp.

"Now, that's creepy," Diana said.

Jack's skin crawled as he wrapped it back up. No matter how much he'd seen or the Crosses had told him, the supernatural still gave him the willies. He liked to fight things he could see, understand and that stayed dead when he shot them.

He nudged it back into place beneath a copper plate with a long handle that hung on the wall.

"I've seen this," Diana said as she pointed to a large necklace in a glass bookcase next to the sideboard. "I can't remember where though."

Artifacts Jack couldn't identify lined the shelves. The few he could, were an ankh and some sort of scepter, but two of the four scarabs that were embedded on each side were missing. There was also an ornate copper dagger with a long runnel and a matching chalice.

"What do you—"

Jack heard something and put his finger to his lips. Diana fell silent and they both listened. There it was again. Footsteps. Close by. Jack's heart hammered in his chest.

He held his breath as the footsteps stopped right outside the door. His hand balled into a ready fist as he heard the doorknob begin to turn. Diana's hand gripped his forearm and her eyes went wide with alarm.

But the door didn't open. The knob rattled as the person on the other side checked to make sure it was locked. Thank God, it was.

Satisfied, the person stopped twisting the knob and the footsteps moved on.

Jack slowly let out his breath and jabbed his thumb toward the window. Diana nodded and they made their escape. That had been foolish, he thought. Reckless. And he'd loved it.

Jack started the car and didn't waste time driving away. "What the hell was all that?"

Diana shook her head. "Nothing good."

CHAPTER TWENTY-SEVEN

"Magic," Whiteside said.

Elizabeth cringed a little, even though she had a feeling that's what he was going to say before he said it. She knew in her heart that someone as crazy pants as Vale couldn't come to a place like Egypt and not get caught up in something nutty.

After Diana and Jack had told Simon and her what they'd discovered, they knew they had to get an expert opinion. They'd found Whiteside and invited him to come to their suite to answer a few curious questions.

He'd come alone, as they'd asked. Elizabeth had argued for Christina's involvement, but had been overruled by both Simon and Jack, and surprisingly, Diana.

"Let her enjoy things while she can," she'd said.

In the end, they'd left Christina to the peace and serenity of the Winter Palace's back veranda and set off to find out what light Whiteside could shed on what the heck Katherine Vale was up to.

"Wax figures," Whiteside continued, "they were commonly used in ceremonies in ancient times."

"So not actual magic?" Jack said, his eyes shifting anxiously to Simon and Elizabeth. "Just ceremonies."

Whiteside smiled. "Oh, no. The Egyptians were renowned in the ancient world for their magic. Sorcerers' duels, secret names, curses, scarabs of immortality, they had the lot."

Jack frowned. "But you don't mean they actually believed—"

"I do. Of course, no doubt some simply employed legerdemain, trickery, but there are descriptions of feats beyond explanation. Great magicians. Powerful necromancers."

Elizabeth and Simon exchanged worried glances. Simon had been convinced that Vale, when they knew her as Madame Petrovka, was no more than a clever charlatan, but Elizabeth was never quite convinced. She'd felt things, heard things, she couldn't explain. And now, after their experience with Mary Stewart in Natchez, she knew firsthand what was possible and what wasn't when it came to communing with spirits. If Vale really could speak with the dead... Elizabeth shivered.

"The other items?" Simon asked. She could see he was as disturbed at the prospect as she was. "Do they point to anything in particular?"

Whiteside frowned in thought. "Are you sure this is proper? I trust you, Diana, all of you," he added glancing around the room. "But I do feel a little uncomfortable with this."

Impatient, and trying not to be, Simon stood and walked over to the window of their suite.

"Arthur," Diana said, moving to sit next to him, "you know that I'm not the sort given to flights of fancy and I don't scare easily."

Whiteside chuckled. "No."

Diana smiled at some shared memory. "There is something about this woman, Arthur. Something...wrong. I know you've sensed it. I don't know what she's up to, but I think we'd damn well better find out. And right now, our best hope of doing that is you."

Whiteside took a deep breath and nodded, accepting his charge. "I'll do what I can. Now, about that necklace...."

"It had the head of a lioness," Jack said.

"Sekhmet most likely," Whiteside said.

"And this sort of...." Jack put both of his hands on his chest and then pulled them apart and slightly up.

"A collar," Diana said.

Whiteside nodded. "An aegis. It's sometimes called a broad collar. One of this sort could be used as protection for the spell caster."

"An aegis," Elizabeth repeated to herself. "Where did I—"

"The museum!" Simon said as he paced back over to the sitting area. "That first day, Jouvet mentioned that one had been stolen."

"That's where I saw it," Diana said, slapping her leg with the realization. "The plot thickens."

Whiteside fiddled with his glasses and pursed his lips. "And this copper plate, you mentioned. Did the handle have a face on it with sort of drooping horns?"

"Yeah."

Whiteside nodded. "Hathor's mirror. Sekhmet is an aspect of Hathor. The mirror is supposed to reflect your power, increase it. There are several magical papyri that have spells utilizing the mirrors for scrying, divination."

Elizabeth felt a lead weight settle in her stomach like a bad burrito.

"And the other wax figure?" Simon asked.

Whiteside frowned. "They were commonly used in curses or spells against your enemies."

She and Simon certainly qualified there, Elizabeth thought. Why make the doll of just the man? Was she after Simon specifically for some reason? She hated the idea of either of them being a voodoo doll in Vale's house of crazy.

Elizabeth glanced over at her husband and could see the wheels spinning in his mind, turning over the question.

Whiteside frowned and stroked his chin. "I am troubled by the athame, the dagger and chalice though."

"Daggers are never good," Elizabeth said.

Whiteside smiled kindly. "No, but in this case doubly so, I'm afraid. You see sacrifices weren't uncommon. Typically, bulls and small animals."

He sighed and continued. "However, the goddess Sekhmet has an unusual proclivity."

His usually jovial face grew quite serious. "According to legend, the God Ra believed man was plotting against him and so he sent Sekhmet to destroy humanity. She cut and maimed and disemboweled nearly all of the men of earth, until the few survivors begged for mercy. Ra granted it, but Sekhmet's savagery once started could not be stopped."

Elizabeth had a sinking feeling.

"Ra cast beer, tinted with red ochre, onto the land and into the Nile," Whiteside continued. "Thinking it was blood, Sekhmet drank until she could be subdued. However, her thirst was never sated. And some say the only way to summon her is by offering her blood. Human blood."

WHITESIDE'S WORDS ECHOED IN Elizabeth's mind. It was hard not to think of them. Blood sacrifices sort of stick with a person. Elizabeth felt a tingle along her breastbone and shivered.

"All right?" Simon asked as he placed his hand on the small of her back as they navigated their way through the crowded vestibule toward the requisite cocktails before dinner.

"Just thinking about what Arthur said."

Simon grunted in agreement. "Yes, vivid imagery. Blood lust and revenge. That, unfortunately, sounds right up Vale's alley, doesn't it?"

Elizabeth saw the Everetts by the long bar and led Simon in the other direction.

Vale had been fixated on vengeance before. That sort of deep-seated hatred didn't just fade away. It was nurtured.

"Do you think she went to all of this trouble for us?" Elizabeth asked. "I mean, why not just..."

"Kill us?" Simon said.

Elizabeth tried to shush him, but he just smiled.

"Saying it doesn't make it come true," he said.

Elizabeth wanted to argue that it might and why chance it, but Simon had already moved on to something else.

"There's one thing that bothers me," he said.

"Just one?"

He gave her a wry smile before continuing. "The blond hair. If the fifth figure is supposed to be me..."

"Unless it's not you," Elizabeth said as she realized the obvious. "This is about revenge, but maybe not against us. There's someone she hates even more."

"Graham." Simon paused and then looked around. Nodding toward an empty spot on the veranda, he put his hand on the small of her back and urged her toward it.

"If it is Graham she's after," he said softly. "Why come here?"

"Because she couldn't find him anywhere else," Elizabeth said, the pieces falling into place. "Travers said Graham was running for his life. What if she tried to find him, but couldn't."

Simon nodded thoughtfully. "The Council sends her here to retrieve the watch and she seizes on the opportunity to use her 'powers' to find the man that betrayed her."

"Now, that sounds like the woman I know and fear."

Simon laughed lightly. "Yes, it does. She spent years crafting her revenge on Graham only to be thwarted—"

"By us," Elizabeth reminded him unnecessarily.

Simon frowned. "We are betrayers," he said. "In her mind, at least."

That was what the cult member in the jail had called them. When you make enemies, Elizabeth thought, try to avoid the rich, powerful, lunatic kind.

"Well," Simon said, "whatever trickery she used to get here, the involvement of the cult and the objects Jack and Diana found point to something more troubling than simply retrieving one of the lost watches."

Elizabeth paused while the waiter took their drink order. Once he was gone, she leaned forward. "I wish you'd let me carry the watch some."

Simon laughed, but not unkindly. His eyes moved up and down her body, appreciating the sheer silk of her dress and the way it clung to her figure. "And you'd put it exactly where?"

Elizabeth pouted. "Ok, but still. I feel like it makes you a target."

Simon took her hand. He smiled, grateful for her concern, but melancholy as well. "Even without the watch..."

They were still targets. They might not be on the top of the hit list, but they were still in the top three. And, despite everything they'd learned, Vale was still one step ahead of them.

They both fell into a thoughtful silence and the cocktail party swirled around them, joyful and blissfully unaware. A small orchestra started to play and the hum of voices increased as more people poured into the parlor bar and veranda.

Elizabeth took a sip of her Gin Rickey and tried to stop dwelling on things she couldn't change and start looking for things she could. That's when she noticed Ahmed.

He was standing at the top of the steps looking out over the garden, clearly searching for someone. A couple paused as they passed and the men shook hands. Ahmed smiled graciously as they exchanged pleasantries and then went right back to his search.

He scanned the garden intently and Elizabeth knew exactly when he'd found what he was looking for. His entire posture changed. He gripped the top rail of the balustrade and his chest heaved as he let out an enormous sigh.

Elizabeth followed his line of sight. Christina.

Ahmed started down the steps, but was briefly distracted by another greeting. When he turned his attention back to Christina, the moment or his courage seemed lost. He looked down into his drink and then turned away, and leaned against the large pillar at the top of the steps and pressed his head back into the marble.

"Back in a sec," Elizabeth said.

Simon looked like he was about to ask where she was going, but saw her glance in Ahmed's direction and sighed. "Elizabeth…"

She arched her eyebrows in feigned innocence. "Just going to say hello."

Simon raised his hand to argue, all the reasons she shouldn't ready on his lips, but from the look in her eyes he knew it was a losing cause and settled for a resigned shake of his head.

Elizabeth kissed his cheek and then crossed the veranda to where Ahmed stood looking absolutely, Shakespearean-level forlorn.

"Hello again," Elizabeth said.

Ahmed jumped to attention as if he'd been stuck with a cattle prod. He cleared his throat. "Hello, Mrs. Cross."

First things first. "Why were you meeting with Katherine Vale today?"

His eyebrows shot up. "How did you—"

Her gut told her he wasn't involved in anything other than regular business things, but she had to be sure. "Are you working for her?"

She watched and carefully gauged his reaction.

"Yes, well, for the museum and the antiquities department for the dig."

Elizabeth narrowed her eyes. Aside from being confused, he was telling the truth. She'd bet her life on it. In fact, she realized, she was. And not just hers. "Avoid Vale as much as you can. She's not someone you want in your life," Elizabeth said.

Still confused, he nodded.

"Unlike someone else," Elizabeth said, her eyes finding Christina in the garden.

His gaze followed hers and instantly got that gauzy, far away look that young lovers and sick kittens got.

Elizabeth slipped her arm through his and led him away from the high traffic area near the steps. "I know it's none of my business," she said, "but that's really never stopped me before, so I'm going to stick my nose in. You can tell me to bugger off, but I'd say you owe me enough to hear me out."

Ahmed nodded, still baffled.

"Why did you break up with Christina?" she asked. "You broke her heart, you know?"

"I did not want that," he said earnestly. "I just...I could see no other way."

"Do you love her?"

Ahmed frowned. "You are very direct."

Elizabeth shrugged. "And also interfering, but that doesn't answer my question. Do you love her?"

She could see him debate whether to walk away or accept her help. After a long moment, he sighed. "With all my heart."

Elizabeth laid a hand on his forearm. "Then there's *always* a way."

Ahmed smiled and shook his head. "Even if she forgave me, her father would never accept me."

"He's not so bad—"

Ahmed held up his hand. "I did not mean to say he was. He is a good man, who does not think I am good enough for his daughter."

Elizabeth felt for him. He was right about Arthur. But there was one trump card in that. "He loves her as much as you do. In the end, that will win out over everything else."

Hope sparked in his eyes and he looked out into the garden. "Do you think there's really a chance she might forgive me?"

"It won't be easy." Elizabeth remembered her own broken heart. She'd stomped around New York with it dangling from her sleeve. "You'll have to grovel."

"I will."

"A lot."

A smile danced on the edges of his eyes. "I would do anything."

"Start with I'm sorry, and end with I love you," Elizabeth said. "And let your heart fill in the gaps in between."

Ahmed grinned. "Yes. Thank you."

He started toward the stairs, but stopped. "Are all American women as…"

"Bossy?" Elizabeth supplied.

He laughed. "Outspoken as you are?"

"If they're from Texas, probably," Elizabeth said with a grin. "Now, go on."

Ahmed nodded and hurried to the stairs, passing Simon on the way.

"Have you finished meddling?" Simon said as he joined her and watched Ahmed approach Christina. "Our table is ready."

Elizabeth gave him a sour look and turned to watch the fruits of her labor as Ahmed spoke with Christina. She'd moved to walk away as soon as he approached, but he reached out to her and, reluctantly, she'd stayed.

From the looks of things, he was groveling and she was listening. It was a start.

"Young love," someone said behind her.

Elizabeth couldn't suppress the chill that ran through her at the sound of Katherine Vale's voice. She and Simon turned to find Vale standing just a few feet away. Elizabeth felt Simon's arm slip around her back.

Vale sauntered over to the railing. "So life affirming, isn't it?" she said and then turned. "Except of course, when it rips your heart out."

She smiled again and Elizabeth could feel the crazy coming off her.

"Her father adores her," Vale said, gazing out at Christina again.

"You'll excuse us," Simon said, and started to usher Elizabeth away.

"What about you?" Vale asked casually before they could leave. "Did you try to have children? And fail?"

Elizabeth glared at her and Vale smiled.

"No," she said, smiling again as if she'd been given a gift. "But you're worried, aren't you?"

Elizabeth hated that Vale could see through her so clearly, but the more she struggled to conceal her feelings the more transparent she became.

Vale glanced back at Christina as Whiteside appeared and bullied Ahmed away. "You never stop worrying, I suppose," Vale said and then turned back, appraising Elizabeth with keen eyes. "Some have more reason than others, of course."

Elizabeth started to take a step forward, but Simon's hold stopped her. "Stay away from her."

"Away from Christina?" Vale said, sounding insulted and surprised. "Why ever would I harm her?"

"You can save your performance for someone else," Simon said. "We know what you are."

Vale feigned shock. "Do you?" She took a step closer, graceful and powerfully confident. "I don't think you have any idea who I am."

Simon stepped between Elizabeth and Vale and steered Elizabeth away.

"I'm sorry you don't have children yet," Vale said behind them. "I'd love to meet them."

The chill Elizabeth felt at the words lingered all through dinner and all through the night.

CHAPTER TWENTY-EIGHT

"G YMKHANA!" ELIZABETH SHOUTED HAPPILY and without reason.

Simon smiled and shook his head.

All she could do was shrug. Some words just begged to be shouted. Gymkhana, like Tequila, was one of them. And besides, she loved races and this one promised water buffalo.

After their run-in with Vale last night, Elizabeth needed something, anything to get rid of the fidgets. Sitting around all day, waiting for something bad to happen just made her as nervous as a fly in a gluepot. Thankfully, Whiteside seemed to be of the same mind and invited them to the weekly gymkhana. Being here was the perfect diversion.

Elizabeth sighed happily and resumed slapping herself with her fly whisk. The only thing there were more of than race day spectators were flies. The fly whisk Whiteside had given her had an ivory handle and long horsehair for swatting. Some were wooden with split palm leaves, but whatever they were made of they were indispensable.

The crowd looked a little like a bunch of horse's backends, the tails swinging and swatting bothersome flies. Elizabeth had felt a little silly at first, slapping herself on the head with it, but soon she fell into the same ten-second rhythm as everyone else and forgot about it and the flies.

"Poor chap!" Whiteside said as one of the donkey racers bounced right off his mount and landed unceremoniously on his rear. Of course, he had no reins to hold onto. The racers had to face backwards, steering by twisting the poor little donkeys' tails. The result was a zigzagging, haphazard race with more donkeys ending up in the crowd than on the course.

Whiteside handed Christina his opera glasses. She pursed her lips, obviously still unhappy with him for his interference in her relationship with Ahmed. But he persisted and she took the glasses, even managing a small smile as the crowd cheered and roared with laughter as the riderless donkey carried merrily on and won.

Even Simon smiled at that. He'd been tense. Heck, they'd both been tense after their run-in with Vale and the platter of heebie-jeebies she brought to every party. They desperately needed a break from it, and nothing could have better served their need. It was more than just a series of races. It was a test of skills, usually with thrilling, sometimes hilarious results.

Elizabeth was sorry Jack had missed this. He and Diana had "other plans." She honestly wasn't sure if that meant hanky-panky or jumping from roof to roof in a race for their lives. Either way, she missed him, but was glad he'd found a partner in crime. She glanced over at hers—Simon. While he was more of an Ascot sort than a fly-swatting gymkhana sort, he still seemed to be enjoying himself, even if only for a few hours.

The races, such as they were, were held on a wide straight course on a small bluff above the river. A few wooden risers had been set-up near the finish line for the wealthy spectators, but most simply lined the two-hundred yard course. First, there had been water bearers with enormous jugs of water on their heads. Then boys and their donkeys, followed by camel races. The camels' legs looked so ungainly and wild, it was a miracle they didn't tangle on the way.

"Oh, Fuzzy-Wuzzies!" Whiteside cried in delight.

"What's that?" Elizabeth said, craning her neck to see.

Whiteside handed her his opera glasses and Elizabeth focused them on the far end of the field and saw tall, handsome North African tribesmen. "Fuzzy-Wuzzies?"

"It's from a Kipling poem," Simon said. "Has to do with their hair. They're actually Hadendoa warriors." He frowned as the racers grew closer. "In a three-legged race."

Elizabeth had her umbrage unpacked and ready to wave around, when she realized that the races were an equal opportunity way to embarrass oneself. The next affinity race was European women riding, but mostly falling off donkeys as they tried to put on hats.

The water buffalo race was unruly and frightening. Shrieks of terror erupted from the crowd as one veered off course and headed straight for them until some brave soul jumped out and rerouted the beast. The young woman won a round of applause for her efforts.

Finally, at the end of the day were the horse races. Beautiful Arabians with their proud, arched necks sped down the track, their bareback riders seeming to float just above them the whole way. They were magnificent.

"Over here now," Whiteside said as the crowd began to funnel toward the river. "Careful, my dear," he said as he held out his hand to help his daughter make her way down the wooden risers.

Elizabeth and Simon followed Whiteside as he led them to the top of a narrow dike where men, women, donkeys, carriages, camels and the rest all rushed headlong and at full-speed in one final race into the river. Donkeys brayed, camels grunted, and people squealed and screeched in delight as the entire throng splashed about in the river. It was absolute chaos, joyous, exhausting chaos.

After the excitement of the gymkhana and the increasing heat of the mid-afternoon, all Elizabeth wanted was a cool bath and a little lie in before afternoon tea and their inevitable dose of Katherine Vale.

The group piled into waiting carriages and enjoyed the refreshing breeze and flyless air as they rode back to the Winter Palace. After agreeing to meet again in a few hours, Simon and Elizabeth split off and headed for their suite.

Simon put their room key down on the side table. "I think I have half the race course on me. I'll start the bath," he said as he went into the bathroom.

Elizabeth took off her sun hat and was just about to toss it onto the table when she noticed a large white box tied up with a silver bow.

She put her hat down. "Simon? Did you do this?"

When there was no answer but the sound of running water, Elizabeth reached for the bow. This was so Simon, always surprising her with little gifts. Although, she thought as she untied the ribbon, this was hardly little. The box was about three feet by two feet and just large enough for a dress.

"You really shouldn't have," she called out as she looked toward the bath and lifted the lid off. But she was glad he had. She loved presents.

Excited now, she set the lid aside and reached to peel back the tissue paper when it moved. It was so subtle she wasn't sure if she'd seen it or imagined it. She reached out again and froze as the pieces of tissue paper parted, and the large brown head of a cobra rose from between them.

The black beady eyes locked onto her as the head rose up, its broad hood fanned out on either side. Elizabeth could barely breathe. She didn't dare move. She was leaning in toward it, her hand hovering in mid-air just inches away from the snake.

"Simon," she said softly, not daring to take her eyes off the cobra.

"Simon," she said again a little louder.

She and the snake stared at each other. His body rising a foot and a half up out of the box now as he held her fixed in place.

She could see the rest of his length curled inside it. Could it smell her fear? Did snakes smell at all? They had noses, so they probably smelled, but maybe they weren't good smellers. Could it hear her heart racing? Could it feel the vibrations the way she did? A series of ridiculous questions and answers tumbled through her mind as she stood rooted in place, afraid to move an inch and sure if she did it would be her last.

"Aren't you co—" Simon started. "Dear God."

Elizabeth's eyes darted toward Simon. He stood in the doorway of the bath, afraid to move. His face was as pale as she knew hers was.

Slowly, he began to move toward her. "Just stay still."

"I'm trying," Elizabeth said, her mouth dry.

As Simon came into the snake's field of view, its dark brown head swayed to the side, but it didn't turn away. It focused on her. It was only thinking of her.

"Careful," Elizabeth whispered in a hoarse rasp.

The minute it took for Simon to get near to her felt like an hour. The snake's black eyes bore into her, frighteningly hypnotic. The markings on his dark gray body and tan underbelly drew her eyes to his. She couldn't have looked away if she'd tried.

She felt Simon approach and with each step the snake swayed just a little. She could hear the length of its body shifting, rustling against the dress it was coiled within. Each sway felt like the moment before the strike. Before she would die. She'd read about Egyptian cobras before they'd come; it wasn't good nighttime reading. Their venom was some of the deadliest in the world, attacking the nervous system and capable of causing death in less than fifteen minutes. Or you could linger with convulsions, blistering, necrosis and paralysis.

"I love you," she said, hoping it wouldn't be the last thing she said.

"It's going to be all right," Simon whispered from behind her. He sounded so calm. How could he sound calm? Ever so slowly, he slipped an arm around her waist.

She was just about to ask him what he was doing when he yanked her back and away from the snake. It lunged forward as Simon pulled her back. But as quickly as he'd moved, the snake had moved that much faster.

She felt it strike her arm, and she screamed.

ELIZABETH'S SCREAM CUT STRAIGHT to Simon's heart. He'd pulled her away from the snake as quickly as he could, but he'd been too slow, too damned slow. What had he been thinking, trying to move faster than a cobra? It was foolhardy at best and at worst...he couldn't think about that now.

His arm still about her waist, Simon spun her away. He turned back to see the snake lying half on and half off the table. He didn't hesitate, and gathered Elizabeth into his arms and strode for the door.

"Simon," she said, breathless.

His heart pounded so quickly in his chest he couldn't speak. He fumbled with the door handle briefly and carried her out into the hall.

"I need help!" he cried.

A few people were already in the hallway, alerted by her scream, and raced toward them.

"I'm all right," she said, but it barely registered with Simon.

"Get a doctor!" he bellowed at a short, stout man. "Now! And someone close that door! There's a snake in there," he ordered another guest.

Both complied with his orders without hesitation.

"It's all right," Elizabeth said again. "I'm okay."

She held out her arm, and where Simon had expected to see two puncture wounds, there was nothing.

"It didn't bite me," she said.

It took a moment for the news to reach Simon's brain. "What?"

"You can put me down," she said with an embarrassed smile.

Slowly, Simon lowered her to the floor of the hall where quite a crowd had gathered, including Jack and Diana.

"What happened?" Jack said, shouldering his way past the other guests. "You okay?"

Elizabeth nodded and then looked up at Simon. "I'm sorry I screamed..."

Simon let out a shuddering breath and cupped her cheeks. "You're sure you're not hurt?" He scanned her quickly. Miraculously, she seemed unharmed.

"I don't understand what happened," she said. "I felt the snake hit my arm."

Jack held up her arm to see for himself. "Snake?"

Simon tilted Elizabeth's head forward and rested his forehead against hers. "Oh, Elizabeth," he whispered. He thought he'd lost her. He thought he'd lost everything.

"I'm okay," she said.

Simon let out another breath, one that barely held back his emotions, before kissing her forehead and pulling her into his arms.

"What happened?"

"Did someone say snake?"

249

The growing crowd buzzed with questions, but Simon ignored them. His only focus was on the woman in his arms.

"All right, all right," Jack said. "Show's over, everybody."

"Come on," Diana said, joining in his crowd control efforts. "Back to your rooms."

Slowly, the guests began to disperse, grumbling and gossiping as they went.

Simon eased Elizabeth back from his embrace. "Are you sure you're all right?"

She nodded and held out her arms, her hands trembling. "Biteless and happy to be."

"What's going on here?" a man's voice came from down the hall. A group of men, including a doctor with his small black bag hurried toward them.

"My wife was nearly bitten by a cobra," Simon said. "In our room."

The hotel manager blanched and waved to two of the other men who had long poles with wire loops on the end. They opened the suite door and disappeared inside.

The doctor stepped toward Elizabeth. "You were not bitten?" he asked as he ran his hands up and down her arms. "You're sure?"

Elizabeth nodded, but it was clear she was still shaken.

"Is there somewhere we can take her to rest?" the doctor asked.

"My room's right here," Jack suggested.

They all moved to Jack's room where Elizabeth was examined by the doctor and declared "very lucky." Simon was hardly going to disagree.

He sat down next to her on the sofa and despite her protests that she was fine, he could see she was still unsettled as she tucked her legs up beneath her. Simon held her hand and tried not to reach for his watch to get them both the hell out of there.

After a few minutes, there was a knock on the door. The men had captured the snake and brought it to show them. Elizabeth pressed into Simon's side at the sight. It was enormous, perhaps four feet long. One of the men grasped it about the neck and held it out. He said something in Arabic and Diana and the doctor both warily approached.

"What are you doing?" Jack said, reaching out to stop her.

"It's all right," Diana said. "It's harmless. Well, relatively." She leaned in to get a closer look before turning back to explain. "I've heard of it, but I've never seen it. The lips have been sewn shut with a fine fishing line."

The doctor cleaned his glassed. "Some of the snake charmers you might find on the streets do this to protect themselves. As you can see, it is an excellent deception, only visible upon close inspection."

Simon didn't know whether to be relieved or angry. It wasn't meant to kill; it was a message. *You are vulnerable.* He glanced down at Elizabeth. They were indeed, and he'd never felt it more acutely.

She squeezed his hand and looked up at him. He could see the same thoughts mirrored in her eyes.

After repeated sweeps and promises that there were no other surprises in their room, Simon and Elizabeth, and Jack and Diana went back into their suite.

"So, it was in the box?" Jack said as he carefully poked the tissue paper inside the box with the tip of an unlit candle.

"I thought it was a gift from Simon," Elizabeth said. She'd regained her color, although, he noticed she kept her feet up off the floor.

"It sure as hell wasn't from me," Simon said as he crossed the room. Sitting inside the box was a small, folded card. He picked it up and opened it. The earlier choice between relief and anger was made. "Jouvet."

"He wouldn't—" Elizabeth said. "I mean, the dress, but not the other."

Simon's rage was white hot. He would break the man's bloody neck.

"Really," Elizabeth said.

Her trust in the man only fueled Simon's anger. With a remarkable veneer of calm considering the anger boiling inside him, he nodded and slipped the card into his pocket. "I'd like to have a word with the manager. Will you be all right?"

Elizabeth eyed him for a moment and he thought she saw through his ruse, but she nodded. "I'm fine, really."

"I'll stay with her," Diana offered.

"I think I'll come with you, if that's all right?" Jack asked.

"I won't be long," Simon dismissed him and left.

He was only a few steps down the hallway when Jack grabbed his arm. "Don't do anything stupid."

Simon stopped and swiftly turned to face Jack. "I am going to hit someone. And unless you get out of my way, you will be the first."

Jack's expression changed from concern to relief. "I thought you were going to kill him," Jack said. "Beating him up sounds good."

He let go and Simon resumed his march down the hall.

"Leave a little for me," Jack said.

CHAPTER TWENTY-NINE

DESPITE THE REPEATED ASSURANCES from the hotel staff that the room was safe, Elizabeth couldn't help but look around nervously. Snakes could hide in places. Like big boxes or small crannies. Nagini's smaller cousin could be hiding somewhere, waiting.

Diana sat down opposite her in the seating area and started to say something, but just offered an awkward, but reassuring smile. Elizabeth gave her one of her own, before the curtain fluttered and she jumped a little.

Diana leaned forward. "I know they said they checked everywhere, but maybe we could give it one more look?"

Grateful for the offer, Elizabeth nodded and got up. She'd definitely feel better if she saw for herself the coast was clear. But she didn't relish the idea of sticking her head under the bed to find out what was there. "We need something pokey."

Diana cocked her head to the side.

Elizabeth mimed jabbing something. "To poke with."

"Right," Diana sad and chewed her lip in thought.

Elizabeth looked around the room for something that would do, but there was nothing long enough.

"I'll be right back!" Diana said suddenly, and bolted from the room.

She was back less than two minutes later with two golf clubs and handed Elizabeth one.

"Courtesy of the Everetts'," she said.

"They let you borrow them?" Elizabeth asked skeptically. The Everetts didn't seem the generous type.

Diana smiled. "Not exactly."

Elizabeth liked this woman more and more.

Diana moved to the window and pulled the curtains back with the club. "You start over there. If you find anything suspicious, don't be a hero."

Elizabeth laughed. "I'm not feeling all that heroic at the moment."

"You could have fooled me." She prodded at the other sheer and looked out on window ledge. "I would have fainted dead away."

Elizabeth found that hard to believe. "You?"

"Snakes," Diana said with a shudder.

Elizabeth laughed and poked behind a potted palm. "You really are like Indiana Jones."

"I don't know him," Diana said, distracted by her search.

Elizabeth smiled. "You'd like him."

They poked and prodded the living area to Elizabeth's satisfaction before moving to the bedroom. "Oh, we should call for ice," she said as she swiped the club under the dresser.

Diana looked at her blankly.

"For Simon's bruised hands."

Diana's eyebrows arched in surprise. "You mean you know why he really left?"

"He's my husband," Elizabeth said simply. "Hopefully, Jack will keep him from getting into too much trouble."

Diana rested her club on the floor. "You know, in spite of how it looks, I don't think Henri has something like this in him."

"I don't either," Elizabeth admitted. "But Katherine Vale can be quite...compelling. In an evil witchypoo sort of way."

Diana thought about it and nodded, before going back to searching the room. "What do you think she's after? Why would she spend all this money on what most people think is a pointless dig?"

Elizabeth paused. "I don't know. All those things you found... There must be something in the tomb she needs," she said. While it wasn't exactly a lie, she didn't like keeping Diana in the dark. Magic spells were one thing and time travelers from the future another.

"Well, we'll—" Diana started as she carefully flipped open the door to the armoire, jumping back a bit as she did.

Elizabeth's heart raced. Diana fished around inside and laughed as she pulled her club back out. One of Simon's belts dangled from the end.

She turned to Elizabeth with a smile as she took the belt off the end of the club. "We'll just have to get it first, won't we?"

SIMON FOUND JOUVET IN one of the salons holding court as usual. He smiled broadly when Simon entered, looking around him and expecting to find Elizabeth. He frowned when he saw Jack instead.

"Where is your beautiful wife?" Jouvet asked, coming to his feet. "The dress, it is—"

Simon's right cross connected with the man's chin so solidly it sounded like a Hollywood sound effect. Jouvet flew back narrowly missing his chair and stumbling around behind it. Simon stalked forward and threw the chair aside. Jouvet's party of sycophants screamed and scrambled out of the way.

Jouvet grabbed his jaw and shook his head, as he slowly backed away. "What are you doing? Are you mad?"

Simon pressed forward. "Stay away from my wife!"

"It was just a dress," Jouvet protested, as he found himself trapped between Simon and the wall. "To replace—"

Simon lunged forward and gripped the man by the lapels. "And the cobra just found its own way into the box, did it?"

Jouvet blinked in confusion. "Cobra?"

Simon shoved Jouvet back against the wall and pressed his forearm against the man's windpipe. "She could have been killed."

"I don't understand," Jouvet croaked.

"Don't play games with me, Jouvet," Simon ground out.

"I have seen jealous husbands before but—"

Simon buried his fist in the man's stomach.

Jouvet grunted and gasped for air.

Simon forced him back against the wall and leaned in. His own chest heaving from effort, from anger. "Tell Vale that your little trick didn't work. We're not going anywhere."

Simon heard voices behind him and shoved Jouvet back against the wall as he released him.

"Vale?" Jouvet croaked out. "What does she—?"

Simon glared at the man and was about to explain things again, when Jack stepped forward. "That present you sent Elizabeth had a little something extra in it."

Jouvet looked surprised. "A snake?"

"Don't pretend—" Simon said, as he balled his fist again.

The voices behind Simon grew louder and he felt Jack's hand grip his arm.

"What is going on here?" the manager said, and then saw Jouvet. He hurried over to him. "Monsieur Jouvet!"

Jouvet stared at Simon for a long moment.

"What has happened?" the manager demanded.

One of the men in Jouvet's entourage stepped forward. "That man," he said, pointing at Simon, "simply attacked poor Mr. Jouvet."

Simon glared at him and the man took a step back, but nodded toward the manager. "You see? He's raving."

Jouvet kept his gaze on Simon and then reached into his jacket pocket and pulled out a handkerchief. "It was simply a misunderstanding."

He wiped the blood from his lip, arching his eyebrow in surprise at how much there was. He looked again at Simon as he dabbed at his lip and then refolded his handkerchief, stuffing it back into his pocket. "Isn't that right, Mr. Cross?"

Simon didn't say anything. What was the man up to?

The manager looked nervously between Simon and Jouvet. "Do you want—"

Jouvet raised his hand to silence the man. "It is a private matter. But thank you for your assistance, Monsieur Taylor. You may return to your work."

The manager hesitated, but bowed and hurried off again.

Simon, his chest still heaving from his efforts, glared at Jouvet.

"Despite your...feelings," Jouvet said as he smoothed his jacket down. "I would never do anything to harm a woman. Especially—"

Simon clenched his jaw and his fist, but Jack stepped in again.

"Better stop while you're ahead, pal," Jack advised him.

Jouvet cocked his head to the side and looked back into Simon's eyes. He raised a hand in surrender and nodded with a small smile.

Jouvet was damned lucky Jack was there. The rage that had built up inside Simon had only partially been sated. He would have happily wiped that smug smile off the man's face with his fist.

"Come on," Jack said, tugging on Simon's arm.

Reluctantly, Simon let Jack pull him away.

"I am happy she was unharmed," Jouvet called out to him.

Simon paused for a moment, clenched his jaw, and then kept walking.

ELIZABETH CHECKED HER PILLOWS, again, before piling them up behind her against the headboard. She smoothed out the blanket. Any wrinkles or rumples looked too much like hidden snakes. Not that there were any snakes in the room. She and Diana had given it a thorough going over, something Simon had repeated when he'd returned from his errand.

He'd calmed considerably since then, but the tension in his jaw and shoulders was still noticeable as he took off his robe.

He reached to turn off the lamp on the end table.

"Would you mind? Just for a while?" she asked, looking meaningfully at the light.

He smiled, a little sadly, and shook his head. "Of course not."

He pulled back the covers and climbed into bed. Leaning closer, he kissed her temple before shifting his pillows to sit against the headboard with her.

He folded the sheet down around his waist and smoothed it with his hands. The ice had done its job; the knuckles of his right hand looked almost normal.

Elizabeth felt a pang of guilt. She should have stopped him. Jouvet hadn't deserved his anger, not all of it anyway. She reached out and let her fingers trace the strong contours of Simon's hand.

"Why do you think Hen—Jouvet didn't want the manager to call the police?" Elizabeth asked.

Simon turned his hand over and held hers. "I don't know. Perhaps he and Vale don't want the police poking around. Might stumble onto something."

Elizabeth hadn't thought of that. "Maybe."

Simon sighed. "It was a mistake. Don't get me wrong," he amended quickly. "It felt incredibly good to hit him, but I'm afraid it might have been short-sighted."

Elizabeth knew what he meant. "We need him to get into the tomb."

Simon nodded. "As much as I hate to admit it, yes."

Elizabeth shifted toward him. "Jack said he looked surprised at the whole snake thing and he didn't call the cops. Maybe he'll look past it, if..."

Simon closed his eyes and leaned his head back against the headboard. "If you ask him." He turned his head toward her. "There are not enough words to express to you how much I hate that."

Elizabeth smiled and kissed him.

He grunted again, and tried to hide his smile. "That helps a little."

"Just a little?" she said.

He leaned toward her, one hand on the back of her neck as he guided her into a deeper kiss. Elizabeth's heart sped up the way it always did when he touched her.

After a lingering moment, he pulled back and smiled. "More than a little."

Elizabeth nestled into his shoulder and he put his arm around her.

"Do you think she can really talk to the dead?" Elizabeth asked.

She could feel Simon's body move as he shifted to look down at her. "Vale? I doubt it. Once an impostor, always an impostor."

"I don't know." Elizabeth tilted her head to look up at Simon. "She knows things."

"Nearly all of which can be explained without witchcraft."

He sounded so sure. Elizabeth wished she shared his certainty. "Why does she keep bringing up children?"

Simon's hand slid down to her arm and urged her to sit up. He looked at her with his Most Serious Face. "It's part of her act, Elizabeth. She finds weaknesses in people and exploits them."

"How does she know that's mine?"

"Ours," Simon said, brushing his knuckles along her cheek. "She's observant, clever," he added reluctantly. "Too clever. But there's no evidence she has any supernatural powers or can speak to the dead the way—"

"Old Nan did?"

Simon paused and then nodded. "Yes."

Elizabeth settled back against Simon, laying her arm across his bare chest. She let the strong steady beat of his heart soothe her for a moment.

"You know when I thought I'd been bitten," she said, "I expected my life to flash in front of my eyes. Like in the movies."

Simon's hand covered hers.

"I guess it did in a way, just not the way I thought it would," she continued. "I saw everything I haven't done yet."

Simon lifted her hand to his lips and kissed it.

Elizabeth remembered the moment, a future life passing by in an instant. "Did you know, I've never been to the top of the Eiffel tower?"

She felt and heard Simon's laugh. "We can easily remedy that, darling."

She smiled against his chest. "It all flashed by so quickly. Going to the Super Bowl, seeing Yellowstone, taking little Charlotte to school…"

"What?"

Elizabeth laughed, a little embarrassed. "When we were first in New York, I sort of fantasized about us having a family. And well, Charlie sort of brought us together…"

She tilted her head up briefly to see Simon's expression, but it was enigmatic.

She knew they both wanted children someday. They'd talked about it in Natchez. But talking about it in theory and giving future children actual names were different things. Not that she was ready to have a child yet, but the image had been clear, so real in her mind.

"Anyway," she said, resting her head back on his chest. "It just surprised me."

Simon's fingers gently touched her hair. "Things to look forward to."

Elizabeth nodded. They were. She stifled a yawn.

"Best to get some sleep if you can," Simon said. "Who knows what excitement tomorrow will bring."

"You can shut off the light now, if you want."

Simon turned the switch and the room fell into darkness. He lay down and Elizabeth repositioned herself in his arms. She'd thought she wouldn't be able to sleep, but felt the weight of it coming on. Simon would stay up worrying, she knew, possibly all night.

Her head felt heavier as she sank into sleep. Just on the edge of consciousness, she heard Simon's voice. Just a whisper in the dark.

"Charlotte."

CHAPTER THIRTY

$\int$ IMON TRIED TO ENJOY the brief, peaceful, twenty-minute carriage ride from the hotel to the party. He knew that once they arrived, the relative safety they'd enjoyed during the day, where they'd lingered close to home at the hotel, would be lost in the darkness and the crowd of the Winter Garden's Karnak Gala.

He really would rather have stayed at the hotel and skipped this altogether, but Elizabeth had convinced him otherwise. She'd been right, of course, but that didn't mean he had to like it.

"It won't be so bad," Elizabeth said next to him.

He looked down at her with a curious frown. "Reading minds now?"

She smiled. "You were grinding your teeth."

She squeezed his arm and moved a little closer to him. "Just look at how beautiful it is," she said, gazing out of the open air carriage.

The Nile stretched out beside them, the moon reflecting off the smooth, glassy surface. A single felucca drifted on a gentle night wind just off the far bank. It was beautiful. Under different circumstances, he would have been happy to enjoy the beauty of Egypt, the pleasure of simply being with his wife, here, now, but not tonight.

Between the what had been and the what was yet to come, Simon couldn't allow himself to relax. When they were home, when the job was done, when she was safe, then, he would rest.

The line of carriages slowed as they turned east away from the river and toward Karnak, a building complex of temples built over the course of 1500 years. Their carriage pulled to a stop at the edge of the massive compound.

Ahead of them, dozens of guests in black-tie walked up the long processional way toward the immense first pylon that served as the portal to the temples inside. Fires from small braziers flickered in front of the two dozen ram-headed sphinxes that lined either side of the pathway.

Simon handed the attendant their tickets and they passed into the Temple of Amun. Most of the great courtyard was in ruins, only a bit of columns, badly damaged statues, and crumbling walls remained.

Music from a small orchestra drifted toward them from somewhere deep inside the complex where the party proper was taking place. Reluctantly, Simon continued on toward it.

Two torches marked the next gateway at the second pylon; beyond that was the Hypostyle Hall and its gigantic columns. Whiteside had said in his pre-party lecture that there were 134 columns in the hall, some measuring as tall as 70 feet and nearly 30 feet around. The ceiling they'd supported was gone and the moon shone down into the temple, the tall columns casting long, dark shadows across the floor.

"It's like a forest," Elizabeth whispered as she looked up at the imposing columns. "Some eerie, stone forest."

It was an apt and unnerving simile and Simon quickened their pace through it and into the next courtyard where a lone remaining obelisk stood sentinel in the dark.

They made their way through the rest of the temple and followed the crowd toward the main party, emerging from the buildings into the middle of a European gala. White linen-covered tables and several bars lined the grounds above a brackish, man-made lake. Tall palm trees and dozens of torches marked the perimeter of the open courtyard where the gala was in full swing.

A waiter, making the rounds with a tray of champagne, paused in front of them. Simon declined and scanned the crowd for the reason they'd come. The sooner he could get this over with, the better.

"Over there," Elizabeth said.

Simon grunted and rolled his shoulders. Standing in a small crowd was Jouvet, laughing with them and regaling them with some ridiculous story, no doubt.

Elizabeth grinned at him, amused by the situation, but her smile faded and she grew serious as she saw the distinct lack of humor in Simon's expression. "I can talk to him," she offered.

Simon sighed, resigned to his fate. "No. I should be the one." He tugged on his cuffs and then held out his arm for Elizabeth. "Let's get this over with."

Jouvet's smile at seeing Elizabeth lost its luster as he noticed Simon by her side. He regained his composure quickly and raised a hand in front of him in dramatic mock surrender. "I do hope we are not in for another round, Monsieur Cross. I am one handed," he said, holding up his champagne glass.

"Jouvet."

Jouvet nodded his head slightly and turned to Elizabeth. "I am so pleased to see that you appear to be in fine health," he said, letting his eyes linger long enough to make the vein in Simon's temple throb. "After your...unpleasant experience."

"I am," Elizabeth said with a warm smile. "Thank you."

Jouvet bowed slightly and then turned back to Simon. He straightened his shoulders and lifted his chin in an imperious and maddeningly French way, as he made a show of waiting for Simon to speak.

Simon cleared his throat. "It appears," Simon said. "That I owe you something of an apology."

He had hoped that Jouvet might have picked it up from there, but, Jouvet cocked an eyebrow and waited, more than content to watch Simon squirm a little.

"I won't lie and say that it wasn't satisfying—"

"Simon," Elizabeth cautioned under her breath.

"But I've since learned that it wasn't entirely deserved," Simon continued. Jouvet's expression was bland and unappeased. "I acted hastily, and quite rudely. I can only say in my defense that I love my wife. However, I realize that does not excuse my behavior. And for that, I am truly sorry."

It took all the strength he had to muster, but Simon held out his hand. "I hope you will accept my most sincere apologies, Monsieur Jouvet."

The damn Frenchman let him stand there hand out for a long moment, before stepping forward and shaking it. With a broad smile, played to the crowd of onlookers, he said, "If I had your wife, I would have probably thrown me into the Nile by now. Hmm?"

Simon managed to force what might pass as an amiable smile on his face as he imagined doing just that. "Very gracious."

"Now," Jouvet said, in full command of the moment. "You will join us tomorrow for the opening of the chamber, yes? I am quite curious to see what treasures await us."

"As am I," Simon said.

"Very good. Ah, Lord Carnarvon," Jouvet said, seeing the tall man arrive with a wake of lackeys and admirers. "You will excuse me?"

Simon did, happily, and let out a sigh of relief as Jouvet hurried over to glad-hand the new arrival.

Elizabeth nudged him once they were alone again. "See? That wasn't so bad."

"I think I'm bleeding internally."

Her laughter was a welcome salve to his bruised ego. As was the glass of champagne she held out. "Have a drink. You've earned it."

Simon took her up on the offer and had to admit the champagne did help wash away the sour taste of the crow he'd just eaten.

Elizabeth stepped forward and placed one hand on his chest. "Better?"

He nodded. She smiled and then looked wistfully out at the torches and moon reflecting off the sacred lake and the fairy lights flickering in the palm trees. He knew she didn't want to go back to the hotel, and that she'd humored him by staying in most of the day.

"I suppose we could stay for a bit," Simon said. "Try to enjoy ourselves."

Elizabeth turned back, her smile broad and beautiful. "I was hoping you'd say that."

JACK SCANNED THE CARVINGS on the outside of one of the temples at Karnak. "History has always been written by the winners, I guess." Having seen some rather interesting history himself, he knew just

266

how much was left out of the official records.

"It's the ritual massacre of the vanquished," Diana said, leaning in to get a closer look at the reliefs on the temple wall. "The kings' military exploits are carved all along here. Some right on top of the others."

"Literally rewriting history," Jack said.

Diana smiled. "Exactly. Not that anyone would do such a thing today," she added with a wink. "One of the spoils of war."

Diana took a sip of her champagne and continued walking along the perimeter. Jack followed her, enjoying the view of her wearing a filmy dress instead of her more practical, mannish clothes. She should do that more often, he thought, knowing just what she'd say to him if he ever voiced that opinion. And somehow he found that even more appealing than the dress.

Jack nursed the same drink he'd gotten when they'd arrived at the gala and caught up with her. As much as he'd like nothing more than to enjoy the party and a private after party with Diana, he had to stay alert. If Katherine Vale was as nutty as Elizabeth said she was, and Jack had no reason to doubt her, there wasn't going to be any downtime from here on out. It wasn't just his life on the line, but hers and Simon's as well. Vale had a personal grudge against them and that made people reckless, unpredictable, and very, very dangerous.

Never let your guard down had been one of the basic rules of his training. That one moment when you think you're safe, where you light that cigarette you've been craving, that's when the bullet with your name on it finds you. He'd seen it happen more times than he cared to count. And it was not going to happen here.

"These are the Hittites, I think," Diana said, her fingers gently tracing a relief.

Jack asked her questions, and listened to her answers, but his attention was really focused on a movement in the shadows, a change in the tenor of someone's voice, a man with his hat on and eyes cast down..."What the hell?"

Jack touched Diana's arm to get her attention. "Isn't that—?"

Her expression darkened. "Nico. That little weasel. What's he doing here?"

The last time they'd seen Nico was in the marketplace in Cairo. Seeing him here was a hell of a coincidence and Jack didn't like coincidence. Coincidence wasn't happenstance, it was a pattern he'd failed to see. And that meant surprises, and this kind didn't end with a naked girl popping out of a cake.

Nico tugged down on the brim of his hat and disappeared around a corner. Silently, Jack and Diana followed. Nico hurried along the edge of the walls of the main gate, and looked around cautiously, before stepping inside the wall. Or at least that's what it looked like. As they arrived at the spot, Jack saw that there was a hidden doorway and narrow stairs.

Diana glanced at him briefly before starting toward the stairs. He reached out and gripped her arm, and then nodded that he should go first. Diana frowned, rolled her eyes and kept going. He wasn't sure whether to feel impressed or emasculated. He settled on a little of both and followed close behind.

The inner section of the rough stone stairwell was pitch black. They had to feel their way along toward the spot of moonlight sixty feet away at the top. As they neared the end of the stairs and the opening to the rooftop, Jack could hear voices—Nico's and one he didn't recognize.

He slipped his hand under his tuxedo jacket and unholstered his gun. Diana squatted down at the entrance, Jack close behind, and they listened for a moment.

"Yes, we are working together now," Nico said.

"Are you?" a man with a Greek accent said.

"You know how women are," Nico said. "They need a man."

"And she settled for you instead?"

Nico's nervous and high-pitched laugh cut through the night. "Why is she not here herself?"

Before Jack could think to stop her, although he hadn't anticipated the move, Diana stood and emerged out onto the rooftop.

"She is."

Jack shook his head. This woman was crazy. He gripped his gun more tightly and slipped it into his pocket, hidden, but ready, as he followed her out onto the roof.

Nico and three men stood on the rooftop. Nico spun around so quickly, it was a miracle he didn't screw himself into the roof. He took off his hat and held it to his chest and tried to smile. "Miss Trent! I was not expecting to see you."

Diana looked from him to the other man. "Apparently not." She eyed the other man, a big barrel-chested guy who looked like he wrestled Krakens in his spare time. "What's going on here, Alexi?"

"Your man contacted me—"

"My man?" Diana repeated with an arched eyebrow and then turned a withering look on Nico. "Hardly."

"So you do not work together?" Alexi said, his already humorless face looking even more grim.

"No," Diana said firmly.

Alexi narrowed his eyes at Nico. "You lied to me."

Nico shook his head. "No, no, no. That is putting too fine a point on it."

Alexi's bodyguards both moved to take a step forward, and Jack tensed, but Alexi held up a meaty hand and they remained where they were. He turned to Diana for confirmation.

"I work alone," she said.

The big man's eyes slid over to Jack. "And he is?"

"For catching spiders," she said looking pointedly at Nico.

Nico held up his hands in front of him and raised his skinny shoulders. "It was just a little joke."

"No one is laughing," the big man said and jerked his head foreword. The two bodyguards moved forward as one and grabbed Nico by the arms. "You like to play games, do you?"

"Alexi—" Diana said, but the man ignored her and with a slight movement of his head gave the command to his men.

They dragged Nico over to the edge.

For the first time, Jack saw Diana tense. He'd thought this was just a ploy, but if Diana was on edge, this was no game.

"Please?" Nico begged.

The men lifted him up and set him down on the wall's edge like a doll on a shelf in a little girl's room.

"I have what you want," Alexi said to Diana, ignoring Nico's pleas.

Diana eyed Nico's precarious position, but responded as casually as Alexi. "It's about time."

Alexi laughed deeply. "I will contact you tomorrow to arrange a meeting." He glanced over at Nico. "Alone."

Diana nodded. "Alone. Thank you."

Alexi inclined his head and then snapped his fingers. His henchmen let go of Nico, leaving him perched precariously on the edge of the stone tower.

"Isn't somebody going to—" Nico said and turned to beg for help, but as he did, one of the loose stones beneath him gave way and he slipped over the edge.

Jack was closest and instinctively lunged forward. Nico turned in mid-air and just managed to grab onto the wall. His fingers gripped the rough stone, but another gave way and he would have fallen to his death if Jack hadn't been able to grab his wrist.

Party goers at the bottom of the pylon screamed as the stones fell and Nico cried out. Jack was bent over the low wall, half his body hanging down as he held on.

Nico might be a coward and a thief, but even he didn't deserve to splat on the pavement like yesterday's lunch. Nico struggled and squirmed, nearly loosing Jack's grip.

"Stop wiggling, you idiot!" Jack yelled as he looked down at the man. As he did, the ground, over sixty feet away, started to swirl and telescope away. Jack's stomach roiled and he felt the world start to tilt.

Blood rushed in his ears drowning out Nico's pleas and prayers.

"It's all right," Diana whispered in his ear. "I'm right here."

He felt her arm go around his waist. "Just close your eyes and pull him up."

The sound of her voice grounded him. He looked down at Nico, whose eyes were wide with terror, the gathering crowd beneath him. Jack took a deep breath and lifted. Once he'd gotten control of himself, pulling Nico up was easy. After all, the man weighed less than a postage stamp.

Once he was high enough, Diana grabbed Nico's other flailing arm and together they pulled him back to the safety of the roof to the cheers of the crowd below.

Nico knelt and began reciting some sort of prayer in Italian.

Jack, still trying to catch his breath, stepped away from the edge.

"Are you all right?" Diana asked.

Jack took a deep breath and nodded, as the vertigo finally subsided.

Nico's offended voice pierced the quiet. "Him? What about me? Who is the one who almost died here? I think I was the one hanging over the edge like dried sausage."

Diana smiled, stepped forward and slipped her arms around Jack's waist. She gazed into his eyes, but it was Nico she spoke to.

"You have five seconds to leave here or we're going to put you back where we found you."

There was a pause. "Fair enough."

Jack heard Nico's hurried footsteps disappear down the stairs.

Diana smiled and pressed herself into Jack. His arms tightened around her. Forget oysters and Spanish fly, there was no better aphrodisiac than nearly dying.

"Nice catch," she said.

"He was kind of small, I probably should have thrown him back."

Diana laughed. "Probably." She leaned forward and kissed his neck.

"You going to tell me what that was all about?" he asked.

She kissed his jaw. "Probably."

Jack felt his blood rush again, but for much more pleasant reasons. "Is this night going to end well?"

Diana pulled back and grinned. "Definitely."

CHAPTER THIRTY-ONE

$\int$ IMON HAD MANAGED TO enjoy himself, for brief moments at least, as he danced with Elizabeth. They'd spent some of the evening chatting with Whiteside who waxed eloquently and endlessly about the difference between Demotic and Meroitic scripts and avoiding the Everetts, who Simon had last seen trying to put a bra on a statue of Seti II.

Elizabeth had convinced him of one more dance and he'd happily obliged as Whiteside launched into a treatise on cuneiform.

As he held her in his arms and listened to the music, he could almost forget the danger they were in. Almost.

"So romantic," Elizabeth said.

Simon was about to agree when he noticed that she hadn't been looking at him when she said it. He followed her eye-line and rolled his eyes. Ahmed had Christina by the hand and was leading her off to what Simon assumed was a dark corner somewhere.

He doubted Whiteside would agree. The man had lost his audience and was clearly standing on the sidelines looking for his daughter.

"Let's just stay out of it," Simon said, as he turned her away in time to the music.

Elizabeth raised her eyebrows in feigned innocence. "Just observing."

"You are the most hands-on observer I've ever known."

Elizabeth smiled and nodded toward a secluded corner. "I think my work is done."

Ahmed leaned down and kissed the girl and Simon heard Elizabeth sigh.

He shook his head. "Promise me it is."

She gave the couple one last lingering look—always the romantic—and then nodded.

"Good," Simon said. "We have more important things to worry about."

Elizabeth fiddled with his collar as they danced. "Like how to steal the watch with Jouvet, the Whitesides and She Who Shall Not Be Named looking on?"

"Yes," he agreed. "And stay alive while doing it."

There was a bright-eyed confidence in Elizabeth's smile. "We'll find a way."

He should have been used to it by now, but he found himself once again amazed by her strength. It wasn't hubris or conceit behind her words. It was faith, simple faith in him, in them.

He'd always shared it, but Katherine Vale's presence had cast a shadow of doubt that left him with a constant sense of unease and worry. They'd injured Vale and a wounded animal was the most dangerous kind.

"Perhaps we should call it a night?" he suggested.

For once, Elizabeth didn't argue and Simon was grateful for that. They said their goodnights to Whiteside and started back toward the main entrance. Most of the guests were either dancing or drinking now and the temples themselves were nearly empty. As they entered the Hypostyle Hall, their footsteps echoed in the silence.

Simon felt the presence before he heard the other set of footfalls. He glanced down at Elizabeth. She'd heard them too. His heart beating faster, he hurried them through the dark colonnade, but the footsteps grew louder and closer.

They were too vulnerable out in the open and he pulled Elizabeth aside suddenly, and forced them into another row of columns and stopped. They pressed themselves up against the cool stone and listened.

He heard two more footsteps and then only the sound of his heart beating in his chest. Glancing down at Elizabeth, he nodded down the aisle and they slowly made their way from column to column, shadow to shadow.

They zigzagged their way toward the door and were only twenty feet away now. They edged around the girth of another column and had just started for the doorway when a man stepped out in front of them.

Elizabeth gasped in shock and Simon cocked his arm back. He was just about to strike when the figure took a small step to the side, out of the shadows and into a shaft of moonlight.

Hands raised in front of him, a broad grin on his face, was Hassan.

Relief coursed through him. "Good God, man," Simon said, letting out a deep breath and lowering his arm. "Why didn't you say something?"

"I am sorry," Hassan said. "I did not mean to startle you."

Elizabeth's laugh betrayed her nerves. "I didn't even hear you at the end. You are light on your feet, Hassan."

He grinned again. "I take dance lessons."

Simon shook his head. "That's fascinating, but *what* are you doing here?"

Hassan's smile fell. "Mister Wells called me several days ago to see what I could find out about your Miss Vale and her...associates."

"Why didn't you just call us?" Simon asked with a growing sense of worry. "Why come all this way?"

Hassan straightened proudly. "Because, in Cairo, you hired me to help you. And after what I have learned, you, Mister Cross, are going to need Hassan's help."

Simon was about to ask just what that meant when a woman screamed and then men shouted. It sounded liked it was coming from the front entrance. A few people hurried past them toward the sound. There was some sort of commotion at the first pylon.

"Don't let anyone else see that you're here. Meet us back at the hotel," Simon said to Hassan as he took Elizabeth by the hand and started toward the gate.

"Thank you, Hassan!" Elizabeth said. "It's good to see you."

"And you! And remember...Trust in Hassan!"

Elizabeth offered Hassan a drink, but he shook his head. He looked around admiringly at their suite in the Winter Palace and she realized, he probably wasn't invited into places like this very often.

He stood, unsure in the middle of the room, until Simon gestured for him to take a seat. He nodded, a little surprised, then brushed the back of his robes with his hands and sat down carefully on the white sofa.

"Go on," Simon prompted.

"I spoke with many people," Hassan said. "But many would not speak with me."

Elizabeth sat down next to Hassan. "They're afraid."

Hassan nodded. "There are some who know of the cult and your Mrs. Vale, but they fear for their lives. They believe she is magic."

She and Simon exchanged a quick glance. Neither was surprised to hear it. As Madame Petrovka, Vale had used her knowledge of the past to fool people into thinking she was a psychic, complete with spooky séances and chats with the dead.

Simon sat down opposite them and leaned forward, elbows on his knees. "And I suppose she performed some feat that convinced them of this?"

Hassan's forehead knit together. "They say she appeared out of thin air."

Simon's eyes shifted briefly to Elizabeth's and she knew he was thinking the same thing she was. They both appeared out of thin air themselves when they arrived.

"She arrived in the middle of a secret ceremony for Sekhmet. She said she was sent by the goddess," Hassan continued.

"And all of these cult members believed her?" Simon said.

Hassan cocked his head to the side. "Not all of them. There was one who challenged her."

"Did you speak with him?" Simon asked.

"He is dead," Hassan said. "And unlike your Mrs. Vale, I cannot speak to the dead."

Elizabeth looked anxiously at Simon who nodded slowly, and pressed on. "Did you learn anything more? How many members are there?"

"Twenty, perhaps thirty. It is difficult to say."

Elizabeth whistled softly. After what the cult member had said in the jail, about being one of the Seven Arrows, she'd kind of been hoping that was it. Seven, they could handle, but...

"Thirty?" Simon said, arching his eyebrows. He cleared his throat. "Right. Anything else that might help us?"

Hassan frowned. "Only that she has been preparing for something. For many months."

"What?" Elizabeth asked.

Hassan shook his head. "I am unsure, but if it involves Sekhmet, it will be blood."

Elizabeth shivered at that.

"Do you believe in the old gods?" Simon said.

Hassan shrugged. "I neither believe, nor disbelieve. Is it so strange though, to think God has many faces?"

Elizabeth could see Simon consider the question, not in an off-handed rhetorical way, but truly consider it. Neither of them were what anyone would call religious. Both of their faiths were best described as vague.

Finally, Simon nodded.

"Thank you for doing all this," Elizabeth said.

Hassan nodded and, taking her statement as his cue to leave, stood.

Simon and Elizabeth followed suit.

"You really could have called," Simon said as Hassan started for the door. "You didn't need to come all this way."

Hassan stopped at the door and turned back. He squared his shoulders and his pot belly stuck out proudly.

"I am your dragoman," he said. "What sort of guide would I be if I abandoned you when the path grew dark?"

CHAPTER THIRTY-TWO

Elizabeth enjoyed the breeze as their carriage trotted down the dirt road and into the Valley of the Kings. It was hot and dusty, but she was glad they didn't have to make the long hike to Henri's dig this time. Carriages had been provided at the ferry on the west bank, and now one carried them toward through the rocky wadi to the moment they'd been waiting for—the opening of the chamber.

Other carriages trundled along ahead and behind, kicking up long trails of dust. Jack and Diana, the Whitesides, the Everetts and the rest of Henri's entourage wound their way through the canyons to witness history.

Despite the tension of their mission and the fact that someone who hated their actual guts was nearby, Elizabeth was excited. She was about to see the opening of an ancient tomb. She was about to step into a room, into dusty footprints, made three thousand years ago.

Anticipation being almost too much to handle, she wriggled in her seat. They couldn't be far now. She leaned out to see for herself, and got a faceful of dust for her trouble. Coughing, she tried to wipe the dust from her eyes when she saw Simon's hand holding out his handkerchief.

Simon smiled at her as she took it, only briefly though, before turning his attention back to the road. He'd been in a state of hyper-focus since they'd gotten up that morning. She could see it in his posture, rigid and controlled, in the set of his jaw, the way his eyes moved, scrutinizing everything around them, leaving nothing unnoticed.

He was right to be on alert, of course. They weren't the only ones after the watch, not to mention, crazy didn't need a reason to do things. Reining in her excitement, she wiped her face and meticulously folded his handkerchief, dirty side in, before handing it back to him.

Their carriage turned and she could see the white tents of Henri's dig.

She took Simon's hand. "Ready?"

Simon was about to say something when his expression hardened. Elizabeth turned and saw the reason. Katherine Vale stood by her car talking with Henri. Elizabeth's excitement was replaced with a healthy dose of fear. She took a deep breath and her fight response told her flight response to stuff it.

As their carriages pulled up, Henri greeted them. "So pleased you could join me. All of you."

Once everyone had disembarked and the carriages retreated to wait in the shade, Henri turned to address the small group. "I hope today will be one to remember."

Vale smiled at the assemblage, her eyes landing on Simon and Elizabeth. Her mouth curled a little tighter. "I am sure it will be."

He gestured toward the entrance, letting Vale precede him. He waved to the rest of the group, ushering them toward the stairs.

Elizabeth looked anxiously at Simon. He clenched his jaw but nodded that they should follow Jouvet.

Simon held her arm as they made their way down the steep, narrow steps and into the first corridor. The hum of the small electric generator was drowned out by the hum of excited voices that echoed in the narrow chambers.

Elizabeth squinted in the dim light. They'd spent the better part of last night going through possible scenarios. What if the watch was sitting out in the open? Surely, Jouvet would notice the blatant incongruity. He'd probably take it immediately to his rooms or the press. That was if, as Simon said, always a ray of sunshine, Katherine Vale didn't shoot him first. While that was possible, it didn't seem probable. Vale had kept a low-profile so far and if they were right, getting the watch wasn't her true end game. She wouldn't risk it all just for the sake of expediency. She'd try to swipe it later, just as they would.

It was also possible the watch was buried in the midst of hundreds of other artifacts. King Tut's tomb had thousands of things in it. If that were the case here, they'd have to come up with a way to beat Vale to it.

The last possibility was one Elizabeth didn't want to think about. What if the watch wasn't there at all? They would have to start over from square one and neither of them had any idea where the heck that square was.

"If you will stop here, please?" Henri said, bringing the chatter to a halt.

"These walls are quite unstable," he continued. "Please do not touch or disturb the bracing struts as we descend into the ante-chamber."

"How unstable?" Trevor Everett asked.

"If these were to give way," Henri said, waving his hands toward the broad support beams, "we would be crushed beyond recognition." He smiled. "So, do not touch them, eh?"

Trevor looked up at the rough ceiling of the tunnel and paled. "I don't know, darling. What's another dusty old tomb?"

His wife seemed to have the same idea. "Yes," she said. "You've seen one, you've seen them all.

"Quite." Trevor turned around. "We'll see you out there," he said, trying not to sound like a man who had just taken the chicken exit.

He and Constance shouldered past the others in the narrow corridor, nearly pushing people out of the way in their haste.

"Anyone else?" Henri asked.

Whiteside looked at his daughter.

"Don't be silly, papa," she said.

He smiled. "That's my girl," he said, but then cast a concerned look at the wooden beams. "But do be careful."

When no one else had any more objections, Henri continued down the sloping corridor to the doorway Elizabeth had seen on their first visit to the tomb. Remembering how that had gone, she made sure to walk in the middle of the path, as far away from the walls as she could.

"The ante-chamber itself appears quite safe." Henri stopped at the bottom of the corridor at the mouth of the doorway. He extended his arm. "Entrez."

One by one the group filed into the large chamber, perhaps fifteen by fifteen. There were no electric lamps, but two workers held aloft large lanterns bright enough to illuminate the brightly painted walls.

Elizabeth looked at the art, and when she turned, the back of her neck tingled with the undeniable sensation that she was being watched. She knew before she looked who it was. She glanced over and saw Vale simply watching her, a small smile on her lips.

Elizabeth looked away. She wasn't going to let her get into her head. Stay focused, Elizabeth, she told herself. Don't let her get to you.

"As you can see," Henri said. "The walls are quite elaborate. We thought at first this was the burial chamber."

He took one of the lanterns and lifted it to better light some of the detailed reliefs. "These are from the Book of Gates. It is a guide for the soul through the trials one must face to reach the next life."

"Each represents an hour of the sun's journey through the underworld during the night," Arthur said, pointing. "The Gate of Teka-Hra, and here the fifth hour, the Judgment of Osiris."

Each section was incredibly detailed with dozens and dozens of figures acting out parts in a complex play.

"These are beautiful, Henri," Diana said. "The colors are still so vivid."

"You thought this was the burial chamber, but..." Elizabeth asked.

Henri smiled and walked over to the far end of the room. "Until we found this." The light from his lamp lit another doorway and a dark corridor beyond.

They all gathered near.

"This is why we were delayed," he said. "It is as though the hand of God pushes down on this place. It was difficult to secure, as you can see."

The corridor had multiple protective struts and cross beams. At the end of the ten-foot tunnel was a doorway with two handles and a rope wound between them.

"This is the seal," Henri said, as he knelt down next to one of the handles and pointed at a wax blob formed over one of the ropes. "Unbroken for thousands of years."

His smiled. "Until today." He held out his hand and one of the workers handed him a small tool.

Butterflies finished their pre-flight checks in Elizabeth's stomach and took off as she and the others waited.

Carefully, Henri broke the seal, trying to preserve as much as he could, but it crumbled at his touch. He sighed and set to work on the rope.

It only took a few minutes, but the anticipation was agonizing. Finally, he unwound the ropes and gripped one of the handles. He nodded for one of his workers to take the other. They both braced their shoulders against the stone. "Un, deux, trois."

Together, they pushed the heavy doors forward. Elizabeth glanced up anxiously at the ceiling to see if any of the struts gave way, but it seemed solid enough. Once the doorway was opened, the first thing she noticed was the horrible stale air. It fled the chamber in a wave. She coughed and raised her hand to cover her mouth and nose and squinted to see into the darkness.

"Merde," Henri whispered.

Elizabeth didn't need a translator for that and craned her neck to see.

Henri took a deep breath and stepped into the empty chamber.

Like the outer chamber, the walls were filled with detailed reliefs, but there was nothing else. No golden thrones or ivory headrests. No royal beds, no chests filled with jewels and, worst of all, no sarcophagus. And no watch.

Elizabeth's heart sank and she and Simon shared a look of disappointment and frustration. They'd been hurtling toward this moment and it ended with a whimper instead of a bang.

Henri stood in the middle of the empty chamber, a look of such utter defeat on his face, it was all Elizabeth could do not to comfort him.

"You were right about this being for Akhenaten, Henri," Whiteside said. "These reliefs were designed for him and no other."

"And here's his cartouche," Christina added excitedly.

"Yes." The despondency in Henri's voice was palpable.

"It's still an amazing find," Diana said. "These paintings are priceless."

Henri forced a smile to his face and nodded. His eyes were downcast as he looked toward the doorway where Katherine Vale stood. "I am sorry, it is not what you hoped for."

Vale glanced at Simon and Elizabeth and her lips curled into a smile. "Isn't it?"

Elizabeth felt the usual chill that came with the Katherine Vale smile and watched as the woman nodded once to Henri and then left the room.

"What was that?" Elizabeth whispered to Simon.

He shook his head. "More theatrics."

Elizabeth looked around the chamber. Maybe there was a hidden panel or another door. After all, the one to this room had been hidden. She slowly walked the perimeter of the room looking for some sign, some unnatural edge, but she didn't find anything, although it was still very dark and she couldn't exactly look thoroughly without drawing attention.

She saw that Simon was doing the same thing as she was, and with the same success.

"Well," Henri said finally. He looked about to say more when he decided against it. With one last forlorn look around the empty chamber, he gave a curt order to one of his men. "Do not linger too long," he said. "The air is unfit."

With that he walked through the doorway and disappeared.

"Poor chap," Whiteside said. "I wish there'd been something. Anything really. Even just one thing."

CHAPTER THIRTY-THREE

ELIZABETH DID HER BEST to look casual, but knew the harder she tried the more awkward she looked. She leaned against one of the large columns and tried to look like she wasn't about to have kittens right there in the lobby of the Winter Palace hotel.

"He'll be here," Simon assured her, but he looked as anxious as he ever allowed himself to be in public.

She and Simon had spent most of the evening trying to figure out what the heck to do. The tomb was empty. Or at least, it looked empty. They all knew that looks could be deceiving though, and they had to be sure. They planned to meet Jack in the lobby at midnight and sneak back into the tomb for one more look.

Elizabeth looked at the grandfather clock in the corner. He was late.

With midnight come and gone and no Jack, Simon went off to find him. Elizabeth waited at the appointed spot in case he showed up while Simon was off looking for him.

She crossed and uncrossed her arms. Trying to look blasé was impossible. She decided to try sitting down instead and found a rattan chair nestled next to a large potted palm.

Despite the hour, the lobby was busy with people. The nightlife in Luxor centered around the Winter Palace and a few other posh hotels. Just as it had been in Cairo, the not-yet-jet set partied well into the night and early morning. Groups of revelers streamed in and out of the large front doors.

Elizabeth watched them a few minutes until she finally saw Simon heading toward her from across the lobby. But he was alone. He caught sight of her and quickened his pace, a deep frown on his face. In his haste, he bumped into a little man with a pencil mustache, nearly knocking him over. Simon apologized brusquely and hurried over to her.

Elizabeth stood up and met him half way.

"Not in his room," he said, his frustration plain on his face.

Elizabeth felt a lump settle into her stomach. If something happened to Jack....

"Damn it," Simon said under his breath.

"Let's give him a few more minutes," she said, leaving out the "and then we'll" part because she had no idea what that would be.

Simon nodded curtly and they lingered near the doorway. After a few incredibly long minutes, Jack appeared and Elizabeth let herself breathe again.

"I'm sorry I'm late," he said, holding up a hand to stave off the dressing down Simon had poised and ready. "I couldn't find Diana."

Simon grunted and ground his teeth, but didn't say anything more than, "We'll just have to go without her then."

Jack's eyes darted toward the lobby, clearly hoping to somehow see her appear there.

"I'm sure she's fine," Elizabeth said, hoping she sounded convincing.

Jack nodded again, unconvinced, and glanced once more around the lobby. "She can take care of herself," he said, but Elizabeth could hear the worry in his voice.

With an effort, he shook that off and looked to Simon, his focus entirely on the matter at hand. "Everything's ready."

"Good." Simon nodded his head toward the front doors. "Let's get this over with. Hassan's waiting."

"ARE YOU SURE YOU know the way?" Elizabeth whispered.

"We've driven it three times," Jack said. "I think we've got it."

They had been down the road three times now, but she couldn't remember the way if her life depended on it. She shook off that thought and hoped it wouldn't come to that.

She sat back in the carriage Hassan had hired and tried to pay attention to the route, but they were nearly there.

Hassan pulled the carriage up to a spot in a nearby ravine and they quietly climbed out.

"We'll have to walk the rest of the way," Jack said.

They'd suspected there might be a guard on duty. Even though the tomb was empty, it was still an important find.

The four of them walked swiftly, hugging the dark edges of the cliffs above them. The moon was bright and while they tried to be quiet, every footstep seemed to echo in the silence.

Before long, they came to the small wadi that held Henri's tomb. Jack peered around the edge as the others pressed themselves against the rocks. He nodded his head. "Clear."

He looked again and then started the dash across the open, moonlit ground toward the steps of the tomb. The others followed until they were all safely on the other side and standing at the entrance.

Hassan held out the two lanterns he'd been carrying. "Do not light them until you are inside," he cautioned.

Simon and Jack each took one. Hassan gave Elizabeth a small rucksack with a few small tools in it.

"I will stay here and keep watch," he continued. "Be quick and be safe."

Elizabeth squeezed his arm in thanks as they passed him and started down the steep stairs. Once they were a dozen feet inside the tomb and the darkness was nearly complete, Jack lit a match and they lifted the glass coverings to light the lanterns.

Simon went first, Elizabeth second with Jack behind her. They made their way through the first and second corridor until they reached the rough walls.

"Be careful," Simon said, needlessly.

Elizabeth had already almost caused a cave-in here, she wasn't looking for a repeat performance. She gathered her skirts close to her body and walked slowly and carefully down the steep sloping stairs.

They passed through the large outer chamber and finally made it into the smaller chamber at the dead end of the tomb. Both Jack and Simon held up their lanterns and quickly scanned the walls before setting them down near the middle of the floor. The room was small enough and the lanterns bright enough that they could see the entire room clearly.

"Jack, you take that wall, I'll take this one," Simon said. "Elizabeth, the back. Feel for any indentations, any seams, any anomaly. We'll search the floor and the ceilings next."

Elizabeth nodded and set to her task. She hated touching these beautiful frescoes, but they had no choice. Gently, she ran her fingers along the outlines and felt for anything out of the ordinary. The reliefs were very detailed making it slow going. The wall was fairly smooth beneath her fingertips. Occasionally, she could feel a chisel mark or a tiny bit of 3000-year-old paint would flake off. She would have to volunteer the rest of her life at a museum doing restorations to make up for this.

Her wall was divided into three large panels. The first showed Akhenaten and Nefertiti seated opposite each other as they held their three children. It was remarkably normal. The king held one of his daughters to kiss her while the others climbed all over their mother. It was something she expected to see at a mall not in a Pharaoh's tomb. It made these people who live millennia ago, so real, so human.

Elizabeth tried not to get caught up in the images and stick with the task at hand, but it was nearly impossible. She was in an ancient tomb and her imagination started to take flight, but she clipped its wings and forced herself to focus. The watch had to be here.

She moved on to the second panel, this one more formal with the King and his family offering something to the Aten. The giant sun disk hung above him, its rays reaching down toward him. She felt around the edges of the Aten disk, hope flaring in her chest, but it was just stone.

The Aten disk was repeated lower, smaller, but it wasn't a relief, just a painting. She ran her fingers over the smaller disk anyway.

"Show me," she whispered to it.

She waited for something magical to happen, but nothing did. "Open sesame?"

The walls didn't speak or move.

"What?" Simon said.

"Nothing." So much for Hollywood.

With a sigh, she continued exploring the outline of the Aten disk when something suddenly gave. She gasped as a bit of clay or plaster or whatever it was, fell away.

"Guys," she whispered, her heart beating just a bit faster with each passing second.

"Have you found something?" Simon asked as he came to her side.

Elizabeth traced the edges of the disk and more clay fell away. Something was embedded in the wall.

Jack brought one of the lanterns closer and as another bit of paint and plaster fell away, a glint of gold caught the light.

"Well, I'll be damned," he said.

Elizabeth turned to smile in triumph at Simon, but he'd gone to retrieve the chisel from their tools.

Carefully, he ran the tip of it around the edges of the disk until he could get a little leverage. With a few gentle pushes, he pried something out of the wall and it fell into his waiting hand. Elizabeth held her breath as he brushed the remaining paint and clay away until all that was left was a gold watch.

Elizabeth laughed, releasing pent up tension. "How about that?"

"Yes," a voice behind them said and Elizabeth's blood ran cold. "How about that?"

As Elizabeth started to turn, she saw Jack out of the corner of her eye reaching for his gun. She was vaguely aware of Simon dropping the chisel and doing the same thing, when a shot rang out, nearly deafening in the small chamber.

Instinct made her duck and cover, but not before she heard Jack grunt and saw him spin away from her. Dear God, he'd been shot. She looked back to see that a bullet had torn through his arm. His gun slipped from his fingers and clattered to the stone floor.

"Jack!" Elizabeth cried.

He groaned and heaved a few deep breaths to try to control the pain. Across the small room, Simon moved to point his gun.

"I would think twice about that if I were you, Mr. Cross," Katherine Vale said, as one of her henchmen leveled his gun at Simon's chest.

Simon had been too slow on the draw and was caught still trying to get his gun from his jacket pocket. And thank God he had. It was the only thing that kept him from being shot.

One of the four henchmen Vale had with her stepped past her in the tunnel and took Simon's gun and retrieved Jack's from the ground.

"Jack?" Elizabeth asked.

He squared his shoulders as best he could. "I'm all right."

But she could see from the pinched look on his face, he was far from that.

"I'll take that as well," Vale said, indicating the watch Simon tried to conceal in his fist.

One of the men took it from his hand.

A smug smile spread across Vale's faced. "And your grandfather's," she said. "I'd like to complete the set."

Simon took a deep breath, glanced over at Elizabeth and then reached into his vest pocket, but something was wrong. Elizabeth could see it in his body language.

"I seem to have misplaced it," Simon said, sounding pleased with himself, but she heard the tint of worry in his voice.

Vale's smile fell. "Search him," she commanded.

One of the men patted Simon down, but found nothing. Elizabeth's heart didn't know whether to sink at the thought they'd lost the watch or soar because Vale couldn't have it.

"Very clever," Vale said. "But I'll find it. I'll find them all."

Simon glanced over at Elizabeth, his expression worried and confused, but he quickly schooled his features. "You have what you came for," he said, his voice steady.

Vale laughed, savoring the flavor of the moment. "Like mice to cheese you came."

So, it had been a trap. Elizabeth's heart sunk even lower. They'd walked right into it. But why such a ruse? Apart from the loathing and wanting to see them eaten alive by dingoes, why not search the tomb herself? What game was she playing now?

"How did you know it was here?" Elizabeth asked.

Vale smiled. "How is it I know so many things you don't? Hmm?"

She looked at Elizabeth with what she must have thought was pity, but that was an emotion Katherine Vale wasn't capable of and her expression just looked pained.

"I will admit, I didn't know you'd be here. Egypt, of all places. I hoped, of course to find you. When they freed me from Bedlam, I had a very short list of things to do and you two," she said, her eyes glittering, "were very near the top."

Vale sighed dramatically. "I was worried for a while. You were so slow to catch on, despite my best efforts to leave a blazing trail here."

Elizabeth shook her head. She'd led them here? To this moment? To this place? She hazarded a glance at Simon and could see him working it through, seeing the pattern he hadn't seen before and knew he would beat himself up for having missed it.

Elizabeth slipped her hand into his and he looked at her, apology in his eyes. Elizabeth shook her head.

"So charming," Vale said, pulling their attention back to her. With a nod of her head, she indicated that she was ready to her men and they stepped forward. Elizabeth reached out and took hold of Jack's hand and held tighter to Simon's. She flinched, closing her eyes, ready to be killed.

"Oh," Vale said in delight. "I'm not going to shoot you, my dear."

She waited until Elizabeth opened her eyes and with a smile she tilted her head. The men picked up the lanterns and ushered them all out into the larger antechamber.

Once there, her men bound their wrists. Jack's arm was bleeding badly and he grunted in pain as the men wrenched it behind his back to bind his hands. Simon caught her eye briefly as he scanned the room for something to use against their captors.

Elizabeth's heart raced as the men tightened the ropes around her wrists. This was the second time she'd been tied up since they'd arrived in Egypt and she had a feeling this one wasn't going to end as well as the first. She joined Simon in a search for something, anything to help them, when she heard footsteps at the door to the outside corridor and turned to look.

"Oh, yes," Vale said.

Two men stepped into the chamber, a man dragged between them. They threw him onto the floor at Elizabeth's feet.

"Hassan!"

Vale looked down at him in disgust. "Got in my way."

Elizabeth swallowed her shame and guilt. When Vale and the others arrived without Hassan, she'd foolishly assumed he'd seen them coming and hidden. That he'd magically gotten away. Tears at her own naiveté stung her eyes as she looked down at him.

He was alive, but barely conscious. Blood ran down his face from a gash on his forehead as he rolled onto his back and blinked up at Elizabeth, his eyes struggling to focus.

"I'm sorry, Hassan," Elizabeth said.

He tried to speak, but couldn't manage it.

"Quite a little party," Vale said. "I'm just sorry your girlfriend couldn't be here," she added to Jack. "I don't like her."

"The feeling is mutual," Jack ground out between clenched teeth.

"She is a loose end I will snip off," Vale said with a laugh. "I will be having another party soon. Perhaps she can join that. I know your darling Christina will be there."

"Leave the girl out of it," Simon said.

"So noble, and yet so thoroughly ineffectual." Vale smiled. "I owe you a debt on that score. I was going to find any old virgin and you served me one on a silver platter. Knowing her death will be because of you is the icing on the cake."

Elizabeth felt sick. Was there anyone they hadn't dragged down with them?

"Please," Elizabeth said. "You don't have to do this. Any of this. Let us help you."

Vale paused and looked at her, her face set in animated shock.

"Help me?" she said with a laugh that didn't just border on insane it had permanent residence there. "Like you helped me in San Francisco?"

Elizabeth flinched.

Abruptly, unnaturally, Vale's laughter stopped. "Oh, no, my dear. I'm going to help *you* this time."

She waved her hand toward the doorway to the burial chamber and one of the men stepped forward toward Elizabeth. She tried to move away, but there was nowhere to go. He clamped his hand around her arms and jerked her forward. Despite herself, she cried out.

"Elizabeth," Simon said. He lunged forward, but was caught by one of Vale's men and held in place.

"You see there are many kinds of prisons," Vale said.

Elizabeth looked back at Simon, who was helpless as the henchmen held both him and Jack, while another dragged her to the mouth of the burial chamber. A darkened tunnel stretched out before her.

"This one's for you, my dear," Vale said and then made a show of looking down into the tunnel toward the burial chamber. "Although, I don't think it or you will last long."

Elizabeth's breath came faster and faster now as she started to realize what Vale was going to do.

"No," she said, struggling against the man who held her.

"Please, don't," Simon begged, but it only seemed to make Vale happier.

"Please don't what? Bury my wife alive?"

Elizabeth gasped as she said it. Somehow she'd known that was Vale's plan, but to hear it. Her breath hitched again as she turned to Simon. His eyes were wild with desperation. His breath came in quick, short bursts as he struggled.

Vale pursed her lips and looked critically back at Elizabeth's room. "Perhaps six or seven hours of oxygen. Less if you struggle? That is if it doesn't crush you, of course."

"Please," Simon repeated.

Elizabeth pulled against the man that held her. "Simon."

"You will have a choice, Mister Cross," Vale said.

Simon pulled his attention away from Elizabeth to Vale.

"Once we leave," she continued, "we will collapse this corridor to the outside." She gestured to the main tunnel.

She looked around the larger antechamber and adjoining tunnel, gauging the size. "You could, perhaps, dig your way out, but of course, then your wife would die. But if you choose to dig your way in, you will use the oxygen you have in here and not have enough time to dig your way out. Save yourself and your friends, or condemn them all to death with your selfishness."

She smiled almost dreamily. "Either way, she will be dead and you, even if you live, you will be a hollow man."

Elizabeth looked at Simon. "Don't listen to her. If you can save yourself—"

Simon shook his head.

"Isn't that romantic?" Vale said. "And do not think help from the outside will come in time. You will all probably be dead before the dawn, long before anyone even knows you're missing."

"You're sick," Jack said.

Vale ignored him and nodded toward one of her men who started to drag Elizabeth down the tunnel and into the burial chamber. Her burial chamber.

Elizabeth protested and dug her heels in, but she was no match for his strength. She turned her head just in time to get one last glimpse of Simon and the pain and agony on his face etched into her memory.

She felt a swell of panic and called out to him. She could hear him and Jack as they struggled. Her mind raced, but she couldn't find a way out. The four walls already seemed to be closing in on her, the air already feeling thinner in her lungs.

"Elizabeth!" Simon cried.

"I'm all right," she called out, even though she wasn't.

She heard his breath catch.

"We'll find a way," she said and in that instant, believed it. As insane as it was, she believed it.

The man who'd held her left the chamber and Vale stood back as two of her men came forward with a huge sledgehammer.

For some reason, Elizabeth thought there'd be a pause. That he'd lift the hammer and Vale would tease them with a chance at their final goodbyes, but it didn't happen that way. The man swung the hammer and one of the struts shifted.

She could hear Simon calling out to her between blows, between the sound of the bits of dust and rock as they rained down into the little corridor.

"Simon!"

She started forward, thinking maybe she could make a run for it. Somehow. She had to do something. She couldn't just stand there and let it happen. She took two steps closer to the opening and the man kept swinging.

It was happening. It was really happening. She stood in the middle of the room, as the blows crashed into the wood and stone. More rock started to fall and she froze in place. Bits of the ceiling in her chamber fell and she backed away.

She heard Simon calling out to her and she closed her eyes, filling her head with thoughts of him.

"We'll find a way," she whispered. Simon's last words to her were lost as the ceiling of the tunnel finally gave way and the stone curtain fell, thunderous and final.

CHAPTER THIRTY-FOUR

Simon called out to Elizabeth again and again as the stones fell, trapping her inside the tomb. His chest heaved with effort and emotion as he tried to go to her, to stop this, to save her. It was all in vain.

His heart lurched in his chest as the cascade of rocks came to an end. Had she been crushed? Was she alive and hurt and calling out to him in the darkness? His breath, when it finally came, was only short rage-filled bursts.

Vale walked up to him and he strained against the two men that held him.

"Such a painful decision," she said. He flinched away from the cold hand she put on his cheek, but kept his eyes fixed on hers, promising revenge if he ever found a way out of this. She gave his cheek a light pat. "But that's what love gets you."

She nodded to her men who shoved Jack and Simon away. Jack took a step toward her, but a gun leveled at his chest stopped him.

Then, Vale and her men left, taking the two lanterns, their only source of light, with them.

She turned back, the glow from the lantern behind her making her no more than a dark specter in the doorway. "I wouldn't try and follow us. Dynamite is so unpredictable."

With one last laugh of triumph, she and her men left. Simon edged forward, but Jack stopped him. "We need to get back, away from the doorway."

The light from the lamps faded as she and her men climbed up the tunnel. Simon turned his back on it all and stood staring at the mountain of rocks that separated him from his wife. If he started digging now....

He heard Jack's voice, urgent with some warning, but he hardly cared. The room grew darker and darker and with each second Elizabeth felt further and further away. He could barely breathe, barely think. Get ahold of yourself, Cross, he berated himself. What can you do?

"Simon," Jack said urgently. "Get back."

Jack nudged him with his shoulder. "Cross," he said, his voice tense. "Get back. We gotta move."

He hardly took notice, but the intensity in Jack's eyes pulled him into the moment.

"Over there," Jack said, nodding to the back wall. Simon felt himself nod and watched, mute, as Jack made his way to Hassan and knelt down. "Can you move?" Jack asked.

Hassan nodded slowly, his eyes blinking, trying to regain his senses.

"Get away from the door," Jack said. "Over here."

Their hands still bound behind them, Jack and Simon moved to the back wall. Hassan got to his feet just as the room fell into total darkness.

Blind now, Simon turned his head toward the chamber that held Elizabeth and tried to force himself to focus. She heard him, he knew. She would have moved back. He believed it. He had to believe it.

"Eliz—"

An earth-shattering explosion swallowed the tomb. Simon could feel a hot gust of wind push against him. He crouched down trying to protect himself as best he could as dust and small rocks flew like shrapnel into the room. Small shards of rock and pebbles sliced into his skin, but the pain meant nothing.

The blast echoed briefly, followed by the thunderous roar of tons of rock collapsing the outer tunnel, sealing them all inside.

Simon coughed as dust filled the air. The rumbling reverberated in the tomb, made louder somehow by the dark. Finally, it came to a stop, but there was no silence. Simon could still hear the ringing of the explosion in his head. All other noise was muffled, dampened as if they'd suddenly been submerged in water.

The deep, but distant timbre of Jack's voice found its way through the murkiness that clogged his ears and thoughts.

"Everyone all right?"

Simon barely heard him and strained to listen for Elizabeth. He heard Hassan instead.

"I have been better."

"Simon?" Jack asked, his body bumping against Simon's in the dark. "You okay?"

Simon didn't answer at first, couldn't answer. He finally caught his breath. "We need to dig," was all he could say.

There was a pause and then Jack said, "Damn right."

Slowly, the ringing began to subside, leaving a dull throb behind. At least he could hear again, Simon thought. If only he could see.

"I will untie you," Hassan said, his voice weak and breathy.

It seemed to take forever. Every second was one breath less for Elizabeth.

"Hurry," Simon bit out.

Finally, Hassan untied his hands and Simon felt his way along the wall until the smooth stone became uneven and jagged—the collapsed tunnel.

He called out for Elizabeth, hoping somehow she could hear him. He waited for her answer, but none came. It didn't mean anything, he told himself. There was too much rock. She couldn't hear him. Not yet.

His hands grasped stones, any stone, and started to pull them away from the pile. They slid down, crashing into his legs, cutting into them, but he didn't care. He felt for more rocks and pulled at them in the darkness. Elizabeth was alive, he told himself. She had to be alive. And he would find her.

It was a Hobson's choice. He would die trying to get to Elizabeth. He would do that again and again without a second's hesitation. Except now, it wasn't just his life in the balance.

It would take their collective strength to dig their way to the outside. If it was even possible. Even if it were, he wouldn't, couldn't abandon Elizabeth, even if it meant only sharing a few more minutes together. But his decision wasn't just a death sentence for him, but for them all.

"Simon," Jack said, his voice loud and close.

Simon paused for a moment and rested his head on the rocks. He knew Jack was going to tell him it was pointless. That she was probably already dead. That the only logical thing to do was to try to dig their way out, not in. That he was thinking only of himself.

"I have to find her," Simon said softly, hoping Jack could find a way to understand, to forgive him.

For a moment the only sound in the room was their breathing, precious oxygen disappearing with each inhalation and lethal carbon dioxide taking its place.

As Simon reached for another stone, he heard the sound of a match being lit. He turned and Jack held out his hand. One tiny flame in the darkness between them.

"*We* will find her," Jack said.

Simon's throat choked and he fought back the emotion that was already nearly pulling him under.

Hassan stepped forward and tipped a small taper candle toward the flame. The wick caught fire and the room glowed with light. "Trust in Hassan."

Simon looked at both men, humbled by their sacrifice. There were no words. All he could do was numbly nod his thanks.

Jack worked his injured arm and winced. Simon looked at him, worried.

"Bigger things to worry about," Jack said, nodding his head toward the enormous pile of rocks that separated them from Elizabeth.

"We need to conserve as much oxygen as we can," Jack continued. "Try to keep your breathing slow and steady."

He stepped forward and ran his hands over the rocks. "We should work along the top, try to clear a narrow path to her on top of the rest."

Simon looked at the upper edge of the doorway. That made sense and he should have realized it. He had to try to slow down, to think. He would have to make smart decisions, if he was going to reach her in time.

"Right," he said, thankful for Jack's clear head.

Jack moved back to Hassan and tilted the other man's head back. "That's nasty looking," he said, noting the gash on Hassan's forehead. "But it looks worse than it is, I think."

It was a lie, but they all pretended it wasn't.

"It'll be tight up there as we dig and, well, no offense..." Jack said, his voice trailing off as he looked at Hassan's large middle.

"I will work over there," Hassan said, gesturing to the blocked doorway to the outside. "And do what I can."

"All right," Jack said. "Just try not breathe too much." He looked around their chamber. "We probably don't have much more than eight or ten hours ourselves."

Hassan looked up anxiously around the room, as if he could see the air itself disappearing in front of his eyes.

"Everything will be all right," Hassan said to himself as he dripped wax onto the floor to secure the candle. He pulled two more from his belt and set them down. "Trust in Hassan."

Jack turned back to Simon, giving him a curt nod. "We'll get out. Diana knows we're here. Help will come."

Simon didn't remind him that Diana could well be dead already and if she wasn't, odds were Vale would see to it that she would be. Help would not be coming. Not in time, anyway.

Pushing that thought aside, Simon turned back to the mountain of stone they had to move. The tunnel had to be at least three feet wide, eight feet high and ten feet long. Digging their way to Elizabeth would mean moving tons of rock.

Jack started to reach out for a stone and Simon could see the blood that covered the back of his hand. His wound was bleeding badly.

"We need to tend to that arm first," Simon said. It took all of his willpower to turn away from the pile of rocks and toward Jack. "You won't be any help to anyone if you pass out."

Jack hesitated and then reluctantly nodded.

Simon felt stronger somehow in that moment. Having his good sense back, perhaps. Jack sucked in a painful breath as he slipped off his jacket. Simon tore away his ripped shirtsleeve to create a makeshift bandage. The bullet had passed all the way through, which was good, but he'd already lost a lot of blood.

Simon wrapped the bandage around Jack's arm and tied if off. It wasn't much, but it would have to do. Staring at this man who was giving him his life, who had saved them time and again, Simon struggled. What could he say to a man who was willing to do what Jack was?

It was insufficient and not worthy, but all he had to offer. "Thank you."

Jack smiled in understanding. "We're not dead yet." He looked up at the rocks. "We'll find a way."

"You sound like Elizabeth," Simon said, almost as a reflex.

Jack nodded and Simon could see him swallow his own emotion. "Let's get to work."

They made good progress at first, clearing what seemed to be a ton of stone, maybe it was. Large rocks and small, gravel and boulders had to be lifted and shifted away.

With discarded rocks and debris, they'd built up a set of steps so they could climb up high enough to work along the ceiling of the tunnel. They were about two feet in when more rocks collapsed down into the cavern they'd created. Simon barely had time to save his arm from being crushed.

All they could do was start again and again. Time slowly ticked away. The small candles Hassan had brought probably had three hours of burn time each, if they were lucky. The first was more than halfway gone. They'd been digging for nearly two hours, and they were barely three feet in.

If they kept this pace, they'd break through in just over six hours, at the very edge of Elizabeth's air supply. That was if she'd stayed calm, hadn't tried to dig herself out.

But he knew his wife. Elizabeth was incapable of sitting by and waiting. If she was alive, and he had to believe she was, she was digging, wasting her air, wasting her energy. Simon's heart clenched at the thought and he redoubled his efforts. His muscles burned and his hands were raw, but he kept on.

Jack had forced them all to pace themselves, to take breaks. They were short but excruciating. When the last one was over, it was Simon's turn in the tunnel and he crawled on top of the jagged rocks, and pulled himself forward. Carefully, he picked rocks from darkness and placed those he could into Jack's discarded jacket. He tied the arms to create a makeshift basket and passed it back to Jack, who emptied and handed it back to repeat the process over and over again.

It was slow and painful, but they made progress. Simon fixated on that. With each inch, he was closer to Elizabeth.

The exchange, though, became more difficult the deeper they went. Simon was fully inside the tunnel now and Jack had to crawl in a bit as well to reach the jacket and larger stones before crawling out backward to dump them.

More debris dislodged as they went, a large stone falling and cutting into the back of Simon's leg, but he didn't stop, they didn't stop.

Hour after hour, they dug and clawed their way closer to Elizabeth.

Simon reached for a large stone, wedged between two others. He pulled and pushed, but couldn't get it to move. He swore at it, feeling his anger rising, feeling it feed the hopelessness he'd somehow kept hidden. How could they have come so far to be stopped now?

He braced his legs against the side of the tunnel and pushed for all he was worth, only stopping when he felt lightheaded from the effort.

"Dammit!"

"What's wrong?" Jack asked.

"I can't—" Simon stopped. He thought he heard something.

"You can't—"

Simon's heart skipped a beat. "Quiet!"

Simon listened again, but all he could hear was Hassan's rocks tumbling down to the chamber floor. "Tell him to stop!"

Jack did and Simon closed his eyes and listened again.

"Simon?"

It was faint, barely a whisper, but it was *her*.

"Elizabeth!"

"You can hear her?" Jack asked.

"Yes," he said, his heart thrumming wildly in his chest. Alive. She was alive. "Elizabeth, we're coming!"

He listened again, but there was no sound. For a moment, he wondered if he'd dreamt it, if he needed to hear her so badly he'd imagined hearing her. But he put that aside and believed.

She was alive.

"We're coming," he called out and redoubled his effort.

Buoyed by the sound of her voice, he found a reservoir of strength and dislodged the large rock. Slowly, he rolled it back toward Jack. The last few feet were a blur. Every part of his body ached. His head was splitting. His hands were cut. And all he could think of was her.

He reached for a stone and it gave way under his hand. He heard it fall, tumbling down, away from him.

"Elizabeth!"

There was no reply and his heart nearly stopped.

He crawled forward and pushed more rocks. He inched his way to the opening and tried to see in the darkness.

"Elizabeth!"

Nothing. He refused to accept it.

"Elizabeth!"

Nothing. And then...

"Simon."

His breath caught and he pulled himself forward and nearly fell out of the hole he'd created. He could hear Jack close behind him.

"Where are you?" Simon asked as he tried to make his way out of the tunnel and into her chamber.

"Simon."

Her voice was faint and weak. But it *was*. It so gloriously *was*.

He could hear Jack above him, and then the spark of a match lit the small room. He squinted in the dim light and then he saw her.

Elizabeth slumped against the far wall, just under the spot where they'd found the watch, the chisel he'd dropped earlier resting in her hand.

Simon rushed to her side. She was barely breathing. Her chest rose and fell in short bursts, but she was alive. He let out a sob and pulled her up and into his arms.

Tears stung his eyes as he crushed her to him. Dear God, she was alive.

"I knew you'd come," she said.

He laughed and eased her away to see her face in the dim light.

"I will *always* come for you."

He kissed her forehead and pulled her back against him.

"Come on," Jack said, as his match burned itself out and he lit another.

Simon helped Elizabeth the short distance to the tunnel. She was nearly too weak to stand and he lifted her up to Jack, who grabbed her with his good arm.

"Jack," she said, sounding far away.

His voice was raw with effort, but reassuring. "Hey, kid." He shook the match out. "Let's get the heck out of here."

Simon helped Elizabeth up into the tunnel and followed close behind. The pile of rocks shifted beneath him as he climbed up to the hole, but he managed to just get on top of them. He could see Elizabeth's silhouette at the end of the tunnel as she climbed out, bathed in the glow of the candlelight.

Simon crawled through the tunnel, feeling bits collapse behind him as he went. Just a few more feet...

Whoever the powers that be were, they listened, and he crawled out safely into the chamber. Elizabeth, who had been holding onto Jack for support, took two wobbly steps toward him. Simon caught her and pulled her to him. She was crying now, sobbing into his chest. He held her tightly, dipped his head down and let his own tears come.

CHAPTER THIRTY-FIVE

THEY HELD EACH OTHER for a few minutes before Elizabeth sniffled and eased back a little. She could finally breathe again and not just because she had air, but because she had him.

She ran her hands over Simon's stubbled cheeks and wiped the dirt and tears away. Pushing herself up on tiptoe, she kissed him. He pulled her to him again and held her tightly.

During all the time she'd been trapped, she'd never stopped believing she'd see him again. Her heart never doubted.

When the kiss ended she could see him, really see him for the first time. See the love and the pain in his eyes. Every minute of the agony he'd endured etched on his face.

"Elizabeth."

The way he said her name always told her everything she needed to know. And this time, she could hear the sorrow in it. She turned and saw Jack and Hassan. The same mix of love and sorrow, triumph and defeat was in their eyes.

And then she realized why.

The passageway to the outside was still filled with rocks. They'd barely made a dent in it and yet they'd moved heaven and earth to get to her. They'd all sacrificed themselves *for her*.

If only they had the watch. If they had that, they could use her key to escape the same way they did in London, but without it...

She bit her lip to keep more tears from coming, but they came anyway. She slipped from Simon's arms and hugged Jack.

"Thank you."

She knelt down and kissed Hassan's cheek. He smiled weakly at her, barely conscious.

Elizabeth stood up and turned back to look at these three men. These wonderful men and swore that it couldn't end this way. It wouldn't.

She turned away from them then and began to dig.

Simon came up behind her and stilled her hands. "It's too much," he said.

He, all of them, had used everything they had to get to her. They were beyond exhausted. Jack was injured and Hassan couldn't even stand.

Simon nodded toward the candle on the ground. "That's the last one. When it goes out..."

She didn't need to hear the rest of the sentence to know what it was. When it burns out, so do we.

She refused to accept that. "I haven't done anything for the last six hours except sit there and wait. I'll dig."

"There just isn't time, Elizabeth" Jack said. "It's impossible."

Elizabeth tossed another rock aside. "That's never stopped us before."

She would not go out without a fight. If they were too tired to fight anymore, she would do it for them.

Elizabeth grabbed another rock and then another. And then Simon and Jack joined her.

They dug and dug, but every hole they made was filled with falling rock. The tunnel was on a slant and every time they moved something at the bottom, something from the top slid down to fill the gap. But Elizabeth didn't stop digging, until nearly two hours later when she felt the same shortness of breath she'd felt inside the burial chamber.

The candle's flame flickered. It was guttering out and so were they.

The rocks were almost too heavy to move now, or she was too weak to move them.

She laid her head down on her arm to rest.

"Elizabeth," Simon said from behind her.

She lifted her head up, her mind getting fuzzy. She tried to grab another stone, but couldn't.

"Just a short break," she said and Simon helped her climb down from her perch inside the tunnel. Slowly, they moved over to the wall where Jack and Hassan sat leaning and joined them.

Her chest rose and fell quickly. She could only get shallow breaths now. Simon put his arm around her and she leaned into his side. Reaching out with her hand, she felt Jack's and held it.

"Just a few minutes," she said between catching breaths. Her eyes felt heavier and heavier, until she couldn't keep them open anymore.

Then she was in a dream. She and Simon were sitting at home on the sofa. She was in his arms and a fire crackled in the fireplace. In her dream, she closed her eyes content to drift off and then, suddenly, there were voices and noises and lights.

And then someone slapped her. She barely felt it until it came again. The sting in her cheeks roused her and she opened her eyes.

"Dieu merci."

Henri smiled down at her. "Are you all right?"

In a rush, the last day came back to her. "Am I dead?"

He laughed and shook his head, before slapping Simon's cheek with the back of his hand. "*Réveillez!*"

Simon's head lolled to the side and for a split second Elizabeth thought he was dead.

"Simon?" She gripped his shirt and shook him.

Henri slapped him again, harder.

Her heart leapt into her throat until, finally, he groaned. With a relieved sob, Elizabeth put her hand on his chest and felt its rise and fall. Even before he was fully conscious his hand sought hers.

The room was a blur of activity. Diana was kneeling in front of Jack and Hassan. Men, maybe a half a dozen, worked like mad on the tunnel entrance, shifting rocks quickly and efficiently. She could hear the voices of even more men in the tunnel.

"Thought that crazy woman...had killed you," Jack said to Diana.

Diana grinned and put her hand to his cheek. "Oh, she tried. But Alexi and his men. Let's just say I owe them one."

"It seems," Simon said, finding his breath. "We owe you...one."

Did they ever, Elizabeth thought. She meant to say it out loud, but she didn't have the energy and could only nod in agreement.

Diana's smile broadened. "Sorry we cut it so close."

"I had no idea anything like this... " Henri said and shook his head.

Elizabeth managed a weak smile for him.

Diana barked some order at the men before turning back to them. "We'll have you out in a jiff."

A man brought them two goat skins of water. He helped Hassan drink some before handing it to Jack. Elizabeth took a few sips before passing hers to Simon.

"I came back to the hotel," Diana said. "And when you weren't there, I knew something was wrong. I thought you sneaked back, so I came here and saw the cave-in."

"Thank you," Elizabeth said.

"Thank Henri," Diana said. "I went back for help. I don't know how he found all of these men, but without them..."

Elizabeth knew there was no way she could ever thank or repay any of these people enough.

Simon took his arm from around Elizabeth and held out his hand to Henri. "Thank you. Both of you. Merci."

Jouvet smiled as he shook Simon's hand. Instead of letting go though, he stood and helped Simon to stand.

"What about Christina?" Elizabeth asked, wobbling a bit and grateful for Simon's help. "Is she all right?"

Diana cocked her head to the side. "What do you mean?"

Elizabeth glanced over at Simon. They both looked over at Jack and Hassan, both of whom were unsteady on their feet and in dire need of a doctor.

"We'll explain it on the way," Simon said. "And hope we're not too late."

THE MORNING SUN WAS painfully bright and Elizabeth shielded her eyes as she watched Hassan being put on a stretcher and taken to a local hospital. She'd made Henri promise to look after him. Still fresh with guilt, he gladly obliged and swore that Hassan would be well taken care of. He would see to it himself.

"You'll all need a doctor," Diana said, her brow wrinkled in concern. "Inhaling all that dust alone—"

She was probably right, Elizabeth realized, but there wasn't time to waste. She expected Simon to agree with Diana, but he cut her off instead with a weary hand.

"We'll be fine. Hassan and Jack, perhaps, but Elizabeth and you and I have more important things to worry about."

"My arm can wait," Jack said. "Let's get going."

As they raced back to the hotel, they explained to Diana what had happened. Exhausted, but pushed on by worry for Christina, they hurried up to the Whiteside's room as soon as they reached the Winter Palace.

Diana knocked loudly on the door. "Arthur?"

The door opened almost instantly. Whiteside's eyes were wide with fear and hope. "Diana! Is she with you?" He moved her aside to see for himself.

"No, Arthur," Diana said as she put an arm around Whiteside. "I'm afraid she's not."

"She must have run off with that boy," Whiteside said angrily as he strode back into his suite. "When I get my hands on him..."

Hope flared in Elizabeth's heart. She hadn't thought of that. Maybe they had run off together before Vale got to her.

"Did you try Ahmed's room?" Elizabeth asked as they followed Whiteside into his suite.

"Of course, I did," Whiteside bit out and then turned back and shook his head in apology, but it died on his lips as he took in their appearances. "What in the name of God happened to you lot?"

"Long story," Diana said, as she started back for the door. "Let me go see what I can find out and get a doctor."

"A doctor?"

She nodded her head toward Jack.

"Good Lord!" Whiteside cried.

"A few more minutes won't kill me," Jack said to Diana before turning to Arthur. "When did you see last see Christina?"

Whiteside lingered in the middle of the room and ran a hand through his hair. "Uhm, last night. She was gone when I got up this morning. I thought she'd gone for a walk."

He looked helplessly at the others. "She does that sometimes, t-to draw."

Jack pointed to a set of doors. "Is that her room?"

Whiteside nodded. "Do you think something's happened to her?"

Jack's eyes slid to Simon's briefly, but his expression remained neutral and he gestured to the door. "May I?"

Arthur spluttered out his permission and Jack disappeared into Christina's room.

Diana went to his side. "Why don't you sit down, Arthur?"

He looked at her quizzically and then with growing worry. "What's happened? What do you know?"

"Sit down," she repeated.

He did and they began to tell him about Katherine Vale and what they knew of her plans.

"But why? Why would she take her?" Whiteside said.

Elizabeth looked at Simon. How could they tell him what Vale had said? It would kill him.

Jack came back in and everyone turned to him, hopeful he'd found something, but he shook his head.

"Arthur," Simon said kindly, as he walked over to sit opposite him. Elizabeth could see the effort even such a simple thing took. His clothes were torn and filthy. His hands raw and bloodied, but he pulled a chair close and sat down next to Whiteside. Choosing his words carefully, but not sugar-coating anything, Simon told him what Vale had told them about her plans for Christina.

Whiteside paled visibly and stammered denials.

"Sacrifice? That's madness."

"It is," Simon agreed.

"But..." Whiteside choked out. He looked to Diana. "You can't be serious."

Diana sat down on the edge of the coffee table and put her hand on Whiteside's knee. "We'll find her, Arthur." She looked over at the rest of them. "We'll find her."

CHAPTER THIRTY-SIX

ELIZABETH COULD HEAR THE changes in the way the water fell as Simon moved inside the shower. The curtain was closed, but she knew dirt and sand and blood mixed at his feet before swirling toward the drain. She'd seen some of it herself when she'd showered and knew it would be far worse for him. His hands and legs had dozens of cuts from the explosion and the jagged edges of the rocks he'd spent hours moving.

Elizabeth had stayed in the bathroom with him as he showered. He hadn't asked her to, but she knew he would need her close for a while. She tried not to think about how badly she needed to stay close to him.

She busied herself by brushing her hair and going through the first aid supplies they'd procured from the hotel doctor. Despite their protests and arguments, Diana had practically forced them to go to their room to clean up and change. Jack's arm was finally being seen to and Diana promised to stay with Arthur to discuss Christina's disappearance with the police. For all the good that would do.

The police were out of their league when it came to someone like Katherine Vale. That was if they even believed the story.

She and Simon wanted to talk to the hotel staff, but Diana had rightly pointed out that they would get more questions than answers in their current state. They'd finally relented and gone to their suite, but as soon as they'd entered the relative safety and quiet it provided, Elizabeth felt her control slip.

She'd held it together so far and she wasn't going to lose it now. They couldn't afford for her to.

She let out a deep breath and looked at herself in the mirror. She looked like hell, but she was alive. They were all alive. That was what mattered. The rest of it could be dealt with later with expensive therapy sessions and a long, ugly cry, but not now. Now, she had to focus on helping Christina.

The thought of Christina with Vale made Elizabeth's stomach drop. And it was all their fault. Taking her was just another twisted part of Vale's revenge on them. And they had no idea where they were or how to find them.

But they would, she told herself. She had to stay focused on that.

She pushed out a long breath. Keeping it together was getting harder by the minute. She could see the shower behind her and noticed that the sound of the water wasn't changing anymore. Simon wasn't moving.

"Everything all right in there?" she asked, wondering if he hadn't fallen asleep on his feet.

There was no answer.

"Simon?"

She could hear him clear his throat and start moving again. "Almost finished."

"Okay," she said, giving him his privacy.

Despite being the most passionate man she'd ever known, Simon was still a man, and an Englishman to boot. Vulnerability was not something he showed easily and she knew that this experience had left more than the skin of his hands raw and aching.

After a few more minutes, Simon turned off the taps and stepped out of the shower. The cuts and bruises looked better than they had before. Elizabeth treated them with iodine and bandaged them.

"Not too bad, all in all," Elizabeth said as she finished the last of them and helped him on with his robe.

As he tied the belt, she started into the bedroom. "I think we should—"

Simon caught her arm and she turned back. She waited for him to say something, but he just stared at her. His eyes, still haunted, fixed on hers. In the silence, they spoke volumes. His hands gently ran up her arms to her shoulders as he reassured himself she was real and alive.

He let out a short, hitched breath and Elizabeth stepped forward and hugged him. The tenuous grip she had on her emotions was sure to fail if Simon lost it. He pulled her tightly against him, his arms wrapping all the way around her, but she was holding him. For a moment, they both stood on the edge. She could hear his heart racing in his chest, feel the raggedness of his breath as he struggled.

Eventually, he eased back and looked down at her. He shook his head and let out a sigh.

Tears burned the back of her throat, but she wouldn't let them out. She swallowed hard and felt her traitorous chin begin to wobble.

"We made it," she reminded him, her voice breaking. "We're here."

Slowly, he nodded and caressed her cheek.

Elizabeth forced herself not to cry. She was teetering on the edge and managed a tremulous smile before easing out of his arms.

"Elizabeth—"

"We should start with the front desk," she said, moving into the bedroom.

She walked over to their trunk and started digging for fresh clothes. She felt Simon come up behind her.

He gently placed his hands on her arms. "Elizabeth."

She turned around, smiled through her tears and shook her head. "I'm fine."

He crooked his finger and lifted her chin.

"I will be," she said. "Right now, though, we've got to find Christina."

He stared at her for a long moment, and she silently asked him not to push. Not now.

Finally, he nodded. "We will."

Grateful he was willing to let her do this her own way, she turned back to finding fresh underthings.

Simon took the ones she offered and found a fresh shirt. He walked over to the bed where she'd laid out another suit.

Elizabeth pushed out a deep, cleansing breath. "Right," she said and felt herself begin to settle.

Simon slipped on his boxers and pants and shed his robe. Sitting down in one of the chairs, he started to put on the socks she'd given him when he stopped. "I'm sorry about the watch; I don't know how I lost it."

Elizabeth brought over his shoes. "Maybe it's a good thing you did."

Simon shook his head. "I don't see how that's possible."

She set the shoes down next to his chair. "If you hadn't, *she'd* have it now."

Simon grunted, unassuaged and then groaned slightly as he gingerly leaned back in his chair. "Either way, we're trapped here without it."

Elizabeth found her own shoes and sat down on the edge of a trunk at the end of the bed. "I've been thinking about that. We can retrace our steps. It's got to be here somewhere."

"And if we don't find it?"

"Cable Teddy?"

Simon sat forward. "Fiske?"

"Unless you know another watchmaker." Elizabeth buckled the clasp to her shoes. "He might still be in San Francisco. And if he isn't, maybe the Eldridges or Max know where we can find him."

"Assuming they're still there and alive," Simon said as he slipped on his shoes. "It has been fourteen years."

Elizabeth nodded. Max was a world traveler; he could be anywhere. And the Eldridges weren't exactly spring chickens.

Simon tilted his head to the side. "It's a good thought," he said and then tied the laces to his shoes.

Elizabeth stared down at Simon's abraded knuckles, signs of his fight. And, she knew they weren't finished fighting yet. "Where do you think she's gone?"

Simon sighed and straightened. He shook his head. "Poor Arthur."

Elizabeth stood and walked over to stand in front of him. "We'll find her. And the watch."

He chuckled. "An optimist to the very end."

Elizabeth laughed with him, but his words were truer than he knew. She hadn't given up hope in the tomb and she sure as heck wasn't going to give up now.

"One thing I know," she said. "We won't find either in here."

She held out her hand. Simon took hold of it, kissed it, and then stood.

"Right."

They went back to Whiteside's suite and she could see the hope and then the disappointment in Arthur's eyes as they came in but didn't have Christina with them. As Elizabeth had feared, the police were of little help. They'd gone to the house Vale had rented only to find it empty.

Jack and Diana made a few inquiries themselves, but no one seemed to have the slightest idea where she'd gone, including Ahmed. They'd found him in the hotel lobby. When Christina hadn't shown for their arranged breakfast, Ahmed had gone looking for her, and only just returned. After learning Christina was missing, he'd tried to help by speaking with the local authorities. Maybe a native Egyptian, and one from a wealthy family, would hopefully have better luck than Jack and Diana had.

But, Elizabeth thought, judging from the way Diana chewed on her thumbnail, they didn't hold out much hope.

Arthur Whiteside sat in his chair and rubbed his temple absently.

"Maybe we should take a look at Vale's house ourselves," Jack suggested. "Police could have missed something."

"That's not a bad idea," Diana said as she sat down next to him. "I don't think they believed a word we said about the cult."

"That," Arthur said. "I...I've been thinking about that. The cult."

"Arthur, don't—" Diana said.

He held up a finger to stop her. "The Cult of Sekhmet. There were several festivals that were important to them. The Purifying Flame, the Time of Offerings and the Feast. This month, Tybi, is the start of Peret, a very important time for the goddess. If this," his voice broke here and he cleared his throat, "person has my daughter and is planning some sort of sacrifice, it makes sense that it would be on one of those sacred days."

He looked up hopefully. "Cults are very particular about those things, you understand."

"Yes," Simon said. "The power of a sacred time. When are, were these festivals?"

"I'd have to do some calculations to be sure, but late November?"

"Right about now," Elizabeth said, hoping now was a few days away.

Whiteside's face paled. "Yes."

"What about a place? Is there somewhere in particular they might...perform this ritual?"

Arthur frowned. "Most of the temples of Sekhmet have been destroyed by now. There is a small one in Karnak."

"Too public," Simon said. "The book you gave me said something about Memphis, I think."

"Yes, that was a focal point, but not at first," Arthur said, obviously feeling more steady on academic ground. "The cult was centered in Leontopolis, north of Cairo before it was moved to Itjtawy near Fayoum, but there's so few buildings of note left there now. Then it was moved to Memphis. It's all conflated a bit with Ptah, but..." His voice trailed off. "How can we know which Vale might choose or if she'd choose any?"

Jack sat forward. "The stuff we found in her house. Was there anything there that might help us narrow it down?"

Whiteside's brow knit together as he thought.

"What about the dagger, Arthur?" Diana said. "The design, that's New Kingdom, isn't it?"

He nodded. "It could be. Perhaps something Amenhotep's priests used." Arthur hmm'd at something, hope stirring. "Amenhotep's reign did begin in Memphis." Then his face fell. "Hardly enough to go on."

"It's something though," Elizabeth said.

Simon stood. "Arthur, I need you to pinpoint the dates of those festivals. I suspect the Offerings will be the one we'll need to target.

The rest of us will see what we can find out. Something like that doesn't go entirely unnoticed. Someone must have seen something."

Arthur set to his task, clearly relieved to have something to do other than wait and the rest went down to the lobby to discuss their plans.

Elizabeth turned to Jack. "Didn't you say something about delivery trucks when you were staking out Vale's house?"

Jack nodded. "Yeah, two of them."

She stopped walking and the group followed suit.

"Maybe they were picking up instead of delivering?"

Jack raised his dark brow and nodded at the idea. "Right," he said. "And if we can find out where to..."

"Good idea," Diana said.

"We should talk to Hassan again," Jack suggested. "See if he remembers anything that might help."

"We'll do that after we trace our steps," Simon said as his eyes started scanning the lobby. "We've got to see if we can find the watch."

Diana's eyebrows arched in a *that seems like an odd use of time* sort of way.

"It's important," Elizabeth assured her, hoping Diana wouldn't ask why. Thankfully, she didn't press the matter.

"When did you have it last?" Jack asked.

"Right here," Simon said, looking at where they stood in the lobby. "I checked the time, then I went to look for you. I didn't take it out or even realize I'd lost it until her men searched me."

Jack frowned. "I guess it could have fallen out of your pocket on the way to the valley."

Simon shook his head. "It must have, but..." He turned to look around the lobby, but knew it was pointless.

"Think of everything you did," Diana suggested. "You checked the watch and then what?"

Simon's brow furrowed as he tried to remember each detail. "I asked Elizabeth to stay here." He pointed to a spot near the front door. "To wait for me there. And I went up to Jack's room, but there was no answer. I tried yours," he added to Diana, "and then came back downstairs."

He shook his head. "Elizabeth and I waited a few more minutes and then Jack arrived and we met Hassan and left."

Diana chewed her lip in thought. "Nothing else? You didn't bump into someone? The lobbies of these hotels are infected with pickpockets."

Simon was about to answer when Elizabeth remembered something. She raised a finger in the air. "Yes. There was a man. You bumped into him, but he was just another guest."

"That's right," Simon said. "Little man." He held up his hand to his mid-chest.

"With a pencil mustache?" Diana asked. "And a weaseley sort of face?"

"How did you know that?" Elizabeth said.

Diana's eyes narrowed and she glared over at Jack who nodded back. "Nico."

THE DOOR GAVE WAY easily as Simon and Jack kicked it in. It was cheap and flimsy like the rest of the hotel they'd found out Nico was staying in. It had taken a bribe of all of two pounds to find out his room number. They could have picked the lock, Simon supposed, but he wouldn't have missed the expression on the little man's face for all the world.

Sitting in a small metal tub in the middle of the room, his skinny legs dangling over the edges, Nico gave a high-pitched scream as the door flew off its hinges and flattened on the floor in front of him. Jack and Simon stepped inside, followed by Elizabeth and Diana.

Nico squirmed in the tub, water splashing over the sides as he tried to cover himself with a small washing cloth. His eyes darted nervously from one person to the next.

"You have something that doesn't belong to you," Diana said.

Nico shook his head rapidly. "No. I-I did as you said. I stayed away from your deal. Ask Alexi. I have nothing."

In the hallway, a man walked by the broken door, looked in and hurried past, head down.

Simon watched as Diana wandered over to the little man's suitcase.

"Really?" She flipped open the lid and then dumped out the contents onto the unmade bed. Dozens of wallets and watches and bits of jewelry tumbled out.

Nico laughed nervously. "Those are...those are gifts."

Simon glared down at the little man and then stalked over to the bed. It didn't take him long to find the watch and when he did he exhaled some of the tension he'd been carrying.

"Thank God," he said, as he held it for the others to see before clenching his fingers tightly around it.

Elizabeth came over to him to see for herself, her relief palpable. They would have managed life in 1920s Egypt, but he was glad they wouldn't have to try. He slipped it into his pocket, but kept his hand around it. He was not going to lose it again.

"So how did you come by that?" Jack asked.

"That was a mistake," Nico said quickly. "Clearly, that—"

"Save it, " Jack said.

Diana walked over to Nico and stood above him in the bath. He pulled his legs close to his chest and hunched over them and shivered.

"You're going to return all of that, " Diana said, nodding toward the suitcase.

He started to protest, but when Jack took a step closer he reluctantly nodded.

"And then you're going home," Diana continued. "Today. Do you understand?"

Nico looked from her to Jack who scowled down at him.

Nico nodded.

Simon didn't believe the man would do it, but now that he had the watch back, he didn't really care. In an odd way, he owed the man a debt. If it hadn't been for the thief, the watch would have been taken by Vale and added to her collection.

"Good," Diana said and turned toward the door only to stop and turn back. "And if you have second thoughts, Alexi's men would be happy to convince you."

Nico swallowed hard and nodded again. "I understand."

Simon and Elizabeth walked to the door, but turned back as Nico spoke.

"I'll see you in Italy," he said boldly.

Diana frowned and shook her head. Jack put his foot on the side of the tub and shoved. It tipped over spilling the water and the naked little man out onto the floor. He spluttered and tried to cover himself.

"Have a safe trip, Nico."

CHAPTER THIRTY-SEVEN

With the watch now in hand, the group split up. Jack and Diana went to find out what they could about Vale's mysterious deliveries and Simon and Elizabeth headed for the hospital.

True to his word, Jouvet had taken care of Hassan, even arranging a private room for him. They entered quietly. Hassan looked to be sleeping. As much as Simon hated to wake him, God knew the man deserved his rest and more after all he'd done for them, there were questions that had to be asked.

Hassan lay in his hospital bed, an enormous white bandage wrapped around his head. It would have been comical if Simon hadn't known how he'd suffered his wounds or why. The risks this man, this relative stranger, had made for them, were humbling.

Despite Hassan's obvious need for rest, Simon called out his name, softly at first, but then a little louder.

Elizabeth laid her hand on Hassan's arm. "Hassan?"

The man's eyes opened slowly and he looked at them, hazy for a moment, before wakefulness and clarity came.

"How are you feeling?" Simon asked.

Hassan's hand lifted to touch his bandage and he groaned. "I am all right."

He closed his eyes and shook his head, but grimaced and stopped. "They came up too quickly to warn you. I am sorry—"

"No," Elizabeth said quickly. "We're sorry we got you mixed up in all this. How can we ever repay you?"

Hassan smiled a little. "I have been well paid."

Simon shook his head. "Hardly, but you will be, I promise you that." When this was over, every pound they had left would go to him.

"You can get more dance lessons," Elizabeth said.

Hassan laughed lightly and then winced.

"I hate to bother you with this now," Simon said, "but it's terribly important."

Hassan nodded.

"When you were asking around Cairo about Katherine Vale," Simon continued, "you said that she was planning something. Do you have any idea where?"

Hassan frowned as he thought. "I do not think so. I am sorry."

Elizabeth squeezed his hand. "It's okay."

"I wish I could do more to help you," he said.

Simon put a hand on Hassan's shoulder. "You've done more than enough."

Elizabeth leaned forward and kissed his cheek. "Thank you for everything."

Simon waited for Elizabeth to come around the bed, but she stopped midway and turned back to Hassan. Simon's interest shot back up when she asked, "Didn't you say that she arrived in the middle of a ceremony?"

Hassan looked up, trying to remember. "Yes."

"Do you know where it was?" Elizabeth said hopefully.

Simon leaned forward. Yes. She was brilliant. He'd forgotten that. If they knew where that had happened....

Hassan's brow wrinkled as he thought. "The vizier," he said. "They said it was near the tomb of the vizier."

"What vizier?" Simon asked. If they could narrow it down, they might be able to find Christina in time.

Hassan blinked as he thought, clearly struggling to put his thoughts together. "I am sorry. I am unsure."

Simon ignored his disappointment and smiled. "It's all right. You've been more help than you know."

"Thank you," Elizabeth said and kissed his cheek again.

He smiled. "Trust in Hassan."

"November 24th," Whiteside said as he consulted his notes. "As near as I can tell, that's when the Ninth day of Tybi should fall and be the Day of Offerings to Sekhmet."

"Tomorrow?" Simon said.

Whiteside closed his notebook and nodded. Elizabeth sat down next to him. "It's good that we know."

"Is it?" Whiteside said, looking old and lost, not that Simon could blame him.

"There's still time," Elizabeth assured him.

In spite of being bone tired, Simon couldn't sit and paced the room as they spoke. "We know the when, now to figure out the where. We spoke—"

A knock on the door interrupted him and he answered it.

Jack and Diana came in.

"Any word?" Diana asked Simon softly.

He shook his head and she nodded. "You were right about the deliveries," she said to Elizabeth. "They were outgoing and not incoming."

"Any idea where to?" Simon asked as he closed the door behind them.

"Cairo," Jack said. "Where they went from there, we don't know. They were picked up at the depot."

"All right," Simon said. "The cult centers were sacred places."

Whiteside nodded.

"I think those are our best bets," Simon continued. "We have three possibilities: Leontopolis, Fayoum and Memphis."

Two lines appeared between Diana's eyes. "If it were Fayoum," she said, "she wouldn't have everything shipped all the way to Cairo when she could just ship it straight to Fayoum."

Simon agreed. "That leaves Leontopolis and Memphis."

"Can't we check out both?" Jack asked.

Whiteside shook his head. He pointed to a map on the table. "Leontopolis is here, about ninety kilometers northeast of Cairo. Memphis is here," he said, pointing to another spot about two inches away. "Thirty kilometers south of Cairo. With the Day of Offerings being tomorrow...."

Simon's jaw tightened. They'd be lucky to get anywhere in time, much less be able to be in two places.

"Hassan said that he'd heard about a cult meeting near the tomb of the vizier," Elizabeth said. "Does that ring any bells?"

Whiteside almost smiled. "Yes. Aperel, the vizier to both Amenhotep III and Akhenaten is buried in Saqqara. That's where the necropolis is, the tombs and pyramids for the ancient capital— Memphis. There are undoubtedly other tombs of viziers he might have been referring to, but...."

Simon felt a surge of anticipation, excitement and dread. "Well, then...."

Jack grimaced and flexed the hand of his injured arm. "It's taking an awful risk, rolling the dice on one place," he said. "Maybe we should split up?"

"No way," Elizabeth said. They'd been there one too many times and nearly bought the farm each time.

"Whatever those supplies were," Diana said. "There was enough for an army."

"And it seems that's just about what she's raised," Simon muttered. He glanced up at Diana. "Up to thirty cult members, at least."

"I guess we'll need an army of our own then," Elizabeth said. "Where's Ahmed?"

"You what?" Whiteside said angrily as he strode toward Ahmed. "You rode with bandits? Kidnapping!"

Normally, Simon would have happily let Whiteside have his way with the boy, but there were more pressing matters. "Arthur—"

The young man lifted his hands. "I am sorry, Mr. Whiteside. I would never do anything to endanger Christina. You must believe me."

Whiteside grunted.

"That is why I told her we should not see each other. I did not want her involved in such things."

"And yet here you are," Whiteside bit out.

Ahmed shook his head helplessly. "I love her."

"You—" Whiteside started, but Simon intercepted him.

"There'll be time for all this later. Right now, we need to know if you can get those men to help us."

Ahmed frowned. "I do not think so. To risk their lives to save an English girl does not help the revolution."

"Money does," Diana said.

Whiteside looked at the boy with disgust, but swallowed his feelings. "I will give them everything I have if it will help save my daughter. I can have a draft sent—"

Ahmed looked at him with sorrow. "They do not take checks, Mr. Whiteside."

Whiteside was desperate now. "I can sell the estate, but it would take time."

Ahmed shook his head. "I'm sorry," he said. "I, too, will offer all I have, but I am afraid it will not be enough. Not for what we are asking."

Diana sighed. Everyone's attention turned to her and she offered Whiteside a smile. "I might have something. Back in a minute."

"We have a thousand pounds or so in the bank in Cairo," Elizabeth said.

Ahmed shook his head. "That might get us a few men, but none that I would trust."

"There has to be something we can do," Whiteside said. "What about the army? The British army?"

"It would difficult to explain to them and there's far too much red tape for them to get through even if they if they did believe us," Simon said. "There just isn't time. I think we're on our own."

"Maybe not," Diana said as she came back in and set something heavy and wrapped in brown burlap down on the table. She untied the ropes that bound it and pulled the wrappings off.

"Holy moley," Elizabeth said.

A golden statue of Horus as a falcon glimmered on the table. It was at least a foot tall and with green jeweled eyes and red jeweled feathers.

"Are those—" Elizabeth asked.

"Emeralds? Rubies?" Diana filled in for her. She nodded, a little sadly. "Yeah."

"Is that what you were picking up last night?" Jack asked, his voice suitably tinged with awe.

"Been looking for it for two weeks," Diana said.

Jack picked it up. "Must weigh sixty pounds."

Diana sighed again. "Solid gold." She turned to Ahmed. "Will that do?"

Ahmed was too dumbstruck to do anything but nod for a moment. Then he cleared his throat. "I think so."

"Diana," Arthur said, but she stopped him.

"It's just a thing." She looked at it sadly. "A beautiful, nearly priceless thing, but just a thing."

"What will you tell your client?" Whiteside asked.

"That I nearly had it, but it got away from me," she said.

Whiteside hugged her. "Thank you, my dear. Thank you."

Simon turned to Ahmed. "Well?"

"It should be more than enough," he said and then frowned. "Now, I just have to find them. And hope we are not too late."

CHAPTER THIRTY-EIGHT

ELIZABETH DEALT HERSELF ANOTHER hand of solitaire and stared down at it. It was a losing hand, she could already tell. She thought about just dealing the cards again and sighed.

"You should try to rest," Simon said as he stretched out on the bunk in their train compartment. His legs were so long, his feet dangled over the edge.

He was right of course. They'd spent a mostly restless night waiting for the morning train. She'd never wished for more mass transit, but she did yesterday. After the whirlwind of discovery, they'd had their legs cut off. They knew where and when, or at least they thought they knew, but they couldn't do a darn thing to get there fast. There were no planes to charter, no cars to rent. They could only take the train and pray they made it in time. It would be close.

Assuming they were right about everything they'd guessed about, which was nearly everything.

Elizabeth shook her head. "I can't sleep."

Simon checked his watch. He'd been doing that a lot lately and not just to see the time.

"We should arrive in Bedrashin in thirteen hours," he said. "That would give us four hours to get to Saqqara before midnight."

Midnight. Another of their guesstimates.

"Right," she said and looked down at her cards. It was an ugly deal, but she decided to play it anyway. "After this hand."

Simon humphed and rolled onto his side. Pushing himself up onto his elbow, he frowned at her and then at the cards. He gestured toward the play with his index finger. "Red seven on the black eight."

Elizabeth smiled and moved the card. Solitaire was always more fun with someone.

The train bumped to another stop and roused Elizabeth from sleep. Learning the rhythm of the train, she'd grown accustomed to the frequent, short stops. This one, however felt more abrupt than the others. She lifted her head and blinked in the darkness of their compartment.

She could hear a few voices, but couldn't make out what they were saying. Careful not to wake Simon, she slipped out of bed and tiptoed over to the window. Pulling back the sash, she peered out into the darkness.

Nighttime, she thought. They couldn't be far now.

But something was wrong. They'd stopped, but she couldn't see very far in the dark. There were no lights or buildings. No town, no station.

She walked over to the door to their compartment and stuck her head out.

"What's the matter?" Simon said, rubbing the sleep from his eyes.

"We're stopped," she said.

Simon sat up. "Bedrashin?"

"No, I don't think so. I don't think we're at a station."

A porter came toward her down the aisle between compartments and she stepped out. "Is there something wrong?" she asked.

"A minor delay," he assured her. "We will be underway soon."

Elizabeth had that sinking feeling. "How soon?"

"An hour," he said. "Two at the most."

An hour or two they didn't have to spare.

Simon appeared behind her. "Let's talk to the others."

They sent Ahmed off to find out what the delay was and gathered the rest in the dining car. Whiteside looked like a man who hadn't slept in two days, and she was sure he hadn't. His face was pale and dark circles hung under his eyes.

"If we get underway within the hour," Simon said, "we should still be able to find transportation and get to Saqqara well before midnight."

Arthur nodded, but she could see he was already beginning to grieve. She couldn't imagine what he must be going through.

"We'll make it," Diana said to him.

The door to the dining car opened and Ahmed came striding in. "Something's wrong with the tracks," he said. "They think they'll have it cleared up in an hour, but…"

"Where are we?" Jack asked.

"About ten miles south of Bedrashin," Ahmed said.

Jack looked out of the train window. On this side of the train, there were a few lights; it looked to be a small village. "Can we get off here, find horses and ride the rest of the way?"

Ahmed shook his head. "Not for so many. There are probably not six horses in the entire village."

"But one?" Simon said.

Ahmed looked at him curiously and then his eyes widened with understanding. "Yes. One."

Their timeline has always been tight, but Ahmed's was nearly impossible. He had to ride south to find the bandits, convince them to join him and then ride back north to Saqqara, all within hours. Maybe this delay was a blessing? They were closer now to where he hoped they were camped than they would be later.

He turned to Whiteside. "I will give my life to save your daughter."

Whiteside's eyes were red and glassy. He cleared his throat. "Let's hope it doesn't come to that, my boy."

Ahmed nodded and looked at the rest of them once more before hurrying away.

"Good," Jack said. "Now, if we can just get this train moving."

It did, but nearly two hours later. They arrived in Bedrashin at nearly ten o'clock and spent another precious hour finding horses.

They rode west toward Saqqara with no idea what they'd find or even if they'd find it. Thankfully, they managed to gather a few weapons. Diana had surprising friends. But even the guns were iffy—one WWI rifle, an old colt and an antique dragoon. It was all they could manage on such short notice, but it would have to do. Not that Elizabeth wanted to use any of them, although, she would if she had to. She still remembered what it felt like to shoot that man in Natchez and she'd only winged him. She had the feeling it would take more than that to save Christina.

They left the fertile lands that clung to the Nile and ventured out into the desert. The moon was nearly full and very bright in the clear night. They rode in silence. And, Elizabeth thought, silence in the desert at night was a whole new kind of silence. There were no sounds at all except for the soft tread of their horse's hooves on the sand and their own hearts beating.

They slowed as they neared the ancient necropolis. The outline of a ragged step pyramid just ahead on the horizon.

"There should be a slight ravine and temple ruins on the far side," Whiteside said, his voice dry and cracking. He was clearly terrified, both for himself and for his daughter. "That-that's the most likely spot."

Elizabeth and Simon shared a nervous look. Whiteside was a liability. He was far from being in good shape and his emotions were likely to make him do something rash. But they couldn't ask him to stay behind while they went on. If their roles had been reversed, nothing could have kept them away. Whiteside would try to save his daughter or die trying.

CHAPTER THIRTY-NINE

ABOUT A HUNDRED YARDS away from the step pyramid now, Elizabeth could see a slight glow emanating from behind it. This was it, she thought with a mixture of relief that they'd guessed right and dread at facing it. The ritual must have started. Her throat felt dry. They dismounted there and continued on foot, running along the edge of what was left of a ruined wall, finding some shelter in its shadow.

She looked up again at the moon. A full moon, she realized. But there was something odd about it.

"Is it just me," she whispered to Simon. "Or is the moon getting darker?"

Simon glanced up and frowned. He nodded and she knew they were both thinking the same thing. Without the benefit of Teddy's key, Vale had to travel with an eclipse. Unless she planned on staying in Egypt for a few more months, and that seemed unlikely, she would be traveling tonight.

And soon.

Elizabeth's heart raced just a little faster.

They reached the edge of the step pyramid and slowly started to edge around the lower level. Elizabeth wished she had a weapon. Not that she wanted to use one, but she just would have felt better having something to hold onto. Anything to hold onto.

She caught Diana's eye, and vaguely wondered if Diana felt the same way. She didn't look worried. But then, Diana never did.

Their three guns were carried by the three men. It wasn't sexist; just practical. Of the five, they had the most shooting experience. Although, they all knew if it did come down to a gunfight, they were all as good as dead.

Elizabeth shivered at the thought and tried to focus on not tripping instead. The ground was littered with fallen rocks, small and large. They moved slower now as they came to the corner of the pyramid.

The light from torches cast a glowing dome over the large temple and the ruins beyond. The temple was two stories, or had been at one time. The second story was little more than a colonnade now, some columns half shorn, others lying on the sand below. One of the cult members appeared from the shadows, obviously on patrol.

Jack held up his hand to stop the group's progress and edged back. Elizabeth had the sudden and absurd thought that she felt like a Navy seal on maneuvers, just without all the training, weapons and expertise. Basically, just a seal. Or maybe a duck, in a shooting gallery.

Between them and the temple were about twenty yards of open sand. There were no shadows, no shelter, no sneaky way from here to there. They would have to run across the open expanse of desert, completely unprotected.

They watched the man patrol the backside of the temple for a minute, pacing back and forth, before he moved on to something else. They didn't have time to wait, to see if there was a predictable pattern. They had to move. Now.

Jack knelt down in the sand and trained his rifle on the last spot they'd seen him. "Run," he whispered.

Elizabeth's heart pounded in her chest, as the four of them ran across the sand. She tried not to breathe, not to make a sound. Sixty feet felt like a mile. Simon lingered at her side, scrubbing his speed to stay close. The dark recesses of the temple grew closer and closer. Finally, she and Simon ducked into the shadows and behind the relative safety of the walls of the temple. Diana and Whiteside weren't far behind them.

Bringing up the rear was Jack. He'd probably waited until they were all safely across before starting across himself. He was about halfway there when Elizabeth heard something. It wasn't until Simon lunged out of the doorway that she realized she'd heard footsteps— the guard's.

Elizabeth followed Simon just in time to see the guard, his rifle trained on Jack, get clocked on the side of the head with the heavy handle of Simon's dragoon. The man stumbled to the side, dazed. Simon dropped his colt into the sand and ripped the rifle from the man's weakened grip. In almost one fluid movement, he swung again. This blow connected more fiercely than even the first. The man fell to the ground with a thump.

Jack skidded to a stop next to them. "Thanks for that."

Simon nodded and shouldered the rifle. The two of them dragged the guard inside the temple. Elizabeth picked up Simon's discarded gun and followed. They bound and gagged him, although, judging from the blood she could see beneath his *keffiyeh*, he might not be waking up any time soon.

Although it was dark in the temple, there were still openings to the outside and bits of moonlight filtered in. Jack made some more hand-signals and Whiteside nodded toward a corner.

Walking as softly as they could, they hurried over the stone floor to the area Whiteside had indicated. Stairs.

As quietly as they could, they climbed the steps to the upper level, Jack in the lead again. Light from the torches was brighter now and Elizabeth could hear voices, indistinct, but there.

Jack poked his head out of the doorway. After a moment, he signaled that it was clear. He went out first, but stayed crouched down. When it was Elizabeth's turn, she realized why. The upper level of the temple was very open here. They were exposed, except for a few fat columns and a very low wall that ringed the perimeter.

The remnants of the temple were a U-shape. The courtyard below was about forty feet across and thirty feet deep. At the end of the stone quad where the back side of the temple would have been, it was open. The only signs of the temple wall that had been there were a few broken columns and small piles of stone. Braziers and a half dozen cult members stood in the courtyard. All but one, a guard judging from the rifle in his hands, stood facing out toward another set of ruins that looked like what was left of a small pyramid.

It all looked like something out of a black and white movie serial. There were three main tiers that served as platforms. The lowest tier had five torches and between each, another cult member, dressed all in black. Above them, on the middle level, a bed of stone had been built. Two cult members, in black and red robes stood on either end of the platform next to large granite statues of a woman with the head of a lion. Sekhmet.

Above them, near the top of the pyramid and on the uppermost level, stood another henchman and Katherine Vale with her arms outstretched. Her blood-red robes made her skin look almost white. A brazier burned at her feet and behind her two torch flames reflected off an enormous copper disk that stood in front of the cap of the pyramid.

Elizabeth scanned the area for the one thing she wanted to see, but Christina was nowhere in sight. For the first time in her life,

Elizabeth wished she had a plan. She'd always been one to rush in and think about it all later, but this time it left her feeling exposed and vulnerable. Of course, the painful truth was there was no plan to make. There just wasn't time. They had to find Christina and do whatever they could to save her. Whatever that might be. Whatever that might mean in the end.

Jack touched Elizabeth's arm and she started, barely containing her scream. His eyes went round with a silent warning and then he pointed in one direction and then another. Simon nodded and took Elizabeth's arm. She and Simon went to the right, and Jack, Diana and Whiteside to the left. She didn't like the idea of splitting up, but she and Simon inched their way to one end of the U and the others to the opposite side.

Simon stretched out and gently placed his rifle on the rock ledge like a sniper. Elizabeth looked down at the heavy dragoon in her hand and did the same although she wouldn't be able to hit the broad side of a pyramid from here with it.

They settled in and waited. Elizabeth scanned the scene again. Where was Christina?

Elizabeth took stock of the scene below, calculating the number of men and distances, as she knew Simon was. There were twelve men that she could see. Twelve against four—not good odds, but not bad from a gambler's perspective. And tonight, they were definitely gamblers.

Vale, her voice rising into the night, spoke the words of some ancient invocation. "Sekhmet, greater than Isis. Sekhmet, greater than Hathor. Sekhmet, greater than Bast, greater than Maat. Light beyond the darkness, ever burning one. Hear my plea. I come to you for guidance, for justice, for vengeance."

The man behind her stepped forward and handed her a small figurine. Vale lifted it to the sky before dropping it into the brazier. "Beloved of Ra, Ruler of the Desert, Mother of the Dead, You who shook and shake the World, You who have swallowed the Ever-living Serpent and daily raise the Disk of the Sun and of the Moon, hear me."

She dropped three more figures into the fire as she spoke. Each gave off a spray of colored sparks as they were engulfed in the flames. And the men began to chant. Elizabeth couldn't tell what they were saying, but it took creepy to a whole new level.

Vale's voice built in intensity and fervor as she was handed a final figure. This one larger than the others. "This is the one I seek," she said, holding it up to the night. "Charles, son of Anna, and betrayer."

The chanting grew louder now as she held the final figure above the flames. She dropped it in and large billowing clouds of smoke rose up from the fire. Behind her the copper disk started to glow.

Elizabeth looked nervously to Simon, but his expression was unchanged. His jaw remained set firmly in a show of disgust and disbelief.

Vale said something in a language Elizabeth didn't understand and turned toward the copper disk—Hathor's mirror, she realized. Slowly, a figure began to take form in the burnished surface. It was wavy and insubstantial, but it was there.

Elizabeth looked for some projection device, but couldn't see anything. She looked back at Vale, to the mirror. Had she really summoned a god?

Vale, arms outstretched, bowed before the shadow. "Terrible One. I have brought you a gift. A gift of blood."

She waved her hand and from a hidden part of the temple two more cult members appeared, Christina held between them. Elizabeth's heart leapt. The girl was alive. Bound and gagged, she struggled against them, trying to twist out of their grip, but it was no use. Her hands were bound and the men far too powerful.

Elizabeth's stomach flipped with fear and anticipation. She saw something move across the roof on the far side of the temple and saw Whiteside start to stand, only to be pulled back down by Jack.

Simon saw it too. He and Jack looked at each other for a moment and then back to Christina as her guards brought her up to the middle level and forced her to lie down on the stone bed.

"Simon," Elizabeth whispered.

He ignored her and focused on Christina, or more aptly, on her guards. His right eye squinted as he lined one up in the site of his rifle.

He could have shot Vale any time, Elizabeth realized. Probably. It was far enough away to be anything but a sure shot. Regardless, it would have meant a sure death for Christina as their captive. But now, Elizabeth wondered if waiting had brought them anything but closer to dying. They could shoot the guards, but then what? There were too many of them.

Vale continued her litany of prayers to Sekhmet. Her helper held out something and Elizabeth knew what it was before the shining blade caught the light. Dagger in hand she descended the steps to the sacrificial altar.

Two men held Christina down as she struggled. Vale stood above and raised the dagger high into the air.

Elizabeth looked back at Jack and then at Simon. What were they waiting for? This was the window of opportunity. They had to do something. Now.

Vale's voice cut through the night as she gave a final invocation. She started to lower the dagger. Simon's finger moved to the trigger. Christina sobbed.

"Wait!" Whiteside stood up and held out his hands. "Please!"

Elizabeth started and nearly lost the hold on her gun.

"Hell," Simon said under his breath.

Vale stopped and turned toward the intrusion. Even from this far away, Elizabeth could see the fury in her eyes. The guard in the courtyard raised his rifle and pointed it at Whiteside.

The moment hung in the air as if someone had pushed a giant pause button.

"Kill him!" Vale said.

Elizabeth saw the guard's finger move. She couldn't just sit there and let him be shot. Without a thought beyond that, she jumped to her feet and waved her arms.

"Over here!"

The guard's head jerked around to find her and the hesitation cost him his life. Two shots rang out in unison and he crumpled to the ground.

"Bloody hell," Simon said as he pulled back the bolt on his rifle to ready another round.

Vale barked out another order, this time in Arabic and the five cult members that stood between the torches on the lower level moved up the rough steps to the altar.

"Christina!" Whiteside called out. The men in the courtyard had scattered.

Jack had already fired off another shot. One of the men fell forward onto the steps, but the others didn't pause.

Elizabeth heard two more shots fired and then heard Simon swear as he slammed his palm against the bolt. It was stuck. He couldn't chamber another round. He tossed the rifle aside and picked up the dragoon.

Elizabeth bent to pick the rifle up, to see if she could loosen it against the stone when she felt an arm wrap around her waist and a knife against her neck.

"Simon!"

CHAPTER FORTY

$\int$ IMON TURNED OVER, GUN ready, but it was no good.
The man who held Elizabeth grunted and pushed the knife point into her skin. She gasped as it broke the skin. A trickle of blood welled under the sharp tip of the blade and then trailed down her neck.

He had no choice. Simon let the gun fall from his hand. Elizabeth's eyes were wide with panic for a moment, but she seemed to realize the same thing he did at the same time. They were alive. The men hadn't killed them. That meant they still had a chance.

Another man came and picked up both the dragoon and the rifle. Now, at gunpoint, Simon and Elizabeth were forced to walk toward the stairs. Simon's mind raced. They couldn't have come so far, endured so much, to die now. He refused to accept it.

Elizabeth looked over at him, as one of the guards shoved her forward. There was blood on her neck and fear in her eyes, but he could see her faith in him. He would not let her down. Whatever it took.

At the stairs, they saw Whiteside, Diana and Jack, and two more armed men. Jack must have put up a fight. A large cut had opened up over one eye and he blinked through the blood that ran down his face. He caught Simon's eye and shook his head in apology.

They'd lost the battle, but the war wasn't over yet. As long as they breathed, it wasn't over.

The group was escorted down into the courtyard and slowly up the steps toward Vale.

Christina struggled and turned her head toward them. Through her gag she cried out a muffled, "Daddy?"

"I'm here, my girl."

Christina looked at him through tears before turning to Vale.

"Please?" Whiteside said. "Let her go."

Vale ignored him and focused on Simon and Elizabeth as her guards forced them all to kneel on the top step at the foot of the altar. The hard stone split open one of the cuts on Simon's knee, but he welcomed the sting of it.

"Oh, Mighty One," she said, almost breathless with delight. "I am here to make offerings to you and you give me these gifts."

The dagger lay in the flat open palms of her hands as she held it out. "I give you their blood in tribute. I will cut out their hearts so you can taste their betrayal."

She looked down at Christina. "But first, as promised, the blood of a virgin."

Vale lifted the knife. Simon tensed, ready to lunge, to do something. He was not going to sit by and watch her gut that poor girl.

Next to him, he felt Elizabeth tense, but he didn't dare look away.

"Sekhmet," Elizabeth said suddenly and Simon jerked in surprise. "Oh, Mighty Goddess, Sekhmet."

Simon whipped his head around to her. The guard's hands clamped more tightly onto his shoulders. What was she doing? And then, when he heard the apprehension in her voice as she struggled with what to say, he knew. She was stalling.

Vale had stopped and glared at the brazen interruption.

"You...you have been tricked," Elizabeth said to the guards. "By this one. The one in red! Lies. She's lying to you."

Vale's rage grew with every word. And while it was sure to be a short-lived distraction, it was the only hope of buying time and hoping to find a way to save Christina. Simon joined her.

"She is the betrayer," he said. "A tool of..." Damn it; he couldn't remember the name.

"Apophis," Whiteside said quickly. "Enemy of Ra. Bringer of Darkness."

Vale shook her head, her eyes wide and wild. "Do not listen to them."

"See her shadow cover the moon," Simon said.

A few of the men actually looked up then and saw the umbral shadow of the earth as it moved across the face of the moon—the eclipse.

"Sekhmet," Whiteside said. "Child of Ra, the Beautiful Light, do not be deceived by this—"

"No!" Vale screeched, pulling her guards' attention back to her. "They are the deceivers. Who has brought the Goddess to you?" she said, gesturing to the copper disk and its shadowy reflection. "I am the hand of the holy one."

Her closest henchman, whom Simon now recognized as the man from jail, stepped forward in solidarity and then another, and the doubters cowered back. Vale had control again and their time, Simon realized with a dull ache in his chest, had run out.

Vale poised the dagger ready to plunge it into Christina's heart. Christina screamed and Whiteside tried to lunge forward as he called out her name.

Simon reached out to hold Elizabeth's hand. Vale, her face, a picture of hatred, began her downstroke.

Simon heard the shot almost at the same moment he saw the knife wrench from Vale's hands. She cried out in pain and rage. Everyone turned toward the source of the gunshot and saw a man poised on a hill and then two dozen riders appeared behind him. Ahmed!

Simon felt the man holding his shoulders shift his grip and Simon took advantage of his lapse. He pushed himself up as quickly as he could, knocking the man off balance. Turning, he hit him square on the jaw, sending him tumbling down the steps.

Next to him, Elizabeth tried to do the same, but her guard was too quick, too big and he gripped her tightly. He let go of one arm, balled his big, meaty hand into a fist, ready to strike her. Enraged and finally free to do something about it, Simon hit him harder than he'd ever hit anyone in his life. The force of the blow stunned the man to near insensibility and he let Elizabeth go.

Simon ignored the pain that shot through his hand and readied for a parrying shot when Elizabeth's tiny fist rocketed out and punched the tall man right in the neck. The guard's eyes went wide with surprise. She looked at Simon almost as stunned as the guard.

Not wasting a second more, Simon grabbed him by the shoulders and brought the man's head down to his knee. He felt and heard the cartilage in the man's nose break. Off-balance now, the guard swayed and Elizabeth pushed him from behind, and he rolled down the steps to the lower level.

The rest was chaos. Jack and Diana fought off men of their own. Freed from the men who restraining her, Christina hurried down to her father, who'd somehow been knocked down the steps as well. Ahmed's bandits flew off their horses and spilled into the temple.

In the maelstrom, Elizabeth called out to Simon. He turned to her and she pointed to the top of the pyramid. "There!"

He turned just in time to see Vale at the top of the steps. She grabbed a torch and ran toward the copper disk. And right through it.

Simon stood stunned for a moment until he realized Elizabeth was running after her.

"Elizabeth!" he called out, but she didn't stop. Simon started to look for a weapon, but realized there wasn't time and followed close behind. "Wait for me!"

Elizabeth stopped and grabbed the second torch. "She's getting away."

When Simon reached the top of the pyramid, he could see that the copper disk stood in front of an opening to the apex of the pyramid. Vale hadn't gone into the disk; she'd gone behind it.

Simon took the torch from Elizabeth's hand and poked it behind the disk. All he could see was a long tunnel, leading down. He was half-tempted to let Vale go, to simply be glad they'd survived, when Elizabeth looked at him.

"We have to stop her," she said.

It was simple, and yet, so very not. But she was right. They had to stop her.

Carefully, Simon led the way into the tunnel. The rough stairwell led down into the darkness. Holding Elizabeth's hand in one hand and the torch in the other, he led them down the steps as quickly as he dared.

The long tunnel finally ended in a small room and another tunnel, this one flat, probably running under the pyramid. He could hear Elizabeth's breathing start to race and he turned back in concern.

Her eyes scanned the walls nervously. Of course, he thought, she'd nearly been buried alive.

"You can wait for—" he started.

"Don't even say it," she said between short breaths. "I'm okay. Let's go."

She clearly wasn't, but they didn't have time to argue. They continued down the narrow tunnel. There were small alcoves along the way and in the dim light, he could just make out small bundles piled on top of each other. Mummies.

"Are those babies?" Elizabeth said, her voice trembling.

"Animals," he said, hoping he was right. He'd read about catacombs filled with animal mummies. The long labyrinthian passageways were found all over Egypt.

Elizabeth eyed the mummies warily and they continued on until Simon thought he could hear someone else's footsteps and ragged breathing. He slowed their progress and stopped to listen. Nothing.

They walked on ahead until the tunnel hit a crossroads. Vale could have gone either way. Simon looked in one direction and then the next, only just catching a glimpse of torchlight down the one to the right. She wasn't far ahead of them now and they quickened their steps. He swore silently to himself as they followed the light. He should have taken the time to find a weapon. If Vale was armed, they'd have no defense.

Simon forced that thought away and saw that the glow from Vale's torchlight was brighter now and slowed as they came to a corner. Simon held Elizabeth back as he peered carefully around it.

Vale was busy fussing with something in her hands, her torch discarded at her feet. He could see the flames reflecting against the wall behind her. A dead end. She was trapped.

Slowly, he and Elizabeth eased around the corner, and stood face to face with Katherine Vale.

Her breathing was heavy and her eyes still wild, but they had more of the woman he'd known in them. And that made him nervous.

"It's over," Elizabeth said.

Vale looked pained and lifted an empty hand. It was bloody and one of the fingers was missing. "Help me?"

She took a step forward. Simon and Elizabeth eased back a step to match her.

"That's far enough," Simon said. She didn't have a knife or a gun, thank God, but she had something in her other hand.

Vale smiled then. "I should have cut your hearts out when I had the chance."

"Sorry to disappoint you," Elizabeth said.

"Oh, there's still time." Vale held out her other hand now. One of the watches rested in her palm. She smiled a terrible, trembling, mad smile. "I have three now, you see."

She patted a small pouch at her waist. "And you with none."

Elizabeth started to say something, but Simon interrupted her. "They won't give you what you need."

Vale sighed contentedly. "Oh, I think they will." She opened the watch and then looked at them again. "I'll find Charles and I'll kill him. And then I'll come for you."

In spite of the chill her words sent coursing through him, Simon didn't react.

Her eyes danced over them. "And you'll learn what suffering really means."

"*Ila-liqaa*,'" she said and pulled the stem of the watch activating it. She stared at them as the electric blue light snaked up her arm. She stood paralyzed, frozen for a moment as the light enveloped her. Her body shook violently and then in a flash, she was gone.

CHAPTER FORTY-ONE

B Y THE TIME SIMON and Elizabeth emerged from the tunnel, the battle was all but over. Simon had never been in a war before, but he suddenly had a sense of what it must be like. The mad rush of men, fighting and killing in a riot of violence and then the surreal quiet when it was over.

Elizabeth ran down the steps to Whiteside and the others. A quick glance told Simon they'd all survived—Jack and Diana, Whiteside and Christina.

Bodies of half a dozen or more cult members lay strewn on the temple grounds. Two lay twisted at the bottom of the pyramid steps, their limbs bent in unnatural repose. More lay dead sprawled over crumbling bits of wall. In the courtyard, Ahmed's bandits kept the remaining survivors prisoner at gunpoint.

He could scarcely believe they were alive. Amid such savagery, they'd somehow managed to survive. Simon joined the others and stood a few steps above them.

Jack looked at him with a relieved grin on his face. "Am I glad to see you two. When all hell broke loose, I lost track of you."

"We're okay," Elizabeth said, frowning at the state of him. His jacket gone, the white sleeve of his shirt red with blood. His stitches must have torn loose.

"Everyone all right?" Simon asked as he took stock of the rest of the group.

"Just a twisted ankle," Whiteside said from his spot on the ground. "Clumsy."

Kneeling at his side, Christina caressed his cheek. "Oh, papa."

Diana stood. "I don't think it's broken."

Simon nodded. "Good."

Diana moved over to tend to Jack next.

"What about...?" Jack asked, jerking his head toward the top of the pyramid.

Simon scowled. "Escaped."

"You mean there are tunnels?" Jack said. "Maybe the men can—"

Simon shook his head. "They can't follow her where she's gone."

It was clear from his expression that Jack didn't quite understand. "She had a watch," Simon said.

Light dawned in Jack's eyes. "Damn."

Simon was about to tell him what Vale had said when Ahmed joined the group.

"Christina," he said, his eyes on her and her alone.

She started and looked away from her father, eyes widening as she realized who had spoken.

He knelt down beside her and helped her stand.

"Are you hurt?" he asked.

She shook her head. "But you are," she said, touching his cheek just below a cut near his temple

He took hold of her hand. "It is nothing. Nothing at all."

He pulled her tightly into his arms as she cried with relief and joy. He kissed her and Whiteside cleared his throat.

It took him a moment, but Ahmed managed to pull away from Christina's embrace. "Are you badly hurt, sir?"

Whiteside looked up at him, forlorn. He looked at his daughter as she clung to Ahmed's side and Simon could see the pain of knowing he was losing his daughter in a way he hadn't imagined at the beginning of the night.

"I'll survive," Whiteside said and then shifted his weight to try to stand.

Ahmed reached out his hand to help Whiteside up. The older man looked at it and then sighed and accepted the offer.

"It was so much easier disliking you."

Ahmed looked nervously to Christina who could only smile.

Once he was up, Whiteside didn't relinquish Ahmed's hand and held it firmly. "Thank you, my boy. Thank you for everything I hold dear."

Whiteside's eyes shifted to his daughter.

Ahmed's followed. "I would do anything for her."

Whiteside nodded, a little sadly. "Well, then you can start by helping her father back to civilization. I desperately need a scotch."

Ahmed smiled and nodded. He took Diana's place at Whiteside's side and Christina slipped under her father's other arm. Together, they helped him down the steps.

The bandit leader barked some orders and the prisoners were marched from the compound. The bodies of the dead were piled onto the backs of horses and led off.

The leader stood at the center of the temple and surveyed the scene before turning to face Simon and his group atop the steps.

His expression was almost amused. His dark features broke into a small smile and he laid his hand over his heart and bowed slightly.

After another quick barked order in Arabic, his horse appeared at his side. In one fluid, powerful movement, he swung himself into the saddle, gave another command and rode off into the night leaving them alone in the temple.

"THE CARRIAGE IS READY," Jack said as he came back into the lobby of Shepheard's hotel, one arm firmly ensconced in a sling.

Simon nodded. "Good."

Jack shook hands with Whiteside. "Take care," he said and then with a wink at Ahmed and Christina added, "You two I'm not worried about."

With that, he walked over to a Diana who was busy giving orders to the men carrying a large crate across the lobby.

"I hate goodbyes," Elizabeth said with a sigh.

"I'm dashed sorry to see you go," Whiteside said, leaning heavily against his cane.

"I thought you'd be heading back to England after all this," Simon said.

Whiteside looked over at his daughter and Ahmed as they lingered, arm in arm, not far away. He sighed resignedly and then turned back to Simon. "I've spent so much time focusing on the past that I nearly missed how precious the present is. And it seems, that is here, now, in Egypt."

His eyes were misty with emotion when he looked back to Simon. He cleared his throat and looked from Simon to Elizabeth. "How can I ever thank you?"

"How can you ever forgive us?" Elizabeth said. "If we hadn't been here, none of—"

"Nonsense," Whiteside said. "I don't know your past with this woman, but I do know you have no blame in this. And without you, my child would be lost to me. I wish there was something I could do to repay you."

Simon reached into his jacket pocket and pulled out an envelope. Inside were the necessary papers to ensure Hassan received all of the money in their Cairo account. Simon held out the envelope. "You can make sure this is taken care of for me. It's for Hassan."

Whiteside took the envelope and slipped it into his pocket. "You have my word."

The awkward silence that always accompanied any unwanted parting hung in the air. No one wanted to be the one to put an end to it. Finally, Simon did.

He held out his hand. "Professor."

Whiteside chuckled and shook his hand. "If you ever return to Egypt..."

Elizabeth glanced up at Simon with a smile. "You never know."

She stepped forward and gave Whiteside a hug, then said goodbye to Christina and Ahmed. Simon followed close behind.

He held Ahmed's handshake for a moment. "Second chances are a rare thing," he said. "Don't screw it up."

Ahmed smiled a bit nervously. Simon was not joking.

"Yes, sir."

Simon looked back once more at Whiteside before joining Elizabeth with Diana and Jack near the front door.

One of Diana's men motioned to her and she turned back to the group. "That's me, I'm afraid," she said.

She looked at Simon and Elizabeth, and quirked a smile. "You two have an interesting way of vacationing. I like it."

Elizabeth winked at Diana. "You should have seen our honeymoon."

Diana laughed. "My usual mayhem will seem dull after this."

Simon smiled. "From what Jack has told me, I find that hard to believe."

She grinned at Jack. "Maybe it is."

Turning back, she pushed out a breath and pulled Elizabeth into a hug. "Oh, I hate goodbyes."

"Me, too."

She smiled and inclined her head politely toward Simon and then walked over to stand in front of Jack. Toying with the material of his sling, she said, "Maybe I'll see you around?"

Simon lowered his gaze, trying not to invade their private moment.

Jack nodded. "You never know."

Grinning, she kissed him and then walked to the door. She stopped there and turned back. "Something to remember me by," she said and patted her jacket pocket before smiling once more and disappearing into the street.

Jack frowned and mimicked her gesture. His eyebrows arched and he pulled out a piece of paper. He unfolded it and smiled. He held it out for Simon and Elizabeth to see. It was the sketch Christina had done of Diana that first day in the Valley of the Kings.

Jack stared down at it for a moment, before folding it back up.

"We don't have to rush home," Elizabeth said. "If you want..."

She nodded toward the doorway.

Jack grinned. "We said our goodbyes last night. If you know what I—"

"Yes, we know," Simon said.

Jack laughed and then sighed. "Well, then."

"I can't wait to sleep in my own bed," Elizabeth said.

"Yes." Simon felt the same way, but he couldn't help but feel that by leaving here and going home, they were leaping from the frying pan into the fire. They'd made a powerful enemy.

Elizabeth sensed his hesitation. "She can't trace the watch. She doesn't know where or when we live. It was just dumb luck that we ended up here together. She won't be able to find us."

Simon wanted to believe that, but knew their life was never so simple.

"Let's go home," she said, slipping her arm into his.

After every mission they'd been on so far, returning home had been a deep cleansing breath. A return to a place of safety and rest. But this time, it was different. The one place he'd always thought they'd be safe left him feeling more vulnerable than ever before. Katherine Vale was not finished with them yet, and Simon had a sinking feeling that what they'd endured would be a pale shadow of what was to come. Her final words echoed in his mind—*Ila-liqaa'*. Until we meet again.

Simon looked down at Elizabeth, who smiled back at him, her boundless faith unblemished by it all. He wished he could share that feeling, but as they started toward the carriage, he knew with a horrible certitude that they hadn't finished anything here. It had only just begun.

The End

NOTE TO THE READERS

Thank you for reading SANDS OF TIME; I truly hope you enjoyed reading it as much as I enjoyed writing it. Look for another adventure in 2014!

If you enjoyed this book, please consider posting a short review. Thanks again for reading!

Have an idea for a time and/or location you'd like to see Simon & Elizabeth (or Jack) visit? Drop me a line or come on by Facebook and let me know. I have quite a few ideas for future adventures, but would love to hear from you!

Sign up for the new releases newsletter!
Visit: http://moniquemartin.weebly.com

ABOUT THE AUTHOR

Monique was born in Houston, Texas, but her family soon moved to Southern California. She grew up on both coasts, living in Connecticut and California. She currently resides in Southern California with her naughty Siamese cat, Monkey.

She's currently working on an adaptation of one of her screenplays, several short stories and novels and the next book in the Out of Time series.

For news and information about Monique and upcoming releases, please visit: http://moniquemartin.weebly.com/

Printed in Great Britain
by Amazon